I0572451

Rakefang

GALLERIES OF STONE - BOOK THREE

C. J. MILBRANDT

OLEXI

Galleries of Stone, Book 3
Rakefang
illustrated edition

Copyright © 2019, 2013, 2012 by C. J. Milbrandt I cjmilbrandt.com
ISBN: 978-1-63123-084-4

All Rights Reserved. No part of this publication may be reproduced, stored in a retrieval system, or transmitted in any form or by any means–electronic, mechanical, photocopy, recording, or any other–except for brief quotations in printed reviews, without the prior permission of the author.

Illustrations: Hannah Lavender I studiolavender.com
Jacket design: Elza Kinde I bumblebess.com

*"Clear as crystal, sure as seasons, and welcome
as a loaf from Pennyflax & Quince."*

table of contents

Rakefang

1

Pennyflax & Quince

The air finally carried the soft, earthy scent of springtime on the morning that someone new entered Pennyflax & Quince. Chelle caught the swing of the door out of the corner of her eye and automatically called, "Welcome ...?" before trailing off.

A young man stood there, holding the ankles of the toddler sitting on his shoulders.

After so many months, she knew everyone in Hayward by sight, and these two were strangers. And strange.

The slender Flox's white-blond hair was overgrown. Not in a messy way. Anyone could see he was clean and even a little fancy, but Chelle had never seen a boy with hair as long as a girl's.

She didn't mean to stare. People stared at her enough that she knew how much it hurt. To be fair, both customers were staring back. Oh. She'd missed it. Had they asked for something?

Taking a deep breath, Chelle concentrated on keeping her voice steady. "May I help you, sir?"

He strolled closer, and she wondered at his clothes. They were finer than anything worn by the local farmers and quarrymen. Was he a merchant? It hardly seemed likely, since he couldn't have been much older than she. Might he be a showman? A traveling circus had once come through Millford, but the feather-clad entertainers had been showy. This young man's manner was quiet.

But the child!

She was staring again, but how could she not? This was the first time she'd ever seen someone else—outside her immediate family—with brown hair.

When the customer stopped on the other side of the counter, his passenger blinked at her with wide, golden eyes, then leaned down and held out clawed hands, begging to go to her. Without a second thought, she reached back.

The young man's face plainly showed surprise, but he swung the little boy down and placed him in her arms. He was heavy, but she was used to lugging youngsters. Settling him on her hip, Chelle touched his hair—silky, auburn waves that were neatly cropped at his chin. The boy was both wild and sweet, and her heart ached for him. Was he teased for having brown hair? Did people stare because his skin was brown as well?

Cuddling him close, she murmured, "Aren't you a beautiful boy?"

He giggled, revealing sharp little canine teeth to match his claws. Maybe these two really were part of a circus, and the Flox was this child's tamer. She shook her head in wonderment, for he was like a baby animal. "Whose cub are you?"

The little charmer was apparently quite willing to be hers, for he leaned his head on her shoulder and tangled pudgy fingers in her hair. She was smiling softly when she glanced up to find the young man leaning with his elbows on the counter, watching them with solemn intensity. Reaching across the counter, he tapped the back of the boy's hand.

He obediently let go of her hair, then stuck his thumb in his mouth.

Chelle stiffened a moment later, for the young man took hold of one of her loose curls and tugged it gently. If her hands hadn't been full, she would have slapped him away, but all she could do was glare, daring him to make fun of her for being different.

Which she immediately realized was silly. He was even odder than she.

He opened his mouth to say something, but then he straightened and hurried to greet two huge, brown men who entered the bakery. One of them had golden eyes, and they fixed on her with the oddest expression. With a twinge of regret, Chelle circled the counter and offered her little cub back to the man who was obviously his papa.

This auburn-haired stranger accepted his son, lightly tossing him to his companion, whose hair was such a dark shade of brown it was nearly black. Then, he propped his hands on his hips and leaned down until he was nearly nose-to-nose with Chelle. She wasn't sure how to react, and he seemed to be waiting for ... *something*.

Oh. Of course. Blushing faintly, she did her job. "Welcome to Pennyflax & Quince. May I help you, sir?"

He actually seemed confused, which was *very* confusing.

Had she done something wrong?

While Aurelius rattled off a ridiculously long list of supplies, Freydolf perched his nephew on his shoulders before elbowing Tupper. "Is she new?"

"She's not from Hayward," he whispered back.

Aurelius's eyebrows slowly arched. In a last-ditch effort, he pressed into the girl's personal space and grumpily said, "Boo."

Frey knew from experience that this tactic usually sent women and children screaming, but the lass folded her arms over her chest and eyed Aurelius skeptically. The sculptor begged, "Stop trying to frighten the child!"

"Does she *look* frightened?" With a put-out expression, Aurelius demanded, "What's wrong with her?"

"Perhaps you're losing your touch?"

"Impossible. *You* may be considered a lesser evil, but I still possess the necessary charisma to send these simple folk skittering!"

"That's hardly something to be proud of," Freydolf muttered, giving the young lady an apologetic nod.

Shaking her head, she retreated behind the counter, calling, "Auntie, some customers have questions."

"What's all this?" demanded a short, plump woman who bustled out of the kitchen, wiping flour-dusted hands on her apron. "Oh, Tupper! It's a sure sign of spring that you're back in town!"

"Yes, Missus Quince."

"And you brought your Pred friends," she said with a strained smile. "Isn't that ... nice."

Freydolf stifled a sigh, but Aurelius smoothly stepped forward. "Melina sent us to restock her supplies, so our list is a lengthy one."

These semi-annual orders utilizing Misters Pennyflax and Quince as middlemen were one method Ewert had proposed for staying on the village's good side after making off with so many Meadowsweets. Frey had balked at bribing the folks in Tupper's hometown, but the extra coin did go a long way toward assuring his welcome in Hayward.

The lady brightened but pointedly addressed Tupper. "How *is* Melina? Any more little ones?"

"Soon."

"Oh, lovely! Does Merona know? It's such a *shame* so many of her children have taken to that mountain. Too far from home, if you know what I mean."

Tupper smiled faintly. "Melina is visiting with Mother now. Once our order is filled, you could probably join them for tea."

"Oh, that's a fine idea! So, what are you needing?"

To Freydolf's surprise, his servant said, "I'd like to meet her, please."

"What? Oh, that's right! 'Twas late last autumn when we took her on, so you wouldn't have met Chelle."

Tupper reached for his nephew, who gladly jumped from one uncle to the next. "Let's introduce you to the pretty lady."

Frey's bushy brows shot up, and he took a longer look at Chelle. She was a mere wisp of a woman, barely more than a girl. Her lavender dress was covered by a neat, white apron, and her eyes were a pale shade of blue very common among her people. She was fair of skin, but her hair set her apart. Flox curls came in many shades—blonde, gold, buff, cream, silver. This young lady's rich, brown hair wasn't simply unusual. It was unheard of.

"Hello, I'm Tupper Meadowsweet. This is my nephew, Quintrell Harrow."

She smiled vaguely and shot Missus Quince a pleading look.

The woman clucked her tongue. "It's no use, Tupp." Fishing a bit of folded paper from her apron pocket, she passed it along with a stubby pencil. "If you have something to say, you'll have to write it out."

Tupper slowly blinked, and Frey could tell the lad was thinking hard.

He accepted the paper and pencil, looking between the women. Finally, Tupper asked, "Why?"

The baker's wife reached up to pat Tupper's shoulder. "Chelle is deaf, dear boy. She can't hear you."

"May I inquire as to the girl's provenance?" asked Aurelius.

Seeing the Quince woman's blank expression, Freydolf helpfully interjected, "Where's she from?"

"Chelle's from out past Millford. Her family's famous for ... well, there's queer things that crop up in her family," the baker's wife explained. "Up their way, they call that coloring *cinnamon*. Her folk always have a hard time finding placements, but Chelle's mother is a cousin to my mother. I gave the girl a chance, and I've no regrets."

While the woman rambled on to Aurelius in increasingly gossipy tones, Tupper eased over to the counter where Chelle stood with back straight, eyes downcast, and a rather sullen expression on her face. It must be awkward to stand there, knowing people are talking about you, but not knowing what was being said. He plunked Quintrell onto the counter and smoothed out the paper Missus Quince had given him. Waving to catch Chelle's attention, he carefully printed **Tupper Meadowsweet** and pointed to himself.

She read and reread his name, then asked, "Are you Ewert's brother?"

"Yes," he replied, nodding for emphasis.

Now that he, Carden, Aggie, and Farley were living up top, it made sense that Ewert was the Meadowsweet she knew. Tupper's older brother and new wife had moved into Carden and Melina's old home.

Chelle nodded, too. "Your mother is very nice."

Tupper smiled to himself. It was good that she could talk. That made things easier. Next, he wrote out, **I live on Morven.**

The young lady frowned. "I don't know that town."

He shook his head. **The mountain.**

Quintrell spied a basket heaped with nut loaves and crawled across the counter toward them. Chelle scooped him up and asked, "May I give him a bun?"

Tupper nodded and mouthed, "Thank you."

While she distracted the youngster with a snack, Tupper tried to think what else to say. There was too much to explain and not much paper to write on. He could hear Missus Quince rattling on.

"... can't overlook the cinnamon hair, but then there's her ears. People are getting used to her, but she doesn't mingle much with the other girls. Sweet as pie to the little ones, though. And a hard worker."

Tupper glanced over to find Aurelius's keen gaze fixed on the young lady who cuddled his son.

"Most of the deaf I've seen in my travels find it difficult to communicate. How is it that the little lady can speak? And write, for that matter?"

"The girl took sick when she was five or six. A fever. She barely scraped through, and it affected her hearing," Missus Quince revealed in confiding tones. "Chelle's always been a clever one. Her mother taught her to read and write early, and it's a mercy."

"That explains it!" Aurelius fluttered his fingers at Chelle. "Frey, this girl isn't afraid of us because she's never *heard* of us!"

From across the room, Freydolf held Tupper's gaze. "Even so, I'd call her brave. Now, shouldn't we see to Melina's order?"

While the conversation swung to bags of flour and sacks of meal, Chelle came out from behind the counter and stood beside Tupper. With her back to the others, she leaned close and whispered, "Why do those men and this boy have brown skin?"

They are Pred.

"They don't have horns. And they have claws."

Tupper nodded and pointed to the previous statement.

"And ... they have brown hair like me."

Indicating his nephew, he wrote, **Quintrell Harrow.**

"Quintrell," she sounded out. "He looks like his papa."

Aurelius Harrow.

She quietly prompted, "And the other man?"

With great pride, he wrote, **Master Freydolf Meadowsweet, Keeper of Morven.**

"Meadowsweet?"

He's my brother.

Chelle shook her head. "How is that possible?"

Tupper had gotten a lot better at explaining that particular relationship. **An oath made us bond-brothers.**

"You're family, even though he's ... brown?"

With a shy glance, he carefully printed, **I like brown.**

Chelle blushed and busied herself with Quintrell, who had finished his treat and had crumbs all down his shirtfront.

Tupper kept right on writing. **I like your name. Shells are pretty.**

She giggled softly and shook her head. Holding out her hand

for the pencil, she said, "My name is spelled this way."

Tupper watched with interest as she spelled out **Chelle.**

Then, she added her surname, and he slowly straightened.

Staring at the name on the paper, he called, "Frey?"

The sculptor turned away from the haggle that occupied Aurelius and Missus Quince. "Aye?"

Rubbing at the base of one horn, Tupper asked, "Is this important ... maybe?"

Freydolf strolled over, quietly answering, "That all depends on what you're referring to, lambkin."

"This," Tupper said, pointing to the young woman's dainty signature. "Chelle's last name is Tremont."

"Tremont," Freydolf echoed. Was it possible, after all these years? "As in Master Tremont?"

Tupper took the pencil from Chelle, who was staring at them with equal parts curiosity and frustration. The lad wrote, **Master Tremont was a past Keeper of Morven.**

Chelle hugged Quintrell close and said, "I don't know anything about a Keeper."

Aurelius broke off negotiations to butt in. "I'll wager Tremont wasn't Flox!"

"Nay, he wasn't," Freydolf slowly replied. "I researched him a few years back, when Tupper discovered the third Triad. He was Clow."

"Hence the cinnamon hair and ... ears! Oh, my dear woman!" Aurelius clasped his hands together and gleamed at Missus Quince. "When you mentioned ears, you *weren't* talking about deaf ones!"

The baker's wife winced. "Now see here, sirs. I don't want you giving this girl any trouble!"

"Nay, not us!" Aurelius pledged. "I have many acquaintances among the Clow. Noble folk. High ideals. Feisty."

Chelle poked Tupper's arm and whispered, "What are they saying?"

He obediently began writing. **Master Tremont was Clow. You're part Clow. Maybe.**

She tapped the new word. "What's Clow?"

"I see some elucidation is in order!" Aurelius rubbed his hands together and demanded, "Bring me a fresh sheet of paper! Something spacious!"

Tupper helped Missus Quince cut a length from the roll of brown paper usually used for wrapping large orders, and they spread it across the entire length of the counter. Aurelius disdained the proffered stub of a pencil, producing a stylish writing utensil from his breast pocket. With a flourish of one ruffled sleeve, he began in an elegant scrawl.

The Clow are the dominant race on First Continent, just as the Grif are on Far Continent and the Pred on this one.

"Continents?" Chelle asked.

Aurelius launched into a written lecture, complete with rough maps. His flowing words quickly filled sections on the paper.

"Is he showing off?" Tupper whispered.

Freydolf chuckled. "Something like that."

The lad rubbed uneasily at the base of one horn. "Should he be using such big words?"

"Your young lady seems to be keeping up just fine," he pointed out. Clearly, Chelle's mother hadn't simply taught her daughter to read. Intelligence shone in her eyes as she took in the impromptu lesson. Frey ruffled Tupper's hair. "She's clever."

"I think so, too."

Chelle swayed where she stood, lulling Quintrell into a contented doze as she closely followed Aurelius's written explanation. "Are Clow brown like you?"

The Pred straightened and struck a pose. "I think I'm offended that I have—nay, my entire race has—been reduced to such a mundane hue!"

She studied his face closely and hesitantly offered, "I'm sorry?"

Tupper borrowed a corner of the paper and hastily wrote. **Brown sounds too plain. Aurelius likes fancy names.**

Her brows drew together, and the lad did his best.

To Freydolf's increasing amusement, he began a list. **Auburn for hair. Bronze for skin. Chestnut for breeches. His vest is emerald. His shirt is celadon. The stitching is viridian.**

She shook her head. "Wouldn't it be simpler to say brown and green?"

Tupper tried to hold back, but a crooked smile snuck onto his face. With a sly glance at Aurelius, he nodded.

The merchant rolled his eyes, then returned to writing.

Nay, the Clow are not exclusively brown, but darker shades of hair are prevalent. It compliments their spots. Other notable features include claws, fangs, slit pupils … and unique ears.

Aurelius underlined the final word and smirked triumphantly. With a sidelong glance at the baker's wife, he said, "I'm deucedly curious if you inherited your several times great-grandsire's ears."

Missus Quince frowned deeply. "Don't let them twit her about her ears, Tupp. She's sensitive!"

"My turn, lambkin," Freydolf rumbled, dropping to one knee before the counter. He plucked the pencil from his bond-brother's hand. Beckoning to the girl, he began a series of sketchy portraits—a slender Flox with curling horns, a powerful Pred with fangs and claws on display, a haughty Grif with a beaky nose.

Chelle gasped softly, and Tupper moved over so she could stand next to Frey.

"You're very good," she said in admiring tones.

The sculptor accepted the compliment with a smile, then continued—a barrel-chested Ursa, a scaled Basq, and a Pika with long, delicate ears. Labeling each race in turn, he added **Clow** and drew a male and female with broad noses, mottled skin at their temples, and lobeless ears that came to triangular points.

Beneath the pair, Aurelius wrote, **Clow traits are reminiscent of a feline's.**

Chelle looked between the men. "And yours?"

Aurelius smiled fiercely. **We're sometimes referred to as wolves.**

With an impish smile, Freydolf drew a comical wolf begging for a loaf of bread.

Aurelius scowled and demanded, "Make it more ferocious. No self-respecting Pred begs!"

The sculptor added a second wolf, all scowl and prowl, then gave it a fluffy pup to defend. Then he added the small ram with soulful eyes.

Chelle giggled softly. "It's all of you!"

Missus Quince stood by, but most of the bustle and bluster had gone out of her. "Do you mean to tell me there's people like *those* living somewhere hereabouts?"

"Nay," Aurelius politely corrected. "They live somewhere quite far away."

"I wouldn't believe a lick of it if it weren't for Chelle. One of them Clow and one of our Flox ...? To think!"

Freydolf said, "Aye, many centuries ago. Long enough ago to be forgotten."

Beckoning for Chelle to turn, Aurelius reached for her hair, saying, "May I, young lady?"

The girl pushed Quintrell into his arms and stepped out of range. "Don't."

Aurelius lifted his hands in a gesture of surrender, then wrote, **The Clow have charming ears. I merely wanted the sprat to see for himself.**

"Sprat?" she asked.

Tupper's shoulders hunched a little, but he raised his hand.

Freydolf crooked his finger to her and used one hand to shield his writing. **I still call him lambkin.**

Chelle laughed softly. "You really are brothers. Family."

Aurelius scrawled, **Do all your family have these fetching ears?**

"No," she answered readily. "Several of us are cinnamon. People don't mind that so much, but when another trait comes up, it's ... harder. Sometimes it's the eyes. Sometimes the claws. Sometimes the ears. None of my brothers or sisters have a defect. Just me."

Tupper grabbed for the pencil and used large letters to

write, **NO!** Patting the sketches of the Clow, he urgently wrote, **It's not bad to be part Clow. Master Tremont was nice.**

Chelle folded her arms over her chest. "How would you know? You just told me he lived centuries ago."

I know his statues.

Frey could see the girl didn't understand, so he took back the pencil and added, **Master Tremont's workmanship shows a kind and loving heart. And a fondness for dancing.**

Tupper nodded adamantly.

With a glance at her auntie, Chelle quietly revealed, "My papa has cat's eyes. Mum thinks they're wonderful. And I have an uncle with teeth like yours."

"Different traits cropping up within the family tree," Aurelius said. Recalling his secretarial duties, he wrote, **It's a pity no one remembers. You carry a proud legacy.**

Chelle's chin lifted as she searched their faces. "You won't make fun of me?"

Aurelius smiled. **You know we wouldn't.**

Freydolf wrote, **No more than you'd mock us for our lack of horns.**

The corner of her mouth quirked, and she blithely said, "You look *very* strange."

Without further ado, she lifted her curls, revealing a lightly-furred, triangular ear set neatly against the side of her head.

Aurelius nodded approvingly. **Classic Clow. Quite adorable. My wife could confirm my assessment if you'd care to meet her.**

She looked from the merchant to the sculptor, and Frey also nodded. **Thank you for trusting us, Chelle Tremont. Please, count us as friends.**

Chelle folded her hands over her heart, then spread them wide in a show of gratitude. Then, she turned her head, again lifting her hair so Tupper could see.

The lad had never been shy about touching things, so Frey wasn't at all surprised when Tupper trailed his fingertips along the edge of her ear. It trembled slightly, and color rose in Chelle's cheeks; but she stood her ground.

"I've always hated my ears," she mumbled. "I thought I always would."

Aurelius made a snide aside. "Oh, can *anyone* change her mind?"

Missus Quince's wrung her apron hem. "I never! A Meadowsweet! You don't suppose he'd be willing to overlook her ears?"

"My dear woman," the merchant drawled. "He's looking right at them."

Freydolf held his tongue but busied his pencil. Once they returned to the Statuary, Chelle would only have this paper to hold on to, so he worked to add to its value. A hasty sketch of Aurelius with Quintrell on his shoulders. A more painstaking portrait of Tupper. And a short message for her to find later.

If you have more questions, entrust your letters to Ewert Meadowsweet.

Finally, he improved upon the silly drawing that had made her laugh earlier. The three wolves and young ram now kept company with a speckled wildcat.

2

The Necessary

Tupper mostly didn't mind bathing, but Flox custom and Pred traditions were vastly different. He'd been raised to seek solitude before undressing, but his master had grown up in a culture where group bathing was a normal part of every day. Ever since he was ten, Tupper had been trying his best to honor *both* traditions. While Frey washed, the young Flox would work on basketry in the corner, eyes carefully averted while the man rambled on about this and that. Then after the sculptor returned to his workshop, he would take his turn in the enormous tub.

By now, Tupper was used to the awkwardness, if not entirely over it. However, their evening routine had changed a lot, especially since Quintrell's weaning. Aurelius had decreed baths a daily occurrence, and Frey hadn't even balked. In fact, Tupper would have wagered that this was the Keeper's favorite part of the day. It was certainly the noisiest.

"That's it. I give up!" Carden exclaimed.

He was attempting to give two-year-old Arni his bath in one of the laundry tubs. The young father's shirt and pants were soaked by his son's repeated attempts to escape.

"The lad's left out," said Freydolf with a sympathetic smile.

Tupper felt bad for Arni. How did you explain to someone

still in diapers why Quintrell was allowed to play with Uncle Ree and Uncle Doff in the big tub, while he had to sit by himself in the sink.

"You're being foolish, apprentice," Torio remarked from where he lounged in the steaming water with the Pred. "Is there a reason these two boys cannot bathe together?"

Carden sighed. "That would require my joining you, and Flox ..."

"... prefer tepid bathwater?" challenged the Grif. "The world will not end if we learn that your backside is as fair as your face. Why are you imposing cultural differences on those who don't know they have any?"

Tupper held his breath as Carden considered Torio's words. Finally, the Flox kissed the top of Arni's head. "You're right. This is ridiculous."

"And thus, after a lengthy siege, the Pred way prevails!" Aurelius gloated as he lathered Quintrell's hair. "Very sensible decision, Mister Meadowsweet."

"Master Freydolf, would you take him?"

"Aye, and gladly," the Pred held out his hands, and Carden passed down Arni.

Then to Tupper's astonishment, his eldest brother stripped right in front of all of them, sat on the edge of the sunken tub, and lowered himself in. Freydolf and Aurelius made room, and the younger man reached for the soap to wash his son's hair.

Tupper was still trying to decide what to think about this turn of events when Farley trundled into the room, hauling an armload of wood for the fire.

"Ah!" the boy yelped. "Carden! You're ...! How come ...? Hey, can I?"

"Ridiculous question," Aurelius drawled. "The invitation has always been open, *even* to you."

Farley shimmied out of his clothes and sprang into the center of the bath, splashing water in every direction.

Aurelius lifted Quintrell above the sloshing water. "*Do* contain your enthusiasm."

Shaking his head, Torio said, "Why am I not surprised that

my energetic lackey can add brazenness to his list of endearing qualities?"

"*I* am," Carden muttered eyeing Farley. "Aren't you even the least bit shy?"

"Nah. It's okay if it's family ... right?" He reached over and tweaked Arni's toes, then held out his hands, "Come to Uncle Far, and I'll teach ya how to spit water between your teeth!"

Torio laughed and turned bright blue eyes to their lone spectator. "Well, young master?"

Tupper rubbed at the base of his horns, thinking it over. There was no mistaking the way Freydolf averted his gaze. To him, sharing a bath meant something different than washing. Family. Friendship. Trust. Togetherness. Brotherhood. Bonding. This was a tradition the man wanted to share ... but would never demand.

No one pressured Tupper. Torio refused to make a big deal of anything. Aurelius treated it like the most natural thing in the world. Quintrell and Arni giggled and splashed. It certainly helped that Carden and Farley had taken the plunge first, but *they* weren't going to be Tupper's reason for setting aside his modesty.

He waited patiently until his master stole a glance. "Frey?"

"Aye?"

"Is there room for one more?"

Shortly after he stowed his tools, doused the lanterns, and dropped onto his bed, Freydolf had a visitor. Tupper tiptoed over in his nightshirt. The sculptor wasn't sure why the lad had waited. All the others had left hours ago. Maybe Tupper wanted to be sure he had his distracted master's full attention. Or maybe it was lingering shyness. "Should I be apologizing, lambkin?"

"What for?"

Freydolf smiled at the sound of Tupper's voice. It was still settling, but its timbre was definitely deepening toward manhood. "You don't have to bathe with us if you don't want to."

"Oh." After a lengthy pause, he said, "Make room."

The man chuckled and eased toward the middle of the wide bed. "I'll not begrudge half my pillow to one so brave. But I mean it, Tupper. If you're not comfortable ...."

A hand found his shoulder and patted. "It wasn't so bad. Much."

"You were embarrassed. I could tell."

"Yes. But you weren't. That helped." Tupper turned Olexi loose in the space between them and nestled down. "Do Pred always have lessons at bathtime?"

"Aye. Fathers keep their sons close and teach them all manner of things, just as mothers do for their daughters."

"Aggie's been bathing with Ulrica since she got here," the lad revealed. "And Melina lets Dulcie and Yona share, too."

Frey hummed thoughtfully. That would explain why the girls had picked up Terse so quickly. Ulrica had been giving extra lessons to her pets. Reaching across to mess up Tupper's hair, he asked, "Is *that* what you came over here to talk about?"

"No." His servant lowered his voice to the barest of whispers. "What should I do?"

"About?"

"Chelle."

A smile warmed Freydolf's tones. "Does something need to be done?"

"Maybe. Probably."

"And why's that?"

The lad bluntly said, "I'll pick her. If she wants."

"But you hardly know the girl. Would you want to be chosen simply because ...."

Tupper sat up. "What?"

"I was *going* to say, would you want to be chosen simply because you were brave enough to stand your ground before a Pred."

"Like me?"

"Aye, and that worked out well enough."

Tupper lay back down. "Yes. But that's not all."

"Oh? Was it her 'fetching' ears?"

"No. I picked her before I knew about those."

"What then?" asked Frey.

"She was good to Quintrell." He bashfully added, "She called him *cub*. That was cute."

"Aye." Rubbing the back of his neck, the Pred said, "Maybe it would be better to talk to your other brothers about this sort of thing? Carden and Ewert have wives."

"But they didn't talk to Chelle."

"And I don't know anything about Flox courtship."

"But you know *me*."

Freydolf immediately relented. "I'll do my best, lambkin. Feel free to ask me anything."

"Good." Edging closer, the lad solemnly asked, "Do you think I should cut my hair?"

It took a moment for the man to catch up. He'd been bracing himself for a much more uncomfortable line of questioning. "I was under the impression that you're proud of your hair."

"I like it this way," Tupper readily acknowledged. "But Chelle said we looked strange."

"She was probably referring to us Pred."

"I'm not so sure."

The lad had a valid point. Tupper no longer blended in with the rest of the Flox. He dressed too well, walked too carefully, and wore his hair in the Pred manner. According to Aurelius, their young man had even hinted about wanting his ears pierced.

"Are you in a hurry?" asked Frey. "I mean … you're not long enough in the horn to marry, right?"

"No." Tupper touched the tip of a horn that still bore gouges from when Quintrell was teething. "I'll be sixteen in another week, and Carden was eighteen when he married Melina. But Ewert was my age when he made a marriage bargain with Tillie."

"So it's *not* too early for young men to consider their options."

"No. I've been looking for a good pick for a while."

"Since when?" Frey asked in surprise.

"Three years ago." With a small shrug, he said, "Ewert told me not to wait too long, or all the best girls would be taken."

The lad wasn't jumping blind, then. Which made sense. This was Tupper, after all. He took life at his own pace. Honestly curious, Freydolf asked, "What kind of young lady have you been searching for?"

"Brave. Hard-working. Nice," he said vaguely. "And someone who could smile at you."

"Me?"

"No one ever did before, but you even made Chelle laugh. She has a nice laugh."

"Aye," Frey agreed. He gave Tupper's shoulder a friendly poke. "I think it's too early to submit to a shearing. Before you change yourself into what you think Chelle expects, you should find out if she likes your hair the way it is."

"I'll do that."

Freydolf hesitated, trying to put his mixed-up thoughts into simple words. "But it's okay to change."

"Yes. Today's change was good."

The Pred tried to follow this jump to a different trail. "Do you mean the bath?"

Tupper turned onto his side, putting his back to his master. "Yes. When I get married, I won't live in the workshop anymore. But we can still have bathtime. And you can help me teach my sons. And it won't be so bad."

The admission pierced Freydolf's heart. Tupper was worried about more than changing his hairstyle. "Not so bad?" he echoed in a warm rumble. "Your plans sound *good*, lambkin. I'll back you up no matter what you decide."

"Because we're brothers?"

"Aye. Always."

Tupper swept with extreme care, paying special attention to the corners and crevices. He hummed as he worked, hoping to soothe Dessa, who always whimpered when Frey brought out his tools. The sculptor hardly noticed his servant's puttering; he was too busy daubing white paint in curving lines along the surface of the small mountain that occupied the far side of their room.

"You missed a piece," Torio said from his seat in the corner.

The lanky Grif lounged sideways in the chair, one leg swinging over its arm while he flipped the pages of a substantial tome on loan from Morven's archives.

Scanning the wood planking, Tupper asked, "Where?"

Aurelius had impressed upon him the importance of collecting every pebble and speck of black stone, for these scraps were the only payment Freydolf had agreed to take from the Grif in exchange for giving shape to his mountain.

With a twinkle in his eyes, Torio pointed up. "You're harboring a petty thief."

Tupper leaned on his broom and looked into the array of lanterns suspended over this secondary work area and smiled. Nott perched atop one of the highest, cradling a precious chunk of magical stone to her chest. "Did you find a good one? Show me."

Nott dropped onto his outstretched palms and swung around. Changing direction, the little monkey frisked up his shoulder, and after a short rollick through Tupper's curving horns, she ducked under the abundance of his blond curls. From this safe haven, she made faces at Torio.

Tupper lifted a hand, and Nott surrendered a fragment about the size of a walnut. Inspecting it briefly, he slipped it into his pocket before stroking the little guardian's fur. "Thank you, Nott. You're a good picker."

Torio smirked. "She's hardly worthy of praise. It's not as though she could find a dud."

It was true. None of the other mountains had such a strong concentration of magic. "All of Dessa's get will be strong," Tupper agreed.

After endless months of research, sketching, and debate, Freydolf had finally come to the conclusion that more than one statue waited inside the mysterious rock. Once he put his mind to it, Tupper was able to differentiate five strong voices.

Torio had dubbed the loudest one Dessa. She was the mountain's heart.

The lesser voices that emerged from the babble would become guardians, assuming Freydolf discovered how to wake black stone. He straightened from his meticulous task and folded his arms over his chest. "Torio, would you please reassure your mountain? I've barely started for the day, and she's already complaining."

Waving a hand dismissively, the Grif said, "You cannot hold me responsible for her moods. Just use that mallet of yours and knock her into shape."

"She would prefer your hands to mine."

Torio cheerfully replied, "But *I* am no sculptor."

"Nay, but we'll make a Keeper of you yet." Nodding to the book in the Grif's hands, Freydolf said, "You're turning pages. But are you paying attention to what's written on them?"

"How could I do any less?" Torio replied with a straight face. "Riveting stuff. Utterly absorbing."

Freydolf looked to Tupper. "Make him mind his lessons. There are some things *every* Keeper needs to understand."

Once his master returned to mapping his next cut, Tupper checked to see what the Grif was studying. "Is this book really that good?"

Torio reverently touched the page with one taloned hand. "Fascinating in the extreme."

Tupper didn't normally tackle such thick books, but maybe he should consider it this time. "What's it about?" he asked curiously.

With a sidelong glance in Frey's direction, Torio waved Tupper closer, then whispered, "No clue."

3

A Day to Shine

Tupper was anxious to get back to work, but he somehow managed to sit still long enough to satisfy Ulrica, who was applying copper foil to his fingernails.

"You must let me fix your hair, as well!" the woman exclaimed with a flash of fangs. "*Or* we could shock them all!"

"How?"

Leaning forward, the Pred woman said, "I could gouge through your fair flesh, further mingling our cultures while lending you an air of sophistication. Aurelius has collected several sets of earrings to tempt you."

"I haven't earned them," he declined. "They would suit Aggie better than me."

"Aye. She's like a daughter to me. I would be proud to pierce her."

Tupper wasn't sure Merona Meadowsweet would entirely approve of earrings for Aggie. Actually, their mother would probably be shocked by the manifold skills her daughter had learned from Aurelius and Ulrica Harrow.

Just then, the baby of the Meadowsweet family strode through the room with a basket of laundry propped on one hip and bells jingling at her ankles. She *let* them ring. Tupper had joined this game often enough to know they were a lure.

This was training.

Quintrell soon popped through the door. He didn't call out, but his golden eyes sparkled with happiness. The little Pred had sharp ears, and he loved playing this baby version of hunt-and-catch.

Aggie winked at the boy who was hers to mind, ending the need for him to keep silent.

Immediately, Quin darted over to the table. "Unca Tupp! Shiny!"

Tupper wiggled the fingers of his finished hand. "Yes. For today, I'll shine."

"Me, too?"

"Nay, boy," his mother firmly replied. "You'll wait for your own birth festival. Today is your uncle's."

Quintrell leaned against Tupper's leg. "Hunt?"

Once again, Ulrica said, "Nay, boy. Your uncle has no such responsibilities today."

In point of fact, Tupper had finished most of his chores before breakfast lest anyone try to take them from him. It was easier for him to relax and have fun if he knew his work was done.

Aggie slipped up behind him and wrapped her arms around his shoulders for an affectionate squeeze. He half-expected a knife to appear at his throat, but instead, he felt the cool brush of silk.

"What's this?"

"A present," Aggie replied. Slipping around to stand next to her mistress, she held up a celebratory tunic, like those worn by Pred on their birth festivals. Pure white with copper trim. "From us. Do you like it?"

Tupper had never been one to stand out, which may have been why he loved this tradition so much. The fuss and fancy clothes made him feel special. "Yes. I'll change as soon as Ulrica's done."

"Which I am," the woman announced. "So dress the part, then play it. No more work."

Tupper politely argued, "I only have a few things left t–"

And *there* was the blade. But it wasn't Aggie.

Quintrell giggled at his father's success and patted Tupper's leg. "He caught you!"

"I let my guard down," he gravely replied, tipping his head back to meet Aurelius's smug gaze. "Your papa *always* wins this game."

"He's best!" Quintrell boasted.

"Yes." Addressing his captor, Tupper asked, "Did you need something?"

"Not from you, sprat," the man drawled. "Did you mistake my wife's words? No more work."

Relaxing in the Pred's clutches, he asked, "You want me to shirk my responsibilities?"

"Aye. Choose a diversion or two and while away the hours until dinner. Give us time to prepare a proper feast to honor your attainment. Carden says you're long enough in the horn to be called a man by your people."

Tupper caught the qualifying tone. "But not by you?"

"Nay." The deadly hold became a solid embrace, and the Pred swore, "You shall *always* be a sprat in my eyes."

That promise may have been the nicest thing Aurelius had ever said to him, so it felt like a gift. With a small smile, Tupper whispered, "Thanks."

Chelle had never been gladder to see the back of a customer than when Mister Thistledown stumped out the door with the last of their day's baking in his arms. He was a spleenful old goat who always dragged Missus Quince out of the kitchens to complain. Nothing satisfied him—the size of loaves, the filling in turnovers, and most especially *her*. Although Chelle couldn't hear the words, she'd received enough suspicious glances and sneers to know the man wanted her gone.

At least today he'd been quick about it. How he'd found coin enough to clear their shelves mattered little to her. Riddance was good.

She hung the **CLOSED** sign in the window, bolted the door, and rested her forehead against it for a few moments. Another day done. Another waiting tomorrow. She could do this. She was getting by.

When she turned, Chelle leaped backward with a startled gasp, thudding against the door. Tupper Meadowsweet stood there with hands upraised and apology written all over his face. With one hand over her hammering heart, she concentrated on keeping her voice steady. "How did you get in here?"

He pointed toward the back door.

That meant he'd come through the kitchen. "Nobody saw you?"

He shook his head.

Which made no sense. Unless. "Because they've all left?" she asked wearily.

After a moment's hesitation, he shook his head again.

How odd. It wasn't like the Quinces or Mister Pennyflax to let people come through the back. Setting that aside, she gestured toward the empty shelves. "We're all out of bread. I can't sell you any."

Tupper nodded again.

She hadn't expected to see him again so soon. According to Missus Quince, they had their own bread oven up on the mountain, so the Pred didn't come into Hayward very often. She couldn't help asking, "Is Quintrell with you?"

The young man tapped his chest, then raised one finger.

"Just you," she murmured, staring fixedly at the shining nails. "What happened to your hands?"

He glanced at his nails, which seemed to have been coated with metal, then held out his hand. Palm up.

Chelle stared at it, then him. He wasn't showing her. "You want me to go with you?"

Tupper nodded, hand steady as he waited for her answer to his wordless invitation. It was strange to face someone who wasn't perturbed by the communication gap. Many people grew impatient, pushed her aside, demanding to speak with someone who could hear. But this fellow hadn't opened his mouth once.

"You're not a very talkative person, are you?" Chelle guessed.

He frowned slightly, thinking it over. With a small shrug, he shook his head.

That was a switch. It was up to her to keep the conversation rolling. "Where did you want to go?"

He pointed in the direction of the bakery's back door.

"Far?"

Tupper shook his head.

Making up her mind, Chelle nodded and waved for him to lead the way. Tupper accepted this with a nod and hurried toward the kitchen door. To her surprise, he moved so stealthily, no one in the kitchen noticed him slip past and out the door.

When she followed, Missus Quince turned and asked a question her worker couldn't hear. Chelle sighed. After so many months, why did the woman bother? "We're sold out. I locked up. May I go?" she asked.

The woman made a shooing motion, and Chelle took her shawl from its peg and stepped outside.

Tupper leaned against the wall beside the door. Sunlight made him brilliant—white-blonde hair, white shirt, and gleaming copper. He held out his hand once more, and this time she took it.

True to his word—or at least his headshake—he didn't take her any further than around the corner of the building, into the small, walled garden behind the bakery. Chelle helped tend the herbs the Pennyflaxes grew in great quantity to use in their baking.

He waved for her to sit at one end of the short bench next to the rosemary shrubs, then sat beside her.

And that was it.

They sat.

In silence.

Chelle wasn't sure what to make of this turn of events. Tupper didn't try to talk. He certainly wasn't in a hurry. The young man's expression was peaceful. Happy, even.

Once again, she took charge. "Should I get some paper?"

The idea clearly startled him, and he looked between her and the bakery, then shook his head.

This wasn't normal.

"I'm confused," she said. "Did you come all this way just to sit here?"

Tupper nodded.

"That doesn't make any sense," Chelle said flatly.

His face fell, and he dipped his head in apology, moving to rise.

"Wait!" she exclaimed, and he did. Sighing, she explained, "This is frustrating for me. Let me get some paper, and you can help me understand what's going on."

From a pocket, he produced a small notebook and pencil.

She couldn't have been more baffled. "You had paper all along?"

He held it up demonstratively.

"Then why haven't you been using it?"

Tupper opened to a blank page and quickly printed his answer, turning the book for her to see. **I didn't have anything to say.**

Chelle laughed.

He offered a sheepish smile.

"Did you *really* come down from your mountain just to sit in an herb garden?"

Tupper slowly shook his head.

"Well?" she prompted.

He wrote slowly, as if reluctant to commit his thoughts to paper. When he finally handed her the notebook, he was still beating around the bush. It said, **I did want to ask you something.**

She tapped the page. "Then ask."

With a small nod, he busied his pencil again. **Do you think I'm strange?**

Chelle thought his earnestness sweet, and his question silly. With a soft laugh, she replied, "Very." Tupper looked so abashed, Chelle generously said, "I'm strange, too. You know that better than most people in Hayward."

His gaze drifted to where her ears were hidden under an abundance of cinnamon curls.

"You're wearing white, and you did something to your fingernails," she candidly pointed out. "You *have* to know how unusual that is around here."

He held out his hand, scrutinizing the copper-gilt nails. Then he wrote, **A Pred birthday tradition.**

"Oooh," she said softly. "Happy birthday."

The young man dipped his head and wrote, **I'm sixteen.**

She felt oddly shy, since people rarely took the time to share such details with her. "I won't be sixteen until late summer."

This trade of information seemed to embolden him, and he wrote a new question. **My hair?**

Chelle checked, "You want to know what I think of your hair?"

Tupper nodded several times.

This was obviously important for some reason. She sat back to study the young man, who stoically endured her scrutiny. He certainly didn't bear much resemblance to Ewert Meadowsweet, who laughed and talked a lot. Holding still. Walking smoothly. Nodding often. Saying little. This brother wasn't just different from his sibling, he was different from anyone Chelle had ever seen.

With a start, she realized Tupper was patiently waiting for a reply. "It's very long."

He quickly wrote, **Is that bad?**

"Not necessarily. Why do you ask?"

Tupper's expression wavered, and he grimly wrote, **If it's too strange, I could cut it.**

Chelle laughed softly. "Do you think *my* hair is strange?"

He slowly shook his head.

"Everyone else does."

To her surprise, Tupper gently touched one of the stray curls that lay against her shoulder, murmuring something. At her questioning look, he wrote one word in very small letters, as if he were whispering. **Pretty.**

He meant it, too. Someone with as open an expression as his couldn't possibly be lying. Chelle blushed and said, "You're not a normal Flox."

Tupper shook his head, still holding her gaze with quiet intensity.

Smoothing her skirt, she folded her hands in her lap before saying, "I can't change the way I look, so I don't think I could honestly ask someone else to change."

He seemed to need time to think her words over. It was strange to see disappointment overtake his features, and he lowered his gaze to study his fingernails.

Chelle's heart lurched, then skipped. This young man didn't care about generalities. His question had been very specific. Very personal.

"Tupper?"

Gray-green eyes lifted.

"I like your hair, Tupper." Mimicking him, she reached up to touch a fair lock. "Please, don't cut it."

His whole expression changed—happy and hopeful. He also turned a little pink in the ears, which made her suspect that he didn't receive any more compliments than she did. Then, he reached into one of his pockets and withdrew something, offering it to her.

When she extended her hands, he set something small and pink on her palm. Its delicate whorl was quite lovely. After admiring it, she admitted, "I've never seen anything like this. What is it?"

Tupper printed, **A shell.**

Her lips quirked at the word she knew sounded the same as her own name. She was familiar with nut shells and egg shells, but this was totally new. "Is it stone?"

He nodded and wrote, **It's dawnstone. Frey made it for me. It's mine to give.** Then, he closed her fingers around it.

Chelle's heart began to thud. Did Tupper realize how his gesture might be misconstrued? The bestowal of a gift was the first step in Flox courtship.

"You're giving this to me?"

He nodded.

She whispered, "Why?"

Tupper sighed and reached for her free hand. With a pleading look, he slowly lifted it, and her breath caught when he placed it against his horn. There was no mistaking his intent. This was a plea for patience until his horns finished their final curl. He wanted her to wait for him.

"Me?"

He nodded.

Most cinnamon Flox never married, so courtship had been the farthest thing from her mind when Tupper began. She wanted to ask him so many questions, but his writing hand was occupied. It was a strong hand—large, steady, work-hardened. Tupper's grasp was loose enough that she could have pulled away, but she couldn't bring herself to refuse. "Are you sure?"

His nod was just the tiniest bit shaky. As were her fingers, so she steadied them by taking hold of his horn, accepting Tupper Meadowsweet as a suitor. His hand closed gently over hers, and he smiled at her with such tenderness, her ears began to quiver. They always did when something good happened. And this was uncommonly good.

Tupper's heart was as light as his feet when he skipped down a familiar set of stairs. Dinner would be ready soon, so Ulrica had sent him to collect his nieces. Judging by the girlish chatter coming from below, Dulcie and Yona were in their usual spot.

Haimish trailed after him, tail swaying as he navigated the narrow path that cut through gray rock. The brownstone statue helpfully carried a lantern and the two small shawls Melina had sent along. Sunset wasn't far off, and evenings were cool.

"Uncle Tupp!" Dulcie cheered. "Happy birthday!"

He gazed around the terrace in surprise. "Where did you find so many flowers?"

The six-year-old giggled. "Papa and Uncle Kite climbed *so* high! They picked whole bunches for you!"

"Yes. Lots," Tupper agreed, traces of awe in his tone.

Dozens of flowering branches stood in urns all along the

edge of the terrace railing, their creamy white petals blushed pink and gold by the setting sun.

"Bend down!" the little girl ordered, and he dropped to one knee so she could wrap a garland of flowers through his horns.

As their familiar spicy-sweet scent surrounded him, Tupper pulled her close for a quick hug. "Thank you very much. These are my favorite."

Dulcie giggled again and patted her own floral crown. "I know!"

"Mish! Mish!" Yona chanted, bouncing with her arms upraised.

Haimish carefully hung his lantern from one of the hooks beside the stairs before sitting on the ground and opening his arms to his three-year-old darling.

Life in the Statuary had settled into too many new routines to count during the past few winters, but ever since this last autumn—when Melina's new pregnancy had left her wrung out—clear evenings found Tupper and the girls right here. While their mother put her feet up, the three of them chased straggling chickens with Dag, collected any late eggs, and greeted the sunset that would extend Haimish's day into night.

Yona had still been very small when Arni was due, so at Freydolf's urging, Melina had accepted Haimish as an extra pair of hands. She'd been hesitant at first, not wanting to take the stone Pred away from his maker. But Yona spent most of her young life in the stone guardian's arms.

Her first words had been Papa, Mama, Tupp, and Mish—though *not* in that order. She adored Haimish, and his gaze never strayed far from her sweet face. His pedestal now stood beside Melina's bread oven, and he woke each day to the smell of her spice-laden breakfast cake.

Accepting his own crown of oldtree flowers, Haimish wrapped Yona in her shawl, then passed Dulcie's to Tupper. As the young man draped it around his niece's shoulders, he asked, "Did you check for eggs?"

"Not without you, Uncle Tupp," promised Dulcie. "We always look together!"

So they joined the procession of clucking stragglers that Dag hustled toward their roosts. Tupper took the top row of nests, which was still too high for Dulcie to see into, and she checked the bottom ones. One white egg, two brown, and four speckled found their way into the little girl's gathering basket.

Back outside, Dag leaned into Tupper's leg, tail thumping against the ground. "Almost time for a rest," the young man said, scratching the golden wolf's ear. The sunstone guardian wore a ring of flowers around his neck, as did the moonstone she-wolf whose pedestal stood next to his. "Where's Nott?"

Dulcie pursed her lips thoughtfully. "Maybe petting Uncle Doff. Maybe pestering Uncle Kite."

He nodded. The little monkey loved Frey and loved to tease Torio. Either way, she would be back soon. Though an exchange of collars allowed both Dag and Nott to range about the Statuary by day or night, they still had to return to their pedestals at sunset to await moonrise.

Tupper sat beside Haimish, who'd carefully positioned himself so the setting sun's rays would reach his titian jade accessories. Yona reached over to pat her uncle's hand, silently begging to see his special nail treatment.

Dulcie plopped down on Tupper's lap and said, "Birthdays are pretty."

Her little sister nodded solemnly. Then, Yona kissed his knuckles and softly said, "Luff you, Unca Tupp."

"Love you, too," he whispered back.

With his chin resting atop Dulcie's curly head, Tupper watched the sky turn orange and purple. There had never been a day like this, and he almost wished it could go on and on. But then Nott tore past and sprang onto Dag's back, nuzzling her mate before tucking herself between the she-wolf's forepaws. Ember leapt daintily off his pedestal and frisked over to greet them, his crown of oldtree blooms tipped sideways like a crooked halo.

One thing ended. Another began. That's just the way life worked.

Tupper understood what that meant for the statues he loved, but he'd never really thought about what it meant for him. By Flox reckoning, his boyhood had ended. He was a man now, not that he felt any different. But things had changed again, and they would keep changing.

As the sunset guardian placed his paws on the young man's shoulder and wriggled with excitement, Tupper stroked Ember's narrow muzzle and hoped that he could face each turning day with half as much delight.

Freydolf *knew* Tupper. Not only had they been near-constant companions for more than six years, they were both bound to the same mountain. The lad's happiness rang like a song through Morven's magic, hinting at some untold secret. The Pred fully intended to corner his servant later and find out how he'd spent his free day. Maybe that would give him some clue to the melancholy mountain's celebratory mood.

For now, he was enjoying the show. While Aurelius and Torio taught Quintrell and Arni the Terse alphabet with a silly little sing-song rhyme, Frey moved to the edge of the tub and propped his chin on his fists.

"Tupp's not the only one getting older!" Farley grumbled. "I'm practically a man!"

Carden leaned close to tap horns with his youngest brother. "These say otherwise."

"No fair!"

"Today's Tupper's day. Stop trying to horn in."

Farley fidgeted. "That's not what I'm trying to do. It just happened to come up today is all."

With a soft sigh, Carden warned, "Farley ...."

But Tupper surprised them both by reaching over to chuff his little brother under the chin like he did to Rimbles. "Yes. It's definitely time. We should teach him."

"See!" Farley exulted.

Freydolf smothered a chuckle as Carden gave in and handed

down the time-honored Flox tradition of shaving. The brat couldn't have had more than seven downy hairs upon his chin, but he could hardly wait for permission to take a blade to them.

Carden calmly explained the importance of keen edges, steady hands, and thick lather. Then the three lined up side-by-side-by-side in front of the row of sinks.

They made quite the picture, dressed in naught but the towels at their waists.

"No doubt to their heritage," drawled Aurelius as he eased over next to his brother-in-law.

"Aye."

Freydolf had always thought that Tupper resembled Carden, but the likeness Tupper and Farley shared was uncanny. If it weren't for the younger boy's blue eyes and energetic personality, the Keeper might have thought time had turned back.

"Same height. Same build. Same hair," Torio listed. Tapping Arni's pert nose, the Grif said, "And you were hatched from the same nest."

Aurelius fluttered his fingers at the wet curls straggling halfway down Tupper's back. "The sprat *did* find a way to distinguish himself."

"Quite true," said Torio. "The fairest Pred in all the land."

Freydolf laughed, and the three Flox turned at once, matching quizzical expressions on their faces.

Tupper asked, "What?"

Grinning broadly, the sculptor said, "I was just thinking I should create a Triad of my own. Instead of Master Tremont's daughters, it'll be Master Meadowsweet's brothers. Future generations will herald you as my greatest accomplishment."

Farley jostled Tupper. "We're gonna be a masterpiece?"

"Don't be ridiculous," Aurelius scoffed. "I've already decided. Dessa will be Frey's masterpiece."

"*You* decided?" Freydolf echoed.

"Aye. Which is why I've been documenting your progress with the Lost Mountain," he smoothly revealed.

"I wonder if Dessa will hate that title as much as I do," Torio muttered sourly.

"Don't you think you're overstepping your bounds, Aurelius?" Frey asked. "Dessa belongs to Torio."

The Grif rolled his eyes. "Are you sure it's not the other way around?"

Aurelius slapped his hand on the stone tiles that surrounded the bath. "Frey, your efforts on her Keeper's behalf will fascinate sculptors all over the world! You'll be heralded as the expert in waking the unknown!"

Freydolf rubbed the back of his neck. "She's far from stirring. Don't get ahead of ...."

"Mark my words!" Aurelius exclaimed, his voice ringing with authority. "Dessa is a mountain like no other—pure magic, raw power. Other Keepers fled from this opportunity, but a Pred embraced the challenge. Master Freydolf Meadowsweet, Keeper of Morven, will go down in history as the only man brave enough to tame the legendary black mountain!"

4

Mix and Mingle

It was late when the men gathered in the balcony to officially welcome Tupper into their ranks. Farley had angled to be included, but Carden turned the boy over to Ulrica with the promise that his day would come. Assuming he lived two more years.

The Harrows were fond of pointing out that Farley's continued survival depended heavily on his attitude, behavior, and usefulness. That usually kept their resident mischief-maker on his toes.

So while Uncle Far helped tuck in the youngsters, Tupper bravely faced his future.

Carden took one look at his face and laughed. "Relax, Tupp. Your bravery isn't required for this particular rite of passage."

Aurelius produced a bottle from his private store, and Torio's low whistle testified to its quality. "You'll spoil him if *that's* his first taste," the Grif warned.

"As if I'd ever give him common swill!"

Carden explained, "We're mixing and mingling a little. Usually, it's a mug of ale with the village men, followed by a night of wild stories and bad advice. But since we're already combining Flox and Pred birthday traditions ..."

Freydolf reached for his hand and pressed something cool

against his palm. "... we didn't think you'd mind trading your mug for a goblet."

Tupper's fingers automatically closed around his gift. The stone goblet was definitely his bond-brother's workmanship, a masterpiece in heliotrope crystal. With a slow smile, Tupper smoothed his thumb over the decorative band just below the rim—Frey's signature whorled sea shells mingled with oldtree flowers. "Perfect," he murmured.

"Are you sure?" the sculptor asked in a low voice. "Torio pressed for this color, but I have others."

The Grif tapped his nose and winked.

"This is good. It's my favorite." Looking from face to face, Tupper earnestly added, "Thank you."

Aurelius poured, and Tupper held the goblet up to the firelight, admiring the crystal's translucence. Deep lavender and rich red. That's when he noticed the maker's mark wreathed in meadowsweet on the goblet's base. There was also an inscription. One word. **Always.**

He peeked at Freydolf, who was rubbing the back of his neck in embarrassment.

When Aurelius muttered something about sentimental old fools, Torio snorted. "Your plans for the remainder of the night are proof that your own fangs are also in that boy's pocket."

"That *man*'s pocket," Carden corrected, amusement sparkling in his eyes.

Lifting his glass, Torio inclined his head. "No offense intended, young master."

"What plans?" Tupper asked.

Aurelius pointed to the filled goblet, refusing to answer until his offering was tasted. Then the Pred drew himself up. "Flox traditions are deucedly tame, so we'll liven up the sprat's attainment ceremony with Pred ingenuity."

Tupper took another sip to give himself time to think. Aurelius's *ingenuity* usually led to the kinds of things that *did* require bravery. "How?"

The man smirked. "I propose a test. Little more than a game. Prove yourself, and I'll bestow the finest gift any father can grant his son."

Freydolf quickly added, "*Only* if he wants it."

"Aye, with his consent."

Tupper looked blankly from face to face. "But Aurelius isn't my father."

"A paltry detail I'm willing to overlook in the interest of cultural exchange!" Aurelius prowled closer to Tupper and flicked one of his horns with a clawtip. "Come with me to the Cavern. Show me what you're capable of. *Impress* me, and I'll pierce you."

By the time they reached the Cavern, the moon had crested, and its silvery light swept across the central gallery's floor from the clerestories, stirring the statues. Morven's children were on the move, with Thrall presiding.

The enormous dragon reared up and bared her teeth when the five men entered through the double doors. Only Tupper didn't hesitate. He knew Thrall too well to be bothered by her posturing. And now that he'd met Dessa, he could understand why she was so protective of her egg.

The heart of a mountain was precious.

Carden helped Freydolf wake a few torch-bearers, but Torio hung back, his gaze fixed on Thrall. "You'd *better* not give Dessa that many teeth," he called to the other Keeper.

"A dragon might be good," Tupper said. "Dessa likes to snap."

"All the more reason *not* to give her fangs!" protested the Grif. "I'm quite sure Harrow said the goal was to *tame* the black mountain. Not arm her."

Frey chuckled. "When she makes up her mind, you'll be the first to know what form Dessa will take."

"Speaking of weapons," Tupper ventured. "Do I need mine?"

Aurelius quirked a brow. "Planning to attack someone?"

He rubbed at the base of one horn. "Not sure. Pred games usually work that way."

"The purpose of *this* test isn't to demonstrate your dismal lack of skill, sprat."

Tupper nodded. "I can't defeat you."

Leaning down to stare directly into his eyes, Aurelius smirked. "I never said you had to *defeat* me. Your goal is to *impress* me."

"How?"

Straightening, the Pred fluttered his fingers in a vague way. "Show me what you can do."

Tupper was stumped, but Freydolf came to the rescue. "I've been meaning to test your affinity for stone," he said. "The four of us have hidden thirteen stones. One for each mountain. I want you to see if you can find them."

Shuffling his feet, Tupper asked, "That's all?"

"Aye. There's no hurry," the sculptor said reassuringly. "And they're all right here in the Cavern."

"I know. Does it matter what order?"

Freydolf bemusedly replied, "I'll set no other restrictions."

Tupper wasn't sure how else to respond, so he simply obeyed.

Brand trailed after him as he slipped silently through the crowd of waking statues, touching hands with several. It took no time at all to locate the burly minotaur who held a prize.

The statue's ears flickered when the young man lifted his hands, saying, "Please?"

With a toss of his impressive horns, the bullheaded statue relinquished a redstone sphere, and Tupper patted it. No wonder its voice had sounded so familiar. This wouldn't take long.

"Already?" Freydolf asked when Tupper offered him the first stone.

"You must have hidden it too easily!" Aurelius accused.

Torio suggested, "Beginner's luck?"

Carden chuckled. "Does that mean you're impressed?"

With a small shake of his head, Tupper strolled back into

the gallery, soon returning with dawnstone. He brought the titian jade sphere next.

"Are you doing that on purpose?" Aurelius demanded.

Freydolf shot his brother-in-law a stern look. "*Of course* he's finding them on purpose. That's the whole point."

"But in order?" the merchant pressed. "These are all from Far Continent."

"Yes," Tupper said. "It's more interesting this way."

He disappeared back into the dark recesses of the Cavern, leaving behind four speechless men.

Tupper brought First Continent stones next—blue, green, and crystal.

Torio opted to join him while he collected the next set— brownstone, dapple, and dazzle.

When Tupper placed the ecru sphere with its signature copper threading into his master's hands, Aurelius demanded, "Can you tell how he's doing it, Kite?"

The Grif tapped his nose. "Yes and no."

"Is that meant to be helpful?" he retorted peevishly.

"There's no cheat, but there's also no challenge," Torio said. "The young master simply walks to the hiding places, takes the stones, and carries them back."

Tupper frankly said, "If you wanted to make this difficult, you shouldn't have used stones I *know*."

Freydolf crouched beside the incomplete set on the ground beside the door and plucked up the closest sphere. "These are unmarked stones with little or no magic, lambkin. Are you saying they have voices?"

"Yes, and splitting them up made them grumpy." Tupper hovered uncertainly. "Should I go get the rest."

"Aye, lambkin. You're doing well."

"If you say so," he murmured, jogging away. He was anxious to finish, and the next three stones were close by—sunstone, moonstone, and starstone.

Tupper saved the black rock for last, mostly because of where it had been stashed. "I'll need more time for this one," he said apologetically.

Carden frowned in concern. "Why, Tupp?"

He hesitated, then asked, "Who hid this one?"

Three fingers pointed to Torio.

Tupper smiled at the man. "Was its hiding place your idea ... or Dessa's?"

Tupper wended his way toward the Cavern's central figure, remembering the day Freydolf had shown her to him. He'd loved Thrall at first sight, but probably not for the right reasons. When Tupper was ten, he'd wanted nothing more than to see the view from atop her head, but eventually, he'd understood that the great dragon was a piece of Morven's history. One with a fearsome purpose.

Thrall had been guarding the heart of this mountain ever since ancient times, when wars raged over the right to possess Morven's magic. The dragon's ferocity was meant to strike fear into the hearts of all, and she did a good job. Even brave men quailed in the face of her soundless roars.

Tupper had been content to let Thrall have her way up until his young nieces were ready to move into the Statuary. That's when he decided he'd better get to know their oldest guardian. IIc'd needed to know if she was truly dangerous. Especially where little girls were concerned.

"Hello, Thrall," he greeted, keeping his voice low.

The dragon's scales slithered together in eerie silence as she lowered her torso enough to rest one set of forearms upon her coils. He glanced over his shoulder as her tail slipped into position behind him, barring his escape.

"Freydolf wants me to bring him the stone you're holding close to your heart. May I take it back?"

Thrall's long-fingered hands flexed as they inched closer.

Rubbing at the base of one horn, he said, "I guess it *has* been a while since we visited. Do you mind if we keep it short? I'm in the middle of a tes- "

Tupper's breath left his body in a *whoosh* as she snatched him up.

Aurelius's shout was soon followed by Freydolf's deep bellow. "Tupper! Are you all right?"

"Yes!" This is exactly why he'd told them he might take a while. It wasn't because Thrall would fend him off. It was because whenever she caught him in her coils, she refused to let him go. Reaching up to tickle the long whiskers on her muzzle, he called, "She just misses me."

A strangled sound caught his ear, and Tupper craned his neck to see if the others had run into trouble. In the light of Brand's lantern, he could see the expression of disbelief on Aurelius's face as he slowly sheathed his daggers.

The other three men were doubled over. Laughing.

Tupper was impressed. Freydolf wasn't Keeper of Morven for nothing. A few stern words were enough to convince Thrall to relinquish her hold, allowing the young man to slip down into the dragon's nest of coils. He gently caressed her egg before retrieving the chunk of black stone tucked against its base.

When he turned it over to Frey, Tupper said, "You should make this one into a sphere as well. I think she'll cooperate. She feels left out."

With a startled blink, the sculptor scrutinized Dessa's fragment. "Aye. That's easily managed."

To Aurelius, Tupper murmured, "Sorry."

The Pred peered down his nose at him. "For?"

He offered a small shrug. "I couldn't do anything impressive."

"Is *that* what you think?"

Tupper couldn't understand Aurelius's tone. He'd done what

they asked, but it hadn't been much of anything. Maybe they didn't think he could handle anything harder? Feeling ten all over again, he touched one of his horns, reassuring himself that he was no longer a child. "Maybe you could give me a different test? I'll do my best."

Carden asked, "Was that less than your best, Tupp?"

Fidgeting under so many amused gazes, Tupper wished he understood the joke. "I probably could have gone faster. And I needed help to get away from Thrall."

"Speed wasn't the goal," Torio said. "And that great lizard's affection for you is entirely beside the point."

"The *point*," Freydolf quickly interjected. "Is that you accomplished the task we set."

"It was well within your abilities," the Grif added.

Carden smiled warmly. "You made it look easy."

Tupper shook his head. "But it *was* easy."

Aurelius stepped in front of him, dropping both hands onto Tupper's shoulders and giving him a gentle shake. "Have you *any* idea what you just did?"

With a faint smile, he replied, "Picked up after you ... like usual."

The Pred rolled his eyes expressively, and Freydolf said, "Tupper, *I* wouldn't have been able to do this. I don't know *anyone* who could. Your affinity for stone is ...."

When words failed the sculptor, Aurelius finished for him. "*Impressive.*"

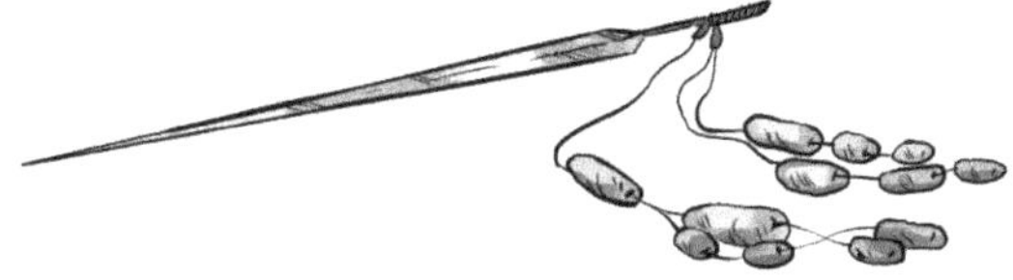

Freydolf couldn't help asking again. "Are you okay?"

"Yes."

In the wee hours of the morning after his birthday, Tupper sat in his nightshirt on the edge of his bed. His feet still didn't reach the floor. They probably never would.

The Pred anxiously pressed, "You're sure?"

"Are you trying to mother me?"

"Aye. You're injured."

His servant's chin came up a fraction. "No. Pierced."

"Does it hurt?"

"A little. But I think this was harder for you. Carden said you almost fainted."

Tupper held out his hand in an invitation Freydolf willingly accepted. As he sat beside his bond-brother, the Pred drew in a shaky breath. "You're braver than I'll ever be."

The lad gazed at him with a thoughtful expression. "I don't feel brave. If anything, I feel vain."

Freydolf chuckled. "Perhaps too many of your formative years were spent with Aurelius."

"I think so, too. But I don't mind."

Gently shifting aside some of Tupper's curls, Frey said, "They'll suit you."

He tentatively touched the slender rod filling the neat hole Aurelius had made through the lobe. "Maybe."

There was no mistaking how pleased he was. With an indulgent grin, Freydolf offered, "I'll fashion rings for you … for after they heal. Or do you want droplets like Aurelius's?"

"Droplets," Tupper said quickly.

The sculptor nodded. "What kind of stone do you want? Jewels? More lavender crystal?"

"No. I want Morven's stone."

Freydolf could tell Tupper had put a lot of thought into this. When answers came so easily, his mind had been made up for a while. "Moonstone it is," he said approvingly. "And speaking of Morven. My mountain has been unusually quiet today."

"You can't hear her singing?" the lad asked in disbelief.

The Keeper slowly nodded. "Aye, I hear her melodies. But she's keeping secrets from me, and I think they're about you."

After some consideration, Tupper asked, "She knows things about us?"

"A Keeper's mood affects his mountain's. And because of your bond, so does yours." Giving the lad's shoulder a nudge, Frey asked, "Has something happened?"

"Yes."

"Is it something you can tell me?"

Tupper's smile was full of sleepy contentment. And perhaps a little too much of the wine Aurelius had insisted the lad drink to brace for his ordeal. "Yes."

"And ...?" he pried.

"Chelle likes my hair."

"You were in Hayward today?" Freydolf hadn't realized the boy had gone so far.

With a nod, Tupper explained. "Graven's fast. It was easy."

Many things seemed to come easily to this lad. Things Frey had always found impossible. "Very good. Do you think she'll look as favorably on pierced ears?"

"I'll ask her next time, but I don't think she'll mind."

The Pred couldn't resist teasing a little. "Already planning to see her again?"

"Yes." The lad's smile took a sly turn that meant he was teasing back. "I'll have to."

Playing along, he asked, "And why's that, lambkin?"

"Because she accepted my gift. We're courting."

Freydolf gawked. Tupper grinned. And the strength of Morven's joyous song doubled.

5

Squawk and Squabble

Aurelius tapped the game board with the tip of one claw. "That was an illegal move, Kite."

"Was it?" the Grif asked, feigning surprise. "Skies above, you're right! A thousand apologies, my good man!"

"Spare me your shams," the Pred scoffed. "You know the rules as well as I."

Tupper smiled to himself. These two were evenly matched where games of strategy were concerned, so they often challenged one another on the quiet evenings they spent in the balcony. Tonight was different, though. One thing had led to another, and there was an intriguing wager riding on the outcome of this game.

"Is Torio going to lose?" Tupper whispered to Frey.

His master's solemn wink was an affirmative.

Aurelius knew it, too. He toyed with the green jewel dangling from one ear lobe. "Shall I take your descent into the underhanded as a sign that you've finally grasped your imminent demise?"

Torio rubbed his nose. "I *shall* defeat you!"

"Perhaps another day, but not this one." With a serene smile, Aurelius generously offered, "If I take one ear and Ulrica the other, the ordeal's end will be doubly swift."

One look at the Grif's pale face, and Freydolf took pity. "At least give him some wine."

"I might spare some swill if he needs to brace himself."

"The *good* wine," Tupper said. "Because Dessa's happy."

"Happy? She's a vindictive harpy," Torio complained.

Freydolf glanced up sharply from his sketchbook. "Is that *really* the shape you'd like her to take?"

"No!"

"Then banish the very thought from your mind," the sculptor sternly instructed. "And resign yourself to rings."

Tupper patted the small black stone that would soon become matched circlets. "Yes. Rings."

Torio grimaced. "Hasn't Dessa claimed enough of my life? Must she pierce my flesh as well?"

Frey gently said, "Maybe she needs it."

"Needs *what*?"

"My mountain calls for tears. Perhaps yours calls for physical contact," the Pred suggested.

"Like dawnstone," Tupper added.

Freydolf leaned forward, resting his elbows on his knees, all jesting aside. "Ask her what she needs, Torio. Help me understand your mountain."

Tupper nodded. "Otherwise, she might never wake."

"Maybe that's for the best," the Grif countered warily.

Aurelius leaned forward and smacked him lightly upside the head. "Think, Kite! If Frey gives her legs, you could travel again! Don't deny your restlessness."

"Aye. You'll likely be the first Keeper *not* confined to one place." Freydolf indicated the sheaf of discarded sketches on the floor beside his chair. "Find her form, and you'll be free."

Torio still balked. "Give her legs, and I'll be giving up what little distance I can keep from her. She'll follow me everywhere!"

"Like a puppy," Frey teased.

The Grif wrinkled his nose. "No dogs!"

"Like a pet dragon," suggested Tupper.

"*No* fangs!"

"Like a jealous lover," Aurelius remarked offhandedly.

Torio reverted to Terse, and Tupper caught enough of his sharp tirade to know his refusal was less than polite. The Grif drummed his fingers on the table as he assessed his position on the game board, then wearily begged, "If I concede now, will you make it two bottles?"

Tupper thought Aurelius's smirk was almost sympathetic as he withdrew a slender blade from his vest pocket. Unsheathing it with a flourish, he purred, "Done."

In the deep of night, with the full moon as witness, Morven's Keeper sneaked into the Cavern like a common thief. If it hadn't been for his mountain's shrill insistence, Freydolf would never have dared something so drastic.

"This is unheard of." Gazing up into the looming dragon's face, he murmured, "Nay, this is criminal!"

Thrall loosened her many coils, exposing her egg to the silvery light pouring down through the clerestories. Even convinced as he was that Morven wanted this, Freydolf balked. "And you're abetting this crime? What kind of Guardian invites vandalism?"

She tapped the smooth curve of its polished shell with one long finger.

"Aye, I know," he grumbled. "But I'm taking not a sliver more than necessary. And from a place not easily noticed."

From this proximity, the force of Morven's triumph buffeted his mind *and* body. Frey chuckled softly. "You should be ashamed of yourself, a mountain your age. I'd have thought you too well-established to be jealous of a youngster like Dessa."

His teasing tones were ignored, for Morven meant to have her way. Magic spun into a tight whorl near the base of Thrall's egg, and Frey knelt to set the keen edge of his chisel against the spot. Taking careful aim lest he bollix the job, he crooned, "Gently, now." And the hammer fell with a sharp *thwack*.

A piece of gray rock clattered to the floor, and Freydolf sat back on his heels and hung his head. Setting aside his tools, he held his hands before him. Now that the deed was done, they were trembling.

"Is all well, Morven?" he asked, his voice low and hoarse.

Delight whirled through her magic, and he nodded. "Aye. That's good."

Once his scattered wits were scraped back together, he plucked up the slender fragment and held it up to the light. Yes. It would be just enough for the task his mountain had set.

Two droplets.

Tears from Morven.

Heartstone for Tupper.

Carden knelt in the street not far from his home, patiently chiseling a decoration into one of the countless cobbles. He glanced up when Aurelius announced his presence by pointedly shuffling his feet. "Good afternoon, Mister Harrow."

"Apprentice work?"

"Yes. Master Freydolf says there is no substitute for repetition, but there's no need for it to be pointless."

The Pred noted the trail of identical carvings behind the man, leading back toward his home. "I see! These are for your little ones?"

"That's right." Carden sat back on his heels, unobtrusively stretching his back. "These will lead them to safe places— the bakery, the necessary, the hen house, the workshop."

"My home?" Aurelius prompted.

"If you'll permit it."

"Aye. That way, my boy can easily track down your brood."

Tilting his head to consider the design Carden had chosen, he asked, "Why bees?"

The younger man's ready smile held a touch of bashfulness. "My wife's name means *honey*."

Aurelius's eyebrow quirked, then he flipped back the full swallowtails of his newest coat, drawing both daggers in one smooth motion. Crouching before the Flox, he displayed the jeweled blades. The heads of two snarling wolves had been figured into the end of each hilt. With a smirk, Aurelius said, "My wife's name means *wolf*."

"Ah," Carden said warmly. "Did you have need of me?"

"In a sense." The Pred kept his gaze on his blades as he said, "In my country, when there are twelve people living together in a place, they may consider themselves a colony. A city unto themselves. When your next child is born, we will be enough."

Frowning thoughtfully, Carden said, "We are already thirteen."

Aurelius waved a clawed hand dismissively. "Torio won't stay, and he'll take Farley with him. They don't count."

"If that's so, then Aggie ...?"

"She's ours," the Pred said sharply. In gentler tones, he murmured, "Nothing could convince Ulrica that your sister isn't the daughter she's always longed for."

"Thanks to you and your wife, Aggie is blossoming into an extraordinary person."

Briskly getting back to the point, Aurelius said, "When your babe is born, we can establish ourselves."

"But most of us are Flox," Carden pointed out. "We hardly qualify as a Pred colony."

"Trifling details. Hardly worth mentioning."

"Then why bring it up?"

Aurelius pursed his lips, then proceeded with delicacy. "The matter of governance must be considered. Frey hardly has time to lead a community. Which leaves ...."

"Us. And I shall defer to you." Carden laughed and asked, "What shall we call you then? Headman, elder, lord ... or do you fancy *your highness*?"

"It's a good day to visit your orphans," Freydolf said, gazing off to the west.

The wind was picking up, and dark clouds smudged the horizon. Tupper could feel the storm building strength. "All day?"

"Aye. Fetch enough bread for two meals from Melina and warn her to latch her shutters. I'll let Aurelius know we'll be working below."

Tupper was braver about storms than he had been as a boy, but he still didn't like foul weather. The rattle of rain against glass and the clap and growl of thunder made him uneasy. So Frey made a habit of hustling him into the deep galleries, sometimes for exploration, but lately to work on the unfinished statues Morven had bequeathed to Tupper.

Chores attended to, messages delivered, he hastily filled a rucksack, then joined Brand in the six-sided room that led down to the fountain colonnade. Fat raindrops splattered against cobblestone by the time Freydolf caught up, his apron over one arm, and his favorite tools bundled under the other.

Over the last two years, Aurelius had been turning away commissions from Frey's usual customers in order to give the Keeper time to work on his masterpiece. But Dessa was slow to trust, so the sculptor's restlessness had been channeled into Tupper's orphans. The Flox was pleased for the abandoned statues and proud of Freydolf for adopting them. Three were completed. Five were close. All had seen some measure of progress, for the Pred worked a little here, and a little there, as his mood took him.

Patting the flank of the starstone unicorn, Frey said, "They will be invaluable to Carden when the time comes to wake them. Some apprentices wait years for one stone or another to come to their mountain. We have all twelve."

"Thirteen."

"Aye. If Dessa cooperates."

Tupper helped Brand light the torches, then moved to the overhead lanterns. Freydolf didn't mind working at these depths so long as they brightened the space. Even before the last flame was lit, the sculptor was tapping away at a dawnstone guardian's many scales.

Pleased by the expression of contentment on his master's face, Tupper quietly moved to the edges of the room. The chamber was his. The statues were his. Therefore, the chunks and chippings were his. Instead of casting them out with the rest of the rubble at the edge of the outer courtyard, Tupper shrewdly saved the leftovers in heaps and stacks along the walls. Small though these pieces were, they were unusually fine stones with strong magic, a trove worth more than most Flox could earn in a lifetime.

Up until now, Tupper's abundant resources had remained untapped. But today, he meant to do some very careful picking. One pile at a time, he sifted through and listened close.

By the time he was done, his pockets were bulging, and his master's stomach was rumbling. So Tupper slipped to Freydolf's side and caught his arm. "Time to eat."

"Aye. Sounds good," the Pred quickly agreed.

Midway through their meal, Tupper emptied his pockets, lining up the stones he'd chosen. One for each mountain—strong of magic, sweet in temperament.

Frey watched closely, but reserved comment.

Once they were arrayed between them, Tupper said, "I need your help."

"What did you have in mind?"

"Something for Chelle." He distractedly touched his horn in the same place she had. "Flox give courting gifts. Mostly little things, but at least one very nice thing."

Indicating the stones, Frey asked, "This will be one of your gifts?"

"Yes. The best one." Tupper explained, "For when she promises to marry me."

Frey nodded seriously. "This gift suits its giver. What shape do you want it to take?"

"Ulrica says that Pred give ankle bracelets."

"Aye, they're very traditional. So these will be beads?"

"Yes." He fidgeted, then asked, "Are beads too easy? For a master sculptor?"

With a low chuckle, Freydolf admitted, "Apprentices shape countless beads during their training, but I'd be proud to fashion this set for your bride-to-be." Leaning forward, he roughed up Tupper's hair, then gently touched the highly-polished perfection of one of his earrings. "I seem to be making a lot of jewelry lately."

"Thank you."

Freydolf quietly asked, "How did you know she was the one?"

How? Tupper placed his hand over his heart as he pondered the question. How did you explain something you didn't entirely understand? He simply *knew*. Down deep. Where everything that mattered was held safe and sacred.

Finally, he asked, "How did you know Morven was calling?"

Freydolf's expression grew thoughtful, and his fingertips lightly tapped his broad chest. Then with a crooked grin, he said, "Aye. I see."

Tupper smiled back. It was nice to be understood.

6

Ties that Bind

Torio abandoned his books. This new life wasn't everything he wanted, but he was used to making the best of things. "Makes me sound ungrateful," he muttered as he skirted a tower, crossed a bridge, and descended a steep set of stairs. Sometimes he wondered if Freydolf assigned so much reading just to give him something to rebel against. "Can't escape *her*, so I run from him instead."

The Grif longed to throw caution to the wind, let it clear his head, and choose his own path. Who would care? It wasn't as if he'd ever be a proper Keeper. No matter how you twisted and turned the truth, his life had been ruined by the mountain he'd killed to save. The heart it left behind was a rare mystery, a priceless treasure, and a heavy shackle.

Touching the glossy ring that pierced one ear, he grumbled, "You make it hard to wander, Dessa."

Her laugh sent shivers down his spine.

She didn't understand. How could she? Mountains had never been meant to rove. Yet he had always been a wanderer. The child of traveling performers, he'd seen the world's marvels at his father's side, held close under the shelter of a feathered cloak.

Posters in every language had billed the Grif's father as a magician, though he knew more about sleight of hand than stone affinities. One man's ordinary was another man's wonder, and wonder-workers were often those who knew something they weren't telling. The informed could see the trick or become the trickster.

Still, Torio had grown up believing in the miraculous. It took little faith when he could *see* magic—sense its presence, follow its ties, discern its intents. His vision had led him to his vocation, making a merchant of him. But one night upon a storm-tossed sea had been enough to destroy everything. Magic had betrayed him.

As he descended through the summer-green forest, Torio slowed his steps, treading stealthily toward the sound of rippling water. Parting the leaves that obscured his view of the stream, he spied a lone Flox dozing upon its banks. Tupper.

The Grif's lips quirked. "He thinks himself ordinary, yet he bears no resemblance to that sad state."

Everything had changed the day Dessa cried out for her Keeper by name. Extraordinary though it sounded, Tupper had taught stone to speak. And to the boy, it was no different than teaching his young nephews.

Impossible. Miraculous. And completely guileless.

In his straightforward simplicity, Tupper had treated the beleaguered Grif no differently than he did his precious stones—listening to the heart's cry, grasping the most urgent needs, and finding practical ways to meet them.

Torio's needs had been few, but desperate. Tupper's grasp of them was uncanny, and his generosity had come in the form of four demands. Stay. Rest. Study. Wait.

And in his obedience, Torio found something precious. In hushed Terse, the Grif quoted, "Doves abide while eagles soar, but both build nests."

Although he didn't have blood ties with these people, they'd welcomed him as an adopted uncle. A fellow Keeper. A board game rival. Torio contributed little more than language lessons to the community, yet in return, they were going to make it possible for him to fly free. And the moment he could, he *would* be gone.

He meant to range far and wide. To sail, to ride, to fly, to see the world and marvel anew. But this time would be different. Thanks to Tupper, Torio Kite would have a home to return to.

"Working on your tan, young master?"

"Not really." Tupper had been wondering if Torio would speak up or move along. Turning his head, he opened his eyes. "It doesn't work."

"Your skin darkens," the Grif said, emerging from the underbrush.

"Yes, but my hair lightens."

Torio chuckled. "Even a summer at sea wouldn't suffice to tan your hide to Pred depths."

"I know."

"Why do you adopt so many Pred traditions?"

Tupper offered a small shrug. "They're useful. Like hunting. And knowing when someone's coming."

"You heard me?"

"Yes," he replied, letting his eyes drift shut again.

"But you didn't reach for your dagger," Torio challenged.

The Flox's dagger lay in easy reach on the bank beside him, and he tapped its hilt with his fingertips, proving he knew right where it was. "I didn't need it."

"Because I'm not a threat?"

"You've never tried to be," Tupper replied. Sitting up to gaze into the man's face, he asked, "Do you want to be?"

"Not especially," said the Grif. "Bad for business."

Tupper shrewdly inquired, "And *do* you have business with me?"

"Yes, if you would be so kind. I want you to straighten out my earrings."

The lad studied the heavy, black rings as Torio came to sit

beside him. "They look the same as before."

"They don't *sound* the same! One is louder than the other." With a scowl, he admitted, "I was hoping you could convince them to cooperate. You're better at asking nicely than I am."

Tupper nodded. Holding out his hands, he asked, "May I?"

Torio lowered his head to make it easier for him to reach. "Please."

He gently tugged, then slipped the tips of his little fingers inside the circlets, smoothing his thumbs over them. He smiled faintly as he lavished them with the attention they were clamoring for. As they calmed, Tupper said, "I wish I knew what they wanted."

"That *would* make things easier for your Pred brother."

Tupper searched the Grif's calm gaze. "Do you know what Dessa needs?"

"No." A brow quirked, and Torio asked, "Do you think I'd hold back if I did?"

"No. At least, not for long."

Talons tapped restlessly. "I want to go."

"Yes. And she wants to go with you." Scooting a little closer and adjusting his grip, Tupper tentatively said, "Can I ask something personal?"

Torio snorted through his nose. "Young master, you are massaging my ear lobes. I hardly think you could get *more* personal."

He froze and blinked. "Does this mean something in your culture?"

"Not for Grif, but I don't recommend your trying this with a Pika." Laughing in the face of Tupper's fascination, Torio urged, "Ask away."

Tupper nodded gratefully. "Something Frey said a long time ago made me wonder," he began, trying to explain. "Maybe it will help?"

"And what might that be?"

"He talked about dreams. So do some of the books. They say when Keepers won't listen, their dreams trouble them." Tupper asked, "What do you dream about, Torio?"

Tupper and Torio lay side-by-side on the bank, Rimbles sprawled between them as they soaked up the sun. The lynx kitten's ear twitched. Tupper's lips quirked, and he whispered, "We're about to be surrounded."

"By trees?" the Grif inquired in an undertone.

"By hunters."

A blue eye cracked open. "What tipped you off?"

Tupper said, "Arni giggles."

"I didn't hear anything."

"Probably because you were half asleep."

Torio rubbed his nose. "Any chance I'll be able to get the rest of the way asleep?"

"No. Quintrell's probably tracking us."

"Reduced to prey," sighed the Grif.

A few moments later, the leaves of a nearby shrub rustled, and Aurelius and Carden strolled into the open, each with a small boy riding on their shoulders. Instead of bared blades, they were armed with small baskets.

"Not a hunting expedition?" Torio called.

"It *is*," Carden replied. "Melina asked for berries, so we're raiding the patches."

Aurelius lowered his son to the ground and folded his arms across his bare chest. "Isn't Mister Kite supposed to be entrenched in the archives?"

The Grif lazily waved one hand. "Those with feathers are meant to fly free."

"You may have a prodigious beak, but your wings have been clipped," Aurelius drawled.

"All the more reason to leave me in peace," Torio retorted. "Let me mourn the loss in my own way."

Before they could see who could wax more sententious,

Quintrell pounced on Torio. "Got you!"

With lofty unconcern, the Grif folded his hands behind his head. "I am at your mercy, little Harrow. Be as kind as you can."

After giving the challenge careful consideration, the little boy dropped a kiss on the man's nose. "Luff you, Unca Kite!"

Tupper sat up and traded a speaking glance with Carden, who was hiding his smile. The brothers Meadowsweet were of the opinion that little Quinn took after his Uncle Doff. Aurelius rolled his eyes at the boy's un-Pred-like behavior, but let it pass. Arni giggled and wriggled to be let down. "Me, next!"

Carden held the two-year-old's hand, steadying his son's less-than-stealthy attack. Once Arni delivered a noisy smack, Tupper asked, "How many berries did you find?"

"Dis many!" Quintrell reported, showing off fingers that were stained red.

With a nod, Tupper asked, "Did you come down to wash?"

"Aye!"

"Aye! Wash!" echoed Arni.

"Let Unca Tupp help," he offered, wading into the stream with them to scrub off the berry juices.

Aurelius joined them, eager as always to clean up. "So why are you two loitering down here?"

"We were discussing matters of magical importance," Torio said in breezy tones. "Nothing a dullard like you could grasp."

"Dreams," interjected Tupper. "Do you dream, Aurelius?"

"Aye," he replied.

"Do Pred dream as viciously as they daydream?" asked Torio.

With a small shake of his head Aurelius calmly corrected the man. "Naturally, I dream of Ulrica. And lately, about my sons."

Tupper's tones were all innocence as he said, "When you dozed off in front of the fire the other night, you were muttering instructions to your tailor."

The Pred puffed up, but Carden stepped in before he could bluster. "Do you mean everyday dreams, or the sort sent by mountains? Because when Morven was calling to me, I always dreamed of the moon. And I would wake up with tears on my face." Shaking his head, he added, "I didn't know until Master

Freydolf told me that those things *meant* something."

"Aye, I see." Aurelius's keen gaze narrowed on the Grif. "Do the dreams of Dessa's Keeper hold some deeper significance?"

"What if I told you I *don't* dream?"

"I'd call you a liar," the Pred said sweetly.

Torio sat up, shoulders hunching as he tugged an earring. "And what if I told you my dreams are all sweetness and light."

"I'd call you a *bad* liar," Aurelius said, frowning now. "What's he hiding, sprat?"

Tupper simply shook his head.

After muttering a few choice words in Terse, Torio admitted, "My dreams are nothing but nostalgic nightmares. Dessa is forever casting me onto the black rock where I found her."

"The island?" Carden asked.

"Such as it was," Torio acknowledged. "I'm thrown onto jagged stones from a great height, surrounded by wind and waves, under a starless sky, with the sting of salt in my wounds."

"Dessa could be trying to tell you something," Carden pointed out excitedly. "One of those things—or a combination of those things—could be the key to waking her!"

Tupper held Torio's gaze over the top of Arni's head. "You don't like the dreams."

"Who would?" the Grif complained. "I'm alone. Cold. Wet. Miserable."

"And Dessa?" Tupper pressed.

Torio grimaced. "Oh, she's cold, wet, and miserable, too. But happy. *So* happy."

"But why?" Carden murmured.

The Grif hid his face, so Tupper answered for him. "Because she's *not* alone."

Visits from Chelle's new suitor were erratic. He didn't turn up often, and he never stayed for long. But he checked in on her at intervals, usually bringing small gifts. Tupper's courting gifts were unusual, though very practical. The seeds and slips for the garden had pleased Missus Quince almost as much as her. And Mister Pennyflax had built her a tiny coop when Tupper brought her a basket with half a dozen black chicks inside.

Checking the faint blush in the early morning sky, Chelle dressed with care, her heart already skipping. Fair mornings often brought good things from the mountain. Maybe today. She hoped so. She wanted to see him again.

Shortly after sun-up, Chelle was picking herbs in the walled garden behind the bakery when she caught a movement out of the corner of her eye. Tupper stood just outside the low gate, and he raised a hand in silent greeting.

With a bright smile, she called, "Good morning."

He glanced toward the bakery door, then beckoned to her.

Setting aside a bundle of lemon thyme, she brushed her hands on her apron and hurried over. Tupper seemed nervous about something, so she kept her voice low. "Is something wrong?"

Shaking his head, he held out his hand.

This was new. Usually, they visited right here in the garden, sitting on their bench. "Are we going somewhere?"

He nodded.

She hesitated. "Will it take long? I have to work."

Tupper withdrew a small notebook from his pocket and quickly jotted a message. **Not far. Not long. Nothing bad. But secret.**

Chelle found his odd bluntness sweet. It made an interesting contrast to the smooth way he moved. Placing her hand in his, she said, "Let's go."

He tucked her arm through his, walking by her side instead of leading her along by the hand. Although it wasn't an uncommon courtesy, he was the first young man to treat her like a lady.

Her fluster quickly turned to uncertainty when she realized where Tupper was leading her. "The woods?"

A nod.

Having recently endured a long and embarrassing written exchange with Missus Quince about the kinds of things good girls did and didn't do when courting, Chelle balked. While the young woman had been fascinated to learn about courting games that were unique to Hayward, the rest had been awkward.

While Missus Quince assured her that Meadowsweet boys were raised better than to take advantage of a young lady's innocence, she'd firmly drawn the line of propriety. Going alone into the woods with a boy definitely crossed that line.

Coming to an abrupt halt, Chelle calmly demanded, "Why the woods?"

Tupper searched her face, then released her. Retrieving his little notebook, he showed her the page, carefully underlining, **Nothing bad.** Then he printed more of an explanation. **I want you to meet Rimbles. She's mine.**

"Rimbles?"

With a nod, Tupper pointed to the phrase, **Not far.**

When he slipped into the woods, she followed. And it *wasn't* far. As soon as the trees shielded them from view, the young man dropped to one knee in front of a stand of ferns. Chelle could tell he was saying something, perhaps calling out, and then the fronds rustled, parting as an animal emerged and leapt into his arms.

A pet? She shook her head, feeling foolish. "You have a kitten?"

Tupper nodded and turned, holding the tawny creature against his chest. He scratched under the little one's chin, tickled her ears, then stroked her arching back. All the while, he watched Chelle's face, silently pleading with her for ... what?

Then, the feline turned its face toward Chelle and blinked, and the young woman started. There was something very wrong with this cat.

"Everything's the same," she muttered. "Why is she all one color?"

He eased closer and reached for her hand, encouraging her to touch the bundle of golden fur. Rimbles was as fuzzy as a new kitten, despite the odd coloring. Soon, the little one was leaning into Chelle's touch, and Tupper transferred her into her arms.

She gasped at the unexpected weight. "So heavy!"

Tupper located his pencil again. **Rimbles is a statue. Stone is heavy.**

"But she's alive!"

Tupper nodded happily.

"How?" Chelle demanded, playing with the kitten's tufted ears. **Magic.**

She gaped at him, but her mind quickly whirled through what information she had. "Does this have something to do with Master Freydolf?"

His approving smile brought color to her cheeks, and he busied his pencil, filling the rest of the page with a scanty explanation. **Some stones have magic. Some sculptors can use it. Frey is a master. He made Rimbles. He woke her. She's a stone guardian.**

"Magic," she breathed. Looking off in the direction of the gray mountain, she asked, "You live in a magical place?"

Tupper nodded solemnly.

"I don't really understand, but Rimbles is cute." Touching the baby lynx's over-large paws, she asked, "So why is she a secret from everyone?"

Turning a page in his little book, Tupper carefully wrote, **People are afraid of Freydolf. They think there are monsters on the mountain.**

"Are there?"

Tupper paused, then answered, **There are many, many statues. Some are big. Some are scary. Freydolf doesn't like to scare people. He keeps his mountain's secrets.**

Chelle couldn't see how something as gentle as this kitten could frighten people. But then she'd been shunned all her life because of her ears and her hair color. Being different made a difference.

"That's sad," she mused aloud. "Because magic seems quite wonderful."

When she glanced up, Tupper's awed expression caught her off guard. So did his gentle embrace. Rimbles squirmed between them when he gathered Chelle close, her cheek resting against soft fabric as Tupper rested his chin atop her head.

He'd shared a great secret. Something dear to him, but also dangerous. More than any of his other gifts, this showed the depth of his commitment.

"I'd like to see this magical place for myself someday," she admitted.

She could feel his nod.

Daring to press the matter, Chelle asked, "Soon?"

His arms tightened, and she smiled. Then giggled as a small vibration started up, for it seemed that magical stone cats could purr. Feeling incredibly bold, she asked, "Is Rimbles happy because you're happy?"

Chelle expected another nod, but Tupper eased back. When she glanced up to search his face, his eyes were shining. And then he surprised her again by leaning down just enough to drop a light kiss on the tip of her nose.

7

Welcome News

Ewert burst through the workshop door, breathless and beaming. "Good morning!"

His enthusiasm dwindled somewhat when Freydolf didn't even glance up from the black stone he was shaping. Not to be discouraged, the man strode into the kitchen, located a heel of bread, and hurried back out to wave it under the sculptor's nose.

Dark eyes blinked, then focused. "Ewert! I wasn't expecting you today. Was I?"

The second Meadowsweet brother laughed. "No, sir. I'm not the one who was due. Where is everyone?"

Freydolf glanced out the window. "It's not even mid-morning. They're here and there—lessons, gardens, stables. Do you need anyone in particular?"

"Oh, I want *everyone* to hear this, but you'll be the first." Thumping his chest, Ewert announced, "I'm a father!"

Hastily setting aside his tools, Freydolf gripped the young man's shoulders. "That's welcome news! How's Tillie?"

"Tired, but good. Mother said she was so strong through the whole thing," he shared with obvious pride.

"And the baby?"

The younger man's blue eyes took on a twinkle. "That all depends."

"On what?"

"On which one you're referring to. Tupper was right!"

Freydolf grinned. "So Tillie *was* carrying twins. Boys? Girls?"

"One of each. The little girl has a strong grip and a stronger voice, but her brother's a wee little thing. Mother's fussing over him now. Thinks he's too quiet."

"Maybe he's just letting his sister have her say first," Frey offered in gentle tones.

With a crooked smile, Ewert said, "Hope so."

Slipping free of his apron, the sculptor said, "Let's spread the word! I'm sure you're anxious to get back to your family."

"With reinforcements, I hope. Mother wants everyone who can to pay a visit." Chuckling, Ewert confided, "I don't think she likes it that the Butternuts currently outnumber the Meadowsweets in our front room."

"Baby?" Arni asked, wide eyes fixed on his father's face. "Mine?"

"Not yet, little man," Carden corrected. "Our baby is coming soon, but Aunt Tillie had hers before your mama could get around to it."

Melina grumbled, "You make me sound lazy."

"Hardly," her husband laughed.

"Can we go visit?" Dulcie begged. "I want to see!"

"Mish, too?" Yona asked softly.

Carden smiled at his daughters. "Haimish and I should stay home with your mama. It's too far for her to walk."

"Uncle Doff could carry Mama," Dulcie suggested. "He's strong."

The Pred chuckled. "She's naught but a wisp, but I don't think your mother wants to be treated like a sack of oats."

"Wisp," Melina said with a wan smile. "I feel more like one of your ocean's whales."

"Soon," Carden murmured comfortingly.

His wife nodded, then said, "But you should go. It's plain that Merona and Ewert want you. You're head of the family."

Ewert nodded. "We'd be grateful."

Carden hesitated, and Tupper spoke up. "You need to welcome them as Meadowsweets, and sooner is better for their naming. I'll stay with Melina. We'll be fine."

"Aye. We'll be back before nightfall," interjected Aurelius, who leaned through the door. "Ulrica has Quintrell ready. And Kite is offering his shoulders to young travelers."

"Me!" Yona exclaimed.

Dulcie smiled sweetly up at her Uncle Doff and asked, "Will you carry me?"

"Nay, Miss Dulcie," Frey answered. "I'll stay back with your Uncle Tupp. He and I will meet your new cousins tomorrow instead."

Carden finally nodded. "I'll just put Melina to bed."

His wife snorted. "I'm not sleepy."

"You should rest." To Tupper, he said, "Make sure she takes advantage of the quiet."

"Aye, mother her properly, sprat," Aurelius drawled. "Now enough of this palter! We must drive out those Butternuts!"

Freydolf's brows drew down, "It's *not* an invasion."

"I will merely ensure that the Meadowsweets can lay proper claim to Ewert's progeny. The retreat of Tillie's relatives will be purely coincidental!"

"A coincidence you'll enjoy," Frey accused.

"Aye. Immensely."

Freydolf stepped on a sharp stone and automatically lifted his foot, rubbing it against his other leg. Dessa was in a fine mood today, so he was splitting off another section of her block. Although he still couldn't see what form the central column would take, this piece's personality had quickly resolved under his hands. Very little stone would be wasted in bringing out a life-sized lioness.

"Torio is fond of lions, but you knew that, didn't you?" he murmured to the yet-formless feline. "Dessa isn't the only one who wants to please her Keeper."

It was exhilarating, working with such potent stone. He knocked away corners, then smoothed his palms reassuringly over the raw surfaces, pleased by the strong magic rising to meet his touch. This guardian would be magnificent, and he told her so in every language he knew.

However, before he began sculpting in earnest, he wanted to share his news with someone. Gazing around the empty workshop, Frey rubbed the back of his neck in consternation. "Where did Tupper get to?"

He dropped his apron across a workbench and paused to touch the larger, central section of black stone. "This is a good start, Dessa. Your first guardian shows great promise."

The heartstone radiated pride, and Freydolf smiled to himself. Perhaps in seeing her "children" come into their own, Dessa would discover what shape she wanted her existence to take. Pleased with the progress they'd made in a few short hours, the Keeper went in search of his bond-brother.

He ambled toward the outer courtyard, which seemed the likeliest place to find Tupper. Along the way, it occurred to him that the Statuary was unusually quiet with most everyone down in Hayward. "Strange how quickly one gets used to noise," he remarked to a stone turtle. Patting its knobbly shell, he lengthened his stride. There was a good chance the lad was with Melina.

But then he picked up the sound of splashing and a low laugh coming from the entrance to the Harrow's courtyard.

Slipping up to the gate, Freydolf grinned at the sight of Tupper visiting with Phineas and Nerine. The freshstone set into the front of the Basq prince's turban gleamed wetly as he gazed upward with a serene expression.

Strolling toward the fountain, Frey said, "Not many starstone guardians ever see blue skies."

Phineas dipped his head in greeting, and Nerine playfully waved her finned tail. Tupper kept right on tending to Graven, who blinked contentedly as the lad trailed wet fingers along each blue stripe.

With a sidelong glance, he shared, "Phineas usually stays in his niche during the day."

"Aye. Ulrica mentioned something about that. Called him shy."

"Children make him nervous," Tupper explained. "So he waits until they're tucked in."

Freydolf thumped the starstone statue's shoulder. "No harm in sticking to your strengths," he said generously.

"Tupp?" came a low voice. "F-frey?"

They turned to see Melina at the gate, leaning heavily on Haimish's arm. The brownstone statue's tail was puffed out like a bottle-brush, and his gaze was filled with silent pleas. To Freydolf's recollection, Melina had never called him by his nickname before. He wasn't truly sure if she'd done so now, or if she'd simply lost the breath needed to finish. Something felt off.

He asked, "Shouldn't you be resting?"

Her expression was grim. "I'm sorry to impose," she managed between clenched teeth. "But I'll be needing your help."

With a soft cry of dismay, Tupper rushed to her side and lifted a sodden patch on her skirts. "Melina," he groaned. "Oh, no!"

"Oh, *yes*," she replied, steel in her tones. "We don't have much time, and we don't have much choice."

Freydolf's eyes slowly widened with horror. "I'll go get ...!"

"*No!*" The woman held his gaze and sternly said, "And if you faint, I'll give you naught but stale bread until you're toothless, then scorch your mush."

The Pred paled, but mumbled, "Aye."

Freydolf gingerly lifted Melina into his arms and strode toward the workshop, Tupper jogging alongside. She made a scanty burden but cradling her close nearly drove him to his knees. Melina was trembling.

He opened his mouth to apologize, but he choked on his words.

Suddenly, she stiffened, and the Pred skidded to a stop. "What is it? Melina?"

The unfailingly sweet-tempered woman actually *glared* at him.

"Birthing *hurts*, Frey."

Peering up into his sister-in-law's face, Tupper asked, "Should you hold your breath like that?"

Melina writhed as if trying to escape the pain, and the Keeper tightened his hold, mindful of his claws. When she was finally able to draw air into her lungs, she ordered, "Inside. Old sheets. Clean knife. Swaddling. *Now!*"

"Yes, Melina," said the lad, clearly relieved to have direction.

Unwilling to be left alone with such an enormous responsibility, Freydolf rushed after him, keeping his stride smooth so he wouldn't jostle Melina. Tupper held open the door, and the Pred hurried through it, but paused uncertainly. "My bed?" he offered.

"No, no," she said, waving toward the far end of the room. "An old sheet on the floor. Something we can bundle up and burn later."

"Birthing is messy," Tupper helpfully interjected.

Frey winced. "Aye, Ulrica likes to describe her travail in excruciating detail."

His servant brightened. "Then you know what to do?"

"Nay. By the time she reaches the part where her 'waters drench the barren earth,' I've fled the room with my hands over my ears."

"Too bad. We've passed that part." Tupper pulled a little-used tablecloth from one of the cupboards, kicked aside several stray chunks of black stone that littered the floor, then spread the heavy cloth. Running to his bed, he pulled off a sheet, then called Haimish over to help him spread it neatly. "Pillows?"

"Please," Melina replied. "And some water."

"Am I supposed to boil it?" Tupper asked uncertainly.

"Just pour it into a mug, Tupp," she said wearily. "I'm *thirsty*."

With a sheepish smile, he disappeared into the kitchen.

Freydolf fixed his gaze on the ceiling high above in a feeble attempt to give Melina some privacy. "I shouldn't have encouraged your husband to go," he murmured. "I'm so sorry."

"It's Ulrica I'm missing."

"Aye. I *could* go get her. Riding Graven, it wouldn't take long."

Melina gasped as another birth pang took hold, and she hid her face against his broad chest until it eased. "No," she hissed. "It's happening too fast. Put me down."

Freydolf steadied her to her feet. "Are you sure you want to be on the floor? The bed would be more comfortable."

"You'll thank me later. Tupp's right about the mess," Melina said. "Besides, this is how we do things. For that matter, it's also how Pred give birth."

"I've never given it much thought," he admitted.

Tupper returned with the mug of water and bulging pockets. When Melina's hands shook lifting the cup to her lips, Frey quickly wrapped his around hers, not that it did much good. He was quaking right down to his core.

Thankfully, Tupper had entered mothering mode. "Your spot is ready. Kettle's on. Swaddling's warming in front of the fire. I have my knife and some string. What else?"

"Oh, yes. String," she murmured. "How did you know?"

"Frey ran out, but *I* listened when Ulrica told about Quin's birth. It was interesting."

Melina stared up at him, but before she could respond, another contraction doubled her over. Freydolf dropped to his knees in front of her, giving him a perfect view of her face when she grabbed his shoulders for support. Raw emotions gave her away. "Melina, don't be afraid," he begged. "When a sculptor shapes a statue, the state of his heart touches his creation. Let this child wake to naught but love and joy."

The woman's fingers dug into his muscles with astonishing strength, but when the pain passed, Melina seemed to have found a reserve of courage. Collecting herself, she touched her lips, then placed her fingertips against his mouth. An apology. "You're a good man, Freydolf Meadowsweet."

"Yes. He is," Tupper agreed, returning from a rummage in one of the chests with a chartreuse nightshirt.

"Good intentions may not be enough to keep me conscious," Frey wryly admitted.

"You'll be fine," the lad assured. "Remember when the chicks hatched into your hands?"

The Pred had fond memories of those tiny, damp puffballs. "Aye."

"This will be a little like that, only instead of a bird, there will be a baby."

Judging by Melina's bemusement, Tupper had glossed over much of what was about to happen, but Freydolf accepted his bond-brother's words with a firm nod. "I'll do my best."

Another contraction seized Melina, and once it passed, she panted, "I must ... change clothes."

"Will you need assistance?" Freydolf asked in a low voice.

She bit her lip, then said, "Haimish can help me."

"Yes!" Tupper exclaimed in relieved tones. "Yes, that's good. We'll go. Call us back when you're ready."

In the kitchen, the lad checked the kettle, rummaged through his collection of herbal teas, then turned to face his master. "You'll do your best?"

"Aye."

"How good is your best?"

"Not very," Frey confessed. "When there's blood ...."

Tupper shook his head. "But this isn't a killing kind of bloodshed. This is what's needed to bring out a baby."

"Piercing your ears wasn't murder either, lambkin." As much as it pained him to admit it, he said, "Midwifery is beyond me."

Tupper nodded. "Then I'll do it. I've helped Aurelius and Old Gruff with colts and calves."

Melina's voice came from the workshop, and they hastened back. Haimish hovered protectively behind the woman, whose grip on the nightshirt's collar may have been the only thing keeping it from slipping from her shoulders. "This is far too big," she complained.

Stepping to her side, Tupper said, "It looks better on you than it did on Carden."

"*He* wore this?"

"Yes. He looked like a green butterfly." Tupper took Melina's arm and led her across the room to the sheet and small heap of pillows, bumping aside more small stones as they went. "This color is nice for your eyes. We should have Aurelius look for a bolt of cloth like this next time he goes to Drom."

It was odd, hearing the lad talk so much. He didn't normally ramble ... unless he was trying to soothe a frightened child or a new-found statue. *Ah.* Taking a deep breath, Freydolf resolved to do the same. He couldn't lend strength or skill, but comfort was within his abilities.

"We'll need your help, Haimish. Kneel here, beside Dessa." To Melina, Tupper said, "See? He'll be your backrest, and no matter how hard you squeeze his hands, you can't hurt him."

"Aye." Freydolf forced out a halfhearted chuckle. "After Arni was born, it took two days before Carden could hold a chisel properly again."

"Only because he refused to put down his son," Melina retorted. Her tone was crisp, but her glance was grateful. The brownstone guardian opened his arms as he usually did for Yona, and with Freydolf's help, Melina lowered herself into his protective embrace. "Thank you, Haimish."

Tupper arranged and rearranged the pillows, but they didn't do much for the pain. The pangs came in waves. Dragging closer. Pulling harder.

Freydolf felt so helpless.

"Drink," Tupper coaxed, holding the mug to her lips. "Take a sip."

"Tupp," she whimpered. "It's not supposed to be like this."

He nodded, then bluntly addressed what they'd all been avoiding. "You're my brother's wife, and you're a good wife. I know you don't want to lift your skirts for another man, but I *need* to see."

Tears slipped down Melina's cheeks. "I'm so embarrassed."

"I know. So are we. But like you said, we don't have a choice." Tupper kissed his fingertips and briefly touched them to her lips in earnest apology. "For a long time, I was the mother Frey needed. I'm sorry I can't be a sister for you, but brothers are family, too."

Another contraction ripped Melina's concentration away, and Tupper waited patiently.

When she was ready to hear him again, he put himself in charge. "It's simple. Frey will take care of your baby. I will take care of you. And Carden will forgive me later. Probably."

Melina sniffled and nodded. Permission to proceed.

Moving into position, Tupper said, "In a way, there *are* other girls with you. Dessa's here. This will be her first time seeing a baby born. How old were you when you attended a birthing?"

"Seven," Melina replied. "Mama let me stay with her when my little brother was born."

He nodded. "That's about right. Dessa's been with Torio for eight years. She's ready to learn about such things." Tupper lifted back the green nightshirt's hem, and kept right on talking. "And Morven has been a mother many times over. She's pleased with you."

"Me?"

"Yes. You've given her many tears today, and she thinks they're nice. I know you can't sense it, but there's magic all around us, like music at the midsummer dance. It won't make things easier for you, but I feel braver." Tupper carefully pulled the nightshirt back into place, then said, "Now it's time for Uncle Doff to make himself useful."

Frey had been staring out the windows with all his might, and he started at the sound of his name. "What do you need?"

"Light the lanterns, please. And give us something else to think about." Tupper rubbed at the base of one horn, blushing badly. "Maybe tell us a story? A long one."

"Aye, I can do that." He leapt to his feet and busied himself with wick and flame, searching his mind for a story that would do the job. If this was to be his contribution, he would make it an admirable one.

Melina was shuddering free of another contraction when inspiration struck. With a low laugh, the Pred announced, "I'll tell you how Aurelius and Ulrica first met. It *never* should have happened, but one of them crossed a boundary that *should* have been well-marked. Each still accuses the other of getting lost."

Tupper said, "I thought they met at a festival and danced together."

"Aye, officially," Frey acknowledged. "But they knew one another for years before that."

"Were they childhood friends?" Melina asked.

The man snorted. "More like *rivals*."

And so Freydolf spun out a tale of stubbornness, squabbling, and surprising sweetness, dragging out all sorts of embarrassing details that his sister and her husband would probably kill him for later. When Melina's groans grew louder, he simply raised his voice and talked over her. He'd always enjoyed telling stories, and theirs was a particularly amusing one.

Once he caught a low chuckle from Tupper, who said, "That's just like her."

Not long after, Melina managed a breathy laugh. "It's a wonder Aurelius survived."

"Aye. I've always thought that was the surest sign that my sister truly cared about him." Freydolf grinned broadly. "Time and again, she let him live."

Suddenly, Tupper's tone sharpened. "Melina?"

Freydolf felt a shift in Morven's mood and risked a glance over his shoulder. The woman's face was a picture of concentration as she strained. Fabric fluttered, and his gaze snapped to the ceiling. "Wh-where did I leave off ...?"

"The fall festival, when Ulrica was my age," the lad prompted.

He valiantly picked up the threads of his story, detailing the string of scandals that had marked his sister's chaotic courtship, but the telling was cut short by a strangled yip, followed by a soft oath that Tupper had probably learned from him.

"What is it?" Frey asked anxiously.

The lad whispered, "It's a *baby*!"

"Knew. That," Melina gritted out.

Tupper sounded entirely pleased when he said, "This *is* interesting! Can you push again?"

She must have found the strength, for the next sound to interrupt the expectant hush in the workshop was a newborn's thin cry.

8

Of All Things

"**M**elina, is this normal?"

"Don't worry, Tupp. It is."

"Thought so." In a stern voice, the lad said, "Frey, *don't* look, but hold out your hands."

When he obeyed, Tupper placed something warm and wriggling on his outstretched palms.

By now, Freydolf was used to holding babies, and he quickly pulled the newborn to his chest. "A boy," he murmured. "You have another son, Melina."

"Carden will be so surprised. He was sure this would be another girl."

"Aye, he'll be surprised," Frey agreed, glancing toward the windows. "A few more hours at most, and they'll be back."

"The swaddling blankets are in the kitchen," Tupper prompted. "Keep him warm."

Freydolf rose smoothly to his feet, tutting and crooning as he carried the little one to the kitchen. The baby *was* a little like the damp and matted chicks he'd held, but peeping was replaced by squeaky wails. "Such noise, little nephew," he rumbled. "Are you anxious to be heard?"

His crying abruptly stopped, and the lad struggled to open his eyes, squinting up at the man.

Chuckling softly at the babe's scrunched gaze, Frey asked, "Would you like a blanket? Your Unca Tupp was thoughtful enough to warm some for you."

Tiny lips pursed. Hazy eyes stared fixedly into Freydolf's face. And the wee lad squeaked.

"Right away, young master Meadowsweet," Frey replied, snatching up one of the dishtowels Tupper had chosen for makeshift bundling. In wrapping the soft cloth around the baby, he rediscovered something he'd first noticed with Arni. A newborn Flox fit neatly into one of his large hands. "Is that better, little mouse?"

Tupper hustled into the kitchen and poured hot water into a bowl, tempered it with a splash of cool from the pitcher, then grabbed soap and some cloths. Pausing to smile down at his nephew, Tupper asked, "Have you checked fingers and toes?"

"Nay."

"Do that while Haimish and I help Melina clean up."

"I shall perform a thorough inspection."

Freydolf talked nonsense to the baby while he tallied up each tiny digit. "You're all here, but you're a mess," he said conversationally. Carrying the baby to the washstand, he poured cool water into the basin, then added enough from the kettle to warm it. Moving to the hearth, he sat before the fire, dipping in the corner of a soft cloth and washing away the worst of the smears. Next, he did what he could for the boy's hair. By the time he was done, white-blond ringlets puffed out around the boy's head.

"You're your father's son," Freydolf said admiringly. "May you be as fine a man one day."

Just then, there was a startled cry from the next room. Tupper's voice shook when he exclaimed, "F-frey!"

The Pred stood. "Is something wrong with Melina?"

"I'm fine," the woman quickly called. "It's Tupper I'm worried about."

Frey strode out into the workshop without giving proper thought to what he might find. Full of concern, he asked, "What is it, lambkin?"

Melina looked over her shoulder at him. She was on her feet, wrapped in a quilt and leaning on Haimish's arm. But Tupper still knelt on the sheet they'd used to cover the floor. A sheet that had once been white. Freydolf dazedly attempted to drag his gaze away, but it was too late. Blood. *So* much blood.

The baby squeaked as his uncle swayed.

Frey groaned, slapping his free hand over his eyes. "Take the baby,"

In a moment, Tupper's voice was at his elbow. "Sorry. I have him. Sit down."

"Nay." The Pred moved to the wall and rested his forehead against cool stone. Taking several deep breaths to steady himself, he said, "Not until we calm Dessa."

"You can feel it, too?"

"Aye. It's been building for a while, hasn't it?" Freydolf risked a glance at the black stone that dominated the other end of the workshop. "I was too wrapped up to notice."

"Yes. She started softly." Tupper said, "Wait until I tuck in Melina and her baby. Then, I'll show you what I found."

Frey grunted.

A thin tang of blood hung in the air, which left him lightheaded and logy. The only thing keeping him on his feet was his responsibility to Dessa, whose giddy outburst wasn't quite enough to take his mind off the mess. The black mountain's magic whirled against his weakened knees and whizzed in increasingly frantic circles around them.

"Have mercy, Dessa," he moaned. "I'm spinning enough as it is."

"She's too excited to listen," Tupper said, pressing a warm mug into his master's hand.

The Pred sniffed at its contents. "Isn't this the medicinal stuff you made for Melina."

"You need it even more than she does. Drink."

Downing the bitter liquid in one go, Freydolf grimaced. Some of the lad's home remedies were truly awful. "One thing's clear. Dessa's doing everything in her power to get our attention, and that's a *lot* of power."

"Yes. It's my fault. I didn't sweep, so there were lots of chippings on the floor."

"This isn't something you should be apologizing for, lambkin. There wasn't time."

"Lots of them got … splashed," Tupper said delicately.

Freydolf winced. "I can imagine. You have one to show me?"

"Are you sure?"

"I *need* to know for certain. Show me."

Tupper nodded, but said, "Stay here. I'll bring some over. That way there'll be … less."

Glancing over his shoulder, Freydolf checked on Melina, who was propped up amidst pillows in his bed. She looked tiny, tired, and serene despite the riot of magic surging through the room. Melina had never shown any sign of magical affinity, but he couldn't help but wonder if her children would. Maybe one day, the newborn she was holding now would want to follow in his father's footsteps.

"I could teach him, too," Frey murmured, perking up a bit at the prospect.

Tupper returned with the same mug, but this time, it didn't hold tea. In the bottom, a black stone sat in a small pool of blood.

Freydolf's heart began to hammer, but he did his best to remain detached as he took the cup and inspected its contents. With the tip of one claw, he poked at the rock. Enough power fizzed along its surface that he probably could have woken the chunk simply by giving it a name.

"Aye, there's no doubt. Dessa needs blood." Lifting a shaky hand to his forehead, the Pred swiped at cold sweat.

Tupper pried the mug from his master's grasp. "Sit down before you fall down."

It was too late for that. Slumping forward, Frey rested his forehead on his bond-brother's shoulder. "Of all things," he muttered.

"It's good we found out," Tupper said. The lad shifted, and Freydolf felt light fingertips brush his lips. "I'm sorry it's not something easier."

Frey managed a hum, but the world was fading fast. He probably should have warned the lad, but he could barely breathe, let alone talk. Blackness as dark as Torio's nightmares swamped him, and the last thing Freydolf heard was Tupper sharply calling, "Haimish, help me!"

Tupper sat on the edge of a workbench, his pant legs rolled up and his feet bare. Watching the wide planks of the wooden floor dry was far from exciting, but he was ready for some peace. If he held still, he could hear the fires crackling in the balcony overhead. And the soft, steady breathing of the three people sleeping in Freydolf's expansive bed.

Melina had insisted she didn't mind sharing, which was really nice of her. Tupper and Haimish had lugged the unconscious Pred up and tucked him in where she could keep an eye on him. From that moment to this one, Tupper had been working as quickly and quietly as he could.

All traces of the baby's birthing had been bundled up and out. Every precious tidbit of black stone had been collected. And he'd only just finished scouring the floorboards. Taking a deep breath, Tupper exhaled in a sigh of satisfaction. When his master finally regained consciousness, he would only smell soap, herbs, and beeswax.

For several long minutes, he contented himself with watching the shadows lengthen across his clean floor. The candles he'd lit made them dance, and their quiet celebration made him happy. Three babies in one day. Did that count as triplets? Probably not. But this new trio of Meadowsweets would always share the same birthday.

Closing his eyes, Tupper listened hard. It was nearly dinner time. The others should be returning soon. More time gently slipped away before he heard the faint voice of a familiar stone.

With a small smile, Tupper whispered, "Here he comes."

When his younger brother sneaked through the workshop door, Tupper hopped from his perch and joined him in the entryway. "The others?"

Farley was breathing hard. "Torio's having fits. Sent me ahead," he said in an undertone. "What's goin' on?"

Tupper asked, "What do you think happened?"

"How would I know?"

He shrugged and waited, watching his brother closely.

Farley straightened and glanced around the room, staring hard at the bed for a moment before stealing a look in Dessa's direction. Shrewd, blue eyes narrowed. "What did you do to her?"

"To Melina?" he asked innocently. "She's fine."

Scowling, Farley whispered, "You *know* I'm talking about Dessa!"

"Why do you think I did something?"

It had always puzzled Tupper that Farley insisted he couldn't sense magic. Usually, he tried to outdo his brothers. The boy must have had a reason, but he gave himself away in moments like this. Aurelius often complained that Farley was either loud or louder, yet he knew enough to whisper. Catching a mountain's mood and truing his tones amounted to affinity.

"Dunno," Farley muttered, his gaze darting back to the black stone once more. "Something's different is all."

Tupper nodded and said, "I thought so."

"What?" Farley asked warily.

"You can hear her, too."

Freydolf came to with a start and pushed up onto his elbows, disorientation fueling his agitation. "Wha–?"

"Calmly, Master Freydolf," Melina said in a soft voice. "Tupp's taken care of everything."

He glanced at the woman next to him, groaned, and fell back on his pillow, hands covering his face. How mortifying. "How long has it been?"

"A few hours," she replied. "He insisted we all have a nap while he set your home to rights."

Taking a cautious survey of his senses, Frey detected no giddying smells. The clenching in his gut was all hunger. He sighed and sat up, swinging his feet to the pristine floor as he gazed out the windows. Evening was coming on fast, and the soft glow of candles barely touched the deepening shadows. He should light the lanterns.

"Where is the lad?"

"Farley was here ahead of the rest. He and Tupp went down to meet the others. They should be here soon."

"Good." Peering at her over his shoulder he asked, "Do you need anything?"

Color tinged her cheeks. "Yes. I'd like to visit the necessary." Anticipating his next questions, she added, "Haimish will come with me. Could you watch over my son while I change? "

"Aye, and gladly." Holding out his hands, he said, "This young man and I are already on friendly terms."

Before relinquishing the baby, Melina held his gaze. "Thank you, sir."

"Tupper's the only one who was any use, missus."

"But you carried me, and you stayed when I asked." Her forehead creased as she searched for words. "With you here, I felt ...."

"Embarrassed?"

"Definitely," she said, her cheeks darkening further. "But that's not what I meant. It's hard to explain, but this is your mountain, your home. Everything happens because of you. So when you're here, I feel safe."

There was an old saying that turned up a lot in the journals of past keepers. **Those with magic look to the mountain, but those without look to her Keeper.** For the first time, Freydolf realized that the mountain was no longer the only one in his care.

Fearsome claws slipped gently through downy curls as Freydolf quietly recited sculptors' lore in a sing-song voice. "Blue for sweet waters; white for the brine. Gray under moonlight; gold calls for wine." Hairy knuckles brushed the sleeping baby's cheek as he continued, "Touch pink at dawn; jade when day wanes. Warble for green, dapple needs rains ...."

He heard the workshop door swing open and expected to greet Melina, but Carden stood in the fading light. Glancing around uncertainly, the Flox hovered on the threshold. "Tupp and Farley refused to say *why*, but they told me Melina is here."

"Aye, she was. And she'll be back," Freydolf answered. So the boys hadn't told? Sly things. With a low chuckle, he beckoned to his apprentice. "Come see what she left for you to find."

Carden's gaze skimmed the hushed, candlelit workroom, resting for several moments on the gleaming sections of black rock. His forehead creased thoughtfully, and he seemed about to ask something. Until he came close enough to the bed to properly see the bundle in the crook of Frey's arm.

"Sir, is that ...?"

"A baby. Aye. Surely you're familiar with such things by now?"

"Yes, but ... sir?"

Freydolf warmly answered, "Aye, Mister Meadowsweet. Come, take your son."

His apprentice wasted no time in joining him on the bed. Carden knelt beside him and accepted the infant, lapsing into a soft series of *ohs* and *ahs*.

The sculptor stared in wonder at the sight of a father falling in love with his child. It was indelibly sweet.

Though he only had eyes for his son, Carden soon asked, "Melina?"

"She assures me she's fine. Haimish is attending her." At the Flox's prompting, Freydolf briefly explained what had happened while he and the others were away for the day. Then he nudged Carden with his elbow. "Did the naming go well for Ewert's twins?"

"Very well. And it seems we'll be going through the formalities again."

"Tonight?"

"If we can settle on a name," Carden said with some chagrin. "I only gave thought to ones for girls."

Freydolf reached over to slip one large finger under the newborn's tiny hand. "Although I've never been a father, I've woken countless statues. It's part of a sculptor's work, so there are several books in the archives dedicated to naming in many languages ... from many generations ... and with many meanings."

"Maybe we should let *you* do the choosing."

"Me? Nay. If anyone has earned that right, it's Tupper."

Carden nodded slowly. "If Melina agrees, I'd like that. Tupp can choose the name, and you can preside over the naming."

"But ...!"

"Please?" The soft request cut across Freydolf's protest. "I'd consider it an honor to have the renowned Keeper of the mountain who called me pronounce my son's name and welcome him into our family."

Swallowing past the lump in his throat, Frey said, "Aye. I would count it a privilege."

Chelle felt the small gust of air that meant someone had opened her bedroom door and glanced up from the letter she was writing to her family back in Millford.

Missus Quince leaned in from the hallway, flapping her hand and talking nonstop.

What now? Chelle asked, "Is it the boys?"

The baker's wife shook her head and waved impatiently for her to come downstairs, and as Chelle followed, she searched her mind. Dinner was done, as were the dishes. Her chickens were snug in their coop, and it was too early for baths. Maybe one of the neighbors wanted something? The Pennyflaxes sometimes called on her when they needed an extra pair of hands. But at this hour?

When they reached the kitchen, Chelle stopped in her tracks. *Tupper* sat at the table, hands folded over a thick book as he listened to Mister Quince, who gesticulated jovially. The baker seemed to be in the middle of a story, but as soon as she entered the room, Tupper looked her way with an expression of relief. Was the older man being tiresome? Or was something wrong?

"Good evening," she offered.

Tupper patted the back of the chair next to his—an invitation.

This seemed rather bold. It wasn't that Tupper's visits had been a secret. But coming to the place where she lived was different than dropping by the place she worked.

Mister Quince beamed at Tupper, cuffing his shoulder and winking at her before his wife could hustle him out of the kitchen.

She slid into the chair beside Tupper, who was already bent over his little notebook. When he pushed it toward her so she could read what he'd written, she sat a little straighter. It said, **I need your help.**

"With what?"

Tupper started writing again, his messy scrawl communicating urgency. Chelle leaned close to see what he was writing. **With rocks, I'm a good picker.**

That didn't make sense. He wouldn't need her help with

stones. She knew almost nothing about the special rocks he loved so well.

But with most other stuff, I'm ….

He trailed off, his forehead creased in thought. For several moments, the tip of his pencil tapped lightly against the page while he tried to find the right word. Finally, he settled on one.

Slow.

Chelle laughed softly, but Tupper's gaze was so hopeful. She shook her head and asked, "Is there a hurry?"

He nodded and continued to write, filling up the rest of the page with a disjointed explanation. **Birthing today. Melina's baby. Carden's wife. My nephew. A boy. Frey did his best. It was interesting. And the naming is soon. Tonight. But I don't know what to pick. You're smart. Help me?**

Rereading everything twice, she pieced enough together to ask, "They want you to choose the name?"

A quick nod, and he offered her the book he'd brought. Turning to a fresh page in his notebook, Tupper wrote, **Too many.**

She lifted the cover and turned a few pages. "These are all names!" she exclaimed in an undertone. It was fascinating, and she skimmed through several pages. When she finally recalled her companion, Chelle glanced up guiltily.

Tupper sat patiently, clearly awaiting her decision.

"You want *me* to pick?"

He nodded.

"But is that all right? I'm not family or anything."

Tupper seemed momentarily stumped. Then he wrote, **Our secret.**

Chelle laughed and went back to flipping pages. "If the naming is tonight, how will you get back to the top of the mountain in time?"

My secret.

"Do you have a lot of secrets?"

He nodded, but then brows lifted. She followed his gaze to find the two youngest Quinces spying on them. Caught, they jostled and grinned, and when Tupper spoke to them, they tumbled into the room.

Chelle kept turning pages, but she spent more time watching

the two little boys mob her suitor. The young man faced their questions with the same seriousness he showed her, and he didn't complain when they poked at his earrings and pulled his long ponytail.

When Missus Quince ended the fracas and herded them back out, Chelle said, "You're pretty good at handling youngsters."

With a sidelong glance, Tupper wrote, **I want lots.**

Her lips quirked as she perused the neat rows of names. "Even though you won't have any idea what to call them?"

Tupper took a long time to answer. And when he pushed the notebook over so she could see, he'd written his response in tiny letters. They whispered, **You can pick.**

9

Brothers and Backup

It was a few days later when Tupper pulled Arni onto his lap and rested his chin atop the little boy's head. "Can you see?"

"Uh-huh!"

"Just a little longer," Freydolf promised. Ulrica had reminded them that the birth of a younger sibling was usually the time when children were deemed ready for a very special privilege, so the sculptor was putting the finishing touches on Arni's first night guardian. "Bring the lantern closer, Brand?"

The redstone Grif lifted his light higher. There was a secretive air to this courtyard meeting, for it was well past bedtime, and there were no parents present. Warm breezes stirred fair curls as Dulcie, Yona, and Arni crowded close to Freydolf and Tupper.

Quintrell, who sat between the two men, poked his uncle's arm. "Will it roar?"

"Nay, lad. Stone is silent, like a Pred on the prowl."

The little boy's fangs flashed, but any trace of fierceness was undone when he snuggled close and whispered, "I like kitties."

All the children had at least one stone guardian, gifts from a doting uncle.

Tupper was almost positive that Arni had asked for a feline

because they were Quintrell's favorite. The young Harrow had a fluffy starstone kitten named Cream, and now Arni would have a match. Sort of. Torio had been the only one bold enough to point out how funny it was that the Pred child had been given an innocent pet while the Flox child would have a young tiger for a guardian.

Tupper thought Frey had made a good match. It wasn't that Quintrell wasn't brave. Arni was simply braver. Giving his nephew a squeeze, Tupper said, "You're a big brother now, Arni. And brothers are for back-up."

The little boy kicked his feet. "Imma brother."

Yona quietly asked, "Are *you* a brother, Unca Tupp?"

"Your papa is my brother."

"I knew that!" Dulcie boasted. She sat on the ground next to the bench, petting Ember and playing with her own night guardian—a small, white fox kit. "So's Uncle Far!"

"Yes, Farley is my younger brother," Tupper confirmed. "And don't forget your Uncle Ewert. He doesn't live with us, but he's ours, too."

"He got two babies," Quintrell said. "Lucky."

Arni squirmed. "What 'bout Unca Doff?"

Tupper glanced at the man, who wasn't so wrapped up in his work that he didn't hear. Frey's smile was pure contentment. "Your Uncle Doff is my bond-brother," said Tupper. "Did you think I forgot?"

"Best for last," Yona said.

Dulcie nodded wisely. "He's Uncle Tupp's favorite."

"Mine's Quin," Arni said, reaching out to his best friend.

Quintrell's clawed hand reached back, and he haughtily replied, "'Course."

Freydolf chuckled, then presented the tiny tiger for Arni's inspection. "A statue needs to hear their name to wake up. Do you know any good ones?"

The boy's lips pursed. "Ha-nee?"

Tupper ruffled the boy's hair. "Hanley is your new brother's name."

"It's taken," said Dulcie. "Pick something else."

"What do you like best about kitties?" Freydolf asked in

coaxing tones. "Maybe that will help us choose."

Arni gazed up at his uncle, then shrugged. "Dunno."

"That's all right, Floxling. I'll think on it while we get everything else ready." The Keeper looked to Brand and said, "Step back, please? I want the starlight good and strong for this."

The fire-bearer inclined his head and retreated several paces.

Cherished memories of Olexi's waking were foremost in Tupper's mind as his master drew out the moment for his appreciative audience. Magic swirled, and Tupper felt the gentle push as Freydolf connected the guardian to Arni.

Pressing a tear-damp thumb over his mark, the master sculptor called, "Wake up, Stripe."

Yona gasped, and Dulcie giggled.

Tupper smiled crookedly as Frey cupped his hand under both of Arni's and dropped a lithe tiger onto his pudgy palms. It stretched, tail slashing from side to side as it stared up into his new charge's wide eyes.

"Say his name," Tupper gently prompted.

With a giggle, Arni accepted Freydolf's gift. "'Lo, Stripe."

Tupper was near Morven's summit inspecting their pasture when Quintrell popped into view. "Found you!"

"All by yourself?" he asked in surprise, dropping to one knee in order to hug the three-year-old. He shook his head and gravely said, "I don't need to remind you about Unca Doff's rule against wandering on his mountain. This was good tracking, but you're out of bounds."

The scolding didn't faze the boy, whose wide, golden eyes slid to one side. Tupper turned to see Aurelius lounging on the topmost step.

"Papa followed."

"That's okay, then." Lifting a hand to greet the merchant, Tupper smiled encouragingly at Quintrell. "Is he giving you a lesson?"

"No. Mother sent me."

Half-joking, Tupper asked, "Am I in trouble?"

The boy hesitated, then said, "Not if you come quick."

Tupper slapped his thighs and stood, holding out his hand to Quintrell. "Can you remember the way back?"

Grabbing hold, the youngster exclaimed, "Watch me!"

By the time they got to the top of the stairs, Aurelius had disappeared. Fleetingly, Tupper wondered if that was a bad sign.

In the Harrows' kitchen, Tupper walked in on what seemed to be a tea party. Fancy dishes. Fussy cloths. Flowers aplenty. Ulrica and Melina were already seated at the table, and Aggie stood poised to pour.

"Do sit down, Tupper," Ulrica invited, her tones dangerously sweet.

There was an extra place set. He glanced toward the door, but Quintrell had vanished as swiftly as his father before him. Sliding into the chair, Tupper murmured, "Thanks."

Melina passed him a plate of baked goods, and Aggie filled his cup. He looked from face to face as he nibbled at the corner of a pastry. It was funny how three people could look at him the same way, even though their eyes were all different colors—brown, blue, and green.

Fidgeting under their scrutiny, he asked, "Did you need something?"

As usual, Ulrica took charge. "I was in Shepley this morning with Aggie."

He'd known that, so he nodded.

"And as we were passing through the quarry on our way

back, your brother flagged us down," the woman said, her brows lifting challengingly.

Tupper glanced uncertainly at Melina and Aggie, hoping for a clue to Ulrica's strange mood. "Ewert is back to work already?"

"Just today," Ulrica replied, a faint smirk on her orange-painted lips. "And he gave me something for you."

"That's good." Probably. Or maybe not.

She lifted a small envelope between two fingers. "Can you guess who *this* is from?"

"A letter?" Tupper rubbed at the base of a horn. He wasn't too good at this sort of thing, especially since he didn't have any experience with letters. No one had ever sent him one before. Shaking his head, he guessed, "Ewert?"

"This was passed to him by someone in Hayward," she hinted.

Tupper brightened. "Is it from Chelle?"

"And who is Chelle?" Ulrica inquired archly.

"She works at Pennyflax & Quince in Hayward." Glancing at Melina, he helpfully added, "Has since final harvest last year."

"And why would she be writing to you?"

Tupper blinked. "I don't know. I haven't read it yet."

Melina covered a smile, but Aggie giggled and said, "I tried to tell you."

"Such a shame," Ulrica drawled. "He's *impossible* to tease."

With a small sigh, Tupper said, "I don't understand."

"My husband has been deucedly evasive on the matter, and your forthrightness leaves *much* to be desired!" complained the Pred. "Who *is* she, boy!"

"Chelle is the girl I'm courting."

"That's our Tupp," said Melina. "Blunt as boulders."

"Oh, he's sly as bodkins, thick as blood, and generous as death," Ulrica snapped in a sarcastic collection of multicultural sayings. "But why is *this* the first I've heard about it?"

"Because no one said anything?" Tupper cautiously replied.

Melina jumped to his rescue. "It's a Flox custom to feign ignorance when a boy and girl pair off. Until their respective families announce the upcoming wedding, everyone pretends not to notice."

"It's a secret that the whole village keeps," Aggie added. "Everyone in Hayward probably already knows Tupp's been calling on a girl."

Fiddling with the handle of her teacup, Melina said, "I'll bet Uncle Owen—that's Mister Quince, the baker—is delighted. He was always snooping around when Carden dropped by the bakery to visit me." To Ulrica, she explained, "Plenty of folks make a game of helping young couples along."

Tupper nodded. "Mister and Missus Quince seem happy."

Ulrica clearly wasn't. She surrendered the letter, but her claws drummed on the table. "Who *else* knew that you're pursuing a village girl?"

Tupper self-consciously slipped the envelope into his pocket and took a slow drink of tea while he thought things through. Freydolf, Aurelius, and Quintrell had been with him the day he met Chelle. Frey was the only one he'd told outright that he was courting, but Aurelius was smart. The merchant probably knew about Tupper's trips down the mountain, and he probably knew what they meant. But Aurelius hadn't told his wife. And he was making himself scarce now.

"*Well ...?*" prompted Ulrica.

Because Flox were so circumspect about courting couples, Tupper had taken Aurelius's silence for granted. But now it looked like the merchant had gone against Pred custom by keeping quiet. Bearing in mind Ulrica's love for romantic meddling, Aurelius had probably done him a great favor. One Tupper was happy to repay.

He said, "I only talked to Frey about Chelle."

Aurelius could thank him later.

After much consideration, Tupper escaped to one of his favorite hideaways, an overgrown grotto near his best fishing spot.

Vines draped the arched opening of an abandoned niche that had probably been some past apprentice's getaway. Actually, several bands ringed the walls inside, suggesting that at least six different people had sought privacy here over the years.

Tupper leaned into Graven's bulk and stared at the envelope, tracing the letters of his name, which looked very nice in Chelle's handwriting. "It's my first letter."

The rhythmic flick and curl of the tiger's tail paused for several moments, the only hint that his aloof guardian was paying any attention.

Breaking the seal, Tupper untucked the homemade envelope's flap and withdrew a single piece of paper that had been folded once. The letter was short, so he read it slowly to make it last.

> Tupper–
>
> Thank you for letting me keep the naming book until your next visit. I already read it twice. It mentions all the strange, faraway people your master drew– Pred, Grif, Basq, Clow. When the meaning of a name is explained, the writer talks about cities, countries, and continents I never knew were there. Somehow, it makes me feel very small.
>
> There's so much I don't understand. Would you mind ... is it possible ... do you think Master Freydolf would let me borrow another book? Something about mountains and magic. I want to learn about the place you live.
>
> –Chelle

"That's good," Tupper murmured. He reread the letter, nodding to himself. The false starts in the second part showed how hard it had been for Chelle to make her request. "She was brave to ask."

He was doubly glad because now he knew how to make her happy. Books were easy to come by in the Statuary. Freydolf would share, and Aurelius would know the best ones to start with. Or maybe he should turn this into a peace offering. Yes. That was the best plan. Showing Graven the letter, he said, "I'll ask Ulrica for help."

10

Commanding Presence

Ulrica sashayed boldly through the bakery door in Hayward, Aggie close on her heels, leading Quintrell by the hand. When Chelle caught sight of her new customer, her eyes widened, and Ulrica's lip curled slightly. The local Flox might be impressed with this girl's "unusual" coloring, but brown was brown was brown.

With a soft *tsk*, she muttered, "Is this bland little snippet really worth his time?"

Aggie bluntly asked, "You don't trust Tupp?"

"I trust him to keep Graven out of my garden ... to keep my brother presentable ... and to keep porridge from burning. But that *doesn't* mean he understands the dire consequences of an unwise match!"

"Didn't your parents consider Mister Harrow an unwise match?"

"That's entirely beside the point!"

And then Quintrell pulled away from Aggie and darted across the room, exclaiming, "I 'member you!"

Ulrica opened her mouth to call him back, but Chelle hurried out from around the counter and scooped up her son.

"There you are, little cub!"

As the young woman cuddled the Pred boy, Aggie quietly said, "Seems to me, our Tupp knows what he's about."

"Perhaps the boy's not a complete fool."

Ignorant of the woman's asides, Chelle stepped forward, Quintrell perched on her hip. Her gaze flitted between Ulrica and Aggie, but settled on the Pred. "Missus Harrow? Can I help you?"

"No, but I'll help you," Ulrica replied archly. In commanding tones that rang through the rafters, she called, "I wish to meet the man Melina Meadowsweet calls *Uncle Owen.*"

There was a *bang* and *thump* from the direction of the kitchen, and then Misters Pennyflax and Quince peeped out from the back. Mister Pennyflax gave his cousin a push toward their imposing customer, and after an initial stumble, Owen Quince drew himself up to his full height. "Missus Harrow?"

"Correct."

Stroking his beard in an uncertain manner, the Flox asked, "Is there something you're needing?"

Ulrica peered down her nose at the shorter man, then pointed imperiously at Chelle. "The boy who's chosen that girl is like family to me, so I shall participate in the Floxish schemes surrounding their courtship."

Chelle's brows furrowed as she tried to figure out what was going on, but Owen brightened somewhat. "You like to help the young'uns along?"

She smirked. "Aye, but there's more to it. Tupper Meadowsweet kept his activities a secret from me, and I mean to retaliate for the slight. My husband insists that no blood be shed, so I am resorting to ... *surprise.*"

By the time Chelle sorted out most of what was happening, it was too late to escape. Although, if she was perfectly honest, she didn't want to. The Pred woman had whisked her away, and there was little doubt as to where they were headed. Chelle's hands bunched and smoothed her apron hem by turns. Her thoughts reeled. Her heart raced. But she was happy.

On a wide, plush seat inside the carriage, Quintrell sat tucked up against her side, contentedly munching the bun Mister Quince had given him. Once he was finished, he tugged at her sleeve then pointed out the window at the mountain they were circling.

Chelle asked, "Is that where we're going?"

He nodded eagerly.

"I was hoping," she murmured.

Catching a movement out of the corner of her eye, she turned to look at Missus Harrow. The woman's thick eyebrows lifted haughtily, and she held out a long envelope. When Chelle didn't immediately take it, she rolled her eyes and spoke to her son.

The little boy hopped down from his seat, took it, and returned to drop it into the young woman's lap. His golden eyes shone with delight, and he chattered on for a while. She had no idea what her little brown cub said, but he was happy about it.

Smiling, Chelle included them both in her, "Thank you."

The envelope was heavy, for it was made from thick, creamy parchment, as were the folded pages inside. One glance at the elegant writing told her that the missive was from Aurelius Harrow.

Miss Chelle–

First and foremost, do <u>not</u> be alarmed. You are not kidnapped, and you are in no immediate danger. I presume that your receipt of this letter means that my wife has successfully negotiated a temporary trade with your employers. Aggie Meadowsweet will take your place at the bakery for the remainder of today and all of tomorrow. These arrangements are in answer to your recent request to learn more. I commend your desire to educate yourself about the wider world.

There are numerous books on the subject, and I'll be happy to place several into your hands; however, some things are easier to show than tell. Magic is deucedly hard to explain.

For the duration of your stay, you'll be placed in the keeping of Melina (nee Pennyflax) Meadowsweet. She's wife to Tupper's eldest brother Carden. I'll ease you through the introductions now. They have four children–Dulcie, Yona, Arni, and Hanley.

Chelle paused, taking the time to reread the names of Tupper's nieces and nephews. They really *had* used the one she'd chosen. "Hanley," she whispered with a smile. Thanks to her borrowed book, she knew that it meant "high meadow." Would there be any grass on this mountain?

From the north and the east, Morven looked rugged and steep, but the carriage was taking them around her southern side, where gentler slopes led into thick forests. Tearing her gaze from the window, Chelle continued reading Aurelius's lengthy explanation.

You know my son Quintrell, and my beloved wife is Ulrica. She is Freydolf's younger sister, and I act as his agent. In addition to Flox and Pred, we have a Grif living on the mountain–Torio Kite. He employs another Meadowsweet, Tupper's youngest brother Farley, the cheeky brat currently driving my carriage. Freydolf and Tupper round out our burgeoning community. I trust there are not so many of us that you will feel overwhelmed.

Tupper has no idea that you are about to be delivered to our doorstep. My wife is as vicious in her kindness as she is with her blades. If your arrival is met with naught but rude gawking, do not take it as a sign that you are unwelcome. I'll be on hand to help smooth the way as much as is possible. I only agreed to participate in this escapade because … if I may be so bold … it's best if you know <u>now</u> what you are in for, should you stay the course. Having Pred as a part of your extended family comes with both quirks and consequences. Are you brave enough to live with them?

That was blunt. But there was no sense mincing delicately around the subject. When people had to write out everything they needed to say, they tended to skip the small talk. It had been hard for Chelle's mother to even explain why so much conversation included useless chit-chat, but it put people at ease. So she'd learned to use it. But it made dull reading.

Frowning thoughtfully, Chelle slowly turned to the last page.

Last but not least, I feel it's only fair to warn you that of all the obstacles before you, my wife may be the most formidable. She terrorized our two daughters-in-law, and in many ways, Ulrica considers the sprat one of our own. So gather up your wits, your courage, and my son. He makes an excellent shield.

The final warning took Chelle aback. Was Mister Harrow joking? Or was this another example of the man's ability to cut to the crux of a matter. Folding away the letter, she tucked it into her apron pocket, then pulled Quintrell onto her lap. Maybe Aurelius would tease her later, but something told her that his advice should never be taken lightly.

Graven and Rimbles both turned their heads toward the woods at the same time, ears pricked forward. Tupper tossed one mud-caked boot onto the ground and levered off the other before checking to see who was coming. Shifting his shoulders uncomfortably, he dared to hope it wasn't Farley.

Carden emerged from the forest a little downstream, and the faint smile on his face immediately faded. "Tupp! What happened?"

"Graven made up a new game." Pulling his stained tunic over his head, Tupper knelt and plunged it into the cool water, swishing to dislodge the worst of the muck. "He can wrap his tail around things and pull them."

"Meaning you?"

"Yes."

Carden looked from his brother to the giant feline. "I didn't think cats could use their tails like that."

"They can't. But he can."

Wrinkling his nose, Carden bent closer and plucked a rotted cabbage leaf out of his younger brother's matted hair. "Did he pull you through the cow pen?"

"Compost heap."

The older Flox chuckled. "Aurelius meant for this to be revenge, but I haven't the heart. You need to wash! Now!"

"Yes. I'll rinse off the worst, then go take a bath."

"No time." Pointing urgently to the stream, Carden said, "Be quick, but be thorough. You stink!"

Tupper obediently shed the rest of his clothes and stepped into the stream, wading toward the deepest section. Halfway through washing his hair, he looked back at his brother. "What did you mean ... *revenge*?"

Carden sat on the bank, eyes politely averted. "Remember how you sent me to the workshop in order to see Master Freydolf, but neglected to mention that I'd find a newborn son in his arms?"

"Oh," Tupper replied blankly. "I thought it would make a good surprise."

"And it was! But it would be too cruel to let you draggle home like that."

"Why?"

"No young lady wants a suitor who reeks of decomposing vegetables."

Tupper pushed sodden ringlets out of his face. With a slow shake of his head, he said, "I wasn't planning to go into Hayward to visit Chelle tonight."

"No need. She's *here*."

11

Universal Interest

Chelle's hometown was to the north of Morven. On clear days, you could make out the shapes of buildings tucked in against the north face and up near the summit. When she'd asked her father about them, he'd called them "the Ruins." An ancient city, lost to time. Barren as far back as anyone could remember. Now that Chelle was here, she could see that her father had been wrong, but almost right. Even without hearing, she could tell that the city atop the mountain stood empty.

Mostly empty.

The beginnings of a new village crowded around her— young, eager, and nearly as overwhelming as the architecture. "You must be Dulcie," she said, touching the bright curls of a girl who chattered nonstop. Chelle wasn't sure if anyone had told the child that she couldn't hear. Somehow, she doubted it would have mattered.

When the girl paused for breath, Chelle quickly asked, "And Yona?"

The younger girl nodded in a manner that brought Tupper to mind.

And then Aurelius was there, bowing and flourishing a sketchbook. The dapper Pred dropped to one knee and spoke earnestly to the girls, who promptly directed him to write messages. With a faint smirk, the man turned the page so Chelle could read it. **Dulcie wants to know if it hurts.**

"No, sweetie," she replied. "My ears don't work, but I feel fine." **Yona wants you to know that Haimish can't talk.**

Chelle didn't recognize that name from the list of people living here, but maybe the girl was talking about a pet. "Does it bother you that they can't talk?"

Yona shook her head.

"Do you mind that I can't hear?"

Her second headshake was joined by a reassuring pat.

Melina Meadowsweet welcomed Chelle with a hug and introduced Carden, who had Hanley expertly tucked into the crook of his arm. The man looked a little like Tupper, and Chelle found herself blushing under his thoughtful gaze.

Aurelius rose to his full height and slyly showed her what he'd written. **Everyone wants to know about the girl their Tupp chose. I _did_ warn you about rude gawking!**

Chelle shook her head. She'd been treated rudely many times before, and this wasn't it.

Quintrell marched over leading another little boy by the hand, and she knelt to meet Arni, who reached right out to pet her hair.

When she stood again and glanced around, Chelle ventured, "Will I meet the others?"

Aurelius was quick to respond. **Farley's tending the horses. Kite is fashionably late. Or did you mean the sprat? He's deucedly late. I'll send someone to chase him down.**

She tried to protest, but Carden seemed happy enough to go after his younger brother. Before leaving, he stopped in front of her and said one word, exaggerating it so she could read his lips. "Welcome."

Aurelius displayed his page. **The head of the Meadowsweet clan has accepted you. How momentous!**

Carden only chuckled and strolled away.

Freydolf sidled over and plucked both paper and pen from his brother-in-law. In his hasty scrawl, he warned, **Aurelius is**

fond of embellishments.

"I can see that." She liked this audacious man and his bluntness. Was he dear to Tupper? And did Aurelius's sentiments match his wife's—considering Tupper to be one of his own? If so, did that mean he might welcome her as a daughter? Having honorary Pred in-laws sounded nice ... if Missus Harrow would accept her. Chelle glanced over to the woman lingering on the far edge of the group. Aloof.

Aurelius reclaimed the book, wrote, then nudged her, pointing to his words. **She's softening. In the meantime, Melina proposes a tour of her bakery! Shall we?**

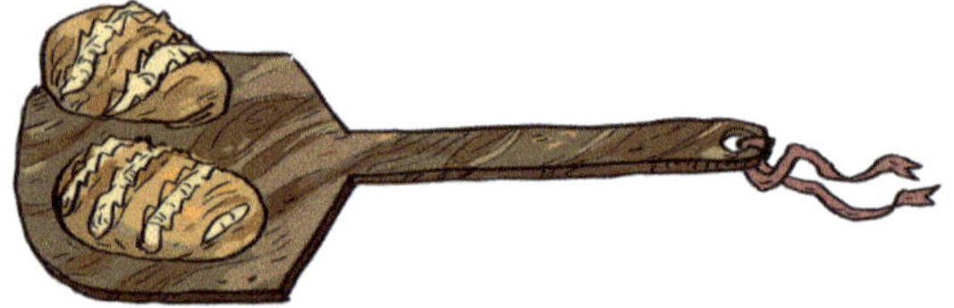

Chelle was startled when Freydolf waded through the crowd of little Meadowsweets in order to reach her side. With a tentative smile, he offered her his arm, and when she immediately accepted the courtesy, his dark eyes took on a shine. Gratitude.

She almost laughed. When his brows lifted inquiringly, she quietly said, "You're used to a different reaction from most people?"

The Pred nodded gravely.

"So am I."

His lip quirked, and then he laughed. The man's whole expression changed to something she liked better than caution. Camaraderie.

Chelle felt as if she'd just made a friend.

Freydolf called out to Aurelius, who took dictation for his brother-in-law. **You're about to meet one of Frey's creations. He doesn't want you to be afraid of Haimish.**

"Is he frightening?"

The merchant waved a hand dismissively, and the sculptor shook his head.

Chelle asked, "What kind of statue is he?"

Aurelius's eyes gleamed. **Brown.**

Their small entourage followed the cobbled road for a short distance, then took an inward turn. Not far down the side street, Chelle spotted one door that was different than all the rest. Huge pots and urns flanked its threshold, overflowing with flowers and herbs.

Melina led the way through the door and up stairs to the second level, from which wonderful yeasty and spicy smells were coming. Her bakery was much grander than Pennyflax & Quince—arched ceilings, tall windows, prettily paved floors.

They were greeted at the top of the stairs by a man made entirely from brown stone.

Chelle gasped in astonishment when he moved, and the statue quickly lowered his eyes, tucking his tail between his legs. But then Yona hurried to him, arms upraised, and the brown man scooped her up, cradling her close to his chest.

The little girl patted her protector's chest and chanted a single word, which Aurelius helpfully jotted down. **Mish. She's always called Haimish that. Pet name. Pet statue.**

"You made him?" she asked Freydolf.

The man nodded, and his agent wrote, **An early work. Fraught with sentimental value. Frey has improved vastly since his apprenticeship.**

"But he's wonderful. He's *alive.*"

Haimish dipped his head, offering a sweet smile.

Thrusting out her hand, she said, "I'm Chelle. It's a pleasure to meet you."

Freydolf added something that caused the statue's eyes to widen and his tail to wag. Haimish set down Yona in order to place his hand palm up under his heart and bow. When he next gathered her hand into both of his, the orange bracelets around his wrists caught her eye. And Chelle was distracted by the gentle pressure of Haimish's hands, cool but pliant.

She really wanted to know what had put so much hope in his gaze, so she asked, "What did they say?"

Aurelius cheerfully supplied, **Like I said, Miss Tremont. Everyone on Morven is interested in what Tupper is interested in. Even the statues.**

Chelle could feel her face heating up. It was odd having her courtship spoken about so freely. In the village, no one remarked on Tupper's regular visits to the bakery.

Freydolf said something more, and Chelle glanced between the men, trying to read their expressions. Aurelius treated his brother-in-law to a sidelong glance, but dutifully transcribed, **Even the mountain is in a tizzy. Frey says Morven is pleased.**

Trying to fathom this, Chelle asked, "Do you mean the mountain is happy?"

Again, she felt the low vibration of Freydolf's voice, and Aurelius wrote, **For the record, this is word-for-word. Frey says: Aye. Which can only mean _one_ thing. Tupper's happy.**

Chelle had lived with a language barrier most of her life, and it was as maddening as it was lonely. Oh, she was always _with_ people, and she was grateful to be included. But when it came right down to it, folks found uses for her.

Conversation was too expensive because paper was precious. But Aurelius seemed to find particular satisfaction in filling page after page, courteously regaling her with gossipy tidbits of information about the Statuary and those who called it home.

Usually, Chelle had to confine herself to questions that could be answered with a simple _yes_ or _no_, but thanks to her glib translator, she didn't need to keep things short.

Aurelius's fancy writing utensil flowed freely across the pages of his book, indulging in the very kind of chit-chat from which she was usually excluded.

And there is young Farley. Horrible child. A lamentable nuisance.

"You don't mean that," she murmured.

Aurelius's gaze lingered on the boy who'd just come out of the stables. **Nay, but he's all sass, and it wouldn't do to encourage him.**

Farley swerved toward them and wiped his hands on his shirtfront before extending one to Chelle. She marveled at how much this younger brother looked like Tupper. If his eyes had been green instead of blue, she might have mixed them up. But then Farley grinned, and the illusion vanished.

Pointing to the page, he fired off several things that Aurelius flatly refused to relay. The merchant said something with a sweet smile on his face that made Farley hold up his hands and back away. Though he sent Chelle a cheerful wink and wave before disappearing into the barn.

"What did he say?"

Six foolish things. Two impertinent things. And one piece of unsolicited advice that I would consider inadvisable at this time.

"That bad?"

He couldn't be <u>bad</u> even if he put some effort into it, but he's at that age. With luck, he'll live long enough to outgrow his irascibility. With an unconcerned flutter of his hand, Aurelius added, **He did compliment your hair.**

Chelle self-consciously touched her brown curls. "I think you're embellishing again, sir."

Nay. And he also informed us that his master is in the chicken yard.

"Master Kite?" she asked.

<u>Mister</u> Kite is respect aplenty for that lay-about.

Aurelius said something that set off the youngsters, who stampeded down a nearby set of stairs. He gestured for her to precede him, and she followed more slowly. The steep passage spilled onto a shady veranda—graceful arches, shapely columns, and a canopy of sun-dappled greenery. And several hens idly picking and pecking at the cobbles. "*This* is a chicken yard?"

Aye, and yon's the biggest fowl on the mountain.

Torio Kite lounged at the far end of the ornate fence that hemmed an imposing drop-off, his lanky frame draped precariously on the stone railing. His head was tipped back, his feathered hat pulled down over his face. Freydolf ambled over and joined him on his perch, and the Grif pushed up the brim of his hat, revealing a beaky nose and bright blue eyes.

"He's Grif?" she whispered.

Instead of answering her, Aurelius smirked and called him over. The tall man obliged, doffing his hat and sweeping into a low bow. When he straightened, Aurelius shoved the book into his chest and proffered his pencil.

Torio muttered to himself as he jotted a few lines on the paper, then turned it for her to see.

Chelle blinked. "I'm sorry. I don't understand."

Aurelius cuffed the other man's shoulder, snatched back the book, and wrote, **Idiot. He claims he wanted to greet you in his own words and in his own way. This is Terse, his native language.**

Different languages? It took a moment for Chelle to process that, but once she did, her curiosity doubled. "What does it say?"

Literally translated... it's a bunch of flowery nonsense. He spouts the most ridiculous drivel.

Holding out her hand, Chelle introduced herself, then shyly said, "When I was little, a circus came through my hometown. I don't remember much, but all the performers wore feathers. Maybe they were Grif?"

Torio said something, and Aurelius penned, **A disreputable lot, no doubt.**

Freydolf intervened, looking amused by the jibes the other men appeared to be trading. The sculptor provided a more faithful translation. **So you've met others of my noble race. I hope the memories are good ones.**

"Oh, yes! I was too shy to say anything, but my father talked to one of the acrobats." Smiling at the memory, she said, "All I really remember was having to look a long, long way up. Everyone there was so tall. Like you."

The Grif rubbed his nose, and Aurelius rolled his eyes expressively. Freydolf chuckled and added their response next to a hasty sketch of a juggler in striped tights with a feathered cape. **Nay, lass. We three must respectfully disagree. It's not that** we're tall. You're simply small.

Torio tapped the paper with a taloned finger, saying something more.

With a crooked smile, Frey added, **And you may call him Torio ... young mistress.**

12

Drop Like a Stone

Heedless of Tupper's sodden tunic, Carden locked his arms around his younger brother's waist. "Do you do this *often*?" he asked, his voice breaking as Graven swerved under an arch before springing to a neighboring rooftop.

"Yes." Tupper said. "This way is fast."

Fast. Talk about understatement.

It had been unnerving enough when Graven lunged up through the woods from the creek bottom, following his nose rather than any kind of path. Then the big cat reached the Statuary walls and performed a vertical leap that put them two-stories above street level. Carden's stomach had dropped like a stone. Now, as their mount took a fluid plunge into an adjoining alley, Carden resorted to a Terse oath Torio often used.

Tupper glanced over his shoulder. "Are you scared?"

Graven jumped, and it took a moment for Carden to catch his breath. "*Terrified.*"

"Don't worry. He won't fall," his brother promised. "Grip with your knees and try to move *with* him."

As they skimmed effortlessly along a wall topped by a series of decorative spikes, Carden considered how often this brother had surprised him over the years. Securing a plum position with the infamous Keeper of Morven, making a pledge of brotherhood with a Pred, negotiating innumerable small comforts to improve Freydolf's way of life, standing up to their mother by refusing to cut his hair. And apparently, possessing the nerve to ride a wild tiger up, over, and through the Statuary's winding galleries.

By the time Carden slid off Graven's back, there was a distinct wobble in his knees. He excused himself to the kitchen while Tupper changed into clean clothes, pouring himself a drink of water to combat his dry mouth and queasy stomach.

On returning, he smiled sympathetically. "Need help?"

Tupper rubbed at the base of a horn, then pointed to the three tunics laid out on the bed. "Which one?"

"Aurelius would serve as a better adviser, but you've always liked green. Wearing something you're comfortable with might help you calm down."

With a nod, Tupper reached for his favorite shirt, but he stopped mid-reach, staring at his hand. "My hands are shaking."

"I noticed."

"Do you think this is how Chelle feels when I show up at the bakery?" he asked.

"Maybe. Melina always seemed very flustered when I turned up unannounced." With a crooked smile, Carden admitted, "It was fun."

Tupper nodded again, finished dressing, then worked his fingers through damp hair. "You met her?" he asked quietly.

"Yes."

"And ...?"

With a soft chuckle, Carden crossed the room and tapped horns with him. "And she makes my courageous younger brother tremble."

Ulrica stood still as a statue at the base of the narrow stairway, her gaze fixed on Chelle, but her ears straining for Carden's return. It was a matter of personal pride that Tupper no longer tromped about like an oaf, but the elder brother always let the heels of his boots scuff cobbles. A quaint habit.

Telltale footfalls sounded, and she turned to glare at the elusive boy who'd made her wait for her prize.

He stopped three stairs from the bottom and drew a shaky breath. "Sorry I'm late."

Searching Tupper's face, she smirked at the numerous signs of his discombobulation—wide eyes, pale face, pink ears, crooked knots, and flyaway ringlets. As Carden slipped past to rejoin Melina, Ulrica asked, "Did your brother have to fish you out of the creek?"

"Yes."

She snorted lightly and retied the lacing on his tunic front, brushing at a crease and fussing with his hair. "I'll have you know that I yielded Aggie to a bunch of unappreciative lackwits in order to see you like this."

The boy blinked. "*You* brought Chelle?"

"Aye." Drawing him down another step so he could peek around the corner to where two Pred and a Grif had his young lady surrounded, she drawled, "They're all quite taken with her."

"And you?"

With a haughty sniff, Ulrica asked, "Does my opinion matter?"

Tupper met her gaze steadily. "*You* matter."

Ulrica scowled, but she couldn't bring herself to trod upon this boy's hopes. Still, it wouldn't do to let him know that he had her by the fangs. Choosing her words carefully, she replied, "I think that Aurelius always wanted daughters."

She nearly missed Tupper's brilliant smile, for he flung his arms around her neck and hugged her the way her sons used to. "I *wanted* to show Chelle, but I couldn't think how to make it work. You're so smart, and I need to thank Aggie. And you. *Thank you,* Ulrica."

Her eyes stung as she held the slender young man as tightly as she dared. Why did they all grow up so fast? At least there was no chance of parting from this one. So long as they both clung to Morven, she could keep him.

"Foolish boy." she muttered huskily. "You should know by now that I'm your *best* conspirator and your *worst* enemy. If you keep something so precious from me again, I'll shave your head and strangle you with your own curls."

Tupper laughed softly and whispered, "Allies?"

Ulrica hummed approvingly. "Lucky for you."

Aurelius and Torio quibbled incessantly, each urging Frey to take their side, as if bringing their case before the village elder. Interesting ideas and good-natured insults flashed past, captured by the perpetual motion of their shared pencil. Chelle's attention was riveted to the sketchbook, which traded hands between the two Pred so fast, the conversation was beginning to feel like a game of snatch the bobbin.

Then she caught a rush of movement out of the corner of her eye and turned to see where the children were going.

Oh.

The youngsters clamored around Tupper, who patted each child's head before looking up. Chelle was painfully conscious of the way everyone's gaze swung to her, but the young man didn't seem to mind the attention. Lifting a hand in the same greeting he always gave, he strolled over, Rimbles chasing around his ankles.

Aurelius nudged her arm, displaying the note, **Carden fished him out of the creek. Such a slacker.**

Tupper tilted his head to one side, read the accusation, and pulled a small notebook from his pocket. Chelle thought he was wise to bypass Aurelius as translator, but his response was as short as ever. **Maybe. Hi. Welcome.**

She replied, "Thank you. I was just telling these gentlemen that if this is the chicken yard, I can't wait to see the rest of the Statuary."

Nodding, Tupper wrote, **I want to show you everything.**

"I'd like that," she replied warmly.

But there's too much.

"I can believe it." Chelle searched his face before suggesting, "Where would be a good place to start?"

Freydolf interrupted by shoving the purloined sketchbook between them. The otherwise empty page held a one-word suggestion. **GRAVEN.**

This time, everyone's attention was pulled toward the entrance, for Ulrica was facing down something on the stairs. Chelle wondered if the woman had been carrying daggers the whole time they were in the carriage together.

Chelle glanced around, trying to figure out how she should be reacting. None of the children seemed perturbed, but Aurelius sidled backwards, putting his brother-in-law's larger bulk between him and ... what?

"Is there something there?" she whispered.

Freydolf, Aurelius, and Torio all pointed to the word on the sketchbook. Graven.

With a sigh, Chelle tried to draw more information out of the men who were suddenly very busy talking amongst themselves. "Is Graven a statue?"

Aye. Frey hastily explained, **And he belongs to Tupper.**

Torio made a flip-flop motion with his hand that suggested it might be the other way around.

Aurelius grabbed the sketchbook and ranted, **A piecemeal pestilence. An unbanishable bane. A sly, striped sneak.**

Freydolf interceded. **Aurelius and Graven have never gotten along, but he's the exception. Don't worry.**

The merchant pouted, then pointed, and Chelle turned in time to see Ulrica step aside, allowing Graven to enter the chicken yard. One large paw was followed by an enormous muzzle, and the moment the huge cat's red eyes fixed on her, Chelle took an involuntary step backwards, bumping into Tupper.

His arms wrapped around her shoulders as he hugged her from behind, which was hardly fair. Now, as the stone tiger prowled toward them, her heart had two reasons to flutter.

Meet Tupper's stone guardian, Graven, the renowned Mosaic Tiger, Freydolf's words read. **He's the masterpiece of Morven's previous Keeper.**

Chelle searched the Pred's face, and he gazed back with sympathy—even amusement—but no trace of worry or doubt. It was reassuring, but then Tupper started talking. She could feel her suitor's voice vibrating against her back, and his breath tickled through the hair, making her ear twitch.

As fresh color crept into her cheeks, she determinedly asked, "What's he saying?"

Aurelius snagged the book and held it so she could see the words form. **The sprat's proclaiming his undying devotion t-**

Freydolf made a grab for the pencil and quickly turned the page. **He said: This is Chelle, and she's ours. Yours and mine, but mostly mine. We can guard her together. If she wants.**

Few words. Much meaning. Just the way Tupper wrote. And it put Chelle's one, tiny, lingering fear to rest.

In the village, everyone knew everyone, so she could tell who was liked, accepted, trusted, or mistrusted. Since Tupper no longer fit into the village where he was born, he was a complete mystery. Oh, people could tell her what they remembered. Nice boy. Quiet. Good family. But Tupper wasn't a ten-year-old any longer, and he'd obviously changed. No one could tell her the things she *really* wanted to know. Until now. This was where he lived. These people knew him best. And the way they treated him told her more than words ever could.

Tupper gave her a small squeeze, then released her and stepped around, shielding her from Graven's baleful glare. Freydolf caught her attention and tapped the sketchbook. **Take it slow. If you're nervous, stay behind Tupper.**

Chelle frowned. "I'm sorry, did I miss something? Take what slow?"

Aurelius elbowed his brother-in-law, who grinned and underlined his previous note. **Try petting Graven under his chin. He likes that.**

"I did miss that," she said, glancing back to Tupper, who had his arms wrapped around the tiger as far as they could reach.

"Will he mind?"

Tupper shook his head and chuffed the big cat under the chin. Chelle followed suit and found the statue's fur was soft to the touch. Bands of bright colors blended with stone-gray fur as it slipped through her fingers. Curious, she delved deeper, scratching at the firm jawline she found beneath the deep plush. Lids drooped over Graven's red eyes, and Tupper looked on with an indulgent smile.

"I can see why they call you a masterpiece," Chelle said, reaching up to trace her fingers along the bright blue bands that rimmed the big cat's eyes. "You certainly look like someone's treasure."

Freydolf reported, **Stones from all twelve magical mountains were combined in this one statue. Graven was my mentor's labor of love.**

Chelle nodded at the sculptor's words, then addressed the tiger. "And you belong to Tupper?"

Graven blinked at her, backed up slightly, then butted his broad forehead *smack* into Tupper's chest. The young man roughed up his guardian's fur, then dropped a quick kiss on the tiger's pink nose.

Chelle touched her own, remembering Tupper's brief display of affection during his last visit into Hayward, and said, "I'm beginning to think you have a special fondness for cats."

Although Tupper didn't answer directly, Freydolf filled in for him, scrawling, **Maybe. Probably.**

Tupper blinked several times, smiled rather sheepishly, then nodded.

Excuses were made, and the group dispersed—naps to take, bread to bake, fish to catch, dinner to start—leaving Chelle alone with the Statuary's original pair. Tupper took her arm, and Freydolf fell in step on her other side, paper and pencil at the ready.

My workshop doubles as bachelor quarters. Tupper wants you to see our home next, the sculptor explained.

"I'd like that."

Tupper nodded, but a dozen tiny worries preoccupied him. He hadn't expected company, and he'd barely given the workshop a glance while hurrying into dry clothes. The wet ones awaited him in the kitchen sink, and he'd left two tunics spread on his bed. If Frey had been sculpting this morning, the floor might need sweeping. And what if Nott had decided to play havoc in the balcony?

He glanced pensively at his bond-brother only to find the Pred's dark eyes resting on him.

"Something wrong, lambkin?"

"Maybe. Is everything clean?"

"I don't really pay attention," Frey admitted. At Chelle's questioning glance, he included her. **The lad's anxious to make a good impression.**

Tupper nodded gravely, and Chelle dipped her head. "That makes two of us."

Make it three.

She laughed softly. "I suppose that means we're all on our best behavior?"

Slowing to a stop, Tupper asked, "Is that bad?"

Once Freydolf had relayed the question, Chelle replied, "No. I appreciate your consideration, but wouldn't it be better to act normally?"

Tupper frowned thoughtfully at this request. Was he making her uncomfortable? Was it possible to be too polite? She was their guest, but maybe she wanted to see how it felt to belong. That idea made him happy, but even more nervous.

Looking to Frey, he asked, "Am I being different?"

"Nay, lambkin. I believe Miss Tremont wants to know you

better, and you're not the easiest person to figure out." He began writing again to bring Chelle into the loop. **Aye, lass. We won't hold back, provided you also make yourself at home.**

Tupper was relieved that Freydolf had found a good way to answer Chelle. But it was confusing. Did she think he would change how he behaved? Bringing out his own notebook, he wrote. **I'm me.**

"Yes, but ...."

With a faint smirk, Frey scrawled, **And I am exactly what I seem—harmless, helpless, hopeless.**

Shaking his head, Tupper set his small notebook over the man's words. **Too humble.**

Freydolf wasn't done. **Miss Chelle, there's no speck of deceit in this lad, but I wouldn't underestimate him. Tupper still surprises me.**

Chelle smiled and said, "I like all the surprises so far. Let's keep going?"

That was certainly fine with Tupper, whose heart skipped to a faster rhythm at her admiring glance. He pointed in the direction they needed to go, then at one of the nearest cobbles, saying, "Tell her about the honeybees."

"Aye," Freydolf replied, quickly sketching one of his apprentice's trail markers.

Even though it was child's play, Tupper was intensely proud when Chelle took in the Keeper's explanation, then used the new information to lead them straight to their own front door. **Clever.**

She blushed lightly under his compliment, and Freydolf opened the door, bowing grandly as he gestured for her to enter. Stepping through, Chelle strolled to the middle of the workshop, sweeping the entire space with one long look. Tupper hardly knew what to think when she burst out laughing.

Catching her breath, she exclaimed, "This isn't what I expected at all!"

Freydolf turned a page. **Why?**

"It's extraordinary," Chelle replied, crossing to touch a half-formed statue on one of Freydolf's worktables. "Everything about the Statuary has been amazing, so I'm not surprised that you live in such grandeur, but these are the *cleanest* bachelor quarters I've ever seen! I didn't know a room so big could feel … cozy."

Tupper stopped in the process of hiding his two extra tunics under his pillow. "Cozy?"

"Aye, and clean," Freydolf said with a chuckle.

Chelle went right on talking. "My uncle—the one who inherited Clow teeth—lives alone. Mother and I have to go in and scour the filth from his house at least once a season. And my two older brothers share an apartment over their shop. They'd let their books pile right up to the ceiling if my little sister and I didn't put them back in order on rest days."

She talked a lot, and Tupper listened eagerly. He hadn't known Chelle had brothers or a sister, nor that Millford had a bookstore owned by Tremonts. As she rambled on about her family, his eagerness for new information ebbed, and his gaze softened. Crossing to her side, he held up his notebook. **You miss them.**

Her smile wobbled. "I suppose I do."

Freydolf eased over, his sketchbook ready. **You like books?**

"Yes, very much."

With a broad wink at Tupper, the Keeper wrote, **Then I propose a trip to the archives.**

13

Hope So

The archives were housed in the Statuary's tallest building, an ancient edifice with numerous windows. Twelve stories towered above the central room, winding upward in a warren of bookcases, cabinets, cubbyholes, and bins.

"Twelve floors of books?" gasped Chelle, staring at the skylights far overhead. Daylight poured through windows on every level, brightening the wide balconies that marched up the walls.

Nay, not just books. There are maps, scrolls, paintings, blueprints, letters … things like that. And the tower only accounts for things stored above ground. The archives stretch as deep into the mountain as they do toward the sky.

"How many have you read?"

Study is part of a Keeper's duty to his mountain, but it would take several lifetimes to read everything here.

"Do you like books, Tupper?"

Yes. And the statues here are nice.

Chelle's expression was all awe and eagerness. Offering her hand, she begged, "Show me?"

Tupper glanced at Frey, who waved them toward the stairs. "Go on, lambkin."

"Aren't you coming?"

"Aye, I'll catch up. While you show your young lady around, I'll pull the books Aurelius and Ulrica recommended."

With a quick nod, Tupper took Chelle's hand, threading his fingers between hers and tugging her toward the curving staircase where Rimbles was already scrambling upward. They climbed three levels before he stopped and pointed down to the floor far below. From above, it was easier to see the floor's mosaic, which depicted all the phases of the moon arrayed around a roaring dragon.

Releasing her to take out his notebook, Tupper wrote, **Thrall is our dragon.**

"You have a *dragon*?"

A dragon statue.

Chelle laughed. "That makes more sense."

They passed shelves packed with stone jars, carved boxes, and bound scrolls. At every turning, there was a niche, and before every window stood a low pedestal, each occupied by the statue of a man or woman.

Chelle paused to study a brownstone Pika. "Why isn't he moving like Haimish?"

He needs spicy smells to wake him. Perfume. Incense. Cake.

Reaching up to touch one of the statue's long, rabbitish ears, she murmured, "And I thought mine were a bother to hide."

Tupper tapped her shoulder, then wrote, **May I see them again?**

"What for?"

He hoped he hadn't offended her. **I like your ears.**

Waving at Rimbles, she inquired, "Because you like cats?"

Tupper glanced around, then drew Chelle over to a bench and sat beside her. **Please? I'll be careful.**

She searched his face before relenting. "Since you asked so nicely."

Lifting aside her hair, Tupper traced the edge of an ear that betrayed her Clow heritage. When Tupper carefully rubbed the delicate point between his thumb and forefinger, her eyes drifted shut. That was interesting. Rimbles always did the same thing. Reaching with his other hand, he sought out her other ear, and she turned her face toward him so he could reach. That was good.

Her peaceful expression brought a smile to Tupper's face, and he slid his fingers behind her ears to massage at the base. To his surprise, Chelle's ears quivered against his palms. She could move them? He ran his fingertips along the lightly furred backsides of each ear, checking to see if she was ticklish.

She sighed and opened her eyes. "Tupper?"

Would she ask him to stop? He didn't want to, but maybe Chelle didn't like people to play with her ears. There was even a chance that it wasn't proper, and he didn't want to do anything for which he'd need to apologize later. Reluctantly, he let go, met her gaze, and lifted his brows inquiringly.

"Do you kiss all your kitties on the nose?"

When Tupper didn't offer an answer, Chelle repeated the question. "Do you kiss all your kitties on the nose?"

He rubbed distractedly at one horn, for her tone had sharpened in the same way Ulrica's did when she was about to bring out her daggers. And that meant he'd messed up. Tupper wished he knew *how*. For now, all he could do was answer her question.

Nodding once, he wrote, **Mostly when no one's looking.**

Chelle coolly replied, "You're very kind to your pets."

He tried not to panic. Women were hard to figure out. Even Aurelius admitted it, and he was just about the smartest person Tupper knew. **Did I hurt you?**

"I am uninjured."

Well, this was interesting. Even though he felt bad for making Chelle angry, Tupper was intrigued by the way her attitude shifted. Chin high. Tone crisp. Eyes flashing. She almost looked dangerous. She definitely made his heart beat faster.

You <u>are</u> hurt. Why?

"You kissed my nose."

That had been weeks ago, and Tupper was certain she'd liked it at the time. But something had changed her mind. Very hesitantly, he asked, **Are you jealous of Graven?**

Her cheeks turned pink as she retorted, "Why would I be *jealous*? You treat us the same."

That didn't make any sense. It's not as if he was courting his guardian. How could Chelle have become so mixed up? It wasn't the same at all. Tupper touched the tip of her nose and firmly shook his head.

"So kissing me was an accident? Or maybe a mistake?"

This time, Tupper understood, and his eyes took on a shine. Tapping her nose gently before removing his hand, he whispered, "No."

Turning to a fresh page in his little notebook, he carefully printed, **You're not a kitty.**

"But you want to pet my ears."

Yes. Lots.

"I don't want to be treated like a pet."

Tupper gazed at her thoughtfully. Then he wrote, **If I was Clow, I'd let you pet my ears. I think it must feel nice.**

She stared at him for a long time before admitting, "It does."

Thought so.

Chelle shook her hair back into place so it covered her ears. "But I'm mostly Flox."

He nodded. **I'll court you in mostly-Flox ways. If you want, I'll ask Ulrica how Clow do things.**

She tipped her head to one side. "Clow courtship?"

Pleased to have coaxed her into a better mood, Tupper pressed the topic. **Is a little Pred okay? Or Grif? You might like their traditions, too.**

All traces of temper vanished, and she leaned closer. "What kinds of things do they do?"

Tupper didn't have the faintest idea. So he bluffed.

When Ulrica was upset, Aurelius always trapped her against his side and traded outrageous threats and oddly insulting endearments until she cheered up. Ewert was quick to apologize to Tillie, wheedling his way back into her good graces. And Carden faced Melina's changing moods calmly, lending his quiet support with casual displays of affection.

Tupper leaned toward the latter approach, but maybe Chelle was right. Hugs and kisses came easily for him, so he was treating her the same as everyone he loved. Could he come up with something special just for her?

And then he remembered something about his father.

Even though Tupper had been very young when their father died, he held onto a few memories. Good ones. And in one of those precious scenes, Father had done something that made Mother smile the way Tupper wanted Chelle to smile.

"I'll try," he murmured.

When Flox needed to apologize, they touched their lips, then placed their fingertips against the mouth of the one they'd wronged. Slipping his arm around Chelle's waist, Tupper pulled her closer, and with his other hand, he mimicked his father's reversal of the standard apology. He skipped the first touch, instead cupping Chelle's face so he could brush his thumb across her bottom lip. Brows furrowing in concentration, he adjusted his hold and tried again. Better. And so soft.

She stared up at him. "What does this mean?"

Since answering her would have required stopping, Tupper opted for repetition, skimming the pad of his thumb over her small pout. This was supposed to mean nice things. And if it worked right, she should smile.

Then her lips curved upward, and she whispered, "Do I have to guess?"

He nodded gravely. Having her so close was turning his mind to mush, so it would help a lot if Chelle could figure it out for him.

"Are you scolding me for being foolish?"

Tupper shook his head.

"Does this mean I talk too much?"

It was fun being on the other side of a guessing game. With a small smile, he shook his head again.

Chelle leaned her cheek against his hand. "Is this how you ask for a kiss?"

"Hope so," he admitted, searching her face to see if she was teasing. This would be a very bad time to mess up. Belatedly realizing she hadn't heard his answer, Tupper nodded.

She said, "Let me try."

Startled, he let his hand fall to his lap as Chelle reached up to touch his cheek, then slide her thumb across his mouth. Tupper's heart thudded. She was a fast learner, but he was much too slow.

Chelle resorted to a much more traditional Flox tactic to stir him from his reverie. She took him by the horn and pulled him into range to kiss his nose.

Slipping from the bench, Chelle hurried along the passage and took the stairs to the next floor. When she glanced over her shoulder to make sure he was following, her eyes sparkled with triumph. She had him by the horns, and they both knew it.

Freydolf lounged on a wide windowsill on the second floor, watching the young couple on the level above. He didn't bother being discreet. Tupper and Chelle were too focused on each other to realize they had an audience.

"And I thought Aurelius was absurdly adorable when he was fawning over Ulrica," he murmured to the moonstone librarian whose pedestal served as his footstool. "These two are even cuter."

He didn't usually play the voyeur, but he was caught between opposing demands. Aurelius had slyly urged him to give the pair some privacy, but Ulrica had insisted he watch them like a hawk. This was his compromise—close enough to see, too far to eavesdrop.

A sunstone statue up on the fifth level waved, and Frey returned the greeting with an upraised hand. He needed to check in with a few of the archive's guardians in order to locate the books

Chelle needed. The librarians were the only ones who could make heads or tails of the Statuary's collection, which was arranged chronologically, with the oldest books occupying the lowest levels.

Most of the books Aurelius had recommended for Chelle were much nearer the top, so gathering them would have to wait until the lovebirds resumed their climb.

It was strange to think of Tupper courting a girl, but the lad seemed to be faring well enough. He treated Chelle very gently, and her responding happiness was lovely to see. Frey stifled a chuckle when the young lady skipped away from her suitor, aiming for the stairs. He felt a little sorry for Tupper, who'd missed his chance at what probably would have been his first kiss.

"No need to rush," he advised in an undertone. Rising to follow, Freydolf chuckled anew, for the young lady had a solid head start, and Tupper was forced to scramble. "Unless he wants to keep up with her."

By the time Frey rejoined them, his sketchbook teetered atop an interesting assortment of books—an atlas, a fat volume about animals from around the world, and another about the various races and their distinctive traditions. He'd even included a personal favorite, a slim book in which twelve legends were collected, one for each of the magical mountain. Sometimes a story could give a better sense of place than facts alone.

"Is this how Flox court? You clean together?" the Pred asked.

Tupper turned and immediately held out his arms to take his master's burden. "These shelves were messy."

"Aye, and that's my fault." Frey surrendered his books, but rescued the sketchbook so he could include Chelle. **Each section has its own guardian, a statue who takes care of the books on those shelves.**

The young woman nodded. "Tupper introduced me to all the ones who weren't too busy to say hello." She gestured toward a sunstone Drom who was chasing imaginary cobwebs out of an alcove. "They're very polite. But I'm surprised. Can statues read?"

It's better to say they know the books they're guarding. These librarians take their job very seriously.

"The books on this shelf are mismatched," Chelle said. "Do they belong in other sections?"

Nay. Frey explained about the Statuary's unique filing system, then admitted, **These are the newest books, and they're untidy because there's no guardian. I'll need to fill this next niche with a statue to tend these shelves.**

Tupper asked, "Do you have a stone in mind?"

"It's been in the back of my mind to use one of your orphan stones."

"The dawnstone lady?"

Frey wasn't surprised that Tupper already knew. "Aye."

The lad nodded. "Yes, she'd like it here."

Without any translation happening, Chelle quietly returned to the shelf she'd been rearranging—picking up each book, whisking the dust from the shelf, and replacing the volumes in neat rows.

Freydolf said, "I'll have to read up on the magic required to bind a stone guardian to books, but I don't think there's any hurry."

Tupper seemed puzzled by the suggestion of delay. "But you don't have any commissions."

"Aye, but I may not need *another* librarian just yet."

The hint only helped a little. Glancing at the niche, Tupper slowly said, "I think the dawnstone would be happy here, even with just a few books to tend."

Freydolf quietly asked, "Wouldn't that rob Miss Tremont of her enjoyment? She makes a fine librarian."

Tupper's eyes widened. "That's a good idea."

"Planning to barter books for the lass's affection?"

"No, but I think I'll look for quarters close by. Since she likes books."

"When the time comes, can I help you search?"

Tupper's eyes lit up. "I'll pack a big lunch."

Relieved to still be included in the lad's plans, the Pred set his hand under his heart and bowed.

"What does that mean?" Chelle inquired, for she'd been stealing glances at them.

Adding a flourish to his gesture of gratitude, Freydolf took up his pencil and changed the subject. **Did you know Aurelius is writing a book...?**

14

Immortalized in Stone

While the others tended to the children's baths, Chelle followed Tupper out to a bench near the garden plots that dotted the wide-open space beyond the Statuary's walls. She was intrigued by the orderly way in which Master Freydolf's statues responded to the turning of the day. At sunset, an orange fox had bounded from his pedestal. When the stars made their appearance, Tupper's white ram frisked about on wee hooves. And as the moon glided high into the sky, the whole mountain seemed to stir.

It was hard to believe, but impossible to deny; atop Morven, stone had a life of its own.

A tiny paw patted her cheek, and Chelle reached up to scratch the tufted chest of the tiny monkey perched on her shoulder. Nott's tail looped around her neck as she played peekaboo with the bristly golden wolf resting his muzzle on Tupper's knee. The young man scratched Dag's ears as he gazed off toward the moon, lost in thoughts Chelle wished he would share.

Graven sprawled on the ground just outside the circle of light cast by Brand's lantern. She glanced up at the stone Grif, and the fire-bearer turned to meet her gaze, lifting his brows the same way Tupper did when inviting her to speak. It dawned on her that Tupper had probably picked up the mannerism from Brand, a statue he obviously counted as a friend.

Chelle nodded, and the redstone warrior inclined his head in the friendliest of manners.

She was beginning to understand something about Tupper, who'd lived among statues from the time he was nubbed. They had quite a bit in common, and that might be why he was so at home with these silent sentinels.

"They don't talk," she remarked. "Statues don't have voices."

Tupper looked her way and nodded.

"What's it like, having friends who can't say anything?"

He patted at his pocket and withdrew his notebook, fiddling with his pencil for a moment. Brand stepped closer, helpfully lifting the light so she could read his response. **What's it like, not hearing?**

"Quiet," she said flatly.

I like quiet. It's peaceful.

She could hardly fault him for loving something she was forced to live with. "Well, I think it's lonely."

He frowned thoughtfully, searching her face as he waited for more.

It had always amazed her that Tupper wasn't afraid of the silence that trapped her. Most people shied away from it, tried to fill it with words she never heard, or fended it off with a scribbling pencil. But he needed to understand her biggest source of frustration.

Chelle explained, "Silence is lonely, but not just because I can't hear what people are saying. Maybe it's because I can't listen to them, but no one listens to me."

Tupper quickly jotted, **Yours.**

His leaps were sometimes hard to follow. "Mine?"

Setting aside his notebook, he took her hands in his, lifting them to press them over his ears.

Laughing softly, she asked, "You're giving me your ears?"

He nodded.

Chelle followed their curve with her fingers, then tapped the earrings that swayed from each lobe. "Are you sure? Because if I was to tell you everything on my mind, you might never have quiet again."

A shrewd light suddenly sparked in his eyes, and Tupper wrote. **Trade.**

He wanted to haggle? Chelle asked, "For what?"

Boldly mirroring her pose, Tupper slipped his hands under her hair in order to tickle her ears.

Tupper gave up on getting any rest, and not because Freydolf was sitting up in the balcony, chipping away at a pretty little piece of moonstone. Head in a whirl, the young man tucked his nightshirt into his breeches and sneaked out into the soft, summer night. He needed to sort out his thoughts, and he knew just the one to help him.

Tiptoeing into the six-sided room at the head of the curving staircase, Tupper polished and refilled Brand's lantern before lighting the wick.

The redstone warrior took one look at him and frowned. Gripping Tupper's shoulder, Brand leaned close, tipping his head to one side as he concernedly searched the Flox's face.

Rubbing at the base of a horn, Tupper answered his unasked questions. "I'm fine. Just muddled. Couldn't sleep."

Brand slipped his arm around his waist, offering him the shelter of his feathered cape. Tupper was only half a head shorter than Grif, but he doubted he'd catch up to his friend. Not that he minded. He liked looking up to Brand, and he liked knowing he always would.

"Frey says I should show Chelle my favorite parts of the Statuary, but they're far and wide and deep. One day isn't enough to reach them all." They descended to the fountain colonnade while he poured out his troubles. "And *my* favorites might not be *her* favorites. How could they be? Shouldn't a person pick their own? Don't you just see something and *know* it's going to be one of your special favorites? Someone else can't choose for you. Can they?"

He hardly noticed that Brand was steering him toward the well. The Grif lifted the cover, then handed his companion the rope, and Tupper automatically pulled up the bucket. When a dipper of fresh, cold water was pressed into his hands, he obediently drank. "Thanks."

His friend smiled. Then taloned fingers took hold of Tupper's chin and turned his face toward the three young women who graced the fountain. Master Tremont's daughters were watching him with amused expressions. It wasn't like him to ignore friends.

Lifting a hand, Tupper sheepishly said, "Hello."

Brand gently flicked his forehead, and Tupper blinked at the warrior. The Grif rolled his eyes, then pointed with his nose at the three ladies.

"Oooh," the Flox breathed. "Oh, that's a *good* idea! Chelle is a Tremont, and visiting all three Triads takes one day."

His friend nodded encouragingly.

Tupper hopped up onto the rim of the fountain and gazed into the faces of the daughters of one of Morven's earliest Keepers. The Clow sculptor had been friendly enough with the locals to have provided a magnificent oven for the baker in Hayward, to have learned all their festival dances, to have married a Flox woman, and to have doted on three daughters ... and at least one son, since the Tremont name had been handed down.

"I'm courting a distant relative of yours. Chelle Tremont."

The young women traded knowing smiles.

Tupper found himself searching for a resemblance to Chelle in their sweet faces. Beckoning to Brand, he asked, "Can you lift the light higher?"

The statue joined him on the fountain's rim and stretched his lantern toward the nearest young woman. Tupper already knew she didn't have claws, and there was no way to tell if she had fangs. If these daughters had inherited Clow ears, they were well-hidden beneath curly hair, but for the first time, Tupper noticed that her pupils were unusually narrow. The effect was uncanny. Cat-like.

And there was something more. Stepping right into the fountain, Tupper waded to the center and clambered up, joining the Triad on their pedestal. They pressed close, welcoming him with a swish of full skirts and a formal clasping of hands. He hadn't been up here since he was ten, and it was funny to have them looking up at him for once.

"Can I see?" he asked politely, tilting one statue's face toward the light.

Now that he was so close, it was easy to tell. He'd always assumed that the rough patches in the stone near their temples was due to the passage of time, but now he understood that the subtle pattern was part of the sculptor's design.

With a wondering smile, Tupper exclaimed, "Spots!"

Chelle was a light sleeper, so she woke the instant her foot was uncovered. Was it already time to start the fires in the bread oven? She glanced toward the window only to be met by a blank stone wall, but then she remembered where she was. Carden and Melina Meadowsweet had made a place for her in their daughters' bedroom.

When small hands wrapped around her ankle, she knew one of the children was trying to get her attention. By the dim light thrown by a shuttered lantern, she could see that Dulcie and Yona were sound asleep in their beds. Did Arni need someone to take him to the necessary? Pushing up on her elbows, Chelle was startled when a dark shape surged forward, and a plump hand stifled her gasp.

Quintrell's golden eyes searched hers for a few moments, and he nodded. When she nodded back, he let go, quickly touching his lips, then hers in a very proper Flox apology.

Sitting back on his heels, he produced a slip of paper.

She angled it toward the faint light and read the short message in Tupper's familiar handwriting. **Dress. Follow. Quiet.**

An age seemed to pass before Carden's front door opened just wide enough for Quintrell and Chelle to step out into the cobbled street where Tupper and Aurelius waited with Brand.

The little boy rushed to his father, who caught him up and demanded, "Were you swift?"

"Yes."

"Were you stealthy?"

"Yes!"

Aurelius caressed his son's silky hair and gravely demanded, "Were you silent?"

"*Yes!*" the boy boasted, giggling when his father's approval came in the form of a skyward toss.

Tupper eased to Chelle's side, his greeting already printed on a fresh page in his notebook. Brand unobtrusively provided enough light for her to see it clearly. **Good morning. Too early?**

"Good morning," she replied, smiling at Aurelius's roughhousing. "And no, the Quinces keep bakers' hours. Are you usually up this early?"

Only sometimes.

"So this is a special occasion?"

He nodded, and glanced at Aurelius, who'd also come prepared. He handed Chelle a single sheet of parchment, the letter of explanation Tupper had asked him to write.

Thank you for your forbearance, Miss Tremont. It's deucedly early, but the sprat wants to share something special with you. My son and I will accompany the two of you into the heights where Morven's third Keeper, Master Tremont—a Clow and your ancestor—hid his dawnstone masterpiece. From what I've read in the archives, Tremont was an unconventional Keeper, but an excellent father. His devotion to his three daughters has been immortalized in stone. Would you like to meet them?

"Yes!" Chelle exclaimed, looking from Aurelius to Tupper. "Yes, *please*!"

Tupper beamed at Brand, who inclined his head and took the lead, lantern held high.

As you can see, Master Tremont's wife was Flox.

"Yes, of course." Chelle strolled between the graceful figures of the sculptor's daughters, looking at the young women from every angle. All three of them were taller than she, which was unusual. Tremonts tended to be bigger than the average Flox, and she was no exception. It was impossible to tell if these women had been dark or fair since they were pink from head to toe, but she noticed something very familiar about them. "They have eyes like my father's. Or I suppose he inherited theirs."

Tupper stood at the ornate window, his gaze fixed on the lightening eastern horizon. When she joined him, he wrote, **Do you like to dance?**

Chelle shook her head. "I never learned. Because I can't hear the music."

Her suitor's expression clouded, then grew thoughtful. **There is no music up here, but we still dance. I taught Frey. I'll teach you. Then we can dance together at the midsummer festival.**

So many words. Chelle recognized the hopefulness in Tupper's expression and reached the obvious conclusion. "*You like dancing.*"

Lots.

Aurelius relieved Tupper of his notebook to cheerfully interject, **Trust me, my dear. The sprat's passion for this genteel form of merrymaking is unrivaled on all four continents. You shall not find a better partner.**

Just then, morning broke, waking the Triad, who spun through several steps of a folk dance before pausing to take partners. Quintrell rushed to one of the young ladies, and she lifted him into her arms before whirling the grinning boy across the room. Aurelius bowed to a second statue and joined her, executing the traditional Floxish steps with aplomb. The remaining dawnstone lady looked between the two of them.

Tupper said something to her, and with a warm smile, she waved her hands, urging them to make the final pair. Chelle tried to hang back, but her suitor firmly drew her into the circle.

That morning, Chelle gained new appreciation for Tupper's infinite patience, unexpected grace, and wholehearted dedication to the things he loved.

15

Uncensored

Chelle sat in Melina's bakery, sipping tea and watching the stone man in the corner for any signs of life. "And you do this every morning?"

The woman nodded as she expertly slid two pans into the oven. Setting aside her long-handled peel, Melina joined her at the table and reached for her pencil. **I wake Haimish before the rest of the family. I don't know what I'd do without him.**

Rereading the wording, Chelle asked, "You consider him family?"

Nodding adamantly, Melina wrote, **He _is_ family. We love him. And he loves us.**

"Do the statues have feelings? They're stone."

With a thoughtful expression, Melina wrote, **They begin as stone. They become something more. And speaking of love, tell me more about Tupp. How often does he drop by the bakery? The sneak.**

Chelle giggled.

After more than an hour of dancing, Aurelius had called a stop to the lesson, so Tupper could escort Chelle here. Melina had scolded her young brother-in-law for making off with their guest, and a faint blush had colored Tupper's explanations.

With a quick note, he'd excused himself to help Farley with their morning's work, promising to return with Freydolf in time for breakfast.

And so Melina drew Chelle into what amounted to a friendly gossip session. Over mugs of tea, she plied the younger woman for news about her family in Hayward, then about city life in Millford. Apparently, one of Tupper's older sisters had hired out to a family up their way, then married a young man from the area.

Before long, the rich smell of spice cake filled the kitchen, and Haimish stepped off his pedestal. Melina turned to address him warmly, and his gaze found Chelle's.

His tail swayed in a hopeful manner.

She said, "Good morning, Haimish. It smells good, doesn't it?"

The statue placed his hand over his heart and dipped his head. Turning to Melina, he showed her his palms, and she gave a reply. Once the brownstone Pred excused himself, the woman wrote, **Carden has a free day, so he's with the children. Haimish will help him. He likes to be useful.**

"And Yona will be asking for him?"

Melina laughed and nodded. **I'm tempted to request another guardian to help with Hanley. Yona doesn't want to share her Mish.**

"For day or night?"

We're spoiled with Haimish. He can do both, thanks to his titian trimmings.

Chelle could see the advantages. "Maybe you should ask Master Freydolf to create a new statue for you."

With a small frown, Melina wrote, **I already have so much. It seems ungrateful to ask for more.**

"There are so many statues here. Couldn't you look in the galleries for a suitable one?"

Her hostess started and glanced guiltily toward the door, and Chelle turned to see a bleary-eyed Pred leaning against the frame of the open door. Freydolf was caught mid-yawn, his fangs on full display. Tupper wasn't anywhere in sight, so his master must have woken early. Or never slept. The latter seemed more likely, and Melina hurried to pour him some tea.

Ambling over to the table, Freydolf pulled over a sturdy stool and dropped onto it, gesturing for pencil and paper. He didn't object when she first turned to a fresh page. **Melina assures me you're talking about nothing, but I don't believe her.**

He glanced at Chelle from under bushy brows, and she fidgeted. It hadn't been her intention to get Melina into trouble. Unsure what to say, she kept her mouth shut.

The Keeper scratched at his messy hair, then sighed. In bold letters, he printed, **How many times do I need to say it? You _and_ Chelle must learn.**

With a jolt, she realized that Frey was speaking each word as he wrote it, giving his message to both women at once.

I welcome any excuse to make you happy. Tell me what you need. Ask, and I will find it ... make it ... give it. Please. He glanced between them as they read his words, then added, **I _want_ to.**

Melina's response was to place a steaming cup in front of the man and kiss his forehead. Chelle thought it was cute, the way Freydolf hunched his shoulders and muttered into his mug.

Unable to resist the urge to tease the flustered man, she said, "If that's how it is, then all we really need is _you._"

The Pred blinked several times, then carefully wrote, **Only as much as I need you. Now, hold out your hands.**

She did, and he dropped a small statue onto her palms—a moonstone ram. She gasped, "For me?"

Aye. Think of a name, and we'll wake him tonight. To keep you company until ...

He hesitated, then finished, **Next time.**

Tupper hung back while Aurelius handled Chelle's questions about the moonstone Triad. The merchant's voice echoed off the walls as he narrated his written explanations for the benefit of the children. Excursions into the galleries with their papas and Uncle Tupp were a normal part of growing up in the Statuary, but all the kids jounced with excitement. It wasn't often that their mothers accompanied them on these outings, and even rarer for Uncle Doff to be lured away from his work.

Today, *everyone* had gathered.

Except Torio. He was late.

Aurelius was still going on about the third Keeper's balmy homeland when a flicker of flames appeared at the far end of the colonnade. Tupper relaxed, only to have Ulrica poke him in the side.

"What are you up to, boy?" she demanded.

"Nothing."

The woman's dark eyes narrowed. "Why is Torio *coming* from the direction we're *going*?"

"We needed fire-bearers."

Torio and his entourage of torch-bearers marched closer, and Ulrica smirked. "And not just *any* block of redstone would do."

He nodded. "Was it a good idea?"

Ulrica patted his flushed cheek and whispered, "Aye. This should be interesting."

Aurelius's voice trailed off as Torio swept into their midst, flanked by four fire-bearers. With a bow to Chelle, the Grif grandly announced, "To light your way, young mistress."

"She can't hear you," Aurelius drawled.

"No matter." Torio casually dropped to a seat on the fountain's rim. "Even if she could, she wouldn't be listening."

Tupper's relief bloomed into satisfaction at the expression of awe on Chelle's face. Forgetting the rest of them, she stepped closer to the nearest statue, who towered over her. Clow were nearly as tall as Pred, and these four were deep-chested and muscular. Torches highlighted noble brows, wide-set eyes, and broad noses. Wild hair spiked back from foreheads roughened to indicate spots, and the sides of their heads seemed to have been shaved, putting their cat-like ears on display. Curved claws added to their imposing demeanor, and they wore short, belted garments without sleeves, beaded arm bands and necklaces, and wrappings on their powerful legs.

Aurelius was quick to take their measure, prowling around to locate their maker's mark. **These are ancient statues, Tremont's own work. Modern Clow show better fashion sense.**

Chelle wasn't listening. Offering her hand to the nearest guardian, she said, "Hello."

The redstone torch-bearer gravely accepted her hand.

Freydolf, who was scrutinizing the mark on one of the Clow's forearm, exclaimed, "I've heard tales about these statues! But Tremont's personal guardians have been lost for *ages*. Where did you find them, lambkin?"

With a small shrug, Tupper replied, "Down, around, and under. They hid themselves, but Morven tattled."

Torio said, "These gentlemen still grieve for the ones they lost. Only news of a daughter of Tremont returning to the Statuary was enough to convince them to come out of seclusion."

Chelle tugged at Aurelius's sleeve, and the Pred obligingly transcribed the conversation so she could follow.

Carden offered his hand to the Clow closest to him, and Melina asked, "Who are they?"

Freydolf said, "Put simply, they were to Tremont's wife and daughters what Haimish is to Yona."

Tupper slipped up behind Chelle and placed his hands on her shoulders. "They like Flox."

"Aye," Freydolf agreed. "Their maker's preference would run deep. Aurelius, ask Chelle if she's willing to show them her ears."

When the message was relayed, Chelle glanced back at Tupper. Taking that as permission, he lifted aside her curls, causing a stir among the astonished children. But the greater response came from the four Clow. Torches held high, they crowded close, exchanged glances with one another, then broke into wide grins.

"They can smile?" Chelle asked in startled tones.

Tupper nodded, but Aurelius's answer was even better. **Aye, lass. Thanks to you.**

Cradling Hanley close, Chelle whispered, "I'm so mixed up. How can we not be lost?"

Melina smiled indulgently. **Don't worry. Tupp knows every nook and cranny of Morven. And the statues that stand in them.** With a nod toward the children who'd taken the lead, she added, **We're in familiar territory.**

"It's so big!"

Believe me, it's <u>bigger</u>, the woman wrote. **Carden has Tupp guide him into the deeper galleries all the time. They're endless!**

Chelle watched Quintrell and Arni leap out from behind a statue, only to have their prey pounce. Aurelius tackled his son, tucking and rolling to his feet with impressive agility. Freydolf scooped up Arni and hung him by his ankles. The passage must have been ringing with their laughter, and Chelle wished fleetingly that she could hear it. She checked on Hanley, but the baby slept right through the noise.

Tupper intervened, rescuing a pink-cheeked Arni from his master's tender mercies. Farley, who was piggybacking Yona, let his steps lag until he was even with them and the Clow torch-bearer bringing up the rear.

Melina listened to something her young brother-in-law said, then wrote, **Yona wants a drink, and Farley wants to say hello. Please excuse me?**

"Yes, of course," Chelle quickly agreed. She was curious about Tupper's younger brother and wondered what he'd say now that no one was censoring his comments.

He took charge of paper and pencil, and as soon as Melina turned her back, he began to write. **Hi. I'm Farley. 'Bout time they let me speak for myself. You sure are strange.**

The comment stung, but she couldn't deny it. "I know."

Not in a bad way. You're sorta like him. Caught in between. It's a good match. He's lucky. You're nice. He searched her face while she read his neat lines. Chelle stared up into bright blue eyes, and he grinned lopsidedly. **Surprised?**

"Yes."

Good. Farley cast a sly glance in his older brother's direction, then hooked his arm through hers, bracing the sketchbook between them so it'd be easy to write while they walked. **There's loads of stuff I can tell you. Like Tupp's voice settled on the high side. Not as low as Carden's or Ewert's. And he hums while he works. Especially if Graven's around. On account of the songstone stripes. And we bathe together. All of us men.**

Chelle's eyes widened, and he seemed pleased to have shocked her.

It's a Pred thing. Tupp was real shy, but I bet he'd do just about anything to make Freydolf happy. They're knotted up tight on account of Morven. Can you feel it? Hear it? See it?

Clearly, Farley wasn't cut from the same cloth as his brother. He was a fast-talker. Shaking her head, Chelle admitted, "I'm not sure what you mean."

Guess not, then. Too bad. I'm talking about magic. This here's a magic mountain, and there's plenty of it around, but not many people have an affinity. Tupp does. But not in the usual way. Did you know?

"Nobody mentioned it."

Farley rolled his eyes. **Figured they didn't bring it up. They're so used to it, they don't notice anymore. Here's the deal. The magic here <u>likes</u> Tupp. You should see it. Chasing after him. Looping around him. Fixing itself to him.**

Chelle wasn't familiar with the mysteries of mountains, but one thing was obvious. "Are you saying *you* can see magic?"

Her companion muttered something, glanced toward the Keeper, then gave a small nod. **But I'll deny it.**

If he was prepared to lie about it, why was he telling her the truth? "I can keep secrets. But why?"

Would you mind being stuck here?

"No."

That's good, but I don't aim to stay. Once Dessa's set—that's Torio's mountain—we're gonna travel. I'll see the world. Every part

of it. Just like Torio. But Tupp has no choice. Morven got greedy, and he belongs to her just like her Keeper does.

"I'm not sure what that means," Chelle admitted. "They have books for me to read once I get home, but ...."

Farley cut her off. **He can't leave. Ever.**

That sounded very strange. Even a little ominous. "What would happen if he did?"

Farley glanced toward his master, brows furrowed. **Torio tried it once, and it just about killed him.**

Torio was a Keeper, too? Clearly, she hadn't been asking the right kinds of questions. But for the moment, she set aside her desire for more details. "Why does it feel like you're warning me?"

I kinda am. But not to scare you away. You gotta understand this, or you don't understand him. He pointed to his brother, then wrote, **Knowing Tupp, he couldn't explain it if he tried. In fact, all he'd say is, "Freydolf needs me. I want to stay." Which is true. But it goes deeper than that. Magic's mixed in. And that's something you can't overlook.**

"You think I'm overlooking something?"

Oh, I <u>know</u> you are. Shaggy hair. Pierced ears. Scuffed horns. Slow wits. Strange taste.

Snatching the pencil out of Farley's hand, Chelle glared up at him. "Hard work. Loyal heart. Steady hands. Slow smile."

He tapped the page. **Sweet kisses?**

Chelle's eyes flashed, and she snapped, "Impertinent brother."

I <u>knew</u> I was right. While she spluttered incoherently, Farley nudged her with his elbow and wrote, **About the match. He's lucky.**

16

Hearing Voices

Chelle hadn't realized she'd dozed off until warm hands closed around hers. Tupper's gentle patting was a nice way to wake, and she opened her eyes with a smile. "Sorry. I fell asleep."

Her kneeling suitor nodded.

The day had been one long, exhausting expedition, filled with delights and dangers—tiny tree frogs, skulking loup-garou, jewel-like flowers, razor-toothed dragons, and more dancing. Sitting up on the oversized couch before the fireplace in the balcony, she asked, "Is the moon shining?"

Tupper sat back on his heels. Nodding, he reached down and lifted Olexi, and the little ram bounded along the springy cushions.

She fumbled around for her gift from Freydolf. "Where did he ...?"

With a small smile, Tupper reached between the cushions and pulled out the gray ram, putting him into her hands.

Chelle set the statue next to Olexi, who capered around the still guardian. To her amusement, Olexi minced forward on tiny hooves to deliver a tap of horns. "They'll be brothers, just like you and Master Freydolf."

A slow smile. A shy glance. A short nod.

Tupper rose up on his knees in order to fuss with her hair, which must have been a mess. Initially, she thought he was trying to get at her ears again, but he seemed content to rearrange her curls. "How did you know where he was?"

He reached for his notebook but came up empty. Without it, he settled for charades, tapping his ear.

"You could hear him?" she guessed.

Another nod.

"But I thought statues are silent. And Master Freydolf hasn't woken him yet."

Tupper rubbed awkwardly at the base of one horn. He nodded again.

Chelle took pity, switching to the kinds of questions he could answer with a *yes* or *no*. "Does this have something to do with magic? Farley said it likes you."

Tupper's eyes widened, and he nodded seriously.

"Can you see it?"

Tupper shook his head, then pointed to his ear.

"You hear it?"

Yet another nod.

"What does it sound like?"

She immediately felt silly because it was the wrong kind of question. Perhaps it was even a foolish question, since she *couldn't* hear. But Tupper seemed prepared to answer. With a series of waves and pats, he coaxed her forward, so she was sitting on the edge of her seat. Then instead of translating thoughts into words, he translated sounds into touch.

He encircled her with his arms. Chelle expected it to turn into an embrace, but Tupper held back. Holding very still, he surrounded her, and it was the oddest sensation. Close enough to touch, to feel, but not quite connecting. "Do you ever reach back?" she whispered.

Tupper eyes sparkled, and he nodded.

"What happens then?"

He eased away from her, a faraway look in his eyes. At that moment, Freydolf strolled into the balcony and spoke to Tupper. Her suitor replied at some length, gesturing broadly.

The Pred sat down on the carpet next to his bond-brother and rubbed his chin. Although she was entirely left out, their mutual puzzlement put her at ease. It was funny to watch the two of them search for a way to explain something Farley said they took for granted.

Finally, Freydolf made a bobbling motion, and Tupper nodded in agreement.

With a hopeful expression, he joined Chelle on the sofa, caught both her hands, and brought them to his ears. Was he offering to listen to her again? No, that didn't make sense. Her confusion increased when Freydolf reached around and covered her hands with his larger ones. The sculptor offered a reassuring smile before closing his eyes, and Tupper's slid shut as well.

Deciding that was her cue, Chelle followed suit and waited to see what would happen.

Something trembled against her palms, the barest of vibrations, and her eyes snapped open. Both men remained calm. Eyes closed. Peaceful expressions.

Could she have imagined that tingle? Chelle took a deep breath and let her eyes drift closed.

This time, the prickle of sensation that began in Tupper's earrings pressed deeper, sending a thrill to the tips of her fingers before dancing up her arms and down her spine. Chelle gasped as the tumult gained strength, thrumming pleasantly between her and Tupper. Emotions stirred in her heart, but she wasn't certain who they belonged to. Impatience. Exhilaration. Possessiveness. Was this what magic felt like?

And then, a voice echoed through her mind, the first she'd heard since she was very small. *Your heart calls to his.*

"Wh-what?" Chelle stammered.

"He wants to be your Keeper."

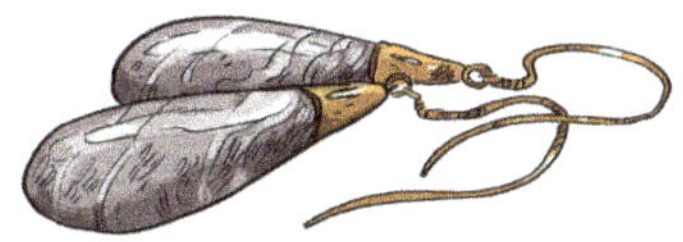

Heartstone was strong stuff. Even dull folk had been known to feel a hint of a mountain's magic when they came in contact with its center. A twinge. A brush. A throb. Just enough to let them know that the invisible was real and present. But magic never behaved itself when Tupper was involved, and Freydolf was regretting his suggestion that they use the lad's earrings as a sort of touchstone.

The master sculptor had taken the young lady's gasp as a good sign that he'd managed to orchestrate some kind of magical tug. But then tears spilled down her cheeks, and he quickly pulled her hands away from the sides of Tupper's head. Flustered, the Keeper called to her. "Chelle? Chelle, what's wrong?"

Blue eyes opened and locked with his. "Who said that?"

Confused beyond the bounds of common sense, he replied. "It's me. Freydolf."

Tupper reacted more slowly, but in his usual hands-on fashion. Turning the young woman to face him, he cupped her face, brushed at her wet cheeks with his thumbs, then pulled her into a hug. Looking over her head at him, the lad said, "She can't hear you, Frey. Chelle's deaf."

"Aye, but ...." He rubbed the back of his neck and gruffly asked, "Did I frighten her?"

His bond-brother shook his head. "Bring paper, please?"

Freydolf hurried to one of the worktables in the corner and pushed aside several half-finished toys and trinkets to get at an old sketchbook. It took longer to find a pencil. Riffling to a fresh page, he strode back to the couple curled together on the couch. Tupper crooned softly as he rocked and patted his teary sweetheart.

To the Pred's amusement, she seemed put-out by his fussing. "Are you humming? Farley said you do."

Tupper blinked, and Freydolf chuckled as he sat on the floor in front of them. "When did your brother put in a good word for you?"

"Not sure."

Chelle's confusion was plain as the tears on her face. "This isn't like me. I'm not the weepy sort. But I can't stop crying."

Nodding, Tupper said, "Morven likes tears."

"Aye, but they'll be the end of me," Frey grumbled. Tupper pointed to the sketchbook, and the sculptor dutifully relayed the message.

As soon as she read it, Chelle asked, "The mountain?"

Aye, this majestic chunk of gray rock that's in my keeping. She's always craved tears and has been known to inspire them. With a small smile, he added, **Those who get close to her usually end up shedding a few.**

"I heard a voice. She said things. But I don't understand." Sniffling softly, Chelle said, "I *can't* hear."

Freydolf cut a look at his servant. "Wonders never cease."

Tupper blushed faintly. "Morven meddles."

For Chelle's benefit, the Pred wrote, **It's said that magic speaks to the soul. I'm very sorry if Morven frightened you.**

"No, no. In a way, it was wonderful, hearing something again. And it felt ... I don't even know how to explain. I do have a question, though." At his nod, she asked, "What's the relationship between a mountain and her Keeper?"

Frey carefully composed a response. **Some say that without a master to keep the mountain in check, her magic will run wild. He tames her.**

Chelle's brow furrowed. "Is that what you think?"

It wasn't. **Morven never asked to be tamed.**

"What then?"

Freydolf glanced at Tupper, who seemed to be trying to hide his face in her hair. "You heard what Morven said, lambkin?"

Tupper nodded.

"Should I be aware of my meddling mountain's remarks before I proceed?"

The lad hesitated, then shook his head. "Tell Chelle the truth."

Frey had heard about other mountains' Keepers, many of whom were known for strong traits—frugality, musicality, rigidity, ambition, strength, beauty. Morven's Keepers didn't fit any particular profile. She'd called to sculptors from diverse lands, races, and backgrounds because those things didn't matter to her. His mountain only cared about one thing.

I think that without her Keeper, a mountain loses heart. Loneliness saps her strength, and her wellspring of magic dwindles away. So in each generation, she searches for a respectable man and entrusts him with her heart. With a soft glance at Tupper, whose cheek rested atop Chelle's head, Freydolf concluded, **He cherishes her.**

"He wants you to stay."

Chelle sat up a little straighter in her chair and glanced at the others crowded around the bakery's broad table. This seemed to be the central gathering point for everyone who lived in the Statuary—warm and welcoming neutral territory. As much as she wanted to linger in the beatitude they shared, her visit to the mountaintop was nearly at its end.

"You want to stay."

She stole a glance at Tupper. The young man showed no sign of having heard Morven's whispers. He was too busy glancing back and forth between Aurelius and Torio, who seemed to be embroiled in a disagreement. Carden slouched in his chair, little Hanley sprawled on his chest. Melina monitored the other children's breakfast with the help of Freydolf, who had a nephew perched on each knee. Quintrell and Arni took turns feeding the big man bits of bread.

"He will make a good Keeper."

With a soft sigh, Chelle rehearsed Freydolf's assurances from the night before. Morven *wasn't* a mind reader, so her private thoughts were safe. But magic stirred with the heart and soul, so the mountain was privy to her strongest emotions. And Tupper's.

Her commentary was a little embarrassing, but it wasn't as

if Morven was spilling any deep, dark secrets. Weren't they courting?

"You are right to admire him."

No wonder Tupper called Morven a meddler. Chelle rolled her eyes, only to find Farley watching her with frank curiosity. The brother who could *see* magic. With a sly glance toward the others at the table, Farley twirled his finger, then pointed at her. She replied with a helpless little shrug. He tugged at his ear, and she nodded. His blue eyes laughed at her, but it wasn't mockery. His attitude seemed to be "join the club."

"He has potential."

Chelle was tempted to ask Morven if she was talking about Tupper or Farley, but Ulrica chose that moment to casually slide into the empty seat beside hers. The woman haughtily met her gaze as she offered a slip of paper. **They're bickering about your return. Tupper planned to carry you upon his tiger, but the others insult your courage, stamina, and resolve. If you want this life, take it. Plunge in your dagger to the hilt.**

As much as Chelle appreciated having these people think of her, she didn't like to have anyone think *for* her. With a grateful nod to Ulrica, she slipped the note into her apron pocket next to Ovis, her precious little guardian, then politely interrupted the debate.

An hour later, Chelle was amply rewarded for her initiative. As Graven sloped through the forested foothills on Morven's southern side, she tangled her fingers into varicolored fur, leaned back into Tupper's embrace, and smiled at the mountain's parting remark.

"He is right to admire you."

17

Brace Yourself

Freydolf wobbled, and Carden made a grab for him. "Easy now! Deep breaths."

Aurelius waved smelling salts under his brother-in-law's nose. "Pathetic."

"Aye, I know it." The master sculptor swatted away the pungent vial and dropped heavily into one of his kitchen chairs.

Torio reached for the goblet standing in the center of the table and held it up to the lantern's light. The smoky crystal helped disguise its contents, but everyone knew exactly what it held. Swirling the sluggish liquid, the Grif asked, "Shouldn't you be used to this by now?

"Sorry."

"No need to apologize," Carden murmured. "The point of these tests isn't to change *you*. It's Dessa's reaction to the blood that matters. And ...?"

"Oh, she likes it," Torio said. "All of it. But especially mine."

Farley took the cup from his master and replaced it on the table. "If you're lucky, she'll only need blood to wake the *first* time."

With a soft grunt, Freydolf said, "It could become a daily ordeal, but it's too early to tell. We should pick a stone, make a guardian, and begin trying to wake it."

Aurelius brandished his favorite writing implement. "Excellent. A new chapter in the saga of the thirteenth mountain can finally begin!"

Frey muttered, "I'd rather you didn't canonize my tendency to keel over every time we try to make some progress."

"If the world at large discovers that your bed doubles as a fainting couch, it will *not* be due to my eloquent descriptions." Flicking the edge of the goblet with a claw, Aurelius asked, "Did you know that Aggie collected this batch for you? Ulrica hopes to pierce her in another year or two."

"Aye, she's a fine huntress," Frey remarked. The girl was often responsible for the meat on his dinner table, and he appreciated her growing skills. Even the suggestion of food was enough to make his stomach rumble.

Tupper noticed. "You should eat."

Grimacing, Frey replied, "If I don't work on an empty stomach, I empty my stomach."

"Your squeamishness is deucedly inconvenient," groused Aurelius. "Hardly befitting a Pred of your lineage."

A loaf of bread found its way into Freydolf's hands, and Tupper quietly said, "Aggie *is* good at catching rabbits, but Frey is *Keeper* and due more respect than you're giving."

The merchant inclined his head and lapsed into silence, and Torio ventured, "I thought you already started on a guardian. That lioness over there."

"Aye, but it'll take *months* to finish her. I want to know how to wake her before then."

Tupper strolled across the workshop, bent, and picked up a small chunk of black stone from the heap in the back corner. "This one."

Aurelius eyed the gleaming rock curiously. "I know you're touted as this mountain's best picker, but why that one? Did it volunteer?"

"Yes."

Carden asked, "Can you tell us anything helpful about that fragment, Tupp?"

Freydolf tore into his bread while waiting for the lad's

answer. Back when he was small, the boy would have lifted the thing to his ear, but that quirk had fallen by the wayside. Frey sort of missed it.

Tupper gave the stone a soft pat, then announced, "He's one of the only males."

"He does look a mite henpecked," Torio interjected. "Has Dessa's son turned to you for rescue?"

"No, he doesn't want me." Crossing to the table, Tupper offered the stone to his brother. "He wants Farley."

Torio was nearly an hour late for his Keeper training session with Freydolf, but the Pred didn't comment. He never did. The Grif sauntered through the workshop's door, crossed to his usual chair, and sprawled.

"*Finally*," complained Aurelius.

"I didn't realize you were pining for me, Harrow. How about we trade dusty tomes for a lengthy game of Pinnacles in the balcony. I'm sure the good Keeper won't miss us."

"Nay," Freydolf replied, all seriousness. "*I'm* in need of a good Keeper today."

"Too bad I'm a *terrible* one!"

"No argument there," Aurelius muttered. "But there's no accounting for tastes."

Torio's eyes narrowed. "What's going on?"

"Dessa's decided what form she'll take," the master sculptor announced.

The Grif's gaze cut to the glittering black column that remained untouched. "Ah. Then by all means, get on with it."

"First, I'll need your help in refining my design," Freydolf said.

"Me? You're the artist. I hardly think it matters what I ...."

Torio's voice trailed off as the Pred unrolled a large sheet of parchment on the low table where his books were usually stacked. No less than two dozen figures had been sketched in considerable detail. Sitting forward, he muttered a series of curt oaths. Every race was included, as well as representatives of famous myths, poetry, legends, and lore.

"I thought you said Dessa had *decided*."

With eyes downcast, Freydolf said, "Aye. She wants to be a woman."

Aurelius unobtrusively crossed to the nearest worktable and inspected the label on a bottle of wine. For the first time, Torio noticed that three goblets stood ready. Wine at this hour? Shifting uneasily, he echoed, "A woman."

Freydolf nodded. "I suppose I shouldn't be surprised. Tupper's been calling her a *pretty lady* from the moment he discovered her."

"True enough," Torio murmured, his gaze returning to the various sketches. "You certainly put a lot of effort into ... diversity."

"Aye, I thought it would help you narrow things down."

Aurelius chimed in. "So many splendiferous choices. You cannot possibly go wrong."

"If none of them appeal to you, I can try again," Freydolf offered.

"I don't care. Whatever works," Torio replied, casting about for a book. Any book.

"Nay," the sculptor said, his voice thick with embarrassment. "Dessa doesn't just want to stand by your side. She wants you to be proud of her."

Aurelius bluntly said, "Nonsense. Like any enamored female, she wants you to find her *beautiful*."

Torio stared in horror at the man who pressed a full goblet into his hand. "Does that mean ...?"

"Aye, Kite," Aurelius confirmed with snide delight. "We're here to discuss your taste in women."

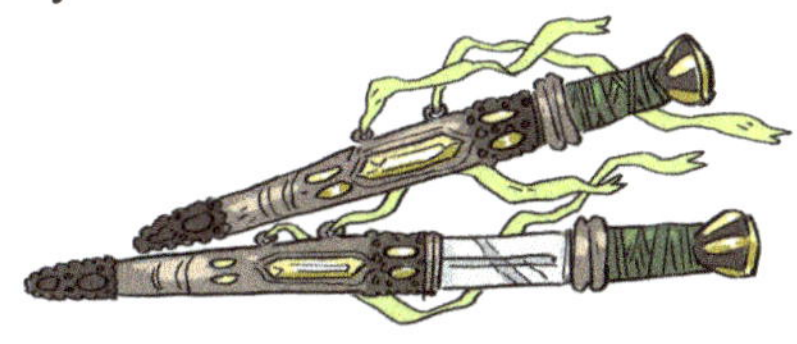

Tupper's siesta came to an abrupt halt when a blade thudded into the grass a few inches from his face. Slowly opening his eyes, he contemplated his own reflection in the gleaming metal of a dagger he knew all too well. The light yellow crystals decorating its hilt were Aggie's favorite.

"Hello," he called softly.

"Were you pretending not to hear me?" she challenged.

He smiled up at his little sister, who was dressed in the fashion of a Pred huntress—a snug tunic, knee-length breeches, and matching daggers slung from her slim hips. Sitting up and stretching, Tupper said, "I was sleeping."

"Rimbles should have warned you that someone was nearby."

"She knows you won't hurt me."

Aggie reclaimed her dagger and inspected its edge. "I caught you fair and square."

"Yes."

"That means you do the gutting."

Tupper nodded. "How many?"

She pointed to a small mound of dun fur at the base of an oldtree.

There had to be a dozen, which meant they'd be eating well tonight. "Good job!" he praised, reaching for his own hunting knife.

Aggie flushed with pleasure.

The Meadowsweet siblings worked side by side, skinning and dressing the rabbits. With a sidelong look at her brother, Aggie asked, "Looking forward to the midsummer festival?"

"Yes."

"Big plans?" she asked sweetly.

Tupper saw no reason to evade the question. "I'm going to ask Chelle for her promise."

"Thought so." With a shrewd glance, she asked, "How long did it take you to find her?"

He rubbed at the base of a horn. "I looked for a long time, but I found her as soon as I saw her."

Aggie giggled. "You make it sound easy."

"It was, and it wasn't." Tupper shrugged. "I worried for nothing."

"You were worried?"

"Yes. Not many Flox like the idea of living with Pred. Even you were nervous about the Harrows."

"At first." The girl kept her hands busy, rinsing fresh meat in clear water. "You're just right for Chelle, but who will be just right for me?"

He blinked. "Isn't it too soon for you to be making plans?"

"Maybe." Aggie paused in her work. "The Harrows are going overseas this winter."

He nodded. "Ulrica said Quintrell's old enough. Arni will miss him."

"Not necessarily. Aurelius invited Carden along to see some of the other mountains. Arni could go, too. If Melina agrees."

Tupper sat back on his heels. "Are you going?"

Aggie fiddled with her blade. "Ulrica invited me."

They finished the gutting in silence, but by the time they were done, Tupper had made up his mind. "Good," he said firmly. "And when you go, keep your eyes open. If a Flox isn't just right for you, pick a nice Clow. Or a Grif. Maybe even an Ursa."

Aggie giggled once again. "Only the biggest and strongest?"

"They'll need to be." With a small smile, Tupper explained, "Since they'll have to get past Aurelius and Ulrica in order to court you."

Farley noticed when Tupper and Aggie returned with a glut of rabbits for dinner, but Freydolf's deft incisions into black stone never faltered. The closer the Pred came to finishing a piece, the tighter its hold on his attention. Which was fine with Farley, since this guardian would be his. Being a Keeper's servant definitely had its perks.

The fourteen-year-old's gaze shifted to his master. Torio

lounged nearby, poring over a book that was holding his interest more than most, which meant it was probably some ancient Keeper's homesick ramblings about a distant shore.

The Grif liked Morven, and he fit in well enough with everyone who lived on the gray mountain. But it was getting harder for the man to stay put. Torio's only escape from the quietude was through books about the lands he'd once traveled. Places Farley hoped to see for himself one day.

Dessa understood, and she did her best to comfort him. As much as the Grif groused about the black mountain's hold on his life, he always relaxed in her presence. Farley enjoyed watching the harmonious ribbons of magic she wove around Torio, coils of power that the man pretended to ignore. But he needed her as much as she needed him. Why else was his usual chair pulled within arms' reach of her column?

"You're unusually quiet, Farley."

Trying to cover his surprise, he replied, "Only because you weren't listening."

"Oh? Was there something you wanted to tell me?"

Freydolf's dark eyes shone with amusement, and Farley had a sneaking suspicion that the Pred knew his secret. "Not really. Are you done?"

"Nearly." Handing Farley the intricately-detailed sculpture, he said, "I've never worked with stone this powerful. He's antsy. And Tupper's right when he said this little guy wants you."

"Is that so?" Farley caressed the coiled snake's gleaming scales, cool and silken as the real thing. He smiled at the little guardian's reaction, for his magic sparked and swirled in an eager bid for attention. His guardian might be small, but he was ten times more powerful than Olexi or Rimbles.

"Aye. It's a *shame* you've no affinity for stone, or you'd realize how attached he's already become."

Grinning unabashedly, Farley replied, "Yep. Terrible shame."

Freydolf didn't push the matter. With a quick flick to Farley's horn, he said, "It's probably just as well he's small because I doubt he'll ever let you out of his sight. If I were you, I'd train him to take a different resting shape—ankle ring, bracelet, arm band."

Farley shook his head. "Won't he keep *this* shape when he's sleeping?"

The master sculptor rubbed the back of his neck. "To be perfectly honest, I don't think *any* of Dessa's get will be easy to constrain once they're free."

"And that goes double for Dessa?"

"Aye."

With a sidelong glance at Torio, Farley asked, "Does he know that?"

Freydolf gazed intently at the Grif. "Better than anyone."

Just beyond the circle of Brand's lantern-light, Tupper lay on Graven's back in the middle of the summit pasture, holding a fragment of black stone up so the moon glinted across its smooth surface. "What does heartstone need?" he asked in a soft sing-song voice.

He hummed snatches of a festival song and tried to think of something Freydolf hadn't already tried. Day and night, every phase of the moon, lapping salt water, fitful breezes, scented smoke, sweat, tears—according to the sculptor, there were so many variables, it could take years to hit on the right combination to trigger an awakening.

"Heartstone?" Torio's clipped accent cut through the darkness. "I thought Harrow was dead set on *blood*stone."

Tupper turned his head and considered the approaching Grif. "Frey doesn't like that name."

"Quite true." Coming even with them, Torio chuckled as he stroked the big tiger's flank with his talons. "This birthing has been even harder on him than young Hanley's."

"How did you know I was here?"

Torio snorted. "You have *no idea* how much Morven is stirred up when you wander about on moonlit nights. The whole mountain trembles with your every footstep."

"Oh. Sorry?"

"No, no." Reaching over to tap the rock held between Tupper's fingers, Torio remarked, "You've done a good job taming this tidbit. What's her destiny?"

"She'll be the last bead on Chelle's bracelet."

"So my Dessa will help seal the marriage pact that will establish your house?"

Tupper took his time sorting out the sentence. Grif had a different way of saying things, but he liked the way he spoke of marriage. Kind of like the things Ulrica said about the noble lineage of the house of Rakefang. Or Aurelius's preening that Quintrell would be carrying on the proud Harrow tradition. Maybe with Chelle, Tupper could establish a noble house with a proud lineage. He finally replied, "That would be nice."

Both of them turned in surprise when the light of Brand's lantern suddenly drew closer. Before either of them could ask if there was cause for alarm, the redstone warrior had drawn his sword and dropped to one knee. Head bowed, he offered its hilt to Tupper.

"Now that's a sight you don't often see," murmured Torio.

The Flox sat up and stared down at his friend. "Brand? What do you want?"

Torio folded his arms across his chest as he leaned into Graven's bulk. "He's pledging himself to your house, young master."

"But I don't have one *yet*."

"Brand's smart to seek a franchise for his future," Torio countered. "Just look at Haimish. That clumsy lout got in early and has Carden's brood all to himself."

Tupper slid to the ground and knelt in front of Brand. "You want to hold my babies?"

The redstone guardian smiled and inclined his head.

Looking up at Torio, he asked, "How do I say yes?"

"Take his sword."

Tupper did and immediately grunted. "Heavier than it looks!"

Torio smirked. "He's a tribute to our people. Strong of arm, true of heart, and wise in aligning himself with a man of similar makings."

To Brand, Tupper whispered, "You've always been a good friend."

With his free hand, the Grif briefly touched the young man's face, a brush of fingertips that was both acknowledgment and reciprocation.

"Now what?" Tupper asked.

"Traditionally, you'd take him under your wings in a symbolic gesture of mutual trust," Torio explained. "You lack the usual trappings, but I believe an embrace would still suffice."

Hugs were something Tupper understood quite well, and granting one to Brand was no chore. With a little bobbling to balance the Grif's sword, he settled his arms around the statue's armored shoulders in a firm embrace that felt like crushed feathers and smelled faintly of lantern oil.

Wanting to add his own dash of formality to the proceedings, he shyly said, "Welcome to the house of Meadowsweet."

18

Face Your Fears

Not many days later, Tupper woke to ominous skies and hastened outside to get through his chores before the storm hit. Distant thunder set his teeth on edge and he jogged through windy passages to the stable.

"Morning," he said shortly.

Glancing up from where he was milking their cow, Farley smirked. "Something wrong, Tupp?"

Filling a pail with chicken feed, he said, "Be right back," and took off for the hen house.

If everything went well, he'd be underground well ahead of the rain. Today might be a good day to clean and organize the storerooms. Or maybe Frey would like a break from gleaning inspiration from the archives and spend the day working with the orphan stones. Either way, he'd have to pack a lunch.

Tupper's mind was made up, but just as he and his bond-brother were ready to leave, Carden interrupted by hustling in with three high-strung children.

"Anyone game for an expedition?" the beleaguered father asked in hopeful tones.

Several pleas for Unca Doff and Unca Tupp to come play were enough to divert the Keeper.

Hoisting Dulcie and Arni onto his broad shoulders, Freydolf

announced, "I know a hiding spot your Uncle Ree hasn't discovered yet. Do you want to try to surprise him?"

"Aye!" shouted Arni.

Dulcie giggled. "Let's go!"

"Mish, too?" asked Yona from her guardian's embrace.

"Oh, aye. There's always room for Haimish." On his way out the door, the Pred added, "Best tell Aurelius that a hunt awaits him, lambkin."

"Yes." Tupper snagged his cloak off the hook beside the door. The first heavy drops of rain were already spattering the cobbles. Thunder rumbled nearer. It was going to be a bad one.

But before he could gather the courage to launch himself outside, Carden gripped his arm, holding the younger man back. "*I'll* issue an invitation to the Harrows. Get below, Tupp."

After a brief pause, he ducked his head gratefully, and they split up. Tupper didn't get far, though. He was just opening the door to the six-sided chamber when someone grabbed his cloak, hauling him to a standstill. Thunder crashed overhead, and he hunched his shoulders defensively. "Not funny, Farley!"

"M'not joking!" his brother countered, his voice raised to be heard over the slap of rain. "C'mon!"

"I don't want ...!"

But Farley wasn't listening. With an insistent tug, he plunged back out into the rain, hollering, "I said *c'mon!*"

He half-pushed, half-dragged Tupper all the way to the workshop, not stopping until they were both panting and dripping on the wooden floorboards next to Dessa. Tupper muttered, "*Now*, look. I'll need to mop."

His brother knocked their horns together hard enough to get Tupper's full attention. Farley snapped, "Stop dithering about the floor and *pay attention!*"

Tupper was losing patience. "To *what*?"

"Wait for the next flash."

"You know I don't like ...."

Just then, pure, white light blazed through the tall windows.

"There!" Farley exclaimed. Grabbing Tupper's hand, he pressed it against black stone just in time for the crackle and roar of thunder to resound overhead.

Tupper's eyes widened.

Farley nodded. "*See*? Where's Freydolf?"

"Halfway to the Cavern by now."

"I'll go get him. You wait here." Glancing over his shoulder at the scowling Grif hovering behind them, he said, "Brand will hold your hand."

"Yes. Tell Frey."

Farley thumped his shoulder, an exultant grin on his face. "This is *it!*"

Once the boy was gone, Brand knelt before Tupper and patted his damp hair. It didn't take much coaxing for the young man to crawl into the warrior's protective embrace. As much as he hated noisy storms, Tupper smiled at the irony. This must be how Freydolf felt. "Of all things ... thunder."

Tupper huddled pitifully under Freydolf's arm, feeling ten years old all over again. It was embarrassing, especially whenever he caught one of the others giving him a concerned look. The men had moved to the outer courtyard, where they were at the mercy of the elements. Wind whipped cloaks and spattered faces despite Carden and Torio tenaciously clinging to the corners of a tarp in an effort to keep off the worst of the rain.

"Are you *sure* it'll be thunder?" demanded Aurelius as he set a small dagger next to the snake sculpture on the bench.

"Aye," Frey replied. "And the louder the better. Sorry, lambkin."

"How much blood will you need?" Aurelius asked.

"Not sure. Not much," the sculptor replied gruffly.

"Do you mean I should prick his finger or open a vein?"

Tupper could feel his bond-brother tremble.

"And *whose* blood? I'd be quite happy to stab either Kite *or* the brat."

Freydolf groaned, "Have pity, you bloodthirsty wretch."

When his shelter swayed, Tupper wrapped one arm tightly around Freydolf's waist and sent the merchant a stern look.

With a disgusted *tut*, Aurelius shoved an aromatic vial under Frey's nose and growled, "Brace yourself." Without skipping a beat, he next waved it in Tupper's direction, then tousled his hair. For once, he offered no sarcastic remarks, perhaps because Quintrell was just as skittish in stormy weather.

Torio gazed at them from under the wide brim of his hat and laughed outright. "Dessa has a gift for forcing men to face their fears!"

"You don't say," Freydolf grumbled. "What's yours?"

The Grif's brows arched. "*Her.*"

Tupper said, "I think it needs to be Farley's blood."

"Aye, that's best." In the next moment, a brilliant flash caused everyone in the huddle to squint, and Frey barked, "Now, Farley!"

The blade flashed, and magic rushed forcefully enough to ring in Tupper's ears. He barely heard Farley's voice over the clap of thunder, but the small statue shivered with delight. The black snake uncoiled from Farley's blood-smeared palm, threading his way between his chosen charge's fingers.

"What's his name?" Tupper asked.

With a triumphant grin, Farley replied, "Nestor."

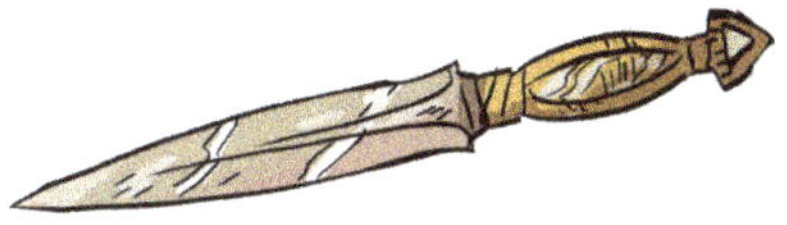

Aurelius sat on the mossy floor in one of the countless niches carved into Morven's rocky slopes. He'd initially chosen this spot for its vantage. Two deer trails meandered through the gully below its access point, making it a prime place from which to take large prey. As far as Ulrica was concerned, he and Quintrell were in the midst of a hunting lesson, but tracking was the last thing on his son's mind.

"Good baby, nice baby, sweet baby," the three-year-old crooned.

Perhaps they'd been cloistered with the Flox for too long. Or maybe Frey was to blame. Aye, that must be it.

Ulrica was fond of pointing out that this was probably the first time in history that a Pred father had surrendered his fangs to a son rather than a daughter. And she was right. But he couldn't bring himself to correct the child for exhibiting a gentler nature than most Pred possessed.

These very same traits had culminated in Freydolf's banishment. Aurelius shuddered to think what might have happened if Ulrica's father had gotten his claws into this child.

"Bunnies are softer than kitties," Quintrell said, his golden eyes shining with happiness.

"Aye."

"But only kitties purr."

Ignoring his son's pleading look, he said, "Nay. I'm *quite* sure your uncle purrs if you scratch him behind his ears."

Quintrell blinked several times. "Unca Doff?"

"The very one!"

With a soft giggle, he asked, "Should I pet Unca Doff?"

"Aye, I think you should."

Aurelius was aware that some Flox kept hutches of the tasty bounders in their gardens and sheds, but he preferred to give his dinner a fighting chance to stay off the menu. He would make certain his son could acquit himself as a Pred, but not today.

The three baby rabbits in Quin's lap would grow quickly, run off into the forest, and procreate another generation of prey. For now, there was no harm in letting the lad cuddle bunnies.

Provided his mother didn't find out. Ulrica would *never* let him live this down.

"Are you done?" Carden asked.

"Aye," Freydolf replied, his voice pitched low so he wouldn't wake Hanley. After much blinking and yawning, the baby had nodded off on the couch between master and apprentice. Holding up the final bead in the set of thirteen, the Pred grunted in satisfaction. "Assuming Tupper is pleased."

"May I see?"

Frey passed along the faceted bead, which glittered darkly. He'd taken great pains in giving the individual beads a touch of personality. The black stone was surprisingly festive.

Carden smiled wryly. "I'm guessing you made this look much easier than it is."

"Aye, the angles are tricky. Show me yours." With a sigh, the Flox turned over an unrefined, freshstone figure. He'd been laboring over a small dove—a bath toy for Yona—and he was still trying to get the hang of feathers. Frey had seen worse, but there was a very long feathered border in Carden's near future. Maybe along the stairway leading down to the chicken yard. "The beak is especially nice. And she has soft eyes. I look forward to when you wake her."

Holding the black bauble between thumb and forefinger, Carden frowned thoughtfully. "This has stronger magic than that bit of blue."

"Aye. Dessa's *dust* could out-dazzle most of the mid-quality stone I've worked with over the years."

"But you don't wake beads?"

"Nay, but that doesn't mean a sculptor can't make sure they're happy with their lot in life." They swapped rocks, and Frey went on, "If a stone is meant to become a guardian, you urge them to be loyal, watchful, and courageous. If a stone is meant to become a bead, you help them to be confident and carefree, poised and playful."

"Shaping their personality?"

"Every stone guardian ever made retains an echo of their maker's hopes for them. One day, you may have to part with them, but you give them the strength to fulfill their chosen purpose."

Carden's eyes took on a shine, and he brushed one finger against his son's cheek. "Preparing them for the future."

With a low chuckle, Freydolf conceded the point. Many would say that the tiny perfection of one bead was nothing compared to a full-fledged stone guardian. And by the same token, even a Keeper's triumphal masterwork was nothing compared to Hanley's tiny perfection. But for Freydolf, those lines of distinction would always blur. His creations took on a life of their own.

Frey was confident that Carden would eventually achieve mastery ... and more. In the realm of magical stones, becoming a Keeper wasn't simply a matter of knowledge and skill. Morven had always favored sculptors whose statues bore a similar imprint. Something Frey had never known. A father's love.

19

Safely in the Majority

Even though Melina's bread had become a staple at their table, there were days when Freydolf wanted nothing more than a batch of Tupper's humble biscuits. "Thank you, lambkin," he murmured when the young man slid a platter of them onto the table.

"More will be ready soon. Eat lots."

Farley made a grab for the jam. "Kinda skimpy for a meal, ain't it?"

"The young master's cookery exceeds my skill," Torio said as he reached for the honey. "Tis a fine feast for a bachelor such as myself."

"Aye," Frey quickly agreed. "His biscuits are life and health and home."

The youngest Meadowsweet drew himself up. "I made the butter *and* the cheese, you know. That's way harder than lumpy biscuits."

"They're not lumpy," Tupper countered in even tones. "And I'm glad for the cheese. It's my favorite."

Mollified by having his efforts recognized, Farley pointed to the lidded cup in the center of the table and asked, "How come they're here?"

"They who?" Frey asked innocently.

"Tupp's beads," the boy mumbled around a mouthful of jammy biscuit.

The Pred feigned surprise. "Is *that* what's in there, lambkin?"

"Yes."

Torio snorted. "Anyone with magical affinity could tell in a trifling. Isn't that right, brat?"

"Leave off," grumbled Farley.

Freydolf held up his hands in a peaceable gesture. "I was hoping you'd agree to help."

"I don't care how much coin it's worth! I *ain't* grubbin' around on my hands and knees, chippin' daisies into doorsteps!"

Torio favored his servant with an arch look. "Do you prefer ceiling work?"

The boy gawked at the Grif, then rounded on Frey. "Look, mister, I *don't* wanna fiddle with rocks, and I *don't* wanna be tied down! I've got plans of my own! I'm gonna travel! With Torio!"

Reaching for his third biscuit, Frey said, "Aye. Sounds exciting."

Farley blinked. "You're not gonna talk me out of it?"

"Do you want me to?"

"No!"

Freydolf chuckled. "What did you think I'd do, lad, chain you to a workbench?"

"Pretty much. On account of my affinity," Farley admitted.

"Not everyone with affinity becomes a sculptor," the Pred patiently explained. "The archives actually indicate that only one in four people with strong magical sense go on to learn the craft. You're safely in the majority."

"I could have told you that much, brat." Reaching over his plate, Torio flicked the covered dish with a talon, producing a clear *ping*. "But I'm curious about our little cabal. Why does an illustrious Keeper need the assistance of magically intuitive lay-abouts like us?"

Tupper began. "The beads are too ...."

When he glanced at Freydolf for help, the Pred finished, "*Feisty*. I'm having difficulty finding a harmonious balance. Until we do, I can't string them."

"They're not listening to you?" Torio asked Tupper in surprise.

"No. They're too busy bickering."

"Master Platt had similar troubles with the stones he chose for Graven," Freydolf said. "He arranged and rearranged rock for almost a decade before he was satisfied."

Farley eyed the covered dish with interest. "Sounds like a puzzle."

"Or a peace treaty." With a wink at Tupper, Torio added, "We shall hammer out the necessary armistice, so you and your lady can forge a convivial alliance."

The lad rubbed at the base of one horn. Freydolf bumped shoulders with him and whispered, "Trust us." At Tupper's grateful glance, the Pred wrapped his arm around his bond-brother's shoulders and rumpled his hair. "Everything will be fine, lambkin. You'll see."

Farley snickered. "Is that some kinda Pred bonding ritual?"

Freydolf frowned in confusion, and Torio chipped in. "Did you say *lambkin* ... or *napkin*?"

Tupper gazed up at him, awaiting an explanation, and that's when the Pred realized what he'd done. Muttering an oath, he dabbed at the sizable glob of preserves he'd smeared into the young man's fair hair. "Jam. Sorry."

With a small sigh, Tupper adopted his mothering tone. "First biscuits, then beads, then bath."

Two in one night. With a longsuffering sigh, Freydolf muttered, "Aye."

Tupper carried the finished bracelet in his pocket for a full week before deciding that enough was enough. Even though the midsummer festival was still two days off, he was ready. Now.

Just before sunup, he crept across the workshop and shook Freydolf's arm.

The Pred snorted, grumbled, peeked, yawned, then finally

budged over so Tupper could crawl into bed with him. "Bad dream?" the man asked, the hint of a smile in his tone.

"No."

"What then?"

"I've been thinking ...."

Freydolf's dark eyes blinked as he sought focus. "Have you been awake all night?"

"Mostly."

The man's fingers sought out the base of Tupper's nearest horn and began to knead. "It's not like you to worry, lambkin."

"I want to see Chelle," he whispered.

"This morning?"

"Yes."

The Pred hummed drowsily. "I'm sure she'd be glad to see you again. You should go."

"And I want to give her the bracelet. Do you think it's too soon?"

After a thoughtful pause, Freydolf replied, "To marry? Aye. To pledge your troth? Nay. If you're in this state, chances are good that she's wishing and wondering, too. Give Chelle your promise. And your fine gift." With another yawn, he concluded, "I'll wait here for your good news."

Tupper plucked at his bond-brother's sleeve. "You're going to sleep in?"

"Aye. It's not as if you'll be wanting me along for the ride."

He pressed closer, hiding his face against Frey's shoulder.

The man chuckled. "You *did* want me there? Lambkin, I don't know much about women, but I'm fairly certain these matters are settled in private."

"You could wait with Graven," he wheedled. "Please, brother?"

"Aye," Freydolf gruffly replied. "I'll back you up."

The first thing Chelle saw when she slipped out the Quince's door on her way to work was Tupper. The young man crouched just inside the garden wall, arms wrapped around his knees and a pensive expression on his face.

Hurrying over, she asked, "What's wrong?"

He smiled a little—a *very* little—and shook his head to reassure her. Slapping his hands against his thighs, he stood, but as soon as he patted his pockets, he froze, all chagrin.

"Forgot your notebook?" she guessed.

Her suitor gave a tiny nod. To her surprise, he touched his lips, then brushed his fingertips across hers in mournful apology.

"Was there something you needed to tell me? I could bring paper from the bakery," she gently reminded.

He rubbed uncertainly at the base of his horn. Apparently, without writing materials, Tupper's plan had been thrown into disarray, and he had no idea how to recover.

Taking pity, Chelle suggested, "How about we see if I can guess what you meant to tell me. I'm pretty good at interpreting your gestures."

With a small nod, he took her hand in his and led her straight to their usual bench in the bakery's herb garden. They sat, and she waited. Tupper closed his eyes, took several deep breaths, then gazed at her much more calmly. Then he reached for her hand and pressed it against his chest.

Not so calm, after all. She could feel his heart hammering. "Nervous?"

He nodded and distractedly touched her brown curls.

Chelle asked, "Did you want to talk about my hair?"

Tupper shook his head sheepishly.

"If I'm going to guess, you'll need to give better hints."

He nodded and dipped into his pocket, withdrawing an exquisite strand of beads. They felt cool and heavy as he placed them in her hand. He tugged her closer, so he could watch over her shoulder as she studied each tiny masterpiece. Chelle took her time admiring each and naming the magical mountains from which it had been taken. Nods, pats, and nuzzles accompanied her soft litany, and she relaxed into her suitor's embrace.

Tipping her head back so she could see Tupper's face, she whispered, "This is a priceless treasure."

Easing away, he knelt on the ground in front of her and took back the beads. Tapping the toe of one of her sturdy work shoes, he encouraged her to lift her foot, and he carefully fastened the strand around her ankle.

"By any chance, is this a Pred tradition?" Chelle asked.

Tupper nodded.

"And does it mean what I hope it means?"

Rising up on his knees, he pressed a swift, soft kiss to her lips.

There was no doubt about it. This was Tupper's pledge.

Taking a deep breath, she cupped the bottom curve of one of his horns. "It's probably too soon for a marriage."

He nodded gravely.

"But we could share a promise until then."

Tupper flung his arms around her waist and hid his face against her knees before nodding again.

Startled, Chelle began to stroke his long hair in a soothing way. "Did you think I would refuse?"

Keeping his face buried, he shook his head.

"Were you *hoping* I'd refuse?" she asked lightly.

That earned her a stern pat.

It also revealed a glistening tear track. And then a voice she hadn't heard in weeks filtered through her mind. *"Your Keeper waits. Complete the vow."*

Chelle nodded, and fresh tears slipped silently down her cheeks as she took Tupper by the horns. He lifted his head, peering at her through damp lashes. "Your mountain is meddling."

He sighed and smiled.

Firming her hold on his horns, Chelle bowed to Morven's demand that she reveal her heart. "You need to know two very important things, Tupper Meadowsweet."

Her suitor's eyes widened slightly, and his head dipped.

"You *will* be my husband," she promised.

Tupper fit his arms more snugly around her waist and raptly waited for more.

Chelle leaned down so her cheek brushed his and whispered into his waiting ear. "Because I love you."

Freydolf leaned his head back against Graven's side and let the tears fall. There was no use fighting them. Morven was all stirred up, and that never led to dry eyes. The insistent flow prevented him from seeing who was coming, but he knew it was Tupper. No other Flox could step lighter than a deer upon its forest trail. Tucking his chin so thick hair would hide his teary state, the Pred batted his lashes, trying to clear his vision.

"Back," the lad called in a low voice.

Frey answered with a sniffle.

Kneeling down in front of his bond-brother, Tupper manfully put his arms around Freydolf's hunched shoulders. "She will be my wife," he reported.

He managed a jerky nod.

Tupper's voice held a tentative note. "Morven is happy."

"Aye."

Lowering himself to try to see into the Pred's face, he asked, "Are *you* happy for me?"

With a soft growl, Freydolf pulled the boy into a fierce hug. "I'm a selfish old fool who only thinks of himself."

"Oh. Do you want your breakfast?" Tupper asked solicitously.

"I want to keep you."

"That's good."

Freydolf confessed, "And I'm *glad* Morven bound you to herself."

"Me, too."

There were so many guilty feelings pigeonholed in his heart, and he felt compelled to bring them to light. "I don't think I could have borne it if you married a village girl and stayed with her."

"I know."

"I would have hated her."

"Maybe."

"I don't want to hate anyone. It's ugly and wrong." Tupper lay his head against Freydolf's shoulder, ever mindful of his horns. "You like Chelle."

"Aye. She's perfect for you."

"Yes." Heaving a deep sigh, he asked, "Then why are you letting in worries?"

The Pred sniffled and grumped, "We've already established that I'm an old fool."

Laughing softly, Tupper asked, "Do *you* need a pledge as well?"

"Nay, lambkin," he hastily demurred.

But the lad ignored every protest. Pulling at the cord he always wore around his neck, he placed Snick in Freydolf's big, brown hand. Wrapping both his around his bond-brother's, he said, "I'm the one who will sweep your floor. Because of me, your water pitcher will always be full. Your hearth is mine to tend, and I'll make sure your favorite tunic is clean." With a gentle pat, he swore, "All my life, I'll serve you."

Even though these were things the Pred already knew, it soothed his heart to hear them spoken. "And make biscuits."

With a happy smile, Tupper promised, "As soon as we get home."

20

Ambitions

Farley wasn't *exactly* jealous of his brother, but it was hard not to compare. Somehow, Tupper had worked it so that Freydolf thought the sun rose and set at his command. An honest-to-goodness Pred let a perfectly harmless Flox boss him around—a good story in its own right. What gave the duo real gloss was that they'd sworn an oath and become bond-brothers.

"It's not fair," he sighed.

Nestor finished exploring the creek bank and slithered across Farley's throat, butting his blunt nose against the reclining teen's cheek. Smiling, he stroked the black guardian's scales. "I *don't* want to be like them. They're too sappy. Always getting teary-eyed over boring stuff. And acting like biscuits *matter*. We'll have something better. Way more interesting. Something *exciting*."

His serpentine companion didn't argue, and why would he? They were excellent plans. The only problem was that Torio wasn't catching on. Farley hadn't quite figured out how to make the Grif understand that they had stiff competition in the master-servant department. They needed to dovetail their ambitions, but it was awkward. How did you explain to someone that you wanted to be important to them?

"Torio probably doesn't love me, but after this morning, I think he'll like me a little more."

It hadn't taken too much convincing to get Aurelius to do some shopping for him. Everyone always made a huge fuss over Freydolf on his birthday, which was fine. He was entitled. But Farley didn't like that *his* Keeper didn't get the same kind of attention. So this morning, while everyone was at a special birthday brunch at Melina's, he'd put a large box on Torio's bed before sneaking down here.

Squinting at the clear, blue sky between the branches overhead, he murmured, "He'll find it pretty soon. And he'll be glad. He's got heaps of pride, even if he hides it."

Aurelius swore that the new feathered cape was both classic and refined, the sort of thing that would command respect among the Grif. Most of Farley's cheese-making money had gone into its procurement, but as far as he was concerned, it was coin well spent.

"Torio's no ordinary Keeper, and Dessa's the most powerful mountain in the whole world. He'll be walking with his head held high."

Nestor's head snapped up, and Farley laughed softly, thinking the snake was acting a part, but then the snake's shape shifted slightly. A cobra's hood flared out, and he bared glittering fangs.

The teen stared at his guardian with wide eyes. "Does Freydolf know you can do that?"

In a flash, the snake was coiled snugly around his neck, his gaze riveted on the wall of greenery on the other side of the creek. That's when Farley noticed that the surrounding forest had grown ominously still.

Rolling into a crouch, he decided that the smart thing was to trust his guardian.

He ran for it.

Ever since taking his rightful place on Morven, Farley had participated in the Harrows' compulsory lessons. The Pred claimed they couldn't abide clumsiness nor ignorance, so training was a regular part of their days. Walking, tracking, hunting, fighting—the games they played together were fun.

Because Aurelius had chased him through this terrain at least a dozen times, Farley knew his pursuer was someone else. Old tricks that didn't work on the Harrows held him in good stead as he zigzagged toward higher ground, ducking under branches and planting his feet on springy moss or bare stone.

Stay low. Tread lightly. Listen close. Hide well.

Without warning, child's play had become a matter of life and death.

Farley jumped feet first into a hidey-hole and fought to steady his breathing. Unwinding Nestor from his throat, he transferred the small guardian to his upper arm while he got his bearings. If he could scale the next outcropping unseen, maybe he could catch a look at his pursuer. See what he was up against.

He darted out, aiming for the rise. Scurrying through a familiar set of finger- and toe-holds, he lay flat, drew his dagger, and crept to the edge.

Ears straining, he watched and waited. One minute slipped by in deafening silence. Another was fading when a swaying branch caught his eye. A stealthy figure stole into view right below Farley's vantage point, just the way he'd planned it.

Except he wasn't feeling terribly proud of himself.

Cold fear shot through his veins, for the hunter was Pred. And not just *any* Pred. The man looked enough like Freydolf to be confusing—height, hair, build, brows. But this one's mouth twisted with disdain, and the dark eyes that singled him out glittered with hatred.

Backing up fast, Farley wracked his brain. If he ran hard, he might still be able to outdistance the man and hide in the galleries. But before he could flee, a cold blade touched his throat.

A smooth voice said, "Yield or die, *lambkin.*"

So there were two of them.

Farley's dagger slipped from his fingers.

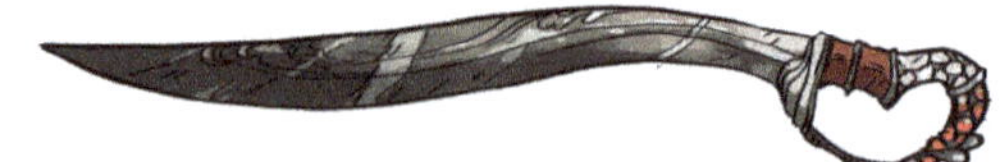

As soon as Farley's weapon hit the ground, his pursuer shoved him into the dirt, and a hand clamped around his neck from behind. The grip was harsh, and the Flox struggled. But then his captor curled his hand so that claws scraped his skin.

"Be still, or you'll be lying in a pool of your own blood."

Farley went limp, but he was far from done. "We don't get many Pred around here."

"Be grateful."

"Didja get lost on your way to the white mountain? 'Cause this one's gray."

"I know where I am, lad."

"You sure? I figured you stopped me to ask directions." The man made a derisive sound, and Farley tried again to get him talking. "So you've been here before? I hear there's a Pred up top. Friend of yours?"

"Don't play the fool. We *know* who you are, Tupper Meadowsweet."

Farley bristled. "Look, mister. You've got the wrong guy."

His captor flipped him onto his back with casual ease. Planting one knee on Farley's chest, he forced the air from his lungs in a rush, adding just enough pressure to make it hard to breathe. "No doubt about it. You're his pet."

From the inside pocket of an exquisitely-tailored vest, he produced a dog-eared parchment and unfolded it, showing Farley the drawing of a sleeping boy. Freydolf's affection for Tupper shone through every line, and the note on the corner in Aurelius's handwriting read, **Frey's lambkin.**

Farley glared at his captor. "No doubt about it. You're a Harrow."

Golden eyes narrowed, and the Pred haughtily retorted, "Rakefang, actually. Hadwin Rakefang."

Out of the corner of his eye, Farley saw branches part, and the Pred who'd been on the trail below stepped through the trees. Now that he was closer, the differences between him and Freydolf became more obvious. This Pred was older, with deep lines framing his scowl and gray grizzling the hair at his temples.

Farley was willing to bet his life savings that this was the Keeper's father. But why would a man who'd banished his own son follow him into exile?

The older Pred looked him up and down, then sheathed his blade. "Let the bleater up."

Hadwin eased off Farley, but he didn't go far. Dagger in hand, he crouched within easy reach, his golden eyes fixed warily on their captive. Farley filled his lungs and slowly sat up, rubbing the back of his head. Nestor was putting out enough outraged sparks to warn off anyone with traces of affinity, but it looked like he was at the mercy of magical dullards. Silently begging his little guardian to stay put, he tried to look as slow-witted as Tupper.

"What have you pried out of him?"

"Nothing yet," Hadwin replied.

Farley didn't like how much the old guy sounded like Freydolf. It was the same deep voice, but all sharp edges and sneers. The boy curled his toes inside his boots and mentally reviewed all the trails on this side of the mountain that led to safety. All he needed to do was get away. Or get them to let him go. He was used to talking his way out of trouble, but would either of these men let him take the lead in a friendly round of give and take?

Adopting a casual tone, Farley took the first step, "I think I know who you are."

"It thinks?" the older Pred mocked.

Hadwin gave his blade a twirl. "It knows the meaning of Harrow gold."

"So *that man* has betrayed us again." With a baleful glare

toward the mountaintop, he growled, "Unforgivable."

The younger Pred searched Farley's face. "Is Aurelius Harrow here?"

"Lookin' for him?"

Hadwin bared his fangs. "Answer the question, or your master will find your entrails strung upon his gates."

Farley doubted anyone would go *that* far. Rolling his eyes, he said, "Nice try, but your mom's way scarier than you are."

He never saw the blow coming.

By the time Farley's vision cleared, his feet no longer touched the ground. He wasn't entirely sure which of the men had walloped him, but the older Pred had him by the horns. That part didn't exactly hurt, but Farley had never been handled so roughly before. With shaking fingers, he touched the side of his face and winced.

The man's heavy brows lifted, mocking his pain, daring him to complain. "If you're fond of your tongue, teach it better manners. Otherwise, it will wag on the ground at your feet."

Limp and mute, Farley stared at the Pred, noticing distractedly that his ears were pierced. He ogled the heavy, red jewels hanging in polished rectangles from his lobes. It was strange that Morven's Keeper had given Haimish the same style earrings. "Are you *really* Master Freydolf's father?"

"I am Lyall Rakefang, and I have no son."

Farley was almost afraid to ask. "Then why are you here?"

"To take back what is mine." Sneering, Lyall sent Farley sprawling. "And to destroy everything *that man* holds dear."

The rattled Flox curled up on the ground, mostly so he could get his hand around Nestor. The little guardian was spitting mad, but a snakebite wasn't going to save the day. Right now,

Farley needed advantages. *Anything* to help get him out of this mess so he could warn the others.

At the moment, they were low in Morven's northwestern foothills, about as far from Hayward as one could get. Farley knew that meant he was on his own, but it also meant that there was a whole mountain between these two Pred and the others. That distance also made it impractical to send Nestor for help, especially since Tupper was the only one on speaking terms with rocks. Still, the snake was an asset.

Would Torio come looking for him? He never had before. The Grif mostly let him do as he pleased, which is why Farley had been *here* in the first place, lazing around by the creek instead of pitching in.

By now, everyone from the Statuary was probably halfway down the eastern trail, on their way to help his mother with festival preparations. Which meant they wouldn't be looking for him anytime soon. Unless Morven meddled. But how could he get the mountain's attention?

Freydolf's father said, "You'll receive no further warnings. Answer my grandson's questions without impudence."

Taking his cue, Hadwin repeated, "Is Aurelius Harrow here?"

Farley hesitated, and the young man's blade was once more at his throat. But this time, Hadwin drew a thin line against exposed skin, and the stunned Flox felt a trickle. Eyes wide, he whispered, "The Harrows live with us on the mountain."

"But merchants travel. Is he *here*?"

"Yeah, your dad's here."

With an oddly blank expression, Hadwin said, "I have no father. He was banished."

Farley stared hard at the Pred, who'd inherited his looks from both parents. Ulrica's thick hair and proud bearing. Aurelius's fine features and fashion sense. Holding the young man's gaze, Farley slowly reached up to pluck at the collar of his shirt, where the fabric had already begun to cling to his skin.

"Probably just as well. He'd disown you for spoiling my best tunic." Working hard to hit the right inflection, Farley added, "Blood is deucedly hard to get out of fine cloth."

Pain flickered briefly through Hadwin's eyes.

Farley grimly hoped it meant another advantage.

He tried reasoning next. "Don't you know *why* Master Freydolf came here? He's a Keeper, an important person in the world."

Lyall Rakefang's jaw tightened. "That man is keeping me from my precious daughter. *She* is the only matter of importance here."

Fair brows drew together. "You make it sound like she's a prisoner."

The Pred's tone darkened. "There is no other explanation."

That was crazy. Only a fool would try to contain Ulrica. Shaking his head, Farley said, "Maybe you should talk to her."

"She will have ample opportunity to thank me when I carry her home a widow."

He was gonna kill Aurelius?

Farley's gaze slanted toward Hadwin, but the young man's face was devoid of expression. "You sure we're talking about the same lady? Because the Missus Harrow I know has both Aurelius and Freydolf by the fangs."

Lip curling, Lyall said, "Those who have been shamed should remain in shame. I will not allow *that man* to subvert my house and ensnare my heirs."

"He's not doing anything like that." There had to be some horrible mistake. "Freydolf's *nothing* like what you're saying."

"As if I'd take the word of the cringing bleater who licks that man's boots."

Farley's face scrunched in utter disbelief, and he muttered, "Shows how much *you* know. He goes around barefoot."

To Hadwin, Lyall said, "I will return your mother to you, just as I have sworn."

The young man placed his hand under his heart and bowed his head. "Shall I go ahead and find her?"

"No!" Farley blurted. "She's ... she's not there. You won't be able to find her."

Hadwin's eyes narrowed. "You're lying."

"I'm *not*. The Harrows are traveling today. Your dad took

your mom dancing."

He shook his head, sending the blue droplets at his ears swaying. "You expect me to believe that?"

Farley shrugged. "Even if you don't, it's true. Nobody's home."

"What foolish disregard." Lyall Rakefang leered malevolently. "I'll scout the grounds ... and leave a message where *that man* is sure to find it. Do you know which stinking hovel he cowers in?"

Hadwin nodded.

"Good. Now, what gift shall we leave at his doorstep?"

Farley didn't like the way the Pred's gaze raked over his body, and he liked it less when Lyall drew his weapon. "We *could* leave a steaming pile of giblets."

"What of carrion birds?"

"Aye." Looming large, the elder Rakefang ordered, "Hold him down."

Before Farley could react, his head slammed into the ground hard enough to stun him. By the time he realized what the Pred were doing, the toe of Lyall's boot pinned his right horn to the ground, and Hadwin knelt over him, holding his body down. With every rasp of Pred's blade, Farley yelled for all he was worth—threats, protests, oaths, pleas. But they didn't listen, and when they let him up, all that remained was an ashen silence.

"Put him in the carriage," Lyall said. "Then meet me at the gate."

Grabbing the Flox's arm, Hadwin hauled him to his feet and muttered, "This way, Tupper."

The words barely registered as the teen stared at the curving section of horn in Lyall's hand. Even when Hadwin snarled at him, barking threats into his face, Farley couldn't shake free of his stupor. Giving up, the Pred threw his captive over one shoulder and stalked off through the trees. Farley hung bonelessly, blood rushing to his head, and hot tears falling to the ground.

21

Prone to Wander

Freydolf's cumbersome frame was draped across Merona Meadowsweet's crowded cottage floor as he played with Quintrell, Arni, and Ewert's twins, but Torio stood silently at the window, gazing out past the garden wall. Beyond the hollyhocks and runner beans, there was a dusty road leading to another world—pink and ocher plains, the striped tents of spice traders, and basking stones where golden guardians lazed. "*Their* summer festival coincides with the melon harvest," the Grif remarked in Terse, stealing a glance at the baby nestled in the crook of his arm.

Hanley's eyes were fixed on his face, and as soon as the youngster realized Torio was looking at him, he broke into a toothless smile. Such innocent trust.

Lips quirking, Torio continued to speak in his native tongue. "It's true, young sir. The Drom are enamored of melons. They cultivate too many varieties to count, and choice seed is as valuable as coin."

A tiny hand waved, reaching, and the Grif lowered his head so Hanley could grab onto his nose. He'd had never thought of himself as a family man, but that didn't stop these people from treating him like a member of theirs.

Merona Meadowsweet slipped up beside him and pressed a

fresh glass of Aurelius's sweetwater into his hand. "You have a faraway look in your eyes, Mister Kite. Is there somewhere else you'd rather be?"

With a low bow that tugged a soft giggle from Hanley, Torio switched to Verit, "Forgive me, my good woman. My thoughts are prone to wander even when my feet cannot. I am most grateful for your hospitality."

The woman waved off his apology and lowered her voice. "I've been hoping for a chance to ask. Has my son been of use to you?"

"Farley is uncommonly clever, utterly incorrigible, completely tactless, and an endless source of entertainment."

Merona laughed lightly. "He's always been energetic."

Torio graciously assured, "I would have it no other way."

She nodded, then bluntly inquired, "If you travel once more, will you retain his services or release him?"

Who could say what might happen down the road? That was one of its allures. Ever-changing. Forever new.

Torio wanted to put her off with a careless reply, but he suspected that Merona's blue eyes would be as keen as her son's at seeing through his little shams. With a small sigh, he answered frankly. "That boy wasn't made for such things. It won't be long before he casts off any pretense of servility."

The woman's brows knit. "But all he speaks of is traveling with you."

"By the time I'm free to leave, Farley will be man enough to choose his own path."

Merona frowned in motherly concern. "Alone?"

Torio rubbed his nose. He hadn't known how to deal with Farley at first. The Grif needed no servant, but the rambunctious lad had needed a master. For a time. Starry-eyed admiration gradually gave way to characteristically presumptuous ambitions. Ones that would change everything. Torio could already see it. Farley would be satisfied with nothing less than equality.

Aware that Merona still awaited his answer, Torio fumbled for a suitable one. What could he say to put a mother's mind at ease without taking on any unwanted responsibilities? He cleared his throat and honestly said, "When that day comes, I would welcome Farley's company."

She patted his arm and warmly replied, "I doubt my son could have found a better ally than you, Mister Kite."

When it was time for Chelle to make her way over to the Meadowsweets' house, Aurelius and his young son were waiting for her at the Quince's gate. With a bow, the Pred offered her a slip of paper that said, **The sprat's too useful for his own good. Since Ewert is keeping him busy, I shall escort you.**

"Thank you," she murmured.

Golden eyes searched her face, and Chelle managed a wan smile. This was her first official meeting with her future in-laws, and she'd been counting on Tupper's calming presence.

The Pred startled her by giving her cheeks a pinch, then briskly patting them.

With a small sigh, Chelle asked, "Do I look *that* nervous?"

Aurelius's brow quirked, and he nodded.

Groaning she ducked down behind one of the rosemary shrubs that lined the Quinces' garden wall and opened her arms to Quintrell. The little boy nearly barreled her over with his enthusiasm, and she hid her face in his glossy hair.

"Why is this so scary, little cub?"

He wriggled close and kissed her cheek, then turned his head to say something to his papa.

Aurelius withdrew a slim book from inside his vest and dropped to one knee. With a wry smile, he wrote, **I can sympathize, Miss Tremont. But trust me. It could be much worse.**

Quintrell pulled out of Chelle's embrace and drew a teensy little knife from his belt. She hardly thought a boy his age should be carrying a weapon, but the blade didn't look terribly sharp. When he pointed it at her, she shook her head in confusion.

Aurelius lifted a finger, his expression stern as he spoke to his son.

Biting his lip in concentration, Quintrell switched his hold, this time laying the small blade across his palm and presenting Chelle with the other end.

With a nod of approval, Aurelius quickly explained, **He offers his defense. To accept, kiss the hilt.**

"I'll be counting on you, little cub," she whispered, doing her part.

When she straightened, she found a second dagger awaiting her. Whether he was backing up his son—or refusing to be outdone—the Pred's haughty chivalry touched her heart. Chelle gratefully kissed the hilt of Aurelius's dagger, right on top of its snarling wolf's head.

Leaning heavily on Aurelius's confidence, Chelle greeted Tupper's mother with a smile. Melina hurried to join them on the front step, tugging along a dainty young woman who was introduced as Ewert's wife Tillie. Chelle recognized her from the bakery, but they'd never done more than nod and smile. Everyone seemed to be chattering at once, but they were armed with what must have been an assortment of Master Freydolf's sketchbooks.

Aurelius had enough of doorstep hovering and shooed the women back inside with a flutter of ruffled sleeves. The first sight that met Chelle's eyes was Freydolf, resplendent in a white tunic trimmed with copper. He sat in the middle of the floor with three children.

Quintrell trotted over to join Arni, whose golden curls shone in bright contrast to his twin cousins. Hazel and Hewett had inherited their mother's silvery hair. The big Pred waved with a flash of gilt claws before self-consciously hiding his hands.

"Your birthday?" she asked.

Freydolf nodded and lowered his eyes, only to catch sight of the beads decorating her ankle. A smile blossomed on his face as if he was greeting old friends, and his chest puffed in obvious pride.

Still firmly in control, Aurelius whisked Chelle over to the table, arranging things so she was seated between him and his wife. Brandishing his fancy writing utensil, he dashed off, **Frey says they look well on you, and I couldn't agree more. If you'll excuse me for a moment, I shall bring something to brace you.**

He said a few words to his wife, then glided over to the punchbowl anchoring one of the counters. While filling glasses, he bantered with Freydolf and Torio. Just by his expression, Chelle could tell he was teasing them about something.

Meanwhile, Ulrica pulled over her husband's pen and pad and began to write. Chelle leaned closer to read the woman's comment. **My husband and son have pledged to defend you.**

"Yes, missus." With a quick glance at Quintrell, she murmured, "It was really very sweet of them."

Weighing a disapproving glance in Aurelius's direction, Ulrica wrote, **Fools.**

"Oh, no," Chelle protested. "I'm sure they were just trying to cheer me up."

Exactly, the Pred wrote, underlining the offending word twice. **Which makes Aurelius's pretty promise the worst kind of neglect. A woman is wise to take <u>surer</u> measures.**

Chelle slowly shook her head. "I'm not sure what you mean."

Under the cover provided by a pristine white tablecloth, Ulrica folded back her skirt just enough to remove a small, sheathed dagger from its hidden pocket. First pressing it into Chelle's hand, the woman wrote, **I could teach you to defend yourself. And your future husband. His aim is mediocre at best.**

Staring up into the imposing woman's dark eyes, Chelle whispered, "Do you think I could learn?"

Ulrica smirked. **My methods are proven.**

Aurelius returned, setting a tall glass of something fruity before her. Noting the addition of a weapon to Chelle's ensemble, he nodded approvingly and plucked his pencil from Ulrica's hand. **Feeling more ready to fight for your place?**

She closed her fingers tightly around the little dagger, holding onto the promise it represented. Much heartened by Ulrica's support and the sweet tang of Aurelius's punch, Chelle relaxed, smiled, and nodded.

Flanked by two Pred. What safer place could there be?

Lunch was long-since cleared away when Tupper rushed into the house carrying a large bundle of the herbs his mother had asked for. Their leaves were as distinctive as their scent, and everyone would know what it meant when he and Chelle wore springs of it to the festival. It was the Flox way of announcing an engagement, and several people had tried to interfere while he gathered enough for the both of them.

Ewert had been no help, saying that every would-be groom had to prove he could fend for himself before he could be expected to fend for a bride. Tupper wasn't sure if he'd cheated or not, heading off on Graven to find a wild patch along Morven's southern slopes.

He checked to see if Chelle had noticed him. The young woman was laughing and passing notes with his mother and Tillie, but she spared him a glance. When she saw what he carried, her cheeks turned pink. That was good. He could tell.

"I'll fix you a plate," Melina offered. "Is Ewert coming?"

"Right behind me."

"And Farley?"

Tupper moved to the washstand and reached for the soap. "Haven't seen him."

Once he dried his hands, Melina handed him a glass of sweetwater, and he turned to eye the two Pred flanking his bride-to-be. Aurelius smiled serenely. Ulrica's chin tilted to a superior angle. Their silent message was easy to read—if you want her, you'll have to go through us.

These weren't the kinds of games he liked to play. Was everyone out to keep him from Chelle?

Just then, a small hand patted his foot, and he glanced down into Hewett's hopeful face. He didn't see Ewert's children very often. "Hello, Hewie."

Hewett had been tiny at birth, and he still quite small. Ewert worried about him, and Tillie babied him, but Tupper thought his nephew was clever for one so young. Wasn't he the first to learn to scoot along the floor?

Tupper settled the silver-haired boy comfortably in the crook of his arm, and Hewett patted his uncle's chest. When Tupper tugged out his money cord, the youngster played contentedly with the key, coins, and beads strung upon it.

Chelle was catching on. By some unspoken agreement, everyone in the room was conspiring to keep Tupper away from her. It was a harmless game, but she could tell her suitor was growing frustrated. Since he was always so calm, Chelle had a hard time picturing him doing anything rash. It was probably a good thing that Farley wasn't there. He was better than any of his brothers at egging on Tupper.

Something brushed against her ankle, and she started. At Aurelius's quizzical glance, she whispered, "Under the table?"

Get used to little ones underfoot, Miss Tremont. It's only Hewett.

Easing back slightly from the table, Chelle was met by a pair of big, blue eyes. She felt his small hands exploring Tupper's gift to her, and she adjusted her foot to make it easier for him to see. Those stones were pretty, and there was no harm in letting him look.

She started more violently when a voice echoed in her mind. *"He has potential."*

Chelle stole a look at Freydolf and Tupper, but neither had reacted to Morven's aside. It seemed the mountain could be subtle when she wished. Scooting back further, Chelle bent to unclasp the beads, then lifted the little one. She soon had a sweet boy with soft eyes nestled in her arms. The precious stones enthralled him, and she asked, "Are you going to be a sculptor like your Uncle Freydolf when you grow up?"

While Hewett gummed the dawnstone bead, Freydolf ambled over, his gaze full of questions.

Aurelius wrote, **Frey's curious about your comment.**

Smoothing her fingers over Hewett's silky curls, she said, "Morven likes him."

The Keeper pointed insistently at the paper, and Aurelius wrote, **How do you know?**

"She said so."

Aurelius's expression grew bland. **If you'll pardon my impertinence, my dear … you're deaf.**

Both Freydolf and Tupper shook their heads, taking turns with an explanation that soon had everyone staring at Chelle. She sighed and said, "Morven still talks to me sometimes."

Rolling his eyes, Aurelius wrote, **Leave it to Tupper to take miracles for granted. He never mentioned this little detail to us.**

Melina held up her page. **What does she say?**

With an apologetic glance, Chelle explained, "Most of the time she says things I wouldn't repeat."

Ulrica took charge of a pencil. **She's probably delighted to have a woman to talk to … for once.**

"Maybe a little," Chelle agreed. "She likes to air her opinions."

Dark eyes flashed, and Ulrica demanded, **What is her opinion of me?**

Since she doubted the mountain could read, Chelle tilted her head to one side and asked, "Morven, what do you think of Missus Harrow?" The answer came swiftly, and she giggled.

Well? Ulrica prodded.

"Morven says she's never known a lady more light on her feet."

With a gratified smile, the woman patted Chelle's head.

Torio pushed his way up to the table, planting his free

hand with a thump before leaning close. He spoke crisply to Aurelius, who gravely took the pencil away from his wife.

Turning to a fresh page, he wrote, **Kite wonders if you can ask Morven why Dessa's out of sorts.**

"I remember Farley saying something about Dessa," Chelle said, searching the Grif's tense face. He'd straightened and kept tugging at one of the black rings piercing his ears. Aware that all eyes were fixed on her, she quietly asked, "Morven, how's Dessa?"

"*Angry.*"

"Why is she angry?"

Everyone at the table exchanged glances, and Chelle looked to Tupper for support. Could he hear as well? His far-off expression suggested that he was attuned to something magical.

There was a long, empty silence, and when Morven's voice came again, she sounded uneasy. Blinking to fight off the tears that prickled against her eyelids, Chelle relayed the mountain's response. "Farley is crying."

22

Hurtful Words

For a long while, Farley was aware of little more than the injustice of his situation. Didn't these Pred realize what a Flox's horns meant? And what kind of fool mistook him for his dim-witted brother? It was plain as mush. Tupper had cost him his pride as a man.

Hadwin's smooth stride ate up the terrain, carrying Farley farther and farther from his place at Torio's side. A change in sounds filtered through his reeling thoughts—the *creak* and *croak* of frogs, and the hoarse calls of leggy marsh birds. He caught the low nicker of a horse and pushed himself up enough to see where the Pred was taking him.

Four black horses stood tethered within a copse of spindly trees beside an overgrown track that stood above boggy ground. It was barely wide enough for the fine carriage waiting there. Sun gleamed against polished metal and dark paint. He remembered Lyall Rakefang's order to put him in the carriage. What then? What chance did he have against men who were plotting murder? In a moment of sheer panic, Farley decided that if he let Hadwin put him in that black box, his fate was sealed.

Grabbing hold of the Pred's belt, he pulled hard hoping to slip the rest of the way over the man's back. Hadwin lost his balance, then his grip, and Farley crashed headfirst to the ground. A hand closed around his arm, but the boy twisted frantically, landing a few good kicks before tearing free.

He ran.

Sprinting through reeds, splashing through shallow pools, he startled birds into flight and frogs into deeper waters. The mountain reared up before him, her heights promising safety, but his lungs were bursting, and his legs were too short. Hadwin tackled him to the ground, snarling curses and threats. Pinned under the Pred's greater weight, Farley sobbed into the soft, dark soil.

"Do you want to die?" growled his captor.

He shook his head, then gave voice to his frustration. "I don't get it! Why are you doing this? Freydolf's a good man!"

Hadwin rolled him onto his back, kneeling over him. "Shut up!"

"Do you realize what hurting me will do to your uncle?"

The man snapped, "I have no uncle."

Farley tried to throw a punch, but Hadwin caught his hand, bending his wrist to a painful angle. Tears brimmed as the Flox accused, "Hearing you say *that* would probably hurt him, too."

"I could end your life here, now."

Was it so easy to kill? More frightened than he wanted to admit, Farley whimpered, "That guy wants to kill your dad."

"I have no father."

What chance did he have against a man who wanted to kill his own son-in-law ... and another who would stand by and watch his father die. Was *this* how things worked in the lands beyond these verdant hills?

Wincing, Farley muttered, "Ulrica must be getting better at raising kids. Your brother's way nicer."

Hadwin blinked. "One of my brothers dared to visit without our grandsire's knowledge?"

"Plenty can happen without that crazy old man knowing about it."

"Who was here?"

Farley thought there was a hint of injury in Hadwin's tone.

"*Is* here. You might be interested to know that *I'm* your little brother's favorite uncle."

He bared his teeth. "You *lie*. My younger brother is halfway around the world, and there's no way he'd claim kinship with a bleater like you."

"I'm talking about Quintrell." Golden eyes narrowed, but Farley held his gaze. "Next festival, your baby brother'll be four."

Some of the frigidity vanished from Hadwin's tone. "A fifth son?"

"A Harrow."

"Torio, wait!" Carden called.

Tupper shook free of his tangled thoughts and watched his eldest brother cross to the Grif, who was halfway out the door.

Torio's confusion quickly lapsed into chagrin, for he still held young Hanley. "My apologies. It seems I'm being a little *too* hasty."

"Do you suspect trouble? Should I accompany you?"

"No, no," Torio replied. "You can leave it to me. I'll sort things out with my servant."

Carden nodded. "Bring him back in time for dancing, or our mother will worry."

The Grif only answered with a bow, then hurried out the door. Tupper stared after him, then blinked. "I need to go."

"Why's that, Tupp?" asked Carden.

He started to answer, then shook his head. It would take too long to explain, so he said, "It's better this way."

His brother studied his face. "If you're sure ...?"

"Yes."

Clearing his throat, Carden jerked his horns toward the

table and quietly advised, "You'd better explain."

Oh. Right. Chelle. Hurrying to her chair, Tupper leaned past her, grabbed the closest pencil, and scrawled, **He needs me. Sorry.**

She whispered, "Hurry."

Nodding once, Tupper strode out the door, racing along the lane in order to catch up to Torio.

The Grif didn't slow his steps. "There's no need for you to follow, young master. You've been waiting for weeks to dance."

Tupper caught the man's arm, hauling him to a stop. With a grim expression, he said, "Something's *wrong*."

Torio heaved a sigh. "Dessa's frantic. What do you hear?"

"Noise." He rubbed at the base of his horn, trying to sift through the clamor. "Haimish is uneasy. Nott is frightened. Phineas is proud."

"Proud?" the Grif asked.

"He defended both the gate and Nerine."

"Against ...?" Tupper shook his head, and Torio demanded, "Why didn't you mention any of this to Freydolf?"

He scuffed his toe in the dust. "What if there's blood?"

"Has it come to that?"

"Maybe." Grimacing, he admitted, "Probably."

Torio spat several choice curses as he pushed Tupper ahead of him along the road out of town. "In that case, you're with me. Where's that beautifully swift tiger of yours?"

He pointed toward the bend in the road, and they broke into a run together.

Tupper was grateful he didn't have to slow down for Torio's sake. Even though it was the man's first time riding Graven, the Grif relaxed comfortably into the tiger's bounding stride. Laying low over their streaking mount's shoulder, Tupper wished he was half as calm. Something bad must have happened for Farley to cry. His little brother never shed tears. And Morven hadn't relished them.

"It's too quiet," Tupper said, needing to break the pensive silence.

"How nice for you." Torio's wry tone suggested that Dessa was shouting in his ear.

Tupper glanced over his shoulder, meeting the Grif's gaze. "Even for daytime, it's very still."

Eyes attuned to the trends of magic raked their surroundings. "I'm not sure I want to be on the mountain when the moon rises."

He knew what the man meant. Every bit of gray rock seemed to strain against the stillness, coiled tight, waiting for the pale beams that would cut them loose.

"You would be safe," Tupper assured.

"*My* safety is the least of my concerns."

The young man lapsed into silence, and Graven proved that he could run even faster.

Minutes later, the Apprentice Gate loomed large, and their mount skidded to a stop between the giant, redstone hounds. Scattered papers fluttered on the ground, and Torio slid off Graven's back in order to pick up one, then another. "These are from one of Freydolf's sketchbooks." He inspected each sheet and held up pages of different sizes. "No, at least two. Who would deface a Keeper's work?"

Tupper moved to help clean up the mess, working steadily toward the largest pile of papers at the gate's threshold. The ruined sketches were anchored by ... was that ...? Tupper couldn't move. "T-torio?" he called, voice shaking.

The Grif turned, followed his gaze, and groaned deep in his chest. He crossed briskly to the gate, stooped, and straightened, the ragged horn cradled in his hands. Taloned fingers smoothed over the ridges as cold fire blazed in blue eyes. "This is his."

Torio offered it to Tupper, who gingerly took it. He rubbed his thumb over the tip, struggling against waves of nausea. On this very spot, he'd given Farley his first tap. His brother had been so proud of his horns. Who would have done something so ... bad?

"Here," Torio called, holding up another of the pages. "There's a message."

Bold words slashed across a playful sketch of gamboling lambs. **RETURN WHAT'S MINE, OR YOUR LAMBKIN'S LIFE IS FORFEIT.**

Tupper sank to his knees.

Torio crouched before him and lightly slapped his cheek. "Stay with me, young master. I need your ears."

"I'm here."

Pointing to the horn clasped to the Flox's chest, Torio asked, "Where's Farley?"

"Not sure."

Sighing, the Grif asked, "Can you hear Nestor?"

Oh. He listened hard, but none of the whispers that reached him belonged to his brother's little guardian. "No, but Dessa can."

Torio rubbed his nose. "Yes, but her sense of direction is definitely lacking. She keeps changing her mind."

Tupper knew Dessa was doing her best, but her tumultuous emotions gave her voice a shrill edge. He did his best to soothe the stone, but she wanted Torio ... and Farley. Focusing on her frantic gibberish made it easier to distance himself from his own fear.

In a flash of clarity, Tupper blurted, "She's right."

"Dessa?"

"Yes. She's not changing her mind. Farley's *moving*."

The Grif straightened. "Then we follow."

23

Confinement

Farley stared at the angle of the sunbeam cutting through a gap in the carriage's heavy curtains. Hours had passed. Slowly. Sweat prickled along his hairline and trickled down his back, for the confined space was stuffy. He twisted and tugged at the ropes binding his hands, worsening the raw patches already showing at his wrists. The knots held, but Farley wasn't ready to give in.

"Too bad you can't bite through rope," he muttered to Nestor.

Obviously, Freydolf really *wasn't* like other Pred. The Harrows had said as much often enough, but reality was sinking in fast. Aggressive confidence. Brutal methods. Casual cruelty.

Nestor slithered onto Farley's shoulder and rubbed his head against the underside of his jaw. Tears threatened. Stupid snake. If Aurelius had designed this little guardian, he would have been better armed.

Nestor nipped his chin, and Farley chuckled weakly. "All right already. I'm glad you're here."

One of the horses nickered, and the boy froze, ears straining for another sound. The carriage dipped slightly to one side, then the other. Springs creaked. The brake disengaged with a *thunk*. Reins slapped, and Farley's head hit the wall behind him as the team jerked forward.

With a Terse oath, he fixed his eyes on that narrow slash of light, hoping to keep his bearings. They trundled along at a fair clip, and to Farley's dismay, they turned neither to the left or the right.

North. Why were they going north? And why were they going so far?

Taking a deep breath, he shouted, "Where are you taking me?"

When no one answered, he bellowed, "Doncha know where you are?"

Silence.

Farley leaned forward and hollered, "Hey, mister! You turnin' tail already?"

At a growled command, the carriage skidded to a sudden halt, and boots hit the road outside.

Shrinking against the wall, the cornered Flox whispered, "You better hide."

When Lyall Rakefang yanked open the door, Farley wished he could slip out of sight as easily as Nestor.

By the time Farley regained consciousness, all the feeling had left his hands. For one panicked moment, he thought Lyall had found and confiscated Nestor, but the little guardian gently tightened his hold around the boy's leg, just above his knee. "Glad you're still here," Farley mumbled, poking at his lip with the tip of his tongue. Fat. Split. Sore.

"Are you? I can't imagine why," drawled Hadwin.

Farley turned his head and squinted into the shadows. The younger Pred lounged on the long seat at the opposite end of the carriage, one leg crossed over the other. Lifting a hand, Hadwin pulled aside the drapes, allowing light and air to filter in. They'd stopped. Possibly for a long time, since the afternoon was more than half spent.

In one graceful movement, Hadwin rose and closed the

distance between them. "You're several times a fool for provoking my grandsire."

"Your dad's always telling me to watch my mouth," Farley said, voice rough.

Hadwin drew his knife and cut him free. As soon as Farley's hands dropped into his lap, pins and needles accompanied the return of blood. He clumsily rubbed at his wrists, while Hadwin sheathed his blade and reached for a canteen.

Sloshing some water into a cup, the Pred said, "You should listen to him."

Farley wrinkled his nose. "That'll be tough if him and me both end up dead."

Ignoring the remark, Hadwin thrust the cup under Farley's nose. "Drink."

"Don't want it."

A brow quirked, and the Pred grabbed a handful of blond curls, yanking back Farley's head. When he yelped in protest, Hadwin poured the whole cupful into his mouth, smiling serenely as the boy choked and sputtered. "If you're this much trouble, why hasn't my mother killed you yet?"

Farley glared at his tormentor. "She says she's raised worse. Guess she meant *you*. Idiot."

Hadwin's dark chuckle bode ill, but he only said, "Your foolishness knows *no* bounds." Refilling the cup, he cast aside the empty canteen. "More?"

This time, Farley grudgingly held out his hand ... and yelped again when Hadwin caught his arm, twisting it upward into the light.

Without expression, he inspected the fresh bruises empurpling his fair skin. "If you anger him again, he's resolved to replace you."

"Replace?"

"Aye. We found evidence of others living on Morven. Easy prey." With a grim expression, Hadwin gave weight to his next words. "You will die, and one of them will know my grandsire's disregard. Do you want that?"

"No."

"Then we have an understanding. Now drink."

The cup pressed against Farley's palm, and he closed his fingers around it, lifted it to his lips, and silently obeyed.

Hadwin returned to his seat, crossed his legs, and gazed out the window. Farley cautiously pushed up onto his knees and peered outside. They were no longer on any kind of road he could see. Trees surrounded the carriage, which meant they were probably somewhere close to the river. Or really, *really* far from home. "Where are we?"

"Out of reach."

Farley leaned out the window and spotted two of the horses tethered a short distance away. Firewood had been gathered. The sun would be setting soon. "Reach of what?"

The Pred pointed up. "There will be a moon tonight. We've fallen back to a safe distance."

That's right. Hadwin would know about the stone guardians. Was there a limit to how far Morven's statues could travel? Probably. Nighttime guardians needed to return to their pedestals before sunrise. But other types could move more freely. And there was Graven. Did these Pred know enough to guard against Tupper's tiger?

"Where's the old guy?"

"Hunting."

Not standing watch. Maybe that was good. Maybe it meant nothing. Farley shook his head in frustration and immediately noticed a change in balance. The absence of one horn left him lopsided. Had they taken the whole thing? He was afraid to find out, but he refused to be a coward.

Letting his gaze slide toward Hadwin, he made sure the man wasn't watching, then casually dragged the back of his hand across his forehead. Before he could lose his nerve, Farley slid his fingers through his hair to the base of his abused horn, then along its curve.

In no time, he found the sharp edge of the break. His left horn had been reduced to a mere few fingers' in length. This wasn't the kind of wound that needed treating, but it would also never heal. Permanent disfigurement.

"Are you half a man now?" the Pred asked.

Farley let his hand fall, and his chin came up. "When folks hear that I lost it in battle against two grown Pred, I'll be considered *twice* the man you'll ever be. Especially once your mother finds out you did this. She'll *un*man you."

"Aye," Hadwin replied dully. "No matter who prevails, I'll meet a bitter end."

Tupper was in a fog, and he rubbed at the base of his horn, quickly recoiling when that brought up the mental image of Farley's broken horn, left at their gates like some hunter's trophy. Which was bad. He didn't really *understand*, but he *knew* that much. His brother was in terrible danger, and they needed to hurry. Tupper's stomach clenched, and he locked his jaw against waves of vertigo. His heart beat crazily, and he buried his trembling hands more deeply into Graven's thick ruff. His head was filled with a distant keening that grew more insistent with every bound.

"–ster? Young master!" Torio's forehead hit his shoulder from behind as the Grif slumped against him, exclaiming, "Tupper! For pity's sake, *STOP!*"

Hauling back on their steed's fur, the young man managed to call Graven to a halt before tumbling to the ground beside his companion.

Torio's hands clamped firmly over his ears, and he roared,

"*Enough*, Dessa! Pinions and pin feathers, woman! I'm *not* leaving you!"

Forehead pressed to the ground, Tupper laughed weakly. "Dessa's not a woman."

"She may as well be." The Grif rolled onto his back, spread-eagled on the ground. "Sorry, young master, but I'm at my limit. How much farther can you go?"

"Not very," Tupper replied. Morven's magic usually whispered all around him, but her voice seemed to shout from a distance, taut with fear.

"This is bad … and for more reasons than one." Torio dragged himself to his feet, leaning heavily against the tiger's striped flank. "As much as it pains me to admit it, we need Harrow."

Tupper sat up and stared along the road they'd been following. It continued on to the north, but they could not. He took a deep breath and exhaled shakily. "Yes. Aurelius will know what to do."

By the time Torio and Tupper made it back to the Statuary, Freydolf was already there, standing at the threshold of the Apprentice Gate, clutching his spoiled drawings to his chest. Tupper had never seen a more bewildered expression on his master's face.

"You're safe. Thank goodness." Frey's clawed hand shook as he held it out to Graven and quietly repeated, "Thank goodness."

From his seat between Itak's forepaws, Aurelius snapped, "Took you long enough. Frey's been in shambles for hours. Please tell me you found the brat lollygagging in the forest and left him to find his own way home."

"No." Tupper glanced around and asked, "Who's here?"

"Just us." Aurelius dropped his tendency to pontificate, briskly demanding, "What did you find?"

They slid from the tiger's back and brought out the severed horn and its accompanying message. Freydolf didn't reach for either, too stricken by the sight, but his brother-in-law studied both items narrowly.

Looking at Tupper over the top of the paper, Aurelius said, "Lambkin? But that's *you*."

"Yes."

Torio said, "We found signs of a struggle. Two men. They had a carriage. Four horses."

Aurelius frowned. "Why didn't you follow."

"We *tried*," the Grif replied, frustration clipping his words even more than usual.

Freydolf spoke up. "I can track them. Show me where you lost the trail!"

Torio grabbed the sculptor's arm. "You can't."

"I can try!"

"No, friend. You misunderstand," the Grif said in a low voice. "Morven won't *let* you."

Freydolf shot a querying glance at Tupper, who nodded. "It's too far. It hurts."

Aurelius bared his fangs in an uncharacteristically ugly snarl. "It's a mercy they snatched the wrong Meadowsweet."

"Just because you don't like the boy ...!" Torio retorted.

"Nay!" Aurelius cut in, eyes flashing. "I bear no ill will toward Farley, and I mean to retrieve him before he comes to further harm. But his loss saved the sprat's life." He clenched his fist, crumpling the torn page. "They knew about Frey's limitations, but not Tupper's."

It took a moment for the import of the Pred's words to sink in. Tupper paled. "If *I* was the one in the carriage ...?"

Aurelius nodded gravely. "You and Kite are both white as chalk and shaking simply from pushing your limits. If you'd been carried beyond Morven's reach, you'd be dead."

Freydolf shook his head dazedly. "But why? What possible reason could anyone have for taking Farley? Or Tupper, for that matter? If it's ransom they want ...."

"*Revenge* is more likely," growled Aurelius, holding up the creased page with its bold message. "And *this* man prefers to be paid in blood."

Tupper hurried to his bond-brother's side, for the man's face became a mask of dread. "What is it?" he begged. "Who has Farley?"

Freydolf swallowed thickly. "My father."

Aurelius knew exactly what it meant to draw the ire of Lyall Rakefang. The man had never forgiven him for eloping with his precious daughter. Not even begetting four fine sons had lessened his father-in-law's disdain for his being a lowly Harrow. Would their grandsire demand the fifth? Perish the thought.

He quickly pondered their priorities. The Statuary was under Aurelius's governance, and its citizens were too vulnerable in the village. Smoothly taking charge, he turned to Torio. "Get a message to my wife."

"Certainly."

Drawing the dagger from its sheath on his left thigh, the Pred twirled the weapon, then offered its hilt.

The Grif took the bare blade, and when Aurelius offered no further comment, he checked, "That's all?"

"Aye. She'll understand."

With a curt nod, Torio strode down the eastern trail.

"*Two* men," Aurelius muttered. He would have given his

best pair of boots to know the identity of the second Pred in the equation. If it was one of their boys, Ulrica would rage and howl, then hunt down the turncoat. *Not* a pleasant prospect.

Aurelius understood what a fine line his sons had learned to walk. Rakefang versus Harrow—the cost of crossing the line in either direction was heavy.

"What can I do?" asked Tupper.

What, indeed? Aurelius fully expected Frey to curl up in ball in the face of conflict, so it made sense to have Tupper coax him into some safe corner and feed him biscuits until the worst was over. He glanced at his brother-in-law, but the gentle, humble, frustratingly passive Pred stood gazing to the north with an unnervingly hard look in his dark eyes.

Signaling to Tupper, Freydolf rumbled, "Bring fire."

24

Maiden Waiting

As the sun dipped lower, the menfolk lit bonfires, and musicians tuned their instruments in preparation for dancing. This was the first time Chelle wasn't off in some corner, minding babies, but her attention kept straying to the road. Would Tupper be back in time for the dances he'd promised her?

There was no sign of her betrothed, but she took a turn once with Ewert and twice with Carden. After some good-natured jostling for the privilege, she was passed along to every Meadowsweet uncle and cousin in Hayward. And they in turn introduced her to their wives, mothers, and sweethearts. It was an unusual way to become acquainted, but by the time she was escorted into the square by Old Gruff, Chelle had unraveled most of the twists in Tupper's family tree.

Her partner beamed at her, and she smiled bravely back ... but her uneasiness only grew. The dance ended, and a patter of applause covered her mournful whisper. "Where *is* he?"

"He is safe. He is home."

As Chelle accepted the hand of a bearded gentleman that she was pretty sure was Tupper's paternal grandfather's younger brother, she tried to be as pleased as Morven. But it wasn't much use. She wanted to see Tupper. To hold his hand. To stand at his side. Maybe even share a kiss.

In her silent struggle, she almost missed the moment when Torio slipped from the shadows and knelt before Ulrica, whose young son slept on her lap. A blade flashed, and the Pred was on her feet, eyes trained on the mountain. Accepting the dagger, she spoke to Melina, who hurried over to Carden.

It was difficult to trace what was happening amidst the twirls and turns of the dance, and Chelle didn't want to be rude to her partner. She smiled apologetically at him and saw the song through.

That was all the time Ulrica needed. When the dance ended, she was gone, having taken every other denizen of the Statuary with her.

Chelle sighed softly and backed toward the bakery, only to bump into Torio.

The Grif gestured for paper.

She hurried to the bench where her shawl and punch glass waited and returned with one of the many small sketchbooks that Freydolf had provided for the day.

Torio sat right down on the ground and began to slowly write. She crouched next to him and studied his visage. Even by firelight, she could see that he was pale and drawn.

He turned the page toward her, displaying his neat—if somewhat boxy—printing. **Tupper is very sorry, young mistress. Farley is missing, and we must hunt.**

"How terrible! I knew something must be wrong. Morven is worried."

The Grif carefully inscribed, **There is no need for you to share her worries.**

"I wish there was something I could do," she protested, her gaze straying toward the mountain. Maybe her eyes were playing tricks on her, but she thought she caught a flicker of distant flames.

Torio shook his head. **Stay close to home and do not add to the young master's worries.**

Which meant—wait. Doing her best to hide her disappointment, Chelle promised, "I will. Thank you for letting me know."

Return message?

Chelle bit her lip, then shook her head. She was afraid anything she might say would sound selfish. Her fragile hopes for the evening were quashed, but poor Farley! She couldn't imagine he was lost, so he must have gotten into a scrape somewhere in or on the mountain. Who knew how many days it might take to search Morven's galleries. "I hope you find him soon."

Torio rose, helped her to her feet, bowed over her hand, and then melted into the shadows.

She was inclined to follow suit. As she gazed toward the Quince's rooftop just beyond the bakery, the mountain's voice wound its way through her soul once more.

"Yes, hide. Hide until your Keeper comes for you."

Odd advice. Or familiar advice. Torio had urged her to do the very same thing.

Wait.

Freydolf kept a firm hand on Ilam's chest while Itak stretched and shook out his fur, scraping great, curving claws on the hard-packed path outside the Apprentice Gate. Tupper scooped up Arni, and Aurelius strode forward with Quintrell perched on his hip. Dulcie and Yona ran ahead of them with arms trustingly upraised, giggling when the enormous hounds pushed at them with their noses, puffing warm air into smiling faces.

"Easy, you over-sized pup," the Keeper urged gruffly. "The family's expanded since you last stirred. Pay attention."

"Time to meet your Uncle Doff's guard dogs, boys," Aurelius said. "They like to know who their friends are."

Carden brought Hanley closer, saying, "Is it any use to introduce one so small?"

"Aye, let them have a look at Hanley," Freydolf urged. "I've never known these guardians to forget friend or family."

Aurelius held out his hand to Itak, then encouraged Quintrell to touch the red hound's muzzle. "Mind the fire. These two are deucedly energetic, and that makes for sparks."

Quintrell chortled. "Puppy!"

Tupper followed suit with Ilam, and Arni petted the red hound, asking, "Ride?"

"*There's* an idea," Aurelius drawled sarcastically. "Mount a howdah on this brute and hie off after Uncle Far."

"And panic the villagers?" Freydolf shook his head. "Besides, you can't track in the dark."

"Nay, but my quarry is leaving a different sort of trail." Sharing a long look with his wife, he said, "I *am* going, and on a statue. Preferably a horse, if there's one to spare."

Tupper nodded. "You could have a horse, unicorn, centaur, or even a big goat. But your own horses might listen better."

"Aye, but statues are silent. And to survive this hunt, I'll need their stealth." Setting Quintrell on his feet, Aurelius pulled aside Freydolf to ask, "Is it true that Itak and Ilam will not stand in the way of anyone they've been told to trust?"

"That's the way of it," the keeper acknowledged.

Aurelius swore softly. "That *may* pose a problem."

Freydolf frowned. "I don't see how, since the only other people I've introduced to these two are ..."

"My sons."

Once Aurelius departed, Tupper urged Torio to come to the workshop. "It's late," the Grif pointed out, his gaze fixed determinedly on the moon.

"Yes, but Dessa's waiting."

Torio sighed. "I know it."

Tupper bluntly said, "She wants to see you. Let her feel your hand."

Although he could have brought up certain *other* young ladies who'd been left waiting this night, Torio only bowed his head. "Lead the way, young master."

Freydolf actually took the lead, prowling along familiar paths with eyes alert. Several guardians from the Cavern mingled with the usual courtyard contingent. A doubling of the guard. From what Aurelius had shared, they were a necessary precaution.

Torio's fingertips briefly grazed the hilt of the short sword Ulrica had pressed upon him. Perhaps he should inspect his own small arsenal, assuming Farley hadn't made off with the collection of weapons in his old wagon.

As soon as Torio entered the workshop, a swell of magic buffeted him, and he stalked over to the column of black stone. Pressing his hand to Dessa's glossy surface, he grumbled, "If you're so worried about being left behind, hurry up and let Freydolf finish you. Now, stop fretting over *me* and spare a thought for Farley. He needs us."

Tupper seconded him with a nod. "I'll bring food. Stay."

Torio glanced at Freydolf, who waved his hand and muttered, "Aye. Stay. It'll do her good to keep you near. She's already calmer."

Ever since they'd settled on a final sketch, the sculptor had started referring to Dessa with greater familiarity. Torio's curiosity had been building for a while, so he asked, "What do you see when you look at her?"

Freydolf tilted his head to one side, assessing the column he'd barely begun to shape. "A shy woman, with her hands like so," he said, folding his demurely over his heart.

"Shy?" the Grif asked, cocking his head to one side, trying to see it. "You jest!"

"Self-conscious, then," Frey amended. "Why? What do *you* see?"

"Formless power," Torio replied, twisting his hand in wavy patterns. "More magic than I've ever seen in one place ... aside from another mountain's heart. And I can see how it connects." He thumped his fist against his chest. "Here."

Frey rubbed the back of his neck. "Aye. That's how it's always felt."

Tupper returned with bread and cheese, saying, "Tea is steeping. Sit."

"I'll sit here," Torio said, dropping to the floor beside Dessa and leaning against her.

The Flox nodded, served him his portion, and pushed the rest into Freydolf's hands. "Eat. We need your strength."

Torio picked up one of the nearest books and paged pointlessly. A subdued voice filtered into his mind. *"See me?"*

"Do you think me blind?" he murmured in Terse, lifting his hand to rap the stone at his back. "You're huge."

"Formless?" Dessa whispered.

He sighed. "If it worries you, show Freydolf what you want me to see. You need to cooperate with him so we can get back onto the road."

"Go?"

"Yes, but not without Farley."

"Too far," she complained, sounding more like her usual self.

Closing his eyes, Torio let his head drop back against black stone. In low tones, he asked, "You can't find Nestor?"

"Too far," she repeated mournfully.

"He's a very little snake. It's not your fault." He felt more of her tension ebb and sighed gustily. Had she really thought he would blame her? "Let's trust Harrow for tonight. Worse comes to worst, I'll toss you in a cart and join the hunt."

Happiness, gratitude, hope—they sparkled through her ever-changing moods. Her ease put his mind more at rest, and he smiled ruefully. Would he be able to defend her any more than Freydolf would be able to defend Morven?

Just then, a pile of pillows tumbled to the floor beside Torio. "Sorry!" Tupper exclaimed, adding an armload of blankets to the heap. "I'll make your bed here."

"That's not necessary, young master."

"Yes. It is."

It wasn't until the Flox was half done with makeshift

sleeping arrangements that Torio realized a similar bundle waited by the door, and Freydolf had shouldered a bulging pack. "Where are you going?"

"The Cavern," the Pred replied gruffly.

Tupper plumped the last of the pillows and sat back on his heels. "Morven wants Frey." Patting Dessa, he added, "You understand?"

"Well enough to know she wants you both."

He nodded readily. "Yes. Me, too."

"So you're going to spend all night warming Thrall's egg?"

Freydolf glanced over his shoulder at the Grif, let his gaze stray to Dessa, then smirked. "And where will you be in two years' time, Keeper?" Frey only had to wait a moment for realization to strike and mortification to set in. The door closed on his deep chuckle.

Torio buried his face in his hands. In clipped tones, he muttered, "See here, Dessa. I sleep alone."

After a lengthy pause, she promised, *"I'll stay awake."*

Tupper chuckled hollowly as Thrall snatched him up. Moonlight poured through the clerestories, and from on high, he could see how many statues milled through the Cavern. Kneeling on the dragon's cupped palms, he peered through prison bars created by four sets of long fingers. "I wasn't done making Frey's bed," he protested. "Don't you want your Keeper to be comfortable?"

She snapped her impressive jaws and tightened her grasp.

"You don't need to hold me." Tracing the pattern of scales on her fingers, the young man promised, "I won't go that far again. I didn't like it."

Thrall slowly loosened her grip, lifting away the upper set of hands and pulling him close to her chest.

Freydolf's voice came from below. "Aye, Thrall. The lad's ours for keeps. Let him down, and you can watch over him all night long."

The mountain's oldest guardian relented, and Tupper slipped and slid down into the nest of her coils. Within minutes, he finished arranging two beds at angles, as close to the dragon's egg as they could be. Freydolf dropped wearily onto his blankets, and Tupper would have followed suit if Graven hadn't tried to join them. "No room!" he gasped through a faceful of fur.

After much useless pushing and pulling, Freydolf said, "Give it up, lambkin. Graven's as rattled as the rest of us and wants to be near you. We can make room."

By the time Tupper pulled free the scattered pillows and re-spread the blankets, he was snugly tucked between Freydolf's broad back and the soft fur of Graven's underbelly. The tiger's chest thrummed with silent purrs, the dragon's coils writhed and twitched, and Olexi marched back and forth along the top of his pillow. If his bond-brother started to snore, Tupper doubted he'd get any sleep at all.

Now that everything was quiet, Tupper was able to think things through. "Frey?"

"Hmm?"

"He's my brother. It was a bad trade. Him for me."

"I understand." The Pred shifted slightly, pulling his blanket more closely around his shoulders. "It's too many kinds of awful to watch a younger sibling take on a burden you were meant to bear."

Tupper thought on that. "Do you mean Ulrica?"

"Aye. I left. She stayed."

"But she says she wanted to."

Freydolf hummed, then quietly said, "And I think if Farley knew your life was on the line, he'd have made that bad trade for your sake."

"Is that what your sister did?"

"In a way." The Pred sighed deeply. "She didn't die in my place, but she lived in it."

Tupper edged closer to Freydolf. "Will Aurelius bring Farley home?"

"Aurelius will do everything he can for Farley, but ... nay. We can't expect him to bring your brother back by morning. Tonight is for scouting. He can only watch and see, assuming he can find them."

The lad gazed toward the windows high above—moon and stars shone in from beyond the glass, while flickering firelight reflected from below. So many torches. Countless redstone guardians. Would they really need so many to stop one man?

In a small voice, Tupper asked, "Are you afraid of your father?"

Sorrow darkened Freydolf's tones. "I'm afraid for Farley."

Hadwin was making his third circuit of the woods surrounding their camp when his father's blade found his throat.

"So it's you," crooned the man who'd raised him to know better. "How shall I interpret my third son's lamentable inattentiveness? Did the peaceful countryside lull you into a false sense of security, or was surrender your object all along?"

Every word bit. Every cut deserved. Closing his eyes in shame, he managed an even tone. "You may consider my capture a compliment to your superior skills."

"Don't patronize, Hadwin. I wouldn't have left you in your grandsire's keeping if I wasn't sure of your capabilities." With brisk ease, the Pred took away all Hadwin's weapons, casting them onto the loamy ground with a series of soft *thuds*. "And as much as I'd like to carry you off, I'm here for the lad."

Hadwin started. "You would give preference to that bleater?"

"That *bleater* is my responsibility," Aurelius growled. "Show me where he's moored. Yield him."

Chuckling hollowly, Hadwin said, "If he's gone, I'm dead."

"Wouldn't it be better to die at your grandsire's hand than at your mother's?" Aurelius asked coolly.

He stiffly replied, "I have no wish to die."

"Then run."

Did his father think so little of him? Hadwin didn't appreciate being baited. Baring his teeth, he countered, "It's in your best interests that I remain. With me here, that idiot boy might survive his captivity."

"Might?" Aurelius scoffed. "Those are scanty assurances."

"He knows no caution, and his tongue's a goad," grumbled Hadwin. "The next time he opens his mouth, Grandfather will either disarm him or dispatch him."

"I see your point." The merchant turned his son to face him and gripped his arms. "Take me to Lyall. I'll barter for the lad's life."

"Nay!"

Aurelius clamped a hand over Hadwin's mouth and narrowed his eyes. In light tones, he inquired, "Whyever not?"

Once he was free to speak, the young man whispered, "He'll kill you."

"For negotiating the return of a single Flox? I'm confident I can make him see the benefits of ..."

Hadwin closed his eyes and shook his head, fighting against frustrated tears.

Aurelius lowered his hand. "Nay?"

"He intends to kill you. If you go to him, you go to your death." Needing to make the situation clear, Hadwin said, "*You* are his prey."

"And your mother?"

"The prize."

"Ah."

Bowing his head, Hadwin begged, "Run."

Pulling his grown son into a gentle embrace, Aurelius said, "Nay. It is in your best interests that I remain."

Hadwin hid his face against his father's shoulder and clung tightly. "I need your help."

Aurelius wryly replied, "The feeling's mutual."

Although Hadwin had been willing to share space with a Flox, when his grandfather was ready to rest, Farley was put out of the carriage. And tethered to the carriage wheel. Like a dog.

Even though the night was warm, a damp chill seeped up through the seat of Farley's pants, contrasting unpleasantly with his new collection of aches and bruises. He was just dozing when Hadwin's voice jerked him from confused dreams.

"The bleater's squirming," he growled. "I'll take him into the woods before he pisses his pants."

From inside the lamplit carriage, his grandsire sourly retorted, "Mind he doesn't piss on your boots."

"If he does, he'll be pissing on his grave."

Farley's lip curled as Hadwin undid his bonds and hauled him to his feet, propelling him into the woods. "I can walk by myself," he muttered.

"Nay, you'd toddle and topple like a milk-faced weanling."

Which was probably true. Farley staggered over every rise and stumbled noisily into bush and fern. How the Pred managed to move silently was beyond understanding. As far as the Flox could tell, they weren't even on a trail. What's more, they weren't stopping. "Where ...?"

"Hush."

Why would Hadwin take him so far from the carriage? The possibilities ranged from bad to worse, and Farley dug in his heels ... only to have his captor stop. Drawing upon what bravado he had left, Farley said, "If you expect me to drop trou in front of you, you don't know squat about Flox. We're real particular about stuff like this. Modest. *Very* modest."

"Hush," the Pred repeated, peering back in the direction from which they'd come. He stood taut as he listened, all his attention focused on the distant carriage and horses.

Thinking this might be his chance, Farley checked to see if there was a dagger handy, but while the sheathes still rode at Hadwin's hip and thigh, no hilts showed. "Hey, mister, how come you're not …?"

Arms slipped around his shoulders from behind, and a familiar voice warned, "Not another word, brat."

He gasped.

Aurelius quickly covered his mouth with one hand, enforcing his order. "Did he follow?"

"Nay," Hadwin replied. "He's probably caught up in one of his books."

Farley began to shake. Tilting his head back to make sure he wasn't fooling himself, he found he couldn't see. His eyes were watering too much.

"Idiot boy," groused Aurelius, turning him around and pulling him close.

Farley grabbed hold, his face crumpling. "You came," he choked out.

"Did you think we'd leave you to the tender mercies of these curs?" With a haughty sniff, Aurelius relayed, "Frey's on the warpath, and Kite's a mess."

Glancing up, Farley asked, "Torio is?"

Aurelius frowned and tilted the Flox's pale face into the moonlight. "Correction. You're a mess." Giving his son a put-out glare, he continued, "You're a great deal of trouble, Mister Meadowsweet. How often have I warned you not to let down your guard?"

"Sorry."

"You should be! Just *look* at your tunic!" Aurelius fussed with the soiled cloth then *tsk*-ed. "It's no use. The stain's set. You're deucedly hard on clothes!"

Was fashion all he cared about? Farley's hands fisted in Aurelius's shirtfront, anchoring himself to the man he respected more than any other. In a broken croak, he drew attention to what truly mattered. "They took my horn."

"Aye," he replied, finally assessing the damage.

Hiding his face, he mumbled, "Is it bad?"

"Worse," Aurelius assured. "If you like, I could hack off the other. Then, at least you'd have some symmetry."

Farley laughed wetly against the Pred's vest. "Try it, and I'll show Graven how to get past Phineas."

His tone grew serious. "I would not trifle with another man's pride in such a low manner, and I'm sorry to learn that my kin had a part in damaging yours. Hadwin's future is far from bright."

"Serves him right."

Aurelius gently prodded some of the lumps Farley had earned, then pet his hair in a manner he usually reserved for the little ones. Holding his gaze, the man quietly said, "I'm in a quandary, Tupper. If I take you now, my son will die. And if I leave you here, your impertinence will get you killed. What do you recommend?"

Farley's mind whirled. Was Aurelius asking to leave him here? And what did he mean by calling him by his brother's name? Aurelius would trust Hadwin with his life, but not with the whole truth? Farley shot a look at his captor and asked, "Are you attached to this guy?"

"Aye. Deeply."

Hadwin's head came up, but he quickly averted his eyes.

Farley grimaced, then grinned. "Then I'll hafta mind my manners a little better."

Aurelius affectionately murmured, "Idiot boy."

"Do you have a plan?"

"Naturally. Support Hadwin without it seeming intentional. Make him look good. Cower. Cringe." To his son, Aurelius said, "Your grandsire will be suspicious if you gain the lad's trust. Fear is all Lyall respects. Be hard. Be harsh."

Hadwin smirked. "Gladly."

"But you're gonna come back for me ... right?" Farley demanded.

"Aye, but from closer quarters." Aurelius turned to Hadwin. "Play up your role as conquerors. Your grandsire's very traditional. Use that to push him into taking unnecessary risks."

"I understand." the young man hesitated, then haggled, "If I can steer him, will you steer Mother?"

"You'll have your chance at redemption. Make sure the lad survives until I can reclaim him." Pulling Farley into one last embrace, Aurelius ordered, "Live."

"Plannin' to."

"Good. Because if you die, Hadwin's fate is sealed, and I would lose two sons."

25

Betrayed

When Thrall stilled, Tupper stirred. His eyes drifted open, and he gazed sleepily at the soft light shining through the windows high overhead. Graven's cool fur brushed his cheek, and Freydolf's deep breathing meant the man had finally managed to get to sleep. Tupper's brow puckered. Why had it been difficult? And why were they *here*? Oh. That's right. Farley.

"Morning, Tupp," came a low voice.

Carden sat on Thrall's stone coils, leaning back against the dragon's chest. Judging by the dark smudges under his eyes, the man hadn't slept much. Tupper started to ask if there was news, but Carden turned and beckoned to someone. Propping himself up on an elbow, Tupper shook Freydolf's shoulder as Torio and Aurelius climbed into view.

"And I thought Dessa was moody," grumbled the Grif.

"Can you blame her?" Carden soothed.

Torio dropped to a seat on Thrall's coils. "I can and I will! She nearly took my arm off with those great fangs of hers. Testy."

Carden chuckled, and Aurelius pointed accusingly. "Don't even pretend you weren't showing off, Mister Meadowsweet."

The younger man simply held up his hands, proclaiming his innocence.

Frey sat up and scratched. "It's only natural that Thrall would favor Carden. He's my apprentice, after all."

Torio smirked at Aurelius. "If you want to talk about playing favorites, Graven has clearly chosen you."

Right on cue, the tiger lifted his head and narrowed red eyes at Aurelius.

"Leave me in peace, you patchwork pest. I've endured enough for one day. Nay, for a dozen days."

To everyone's surprise, the big cat lay back down.

Tupper fidgeted through the banter, but he finally blurted, "Farley?"

"The hunt was only partially successful." Aurelius lowered himself to a seat between Carden and Torio. "I saw him, but I couldn't take him."

"Is he safe?" Tupper pressed.

"Hardly."

"My father has him?" asked Freydolf.

"Aye."

In a soft voice, the sculptor prompted, "And the *other* man?"

"Hadwin Rakefang." Aurelius scrubbed wearily at his face. "My third son."

Freydolf shook his head. "That's almost impossible to believe. How old is Winny now?"

"Nineteen. This autumn's festival will mark his twentieth year."

The Keeper frowned. "Is *this* the task my father set for his rite of passage?"

"Rite?" Carden asked, looking between the Pred.

"Aye," Aurelius replied, bitterness edging his tones. "To take his rightful place in the legendary house of Rakefang, Hadwin must complete a monumental task set by its head."

Tupper rubbed at the base of one horn, trying to sort everything out. "Frey's dad wanted your son to kidnap me to prove he's got the horns to build a house of his own?"

"Something like that," Aurelius replied. "But the ultimate task has little to do with you or Farley."

"What, then?" demanded Freydolf.

Tupper had never seen Aurelius look so angry. "My son has

always been proud, strong, ambitious, and clever. A tribute to both Ulrica and me. But before Lyall will give Hadwin the support he needs, he expects the lad to lure his father to his death."

"He's trying to turn your own son against you?" Carden asked incredulously.

"Aye. In coming here and taking Farley, Hadwin has already betrayed me. But perhaps I betrayed him first ... by leaving him behind."

After an extra-early breakfast in Melina's bakery, Aggie escorted the children outside to play so Aurelius could hold a council of war. From his seat at the head of the table, their governor gave each of them some badly-needed direction.

Beginning with Carden, he said, "Mister Meadowsweet, go down into the quarry. Send all the workers home for an extended break ... with pay. Call it a gift from the Keeper, whose generosity is as great as his appreciation for their labors on his behalf."

"A new midsummer tradition, marking Master Freydolf's birthday?" suggested Carden.

"Aye. I like that," Aurelius agreed. "Have Ewert help you in spreading the word to those already on home days."

Freydolf interjected, "Warn the men to keep their families clear of the mountain. I'm going to give Itak and Ilam more range."

Turning to Carden's wife, Aurelius continued, "Melina, choose new quarters for your family and for mine. Somewhere inside the galleries. Preferably near the Cavern. I want the children out of Lyall's reach."

"Are they in danger?" she asked.

"The move is mostly precautionary," he said with a reassuring smile. "Think of it as establishing a summer home."

Freydolf added, "Wake as many guardians as you need to lend a hand."

Next, Aurelius addressed Torio. "Choose new quarters in the heights. You have sharp eyes, and they'll be easy to spot—a dark carriage drawn by four black horses."

"Hardly typical for this area," agreed the Grif. "Where did they camp?"

"In the north, along the river. They may switch conveyances or saddle the horses."

"If they come near enough, Nestor will give them away," Torio reminded.

"Aye." Turning to Freydolf, Aurelius asked, "What can you do, Keeper?"

"By night, Morven is impenetrable. By day, we are much more vulnerable." Spreading his hands wide, he said, "Few of our sunstone and redstone guardians are warriors, but I'll wake all I can find. Those who cannot fight will stand watch."

Tupper's gaze slid to Ulrica, who seemed completely absorbed in the silent plication and smoothing of the coral-hued fabric of her dress's full sleeves. The woman hadn't taken the news of Hadwin's involvement very well. It worried him.

There was an uncomfortable lull, and Ulrica lifted dark eyes to meet her husband's gaze. "And will you deign to give orders to me?" she inquired in brittle tones.

His brow arched. "Sharpen your blades, my love. Tonight, we hunt."

A soft smile flickered across her lips, and she murmured, "Aye."

Aurelius dismissed everyone to their appointed tasks, leaving Tupper sitting uncertainly at the table. Should he return to his usual duties? Aggie had already milked the cow in Farley's absence, but the eggs needed gathering, and the garden could stand to be watered. With a blink, Tupper realized that Aurelius was waiting for him.

Straightening in his seat, he asked, "Yes?"

"I have great need of your skills, sprat. Can I rely upon you?"

"Yes." Tupper quickly stood, asking, "What do you need?"

Drooping dramatically, Aurelius whined, "A bath."

Despite the heartening knowledge that Aurelius had a plan, Farley spent the remainder of the night cold, thirsty, and miserable. Even after Lyall took over guard duty, slipping off into the woods, Hadwin did nothing to alleviate his prisoner's discomfort. Farley understood that it was important to keep up appearances, but the Pred could have managed a *little* consideration. At *least* a drink.

To ask for one would have been to admit weakness, and there was no way Farley was giving Hadwin any more reasons to feel superior.

As it turned out, Farley didn't need to beg. His stomach did it for him.

Lyall seared his kill over their small fire, and the mouthwatering smell of roasting meat hung thick in the air. Farley's jaw clenched, and he averted his eyes as another gurgle betrayed the enormity of his appetite. The Pred ignored him completely, stripping every bone and licking their fingers clean.

When he'd finished, Hadwin strolled over and crouched before him, and Farley flinched away, curling in on himself. For an instant the young man looked stunned.

But then Lyall barked with laughter. "Put him in his place last night?"

"Aye, he's learned better manners," Hadwin smoothly replied.

Lyall leered. "Did he bleat for his mother?"

"Long and loud. Did it disturb your rest?"

"Nay, nay. His voice must be as feeble as his will."

A flush crept up Farley's neck and face. As if he'd give them the satisfaction! He hadn't so much as whimpered when Lyall beat him!

The elder Pred's tone became indulgent. "Reward your pet's newfound docility."

"Aye," Hadwin agreed, rapping Farley's forehead. "Can you manage horses?"

"Yessir," he murmured.

An eyebrow arched challengingly. "Tend to ours, and I'll let you fill your belly with river water."

How generous. Lowering his gaze to hide his fury, Farley muttered, "Deal."

Claws skimmed down the side of his face, and Hadwin crooned, "What was that, pet?"

Cringing, Farley whispered, "Yessir."

Lyall chuckled darkly. "Well done, Hadwin. I'll leave the arrangements to you. Then on to Hayward. So did that lowborn fool find you last night?"

Farley froze, but his would-be ally calmly replied, "Aye. Harrow came, just as you predicted."

"And did he turn you against me?"

With a serene smile, Hadwin answered, "Any fool believes what he wishes was true."

Tupper kept one eye on Aurelius while preparing the bath. He'd never seen the proud man slouch so disconsolately. Was it the sleepless night? Tipping the copper cauldron, he splashed hot water into the sunken tub. The Pred didn't react, so Tupper reached for the nearby bottles, adding an extravagance of foam and oils to the steaming water. "Ready," he called softly.

Aurelius sat against the wall, elbows on his knees and head bowed so his hair hid his face.

Tupper crossed to kneel in front of him. "Aurelius. Your bath."

Slowly, the man lifted his head, staring blankly into his face. Weariness. Misery. Doubt. This was an unguarded moment, and Tupper understood what it meant to be entrusted with it. Aurelius needed buttressing, so with a soft *tut*, the young man scooted closer and quietly unfastened buckles. It wasn't until he moved on to the vest buttons that Aurelius caught his hands.

"What do you think you're doing?"

"Mothering."

With a rueful smirk, the Pred asked, "How did it come to this, sprat?"

"Not sure." he replied, pulling free so he could tackle the tiny buttons lining Aurelius's cuffs.

The man watched, but his golden eyes were turned inward. Tupper did his best not to interrupt his thoughts. Weapons, jewelry, boots—he took them and tended to them like a proper valet. Finally, Aurelius murmured, "It was deucedly hard to leave Farley in danger."

"Won't your son keep him safe?"

"Not sure," he admitted in a low voice. "Of all my sons, Hadwin is the best haggler. Entering into negotiations with him means taking your life into your hands. He knows how to lie."

Tupper nodded. "Isn't that good? He can trick Frey's father."

"When lies and truths are woven together with such skill, it's nearly impossible to disentangle them. Even for me."

Just then, the door to the necessary slammed open and Torio leaned against the frame, panting. "Harrow, the carriage. Black. Four horses."

Aurelius swiftly stood, barefoot in his breeches. "Aye, that's the one to mark."

"I've marked it," the Grif said tersely. "They're moving south through the eastern foothills."

"Already?"

"Without a doubt."

The Pred lunged for his boots, muttering curses in every language.

Tupper fidgeted, unsure what significance to attach to this turn of events. "Is that bad?"

"Aye," growled Aurelius, grabbing his shirt and striding for the door. "We're not ready."

They were less than an hour outside Hayward when Lyall stopped to water the horses. Hadwin collared Farley to help with the task, warning, "Don't vex the stallions."

"That'd be stupid."

"Aye. But the world is full of fools."

True enough, but Farley wasn't one of them. He might not be able to outrun these Pred, but the horses could. And that made them powerful friends. Reaching up to pat the arching neck of the fieriest of the four, Farley spoke a little louder. "I ain't gonna hurt them just because I can't get at the ones who hurt me."

Hadwin silkily inquired, "What are you implying?"

"Aurelius says you've got wits. Are they slow?"

"Father may find your idiocy quaint, but I do not."

Lyall wasn't nearby, so Farley didn't bother cowering. Meeting the Pred's glare, he asked, "Whose son are you?" Hadwin's lip curled, but an answer wasn't forthcoming. The Flox brazenly continued, "You've got your dad's face, your mom's skill, and your grandsire's name. With all their best, are you gonna do your worst?"

"Are you calling me a traitor?"

"That's the fencepost you're standin' on. But which way are you gonna jump?" With a hard look, he said, "I'm betting you ain't sure, so I'll give you one piece of advice. Don't underestimate your folks."

Hadwin also checked to make sure their conversation wasn't being observed. "Think on *this*. Father's plan is hours old, the product of desperation, based on hearsay. My grandsire's plan is months in the making."

Farley snorted. "So the old guy's slow on the uptake? Is that why he needs you?"

The Pred's mouth twitched. Annoyance or amusement?

Pressing what he hoped was an advantage, the Flox asked, "How come we're going to Hayward?"

"Simple, simpleton. It's your hometown."

"*I* know that, but why do *you*?" Pretending to be more interested in braiding the mane of one of the stallions, he pointed out, "I never said so."

"We've been in this territory long enough to take its measure," Hadwin sourly replied. "The villages are filled with fools willing to hasten us on our way by answering our questions. Every shopkeep in the vicinity knew two names— Meadowsweet and Harrow."

"Bet the old man was peeved that Rakefang didn't ring a bell!"

Another twitch. Definitely amusement.

Farley waved his hands and repeated, "But *why* does he want to go to my hometown?"

Hadwin struck a pose. "It's like Father said. My grandsire is very traditional. He's going to put all who bear the name Meadowsweet under his heel."

In a flash, Farley understood. "He's plannin' to steal our front step?"

"Naturally."

Wow. Just like the legends. But that posed a teensy problem. "There's *no* way I'm leading him to my mom's house."

With an elegant shrug, Hadwin said, "The gesture is largely symbolic. Lead him to the governor's palace, the magistrate's offices, your local treasury, or even the center of commerce. The more prominent the setting, the better."

"No wonder you guys leave us alone. Flox don't have trophies worth taking." Shaking his head, Farley said, "Look, mister, Hayward hasn't got anything worth taking. Except me. And I don't aim to be kept for much longer."

The Pred's expression turned grim. "If Hayward does not properly surrender, its conqueror will become its destroyer."

Farley muttered Terse oaths as he searched his mind for a solution. There was only one, but he didn't like it. "Can you swear no one will get hurt?"

"Will the people of Hayward *voluntarily* cower and cringe?" Hadwin inquired. "Or are they all as foolish as you?"

He'd just have to warn off the concerned or curious. And Ewert. There was no telling what his older brother would do. With luck, he was safely out of the way at the quarry. Sighing, Farley said, "Frey put in the front step of our town's bakery. It's his own workmanship. Master quality. Even signed. That'll satisfy his dad, right?"

Hadwin's brows slowly arched. "Aye. That should do nicely."

The sun was tilting toward mid-afternoon when Lyall Rakefang's carriage rolled to a stop in front of Pennyflax & Quince. By the time the dust settled, Hayward's citizens had scattered, which was a mercy. Farley hadn't counted on having his hands tied behind his back. Or on being forced to his knees in the road. He didn't want anyone seeing him like this.

Hadwin stood over Farley while Lyall surveyed the shops. "Meager pickings," the elder Pred said, grinding the earth under the heels of his boots in a show of disdain.

"Aye, these bleaters are hardly worth your time."

"Then let's make short work of this," Lyall said, approaching the bakery and crouching to inspect the stone step's decorations.

He made a noise of disgust. "What useless scratchings."

"Don't belittle what you don't understand," muttered Farley.

Hadwin kicked him.

Seething inwardly, the Flox managed a halfhearted cringe ... which turned into an honest one when the front door of the bakery flew open. Oh, no. No, no, no, *no*! Even though he shook his head adamantly, he couldn't make Chelle understand quickly enough.

"Farley! What happened? Torio said you were missing!"

"Farley?" Hadwin seized a handful of blond curls, jerking the boy's head backward. "Who's Farley?"

"Great guy. Destined to be the most famous Flox in the whole world. Your dad says he's brazen as blue in the sky ... and kind of an idiot."

"You?"

He smirked. "We seem to have gotten off on the wrong foot. I'm Farley Meadowsweet. Nice to meetcha."

"You denied nothing."

Farley rolled his eyes. "Did so. You weren't listening."

"But my father called you Tupper," Hadwin hissed.

"Kinda makes you wonder, don't it?"

Chelle stepped out onto the bakery's step, concern plain on her face. "Is that blood? What's going on?"

Lyall snagged the hem of her dress, lifting to get a better look at the beads decorating her ankle. She froze as the tip of a claw hooked the strand of precious beads. "This is a rich gift. Do you suppose she's that man's whore? Or do Harrows keep women in every port?"

Farley's jaw dropped, and Hadwin growled, "Nay!"

But before either of them could summon any more outrage, Chelle politely addressed Lyall. "Excuse me, sir. By any chance, are you related to Master Freydolf Meadowsweet?"

The man's head reared back, rage twisting his features, and Chelle paled. Farley struggled to his feet and lurched forward, catching the young woman's attention. He knew his voice couldn't reach her ears, so he urgently mouthed one word. *Run!*

26

Spell it Out

Chelle hadn't wanted to believe anything was wrong, but when Farley stumbled out of the shadow of the Pred standing over him, the sun cast aside all doubt. Dried blood, darkening bruises, a swollen lip, and a missing horn. She wanted to rush to his side, to help him, but his eyes locked with hers with desperation. And he begged her to run.

Kicking free of the man she'd nearly mistaken for Tupper's master, Chelle darted back through the bakery door, slamming it in his glowering face. Would that be enough to stop him?

"No. Run."

Wishing desperately that she understood what was happening, Chelle hurried to the back door, out into the garden beyond, and through the gate. She paused to check if anyone had followed and stiffened when the younger Pred strolled around the corner of the building. She lifted her skirts and sprinted for the woods. But where could she go?

The mountain's voice came again. *"Hide."*

Taking Morven's advice, Chelle ducked behind a tree, leaning against the rough bark and trying to catch her breath. Was it even possible for her to evade a hunter? Fear drenched her, but even worse was the plaguing guilt. How could she have left Farley alone? He needed help. What kind of person was she, leaving him behind? Rooted to the spot by her own confusion, Chelle covered her face and gave vent to tears.

Moments later, strong hands closed around her shoulders, and she was caught. Dashing away tears, she peered up into features that were almost familiar. He was saying something, but she shook her head and murmured, "Your eyes."

He blinked.

In hesitant tones, she asked, "Mister Harrow?"

The oddest expression of regret flitted across his face. He spoke again, harsher words if his grip was any indicator.

Shaking her head, Chelle said, "I don't understand."

Impatience brought a sneer to his handsome face, and he loomed closer. She understood that he was trying to intimidate her, but there was a measure of reluctance in his posturing. He didn't mean whatever he was saying. But knowing that did little good. She couldn't hear the lies.

"Please. I'm sorry," she interrupted. "I can't hear you. I'm deaf."

His hands fell away, and he stared at her in disbelief. Then he pinched the bridge of his nose, muttering to himself. Finally, he threw his hands wide in a gesture of surrender. Meeting her gaze again, he pointed to her, then pressed a finger to her lips.

"Be quiet?"

He nodded briskly.

"I could scream," she threatened.

Tapping one of the many blades strapped at his sides, he said something that was probably a much worse threat.

"What about Farley. Will you take me back to him?"

Frowning deeply, he stepped to her side and caught up her hand. Pressing it open, he traced a letter onto her palm—D.

Oh. Good idea. "I can read. Keep going."

The tip of the Pred's claw moved quickly, but she could follow. D - A - N - G - E - R

"I figured that part out," Chelle said. "But Farley trusts you."

The young man gazed quizzically at her.

"Can I trust you, too?"

Bewilderment inspired another round of spelling. W - H - O -

"Who am I?" she guessed. "I'm Chelle."

But he wasn't quite done. **S – E**

"Whose am I?" Chelle remembered that it was Tupper's gift that had sparked the older man's interest. Lifting her skirt slightly so she could see the beads, she explained, "My suitor likes to follow Pred traditions when he can. This is his betrothal gift. Master Freydolf made it himself."

Y – O – U – & – F – R – E – Y

Chelle forgot her fear and giggle softly. "No, no, no. I'm going to marry Master Freydolf's brother."

The man actually looked sick. **H – A – R – R – O – W**

"You're *very* mixed up. I'm talking about his bond-brother, Tupper Meadowsweet."

With a bland look, the Pred spelled out, **I – D – I – O – T**

"Me?" she asked, bristling.

He jerked his thumb back toward the bakery and mouthed one word. Farley.

"Why is Farley an idiot?"

The Pred's attention swiveled in the direction from which they'd come, and he bared his teeth, then barked a few words. His expression hardened as he searched her face. Once again, he pressed his finger to her lips, and she stayed silent. Then he wrote, **C – O – W – E – R**

Chelle withdrew her hand and propped it at her waist. "You're asking me to keep quiet and pretend I'm afraid of you?"

While the young man was clearly affronted by her choice of words, he nodded.

"Will that help Farley?" she pressed.

He nodded impatiently.

"All right. Show me your dagger."

In an instant, the point of a blade glittered a hairsbreadth from her nose, and he smirked at her surprise.

"Show off," she muttered. "I meant the other end."

With a casual flip, he presented the hilt of his weapon, which was decorated by a rearing stallion with blue jewels for eyes.

Taking hold of his hand with both of hers, she kissed the dagger's hilt, whispering, "We have a deal."

Farley sagged when Hadwin strode around the side of the bakery, his hand firmly clamped around Chelle's upper arm. Lyall hardly spared her a glance but demanded, "Who is she?"

"Nobody!" Farley exclaimed.

"Then no one will weep if I make this her gravestone," he sneered, indicating the upended stair.

Quickly backpedaling, he hung his head. "Please, sir. Don't hurt her."

"Well?" growled Lyall.

Hadwin replied, "She's betrothed to one of the Meadowsweets."

Lyall rubbed his chin. "So she *is* connected to that man."

"Aye. He would count her as kin."

Farley struggled against his bonds, fists clenching as he watched Chelle tremble in Hadwin's grasp. She lifted her hand beseechingly, tearily quavering, "F-farley?"

The older Pred grunted. "And this one?"

"A Meadowsweet, but the wrong one," Hadwin confirmed. "A brother."

"Close enough to cut," Lyall declared. "Lock them both in the carriage."

Hadwin arched his brows at Farley. "Come, pet."

His tone put the Flox's teeth on edge, but he mumbled a docile, "Yessir." Stumbling as he got to his feet, he shuffled over, and once his back was to Lyall, he let the man see his fury. "What did you do to Chelle?"

With a superior smile, Hadwin ignored the question. He ushered Chelle to the carriage and handed her in before sweetly repeating, "Come, pet."

Farley followed, hissing, "Did you hurt her?"

Hadwin roughly grabbed him by belt and collar, hoisting him off the ground. "Your concern comes rather late, considering *you* led your enemy directly to her doorstep." Farley flinched, and Hadwin tossed him through the carriage door, slamming it shut and snapping the lock into place.

Farley landed heavily and lay still, too ashamed to face Chelle. In his haste to protect his family, he'd betrayed someone precious. Trading places with his brother might have played off as noble, but Tupper wouldn't thank him for dragging Chelle into danger.

"I am such an idiot," he moaned.

Chelle touched his shoulder. "Farley? Are you hurt?"

He laughed bitterly. *Everything* hurt—inside and out.

"Sit up so I can see," she ordered.

Farley let her help him up, then knelt with eyes downcast as Chelle's hands fluttered everywhere, touching each bruise and bloodstain, counting each scratch and scrape. "It's not as bad as it looks," he mumbled.

"If that was an apology or a lie, save your breath," she said crisply. "If it was the beginning of an explanation, slow down so I can follow."

Blinking in surprise, he looked up. Instead of a pale and quaking prisoner, he was met by grim determination. Chelle's courage redoubled his shame. "Sorry," he mouthed. "I'm so sorry."

She rolled her eyes. "Farley, I need to understand what's happening. And you're the only one who can tell me." Chelle dipped into her apron pocket and brought out a small dagger he recognized as one of Ulrica's. "Those Pred look related. Is there some kind of family feud I should know about?"

Farley nodded, impressed that she'd sorted that much out already.

"Turn around. I'll cut you loose."

A moment later, he rubbed gratefully at his wrists, then gestured for paper.

Chelle shook her head. Slipping to his side, she offered her hand and whispered, "You'll have to spell it out for me."

By the time Hadwin reentered the carriage, Chelle and Farley had developed a shorthand that combined gestures, guesses, and letters. The Pred didn't remark on his lack of bonds, and as the team hauled them into motion, he draped himself across the bench, closed his eyes, and feigned sleep.

Chelle looked up into Farley's face and whispered, "You trust him?"

He held up thumb and forefinger. A little.

With a small smile, she said, "He trusts you."

Farley's brow furrowed. Since when?

She held up the dagger, brows arching.

He smirked. Point taken. Chelle's quick wits and calm approach to their crisis definitely added to his advantages. Her accessories didn't hurt either. With his finger, he picked up where he'd left off. B - E - A - D - S, he spelled. Making the sign for Tupper, he added, C - A - L - L - I - N - G.

"He can hear them?"

Farley nodded. His brother's picks were dazzling. Every stone vibrated with love and concern for Chelle, and he was certain Tupper would be able to hear their chorus. But only if they were within range. An advantage that they were losing fast.

The horses had picked up considerable speed … away from Morven. Crawling to the window, Farley checked the position of the sun. They were on the eastern road, bound for foreign territories. "Are we going to camp out of reach again?" he asked.

Hadwin didn't open his eyes. "What makes you think we're stopping?"

Although he'd always wanted to make the journey to the Drom capital, Farley doubted it was their destination. "The old guy won't leave without your mom. And she won't leave."

In sulky tones, Hadwin retorted, "If you know all the answers, don't bother me with questions."

The sun was setting when Lyall called out to the team, and they slowed to a standstill. Hadwin rose smoothly from his seat, pulled a bundle from under it, and turned to Chelle with hand outstretched.

Without batting an eye, she surrendered her small weapon.

Hadwin studied it without expression, then slipped it into his belt. "Bring the lantern, pet," he ordered, exiting.

Farley muttered a few rude remarks as he unhooked it, then traded a look with Chelle.

She whispered, "I hope they let me, umm ... take a break."

He nodded, a silent promise to make sure Hadwin allowed her some privacy.

Outside, Farley scanned their surroundings. They stood on a small rise, and to the east lay a wide, empty plain, so different from the green hills at their backs. This land was stark by contrast, and its very strangeness piqued his curiosity. Could he explore? What would he find? He wanted to ask so many questions, if only Torio was here.

At a sudden *creak*, Farley turned as Lyall dropped lightly to the ground. With a sharp command, the Pred slapped the lead stallion, sending the empty carriage on down the road.

Oh. Oh, no.

Feigning confusion, Farley ducked his head when Lyall strode over and snatched the lantern from his grasp. When the big man stepped off the road, the Flox looked to Hadwin, who indicated they should follow. Farley put his arm protectively around Chelle's shoulders, and she gamely supported him as they struck out at an angle across scrub-covered countryside. Before long, they hit upon an overgrown cart track that dipped down behind the rise, putting them out of sight of the main road.

Chelle pointed, whispering, "There's a house."

The term was generous, for the shelter was little more than a shed. A tarp-covered cart stood in its shadow, and Farley could make out a well and animal trough. His sense of foreboding grew when Lyall shouldered his way through its door as if he owned the place and was greeted by the nickers of at least two horses.

Hadwin was right. Lyall had planned ahead.

The younger Pred crossed to the cart—a humble affair that had probably been bought off a local farmer. Lifting one corner of its covering, he revealed a mound of straw and blandly said, "Sleep tight."

"Guess it's better than being tied to the wheel."

"Oh, you will be," Hadwin assured. "And if you try to run, he'll kill you."

Farley's jaw clenched. "Can't run. Can't hardly stand."

"That's the general idea," his captor drawled.

With a sigh, he said, "My sister needs a necessary."

Hadwin rummaged in the cart and came up with a length of rope, then wiggled his fingers toward the surrounding wilderness. "Do what must be done, but don't dawdle. I need to hunt."

"Will you feed us?"

"Perhaps. If you tend to the horses again."

Farley glanced at the well, which boasted nothing more than a rope and bucket. Filling the trough would take some doing, but he'd comply if that's what it took to put food in their bellies. Squaring his shoulders, he said, "Agreed."

"If they're following the carriage, they're going to miss us," Chelle whispered.

Farley pushed at a piece of straw poking the back of his neck. Another blanket would have been good, but he supposed he should be grateful Hadwin had given them anything. With one finger, he slowly traced letters onto Chelle's palm. Even in the dark, she could interpret them if he went slow enough. D - E - C - O - Y.

"I was afraid of that," she sighed. "The Harrows can't sense my beads. And I can't hear Morven anymore, which probably means she can't find me, either."

F – A – R.

"Too far." She edged closer, muttering, "And too cold."

D – E – S – E – R – T.

"I know," she replied. "I've never been this close to Drom before. One of the books Mister Harrow gave me was about this part of the continent. The further you go, the more barren it'll be. All sand." Scooting a little closer, she whined, "Does it get this cold on top of Morven?"

The tarp helped a little, but Chelle was right. And it would probably only get colder. S – H – A – R – E, he offered.

"If you don't mind?"

He could feel his face heating as he slowly spelled, S – I – S – T – E – R.

"And you're my brother." Chelle laughed softly and lifted the corner of her blanket. "I wonder if this is how Tupper felt when he had to deliver Hanley?"

S – O – R – R – Y.

"You know, you remind me of him more than usual today," she said in teasing tones. "All these one-word responses aren't like you."

Two beds became one. He pulled straw around them, and she fussed with the blanket. When they finally settled down again, Chelle lay with her upraised palm between them so they could still talk. Which is exactly what he did. Casting aside their shorthand, Farley spelled out whole sentences, tattling tales. Tupper's embarrassing moments. Torio's farflung adventures. His own plans for the future. She laughed and listened, asked questions and offered opinions. Nestor slithered out of hiding, and Farley boasted about the snake's ability to stay awake by day or night, like redstone.

Their nest grew warm, and her voice lisped sleepily. When they finally drifted off, Farley held tightly to his sister's hand.

27

Shaken to the Core

Ewert left the knot of uneasy Flox gathered in front of Pennyflax & Quince. "Tupp! I was about to make the climb." Nodding to his brother's companions, he solemnly greeted, "Master Freydolf. Mister Harrow."

"What happened?" Frey asked.

Ewert kept it short. "Two Pred arrived by carriage. Farley was with them. They didn't stay long, and when they left, they took Chelle."

Freydolf's bushy brows drew together, and he glanced worriedly at the young man sticking close to his side. When they'd spotted the eastbound carriage from the top of the trail earlier, Tupper had emptied his stomach, and he'd been quieter than usual ever since.

"You knew?" he asked.

"Yes."

The lad started to step forward, hesitated, then gazed toward the east. If anything, Tupper seemed perplexed. Freydolf suspected that things were happening too fast, and the lad couldn't keep up.

"Are you with me?" he asked, wrapping his arm around slender shoulders.

Tupper gazed up at him and gravely said, "Always."

"Where's Chelle?"

"With Farley. And too far."

"Of all the petty …! Frey, come look at this!" Aurelius exclaimed in tones that had a few of the men backing away.

The merchant immediately held up his hands in a peaceable manner. "Don't leave on my account, gentlemen. Indeed, I'd appreciate your telling me what you saw and heard." Gazing from face to face, he smoothly revealed, "You see, I recently swore to protect Miss Tremont. So I'll be going after her."

In a trice, Hayward's men recalled that *this* Pred was their friend, and Freydolf was gratified to see Aurelius's elevation in status to defender of the people. Despite the gravity of their situation, the Keeper smiled to himself. What was next—local hero? If Aurelius could save the day, Frey would be the first to sing his praises.

Tupper broke away, threading through the village men toward the bakery.

Freydolf followed more slowly, already certain what awaited. Pennyflax & Quince's front step lay in three sections, its intricately carved surfaces irreparably marred. Lyall Rakefang had set himself against his son, treating the sculptor's handiwork like a personal insult. Its destruction was a shaming, for he hadn't considered the threshold worthy of carrying off.

Senseless destruction. Calculated cruelty.

Freydolf's heart trembled at the knowledge that Farley and Chelle were at his mercy.

"Why?"

The sculptor knelt beside Tupper, murmuring, "Why what, lambkin?"

He patted the stone, dismay stark on his face. "I can't hear him. He's silent."

"Aye," Freydolf acknowledged. "A stone can withstand chips and cracks, weathering and wear. But a break means the end. The magic fades."

Tupper's hand began to shake. "Stones die? Statues, too?"

"In a way." This had never come up before, and he tried to

think how to explain. "When I work with a stone, it takes on a life of its own. If something like *this* happens ... aye, it's possible for guardians to die."

"And mountains?"

"When Torio carried off Dessa, the rest of her mountain grew dull. In a sense, it died, but she lives on."

Tupper continued his sorrowful patting of the broken step. In a low voice, he asked, "What if Thrall's egg was broken?"

Freydolf couldn't bring himself to put the consequences to words. He simply shook his head.

Clutching the sleeve of the sculptor's red tunic, Tupper tugged urgently. "Does he know?"

"Who? My father?" he asked incredulously.

Aurelius loomed over them, his expression fierce. "The sprat has a point, Frey. If Lyall Rakefang wants you dead, he'll simply carve out your heart. But if he wants you to suffer first, he'll strike hers."

Freydolf had no trouble tracking down his sister, nor in getting past her Basq guardian. Ulrica stood perfectly still in the hushed bedroom where Quintrell slept. Aggie sat on a stool in the corner, minding the candle that served as the little boy's nightlight. Zev, her stone daytime guardian, was still at her feet, but little Near patrolled the room's perimeter. Although the Flox girl's bearing betrayed her attentiveness, she held her peace. Frey was impressed by her devotion to Aurelius and Ulrica. Aggie was truly their daughter, and that made Farley kin.

Clad in snug hunting attire, with her thick hair wound into a knot atop her head—Ulrica was ready for what lay ahead, yet she lingered at home. Freydolf couldn't blame her for clinging to peace. But neither could he take her place in the hunt. "Ulrica, it's time."

She replied in low tones. "I'll protect my son."

"Which one?"

His sister turned, and the golden droplets at her ears swayed, catching the inconstant light of the flame that glinted across her dark eyes. Skirting the question, she declared, "If I fail, you'll raise Quinny."

"Your family would protest—Harrows and Rakefangs alike."

"He's too much like you to survive elsewhere," she replied. Leaning over the boy's bed, she touched his silky hair. "My gentle-hearted son needs his gentle-hearted uncle. I'll trust him with no other."

The man rubbed awkwardly at the back of his neck. "I'd make a terrible mother."

"Leave that part to Tupper. He mothers beautifully."

Aggie giggled softly, bringing a faint smile to Ulrica's face. Just then, her small son stirred and mumbled, "Mama?" Wide eyes blinked, and Quintrell asked, "You going hunting? Can I come?"

"Nay. Mind your Unca Doff while I'm away."

The boy smiled sweetly at Freydolf, then asked, "What will you catch?"

"If Mother prevails, she will bring you a brother," Ulrica replied in lofty tones.

Quintrell gasped, "Baby?"

Freydolf chuckled. Ever since Hanley's birth, Quintrell had been hinting that he wanted a sibling of his own. Ulrica huffed. "Nay, a *big* brother."

His head tipped to one side, considering. "Which one?"

To Frey's surprise, his sister answered, "Hadwin is nearly within my grasp."

"Winny, who likes blue?" Quintrell asked.

"Aye, the very one."

The Keeper hadn't realized Quin even *knew* he had brothers in the capital, let alone their pet names and quirks. It was just like Ulrica to teach her baby about them. Her love for her sons ran deep. Leaving them behind must have cut her more keenly than she ever let on.

Quintrell squirmed happily. "Hurry, Mama. I want to show Winny my kitties."

Ulrica bent to kiss his forehead, then strode out of the room without a backward glance.

Freydolf started to follow, but paused to nod to Aggie. The girl touched her heart and sent him off with a smile.

Once Aurelius was sure of Ilam's gait, he checked to see how his wife fared. Ulrica moved easily with her enormous steed, graceful as ever. Catching his gaze, her lips curved, and the run became a race. Two red hounds bounded across an empty plain with only the moon as witness.

Headlong wasn't Aurelius's style, but Ulrica had a talent for driving him to unusual lengths.

The winds they stirred rushed past his ears and teased at his topknot as he leaned down to offer some encouraging words in Terse. The red hound leapt ahead of his brother, taking the lead in their hunt. If they were going to meet Lyall Rakefang in this barren wilderness, Aurelius meant to get there first.

Ulrica had flown in the face of tradition to bear his name. Tonight, Aurelius would remind her that she'd been correct to place her trust in him the day they met ... the day they wed ... and until the day they died.

Something flickered on the road to the west, and a silent watcher drew his cloak more tightly around his shoulders. In this empty place, the stars blazed and the moon cast shadows deep enough to hide in. Not that he was in danger of discovery. His parents were moving too fast.

Hadwin watched in awe as the two hounds that normally stood guard over the Apprentice Gate rushed past in a silent gale that stirred his hair. Pride stirred in his heart, for this twist would undoubtedly hamper his grandsire's plan. The hunters would overtake the carriage much sooner than expected.

Pondering the consequences of his father's bold move, Hadwin rose slowly, dusted off his breeches, and ran lightly along the edge of the rise before dropping onto the trail it hid. Hadwin stole softly into the shed where Lyall passed the time, poring idly over his books.

Without glancing up, he asked, "Well?"

"They've passed by."

"Good," he grunted. "Go."

With a deferential nod, Hadwin crossed to the nearest stable, held out his hand to one of the horses already standing in harness, and led her outside to hitch to the cart.

Chelle woke with a start, more than a little confused. The smell of straw filled her nose, and someone was holding her hand. "Tupper?" Her companion pinched her arm, and Chelle's head cleared. "Sorry, Farley. What's going on?"

He turned and lifted edge of the tarp, letting in a rush of chilly air. After a quick reconnoiter, he reached for her hand and spelled out, M – I – D – N – I – G – H – T.

"It's only been an hour or two?" she murmured. "Are they taking us to Drom after all?"

Farley shrugged and shook his head. S – L – E – E – P, he urged, trying to get comfortable again.

Under the circumstances, there wasn't much else they could

do. She closed her eyes and tried to relax through the irregular bump and sway of the cart's steady progress. All the while, her mind reeled through the scanty hints she'd been given to the bigger plan underway. Why were they on the move again? Where were they going? What would happen to her and Farley when they arrived?

Just as she was drifting off, Chelle woke with another start and grabbed for her companion, getting a fistful of Farley's shirtfront.

He must have been asleep, because it took a moment for him to fumble for her hand, and his letters were sloppy. S - T - I - L - L / H - E - R - E, he assured, giving her hand a pat.

Chelle pinched his arm and urgently whispered, "We're going *west*. We're getting closer to home!"

H - O - W / K - N - O - W, Farley asked.

"Morven just told me so."

Tupper sat on an outcropping of stone beyond the Apprentice Gate, his feet tucked up and his chin on his knees as he gazed steadily at the eastern road. Aurelius had promised to return by sun-up so the red hounds wouldn't cause a panic in any of the villages, but the Harrows were late.

As soon as dawn broke, Tupper was able to see much farther, and his heart leapt because there *was* someone on the road. In the distance, an old horse plodded along, pulling an ordinary farm cart. Since nothing else was moving, they held his whole attention. A brown nag. A cloaked driver. A tarp-covered load. They were unremarkable, except for the earliness of the hour ... and the faintest of whispers. His eyes narrowed in concentration.

"Did you sleep, young master?"

Tearing his gaze from the oncoming traveler, Tupper shook

his head. "No."

Torio sat beside him, his keen eyes fixed on the horizon. "I don't like waiting. What's taking Harrow?"

Tupper could feel the concern underlying the Grif's complaint. "Do you want to go down to meet them?"

"Can't," he groused. "It would only distress Dessa."

"Morven clings to Frey, but she'd let me go. With Graven."

Torio leaned to one side for a better look at the tiger sprawled across one of the ledges behind them, his pink nose pointed toward the rising sun. "A formidable guardian," the Grif murmured. "If ... *when* Farley returns, I'll see that he's similarly protected."

"Yes. Chelle, too."

Suddenly, Torio pointed east. "*There*! Isn't that them now?"

A smudge on the horizon quickly resolved into two figures raising a cloud of dust as they hurled through the foothills.

"Yes," Tupper breathed, his attention swinging back to the farmer's cart. Would the man be frightened when the hounds overtook him? Could Aurelius steer around to avoid being seen?

In halting tones, Torio asked, "Do you see anyone?"

Tupper thought the question odd until he realized what the Grif meant. Itak and Ilam were riderless.

Without Tupper there to press him into eating, Freydolf hardly touched his breakfast. Instead, he sat kneading his hands together, casting mournful glances between Carden and Melina. The woman finally rounded the table and placed her hand on his shoulder. "What is it you're afraid to say?"

The Keeper's shoulders hunched. "I hate to ask."

She glanced at her husband, who smiled sympathetically. "I was under the impression that apprentices live at their master's beck and call."

"Aye, but under these circumstances." Freydolf shook his head. "I don't want anyone else to be hurt."

"What can we do to help you keep everyone safe?" Melina prompted.

When the sculptor hesitated, Carden spread his hands wide. "We share your concerns. Tell us what you want."

"I want Hayward protected," Frey confessed. "But the kind of protection I can offer may frighten the villagers more than the real danger."

"Statues?" Carden guessed. "You want to send stone guardians."

"Aye. Tupper hand-picked those he wants protecting your village, and he could escort them into place, but people think him odd." With an apologetic glance at Melina, Freydolf said, "I think our neighbors would respond more favorably to your husband. Will you forgive me for sending him from your side?"

She shook her head and said, "From my side and to his mother's, his brother's, and to all of my family's aid? On the contrary, Master Freydolf. I'll *thank* you for lending support to every Flox in Hayward."

"Every village in the vicinity should be graced by a guardian or three." Carden rose from his seat. "But for today, let's take care of the immediate need. Which guardians did Tupp pick, and are they ready to travel now, or do we need to wait for nightfall?"

"They're waiting outside," Frey admitted sheepishly.

Melina laughed. "You *knew* we'd agree."

"I hoped."

Carden crossed to the door and chuckled. "Tupp knows what he's about. I wish the people of Hayward could see this."

Freydolf and Melina joined him in watching the Statuary's youngsters clambering up, over, and around four imposing Clow torch-bearers. One brute of a warrior cradled Arni in the crook of his arm, head tilted so the boy could pet his ear. Quintrell held hands with another. Aggie was introducing Hanley to a third, while her sunstone wolf cub frisked around their ankles. Dulcie sat in the lap of the fourth redstone statue, who was the picture of patience as she chattered nonstop about her dawnstone bunny. His big, clawed hand lightly tousled her fair curls.

Master Tremont's personal guard would defend the gentle folk their creator had loved with all his heart.

Tupper wasn't sure. He *hoped* he was right, but maybe his wishes were getting in the way of what was real. Finally, Morven's voice stirred against his soul in a playful glissade. *"She also longs for you."*

Grabbing Torio's arm, Tupper blurted, "The cart's too early, and the driver's strange. Wouldn't you be afraid of the hounds? A Flox would be."

The Grif frowned. "What are you trying to say, young master?"

Pointing urgently at the traveler Itak and Ilam had left in the dust on their mad dash for home, Tupper exclaimed, "They ignored each other! They *knew* each other!"

"I see what you mean. Very suspicious," Torio mused. Stiffening, he repeated, "I *see* what you mean."

"I can hear them. It's not my imagination?"

"No," the Grif assured. "The magic's there. His *and* hers."

Farley and Chelle were in that cart. Or at the very least, Nestor and Chelle's betrothal gift were. In Tupper's heart of hearts, Morven asked, *"Are you her Keeper?"*

His eyes fixed on the driver who was bringing his loved ones back into reach, he whispered, "Yes."

"Then answer her call."

28

Approach

Farley stole enough peeks from under the edges of the tarp to determine that the Pred was once more approaching Morven. Which was crazy. While it was true that the gray mountain posed a greater threat under the light of the moon, she was by no means unprotected by day. Farley knew dozens of statues who could be mobilized to defend the Statuary. Skirting the mountain was begging for trouble.

"Fine by me," he muttered, petting Nestor with his finger.

Chelle tugged at Farley's sleeve, and he reluctantly gave up his peep hole. Patience wasn't one of his better qualities, but it wasn't her fault that she couldn't hear. Searching her face, he admitted, "It'd drive me crazy to have to wait for people to clue me in." Her mouth thinned, and he grinned unrepentantly. "Guess it bugs you, too. Sorry, sis."

She thrust her hand out. "Can you tell where we are?"

Farley nodded. **S - E.** Using one fist to indicate the mountain, he drew a line with his opposite finger, describing their route thus far, narrating even though she couldn't hear him. "Came in from the east. This is Hayward. We musta drove right on through town, cause we're all the way here now."

"Southeast." She nodded, her eyes fixed on his makeshift map. "Isn't this the way to the quarry?"

Moving his finger around the front of his fist, he showed her where the quarry was situated in the western foothills.

"When I visited, we took a road from there to the top of Morven. Is that where we're headed?"

Farley shrugged, then nodded, then shrugged again.

"Two out of three?" she asked, amusement barely trumping her understandable frustration. "Why did they take us so far into the east, only to drive right back? Don't they realize Tupper can hear stone?"

"I sure didn't tell 'em," he replied, shaking his head.

"So we might be rescued soon?"

Nodding, Farley muttered, "Even if they don't rush for my sake, Tupp won't leave you in the lurch. Him and his tiger are probably halfway down the mountain by now."

She scowled, and he took her hand. G - R - A - V - E - N. Holding his fist up, he let it fall, describing a swift descent from on high.

"You're right. Should we warn Hadwin?"

Farley's eyebrows shot up. T - R - A - I - T - O - R.

Just then, the cart rambled to a standstill, and they edged closer together. At the faint sound of a blade being drawn from its sheath, Farley quickly shielded Chelle with his body. Bright sunlight half-blinded the Flox when Hadwin threw back the tarp covering their nest. The Pred draped his arms on the cart's edge and drawled, "I cut the ropes. You can come out now. Or was I interrupting something?"

Slowly sitting up and reaching for the rope at his ankle, Farley tugged, and the end came free from its mooring. Chelle followed suit. She'd also been cut loose.

Hadwin beckoned to her with both hands, saying, "We're leaving the cart. There's water uphill from here."

"Yeah, I know," Farley muttered, taking a long look around. A light brown mare had been traded for the fine stallions, and Lyall was nowhere to be seen. Pointedly placing himself between Hadwin and Chelle, he helped the young woman climb down before demanding, "Why are we here?"

"This way."

Farley would have turned heel and walked off in the opposite direction, but Chelle took his arm and followed the Pred into the underbrush. Several minutes' climb brought them to one of the many shallow grottoes that dotted Morven's slopes. This one was deep enough to be cool despite its southern exposure, and a trickle of water echoed from the shadows.

Hadwin waved at the recess. "Make sure she drinks something. I'm going to stretch my legs."

With a sigh, Farley spelled W - A - T - E - R into Chelle's hand and pointed.

"Yes, please," she replied, heading toward refreshment.

They drank from cupped hands, and Farley perked up enough to suggest, R - U - N.

"No," she replied evenly. Pulling a handkerchief from her apron pocket, she rinsed it out and tugged him toward better light. "Let's clean you up."

He grimaced. This was so stupid. They should go while they had the chance. All the while she dabbed at his cuts and bruises, he tried to argue. C - L - O - S - E, he pleaded. H - O - M - E.

"We're safe with Hadwin, but he won't be safe without us," she reasoned.

They were staying for *his* sake?

Hadwin strolled out of the woods. "Bickering like siblings, or is this a lovers' quarrel? Can it be you're distressed that she's chosen me? You can hardly fault her."

"Don't mistake pity for preference," Farley grumbled, batting away Chelle's cool cloth. "Now why are we here?"

"I have fond memories of this spot," he replied. "And this is as good a place as any to get rid of you."

Farley's brow furrowed. "I won't let you hurt her."

"Then she's *quite* safe, since I won't allow *anyone* to hurt her."

"Since when?" he asked suspiciously.

Hadwin clammed up, and Farley made a grab for Chelle's hand. W - H - A - T / D - I - D / Y - O - U / D - O, he demanded, pointing at the Pred.

Chelle smiled. "Is he teasing you? You're acting just like

Misters Harrow and Kite."

He gaped at her. Unjust!

"And I didn't *do* anything," she continued. "I simply accepted his offer of protection."

Farley's gaze swung to Hadwin, whose expression had soured considerably. "Aye. Unintentionally. I'd like to know how she knew what to do to seal the pact. And my fate with it."

The boy sat a little straighter. Pointing at Chelle, he spelled out, T – R – I – C – K – E – D / H – I – M.

"Let's call it a good bargain," she demurred. "So long as Mister Hadwin is a man of his word, I have nothing to fear from any quarter."

"Oh, she's good," Farley decreed, grinning broadly.

Sidling over, Hadwin laid claim to Chelle's other hand. H – O – W, he asked, tapping the hilt of his weapon.

"How did I know about kissing the dagger?" Chelle checked. At the Pred's short nod, she softly answered, "Because two days ago, Quintrell Harrow made me the same oath. Actually, so did his father."

Farley whistled between his teeth. "Is your dad gonna be more upset that you were hoodwinked by a girl, or that you kidnapped the girl he swore to protect."

Hadwin tensed, easing away from Chelle. "This entire debacle grows worse by the minute."

Out of the corner of his eye, Farley caught a familiar swirl of magic and turned in time to see Torio spring at their captor. Hadwin smoothly sidestepped the initial lunge, daggers already in hand.

"Run!" the Grif snapped. "Farley, get Chelle out of here!"

At the same time, Chelle exclaimed, "Don't fight! Farley, make them stop!"

"Hadwin, look out!" Farley warned as an enormous tiger crashed onto the scene, fangs bared and tail whipping the air. To everyone's surprise, Graven thrust his big head between the two men, snapping at Torio. The Grif lifted his hands and slowly backed off.

Winding his tail around Hadwin's waist, the tiger pulled

him snugly against his chest. Sitting on his haunches, Graven peered expectantly over his prisoner's head into the woods.

Farley tutted and hollered, "Get a move on, Tupp! We're over here!"

The young man stepped out of the forest and calmly crossed to the tiger, gazing up into Hadwin's face. "Hello, I'm Tupper Meadowsweet."

"Aye."

"Are you Winny?"

"Hadwin Rakefang," he haughtily corrected.

Tupper nodded as he systematically disarmed the Pred, removing all the blades from their various sheathes, letting them drop at the Pred's feet. He held onto the last one, the tiny dagger Ulrica had given to Chelle. Soft and stern, he asked, "Are you our enemy?"

"Nay."

"Then why did you fight Torio?"

Golden eyes rolled. "As if I'd let some Grif preen over cornering me. I was defending myself."

"Graven doesn't want me to hurt you," Tupper announced.

Hadwin looked down his nose at the Flox. "Do *you* want to hurt me?"

"Only as much as you hurt my brother."

He sniffed. "I don't have a horn for you to carve off."

"I meant Frey."

The Pred flinched.

Tupper nodded again, then asked, "Why is my guardian protecting you?"

"I was four the last time we took a family trip to Uncle Frey's home in the wilderness." Hadwin sulkily admitted, "Since I kept wandering off, my uncle made me Graven's responsibility."

"Oh. That makes sense."

Torio stepped forward, taking over the questioning. "Why did you bring these children here?"

"My grandsire expressed a desire that I leave them where my uncle could find them. I have succeeded."

"I'm pretty sure the old guy meant for us to be dead," Farley interjected.

Hadwin smirked. "Since he didn't specify, I took considerable license with my interpretation of his wishes."

"So you're *not* our enemy? Tupper repeated.

"Nay."

Farley could hardly believe his brother was going to let it go at that. This man had hunted him down, humiliated him, and hurt him in ways he didn't want to admit. There should be comeuppance! Fury roiled in his belly, and Nestor responded. The small, black snake dropped noiselessly to the ground, quickly slithering over to where Hadwin stood and spiraling up his right boot. Moments later, the man jerked and swore, for Nestor had buried his fangs into his thigh.

Tupper crouched to retrieve the little guardian, unintentionally providing a ramp for Rimbles, who launched herself into the Pred's face. By the time Tupper caught her and calmed her down, four claw marks scored Hadwin's cheek.

Chelle rushed forward to press her cold cloth to his face, and Farley snorted. Tupper was more upset than he let on. Deep down, he was angry.

Farley said, "Guess that counts for revenge. Right, *Winny*?"

"A light penalty under the circumstances, *pet*."

Was that an apology? It felt like one. Maybe. "Tupp might let you off easy, but your mom won't."

"Aye."

He retrieved Nestor and boasted, "Y'know, Tupp's a good guy, but I'm great."

"Lofty claims from lowly creatures," scoffed the Pred.

Farley knew a fencepost when he was standing on it, and he decided which way to jump. He put a challenge in his tone. "For instance, you'll want to be on Tupp's good side. He's totally got your mom by the fangs. He could keep you alive long enough to grovel for her forgiveness."

Hadwin's eyes narrowed. "I fail to see how this demonstrates any superiority on your part."

Folding his arms over his chest, Farley asked, "Say, Tupp.

You still got Ulrica's dagger there?"

"Yes."

"Hold it out hilt-first to Hadwin."

Without hesitation, Tupper obliged. When Hadwin kissed it, gray-green eyes blinked. "What was that for?"

Chelle chimed in as if on cue. "That's the same promise Hadwin made to me. Now, you're his defense."

Farley tapped his toe while waiting for the facts to filter through his brother's thick skull. Finally, Tupper asked, "Hadwin, did you keep Chelle safe?"

"Aye. With your brother's help."

"Thank you." Turning to his betrothed, Tupper began plucking straw out of her hair. "Does anyone have paper?"

Sauntering over, Farley took Chelle's hand and traced four letters onto her palm. S - L - O - W. With a thin smile, he asked Tupper, "How's your spelling?"

"Good idea," he murmured, reaching out with hands that had begun to tremble. Everyone watched to see what the young man would say, but he simply smoothed his fingers over her palm for several long moments. Farley figured that Chelle was out of luck, but then Tupper gave up trying to find words and placed a soft kiss on her palm.

If Chelle's expression was anything to go by, Tupper wasn't just good or great; he was a genius.

At that point, Torio took Farley by the shoulders, turning him around to study his face. The boy grumbled, "If you try to kiss me, I quit."

The Grif's eyebrows arched. "You need not fear for your virtue, such as it is."

A flush crept into Farley's cheeks. "I didn't really ...."

"Your race is vastly more demonstrative than my own," Torio interrupted. "Fortunately for you, Carden coached me on the proper techniques to comfort you after rescuing you from your tormentors. All seven steps."

"You're *kidding*."

"Naturally."

"I quit."

Torio laughed and pulled him close. "Then your virtue is forfeit."

Farley held on desperately despite his protestations. Torio had come for him, would have fought for him, and was teasing him just like always. Things could go back to normal now. Scrunching shut his eyes, Farley did his level best to keep himself together.

But the contrary man made good on his threat, kissing the top of his head and whispering, "You saved your brother's life. You kept your sister safe. You brought us Harrow's son. Impressive feats."

His chin wobbled. "Glad *somebody* noticed."

"You're a fine young man, Farley Meadowsweet. If today brings an end to your employment, then I'd be proud to call you my friend."

"How much do friends get paid?"

"Precious little," Torio promised.

Farley went for a snort, but it came out as more of a snuffle. "Guess I'll keep milkin' the cow, then."

"Suit yourself," his master replied.

"While I envy you all your easy reunions, I have my own to survive," Hadwin called. "Did my father send back word with the hounds?"

Torio and Tupper exchanged a long look. "You saw Itak and Ilam?"

Hadwin inclined his head. "Hard to miss—coming and going."

The Grif rubbed his nose. "We're not entirely sure what happened. Your parents set out late last night and didn't return. Freydolf fears this means they were embroiled in a confrontation with your grandfather."

"Nay. My father must have reached the carriage and realized it was a diversion. He sent the hounds back to protect the mountain."

"Alone?"

"They are swiftest without riders," Hadwin replied with a shrug.

"Yes. That's true," Tupper confirmed.

"If the old guy didn't go after Aurelius, where is he?" Farley asked, already dreading the answer.

Tupper looked toward the mountaintop. "Is he coming?"

Hadwin's brow quirked. "That's entirely too optimistic."

Farley knew what the tidings must be. "Lyall Rakefang isn't *coming*. He's already here."

Freydolf stood under the wide arch of the Apprentice Gate, turning over a blade so dark, it was nearly black. His father's gift. At the time, the dagger was too big to be practical, but Lyall Rakefang had promised that his son would grow into it. Grand hopes. Bitter disappointments. Frey showed Brand the blade's bent tip. "The last time I used this, I was putting in a mosaic floor. Aurelius caught me and pretended to be horrified that I'd abuse a family heirloom. Later, he asked me why I kept it at all."

Brand held out his hand, took the dagger, weighed it in his hand, then offered it back.

"It should have been stripped from me when I was banished, but I hid it. When Father didn't demand it back, I thought maybe ...." Frey trailed off. "He must have forgotten about it. I wish he'd forgotten about me."

The fire-bearer touched the Keeper's shoulder, a sympathetic expression on his face.

"Unca Doff!" called Quintrell, running lightly over the cobbles in the inner courtyard.

Frey scooped him up, giving him a playful toss. "You're supposed to be helping Missus Melina," he chided.

"Mama said *you* take care of me," the little boy reminded.

"Aye, she did. Does anyone know you're here?"

Quintrell snuggled close. "Nuh-uh. I was loosive."

Chuckling, Freydolf asked, "Aren't you a little young for such big words?"

"Papa *likes* a formible vocablurry."

"He does at that."

"Whatcha doin'?"

The switch to Farley-esque turn of phrase brought a shine to the Keeper's dark eyes. "Talking to you."

"Before that?"

"Talking to Brand."

Quin twisted around and wiggled his fingers at the fire-bearer until the statue offered his hand. With great solemnity, the boy pressed their palms together. "This is how Basq say *peace*."

"Aye, you're right. Did Phineas teach you that?"

Quintrell nodded. "And Mama. She 'splained it since Phin can't talk."

Freydolf offered his palm to the boy. "Do you like peace?"

"Aye." He pressed his small hand to his uncle's. "It's friendly."

"It has been," Frey agreed in a tight voice. "Will you help me, Quin?"

"Do my best," he promised.

"Good lad." Dredging up a smile, Frey said, "I'll show you how to close the gates."

They pushed and pulled at the great doors, which creaked and groaned in protest after decades of disuse. Quintrell cheered when his uncle finally slid the crossbar into place, as if this was a game, and they'd won. Small victories. Necessary precautions.

Helping the boy clamber back onto his shoulders, Freydolf strode toward the galleries, Brand close by his side. "We'd better let Missus Melina know where you are."

Partway through the inner courtyard, they were met by Haimish, whose expressive eyes were filled with fear. Tail tucking between his legs, he proffered a stone flower.

"It broke," Quintrell mourned.

Freydolf inspected the slender stem. "Show me where it happened, Haimish," he urged. "It's a clean break, so I should be able to mend it. But be more careful, please."

The brownstone Pred held up his hands, shaking his head so

vigorously that his jade earrings clicked. Pointing urgently to one side, he drew Freydolf's attention to a sculptural flower bed not more than twenty paces away.

"Oh, no," Frey breathed.

"All the pretty flowers!" his nephew wailed. "Can you fix it?"

Freydolf immediately lifted Quin down from his vulnerable perch, tucking the child protectively against his chest. Someone had methodically snapped scores of intricate stone blossoms from their stems, ruining a centuries' old display of incredible delicacy. Turning his back on the mess, the Keeper ran for the nearest entrance into the galleries.

"Are we going to get tools?" Quintrell asked softly.

"Later," Frey promised. "Right now, we need to get to Missus Melina and the others."

Before *he* does.

29

Group and Regroup

Carden talked as he walked, explaining to the four statues about his hometown and its people. "No one remembers statues or magic. All that's been handed down up until now are rumors. You'll confirm them and correct them by your behavior. Be patient. Be gentle."

The four Clow torch-bearers took his advice in stride, quite literally. Carden had difficulty keeping up with the long-legged guardians. When they suddenly stopped, he bumped into the broad back of the statue in front of him. Two of them hefted weapons. The other two shielded him with their bodies.

A Pred dropped lightly onto the trail in front of them, daggers drawn. She launched herself at the foremost statue, her blades meeting his weapon with a resounding *clang*, but he gave no ground.

"So they *can* sense an ordinary threat, not only magical ones," drawled a voice from overhead. "Serviceable, if somewhat rusty from disuse. One well-thrown dagger, and Mister Meadowsweet would be dead."

"Thank goodness," Carden breathed. "When Itak and Ilam returned without you ... well. We've been worried."

"How insulting," Ulrica murmured, prowling into the midst of the Clow. "Why did my brother fit you with an honor guard?"

"I'm going to introduce this group to the people of Hayward. Master Freydolf wants to protect the village."

Aurelius slipped up behind Carden. "Glad to see Frey's taking advantage of the situation. It's about time the valley folk met their neighbors. What else has been done?"

"Tupp spotted a farmer's cart coming out of the east. He's certain Farley and Chelle are inside, so he and Torio went after it."

"Its driver?" Ulrica asked.

"Just one. Cloaked."

She frowned. "Its speed?"

"Slow."

The Pred exchanged a speaking glance, and Aurelius surmised, "We're spread thin, leaving Frey, Melina, and the children to fend for themselves."

"We woke dozens of statues, and I wouldn't discount Aggie," Carden gently reminded.

Ulrica's fangs flashed. "Aye. Very little would get past my girl."

"Also, Master Freydolf planned to close the gate behind me. You may have trouble getting inside."

"Nay, we'll manage," Ulrica assured with a superior smile.

"Which means *he* could manage," Aurelius reminded. To Carden, he said, "Go carefully. Stay put."

"Shouldn't I return?" Carden asked in surprise.

The merchant shook his head. "Freydolf will be better served if you can put your kinsmen and neighbors at ease where these statues are concerned."

Carden turned to say something more to Ulrica, but the woman had vanished.

Aurelius waved him off. "Trust your family into our keeping. Now hurry along. I have a race to win."

Tupper waited patiently for Torio to reassure himself before approaching Farley. His younger brother bore many marks of suffering, and although he smiled in his usual carefree manner, there was a rawness in his gaze. Reaching up to touch the broken horn, Tupper said, "I gave you your first tap."

"I remember." Farley's smile had a bitter twist. "It's gone now."

"No, I saved it."

"My horn?"

"Yes."

Several emotions flitted across the younger Meadowsweet's face. "You have zero tact."

"Probably," Tupper admitted, but he didn't like the way everyone else pretended Farley's horn wasn't spoiled. Shouldn't they face it? Couldn't he take responsibility? He nodded to himself. "I want a re-do."

Farley understood right away. He was clever like that. Shuffling closer, he whispered, "If you want."

Taking his sibling by the shoulders, Tupper carefully touched the tip of his horn to the stump of his brother's, then delivering a firm tap. "Thank you, Farley," he said solemnly.

"For what? Being in the wrong place at the wrong time?"

Torio interjected, "If your kidnappers had taken Tupper beyond Morven's reach instead of you, the strain on their bond would have been too great. He would have died."

"Oh. Yeah." Farley smiled crookedly and casually retorted, "Welp, what are brothers for?"

"Backup," Tupper replied seriously.

"Say, Tupp. What did you do with my horn?"

"I put it under my pillow."

Farley snorted. "Is that where you keep Frey's fangs, too?"

Tupper smiled faintly as he reached up to finger the rough edges of the break. "I'm in your debt, brother. I'll never forget."

"Never gonna let you!"

Torio stepped to Farley's side and slipped his arm around the boy's waist. "Dessa wants you."

"Yeah?" With a sidelong glance at Hadwin, he quietly asked, "Is she in danger?"

Frowning, the Grif looked to the Pred. "How much does your grandsire know about the inner workings of a magical mountain?"

"We spent part of the winter on the white mountain, learning its mysteries. He knows how to kill a guardian, and he knows how to kill a mountain."

"Lovely thought," Torio murmured. "And how many mountains are there?"

Without missing a beat, Hadwin replied, "Twelve."

Torio smiled winsomely. "Aren't you a clever boy. Any affinity to speak of?"

"Nay."

With a sidelong look at Farley, Torio cheerfully said, "Nope."

"Still, we gotta get up there," Farley said. "Freydolf's no match for his dad."

"You're in no condition to fight," Torio countered flatly.

"I know, but *he* is." Everyone turned to see where Farley was looking.

Hadwin drew himself up, dryly inquiring, "What do you expect *me* to do?"

Farley eyed him shrewdly. "Like your dad said. Redeem yourself."

Freydolf rushed into the quarters Melina had chosen, Haimish and Brand right behind him. The woman was down on her knees with her daughters, singing one of the Flox learning songs while they scrubbed. With the windows open and fresh linens stacked on the table, everything smelled of soap and sunshine.

"Safe," Frey muttered, letting Quintrell down.

"Mish! Mish!" Yona called, scattering soap bubbles as she rushed to her guardian. Haimish picked her up and cradled her close.

"What's happened?" Aggie asked softly.

Conscious of the children, Freydolf kept his tone as even as he could. "We need to move."

Melina sat back on her heels. "I thought we were moving *here*."

The sculptor quietly said, "I barred the doors too late. We need to ... to play a game of hide-and-hunt."

"I see," the woman said evenly. "I'm sure the children would enjoy that."

Frey sighed his relief. She understood. "We'll find a good spot to hide."

"I know good places!" Dulcie cheerfully announced. "Tupper showed me!"

"Aye, we'll need the best possible one." Turning to Brand, who hovered in the doorway, Freydolf ordered, "Wake the other fire-bearers. All you can find."

Inclining his head, the redstone Grif slipped away.

"Are we going deep down?" Dulcie asked. "Is that why we need more lanterns?"

Melina searched the Pred's face. "If that's where your Uncle Doff wants to play, that's where we'll go."

"Going deeper is best for you and yours, but my retreat would leave Morven vulnerable," Frey gruffly replied. "I must protect her heart, at least until Thrall wakes at moonrise."

"That's a *long* game of hide-and-hunt," she murmured. "Aggie, we'll need food, blankets, diapers."

"I gotta go," Quintrell promptly announced, doing a little jig.

Arni joined him in squirming. "Nec'sary, please!"

Stifling a groan, Freydolf offered his hands. "I'll take you."

Melina stopped him with a hand on his arm. "No more dividing. We'll put *all* our eggs in one basket, in a manner of speaking. If Morven's Keeper must protect her heart at all costs, then that's the safest place for us."

"Aye." Freydolf bowed deeply, promising, "At all costs."

With a shuttered lantern in one hand and her dagger in the other, Ulrica led her husband through a series of winding passages. Aurelius remarked, "I wasn't aware you'd familiarized yourself with the galleries to this degree."

"Lost?"

He cleared his throat. "Slightly disoriented."

Flashing a smile over her shoulder, she sweetly said, "Try to keep up."

They passed silently from one set of galleries to the next before emerging onto one of the twelve arteries fanning out from the Statuary's central chamber. Familiar territory.

"Dapple gallery?" Aurelius ventured, touching a particularly fine pierced screen.

"Aye." Ulrica set aside the lantern and drew a second dagger. "My brother will go to the Cavern."

Slipping his arm around her waist, Aurelius asked, "Do you plan to go to him?"

"He cannot defend himself against our father," she growled. "He needs us."

"To crouch with him in a corner?" He shook his head. "Think, my dear. Frey doesn't need more defense. He needs us to turn the tides. We *must* attack."

Her expression clouded, but quickly cleared. "Aye. Can we get higher?"

"Follow me," Aurelius urged, giving her a squeeze before jogging deeper into the gallery. Two turns. A sliding panel. A spiral stair. Within moments, they crouched on a balcony overlooking the Cavern's expanse. Torches blazed at every archway, where fire-bearers stood guard, and other statues stirred—sunstone, brownstone, and even a blue. "I cannot imagine trying to slip through this crowd in order to stage an attack."

"I'd like to try," Ulrica admitted, eyes alight at the challenging prospect.

"Aye," he sighed. "Which means your sire must be equally undaunted."

A soft sound reached them, and Ulrica tensed. "That was Hanley."

Aurelius pointed to where Freydolf and Melina were shepherding the children toward Thrall. "A sensible choice," he murmured. "One with definite potential. There are five more vantages like this. I suggest we move to the second to last one, closest to the heart."

While making the transfer, they stumbled across a broken guardian, redstone head and arms hewn from his torso. Ulrica touched the battered remains of the fire-bearer's lantern, and her eyebrows arched. "Still warm."

"Quickly."

Another panel. A hidden stair. As soon as Ulrica secured the door behind them, Aurelius slipped his arms around his wife. "You're shaking."

"I'm *furious*."

He smiled. "Vent it here. I need you calm."

Resistance only lasted a moment. Blades still in her hands, she wound her arms around him and leaned her forehead upon his shoulder. Taking a deep breath, she whispered, "He used to break my brother's toys. Like that statue. Shatter them and leave them where he would find them. It was supposed to cure his *accursed* weakness."

Aurelius's cheek brushed hers. "Clearly your father has learned nothing from past failures."

With a husky laugh, Ulrica continued. "There was a cave by the seashore. My brother brought them there—his own toys, castoffs of other children, anything that caught his fancy."

"I know," Aurelius said. "He showed me. 'Twas a pitiful gallery. This one suits him better."

"Aye. It suits me as well."

They climbed the stairs and eased onto their new overlook, which afforded a glimpse into Thrall's nest of coils. "You realize what we need to do?" the man whispered.

His wife sighed. "The children. Our child. Bait for the predator who prowls below."

"And from here, we set the trap."

"Nay. One above, one below," Ulrica countered. "I'll go."

"No offense, my dear, but I'm more elusive."

"Aye, but he wants me alive. If he tries to lure me to his side, he'll be inviting death."

Aurelius frowned. "Could you do it?"

Ulrica's gaze shifted to where Quintrell and Arni huddled together next to Thrall's egg. "If necessary to save my son, aye. I will not hesitate."

He tensed, then leaned to one side. "Aggie's not with them."

"I know."

"Where could she have gone?" Aurelius asked worriedly.

Ulrica kissed her husband. "She's *my* daughter. Therefore, she's hunting."

Graven effortlessly carried his five passengers over the walls and into the Statuary's courtyard. Several guardians hurried forward as Tupper slid off the tiger's back, and he paused to greet them and thank them by turns.

After everyone else had dismounted, Farley was the first to grow impatient. "Tupp, where to?"

"This way," he replied, striking off along the cobbled road. Chelle hurried her steps to walk at his side, and he searched her face. The young woman was frightened and frazzled. She needed a safe place to rest, and taking her there was his first priority. Silently begging the frantic statues clamoring for his attention to wait, he took Chelle's arm and promised, "Not much further."

When he went straight to the workshop door, Hadwin drawled, "*This* is your hiding place?"

"Yes."

"Do you hope to hide in plain sight, freezing like rabbits when a predator approaches?"

"He won't approach if you stop him," Tupper reasoned.

"You're sending me after him?"

"Yes. Go to the Cavern."

Hadwin frowned deeply. "What makes you think I won't simply rejoin my grandsire?"

Tupper gazed at him thoughtfully. "Because you're a Harrow." Then he hustled everyone else through the workshop door and closed it in Hadwin's face.

Torio took Farley's arm and steered him over to the block of black stone. "Help me settle Dessa down. She's still anxious from the first time I went after you."

"First time?" the boy echoed.

The Grif thrust the Flox's hand against the heartstone and snapped, "See! Just like I promised. Safe, sound, and nearly in one piece."

With a soft snort, Farley leaned his forehead against the smooth column of rock. "I suppose there are worse ways to be cut in two."

Satisfied by the ebb in Dessa's frantic tones, Tupper escorted Chelle to his bed and pulled aside the curtain. He patted the high mattress, gazing expectantly into her face.

She frowned. "You're putting me to bed?"

Nodding, he cupped her cheek, running his thumb lightly over the dark smudges under her eyes. A bath would have been good, but there was no time.

"Why?" she demanded, looking hurt.

Glancing around, Tupper located paper and quickly scrawled, **You and Farley stay here. Torio will keep you both safe. And Dessa.**

"What about you?"

Frey needs me.

"Do you know how to fight?" she asked.

He shook his head.

"Then why go? What can you do?"

With a vague wave of his hands, he answered, **Start things.**

To Tupper's relief, Chelle accepted this, and he boosted her up. She sat forlornly on his quilt, but he couldn't take her with him. Folding back the covers, he waited for her to crawl under, then tucked her in. This was costing her. He could tell by the rebellion sparking in her eyes. But she trusted him, and he loved her all the more for it.

He lifted Rimbles onto the bed and begged the little guardian to stay with Chelle since he could not. His kitten butted her head against his hand and nipped at his fingers, but she curled up beside the young woman. When he reached up to pull the tapestry back into place, Chelle grabbed his arm. He hesitated, but then she wound her fingers into his long hair and tugged. He was glad to obey. The kiss lasted just long enough for Tupper to wish it could last longer. Maybe Chelle was good at starting things, too.

From across the room, Farley called, "Tupp's way too predictable. Hiding her under his pillow with the rest of his favorite things."

Tupper smiled at the notion, kissed Chelle's nose, closed the bed curtains, and hurried for the door. "Keep her safe!"

Torio doffed an imaginary hat, swept into a low bow, and grandly replied, "Fear not, young master. When you return to hearth and home, you'll doubtless find your bed both warm and welcoming."

Blushing badly, Tupper escaped.

30

Attack and Defend

Hadwin chose a roundabout route through the galleries, descending lower than he needed to go. He doubted either his parents or grandsire would range so far below the Cavern, making a torch feasible. The risks were few, but he quickly discovered that they were real. A slim dagger thudded into the thickest part of the torch he carried, knocking it from his hand. Leaping backward, he crouched in the shadow of a carved pillar.

He held his breath and listened, but the only sound came from the torch guttering on the stone floor. Whoever had robbed him of light had trapped him, for he couldn't leave without it. Not unless he was willing to fumble up four levels in pitch blackness. Though he remembered this part of the galleries from childhood meanderings, he didn't know them *that* well.

"What are you doing here?"

The soft voice sounded feminine. Childish. Easing closer to the torch, hand outstretched, Hadwin replied, "Don't mind me. I'm only passing through."

Another dagger rang off the stones a hairsbreadth from his questing hand, which he snatched back.

The voice came again, and from a different direction. "Leave it, Pred. Or I'll leave you without your fingers."

"You have good aim."

"You don't belong here," she calmly replied, this time from behind him.

Hadwin pressed his back to the pillar. "Nay, I'm within my rights. What are *you* doing here?"

Soft and sweet. "Defending my home."

She'd moved again, but the man was ready. With a quick flick, he threw his dagger at the fallen torch, sending it spinning toward his wily opponent. In a brief shower of sparks, he caught a glimpse of a slender girl with an abundance of golden curls. She moved like a Pred, but she was definitely Flox.

"I could kill you," she announced, sounding unflustered by his tactic.

"I thought the Flox were a peaceful people," Hadwin taunted.

"And I thought Pred were more formidable."

He gritted his teeth but held his temper. Adopting a patronizing air, he said, "We don't prey upon children."

"Liar."

Hadwin sighed and stood, hands upraised. In his silkiest tones, he complained, "You're making it deucedly hard to have a conversation. Come into th–"

Without warning, something hit him in the belly, and when he doubled over, it knocked him onto his back. When he finally caught his breath, he was pinned by a sunstone wolf whose paws anchored his shoulders to the floor. His ribs twinged painfully, and when he turned his head, he winced. There would be a lump.

The slim girl wrested free the dagger from his torch and sheathed it before collecting the second she'd thrown—a matched set with pale yellow jewels glittering in their hilts. Her snug hunting tunic confirmed his first suspicion. She was only a child. "Miss Meadowsweet, I presume?"

Picking up his dagger, she studied the design with some interest before crossing to where he lay. "Do you yield?"

"Aye."

"Off, Zev," she directed.

Hadwin made to rise, but the girl took her guardian's place, pushing him down and straddling his chest. She was light as a feather, and he could have thrown her off in an instant. A dagger point touched the underside of his chin, and he seethed inwardly. "It would take but an instant for me to kill you."

"Likewise."

"I'm ten times stronger than you," he grumbled.

"Yet you yielded your fangs to me," she coolly replied. "You wanted to talk, Pred. Start talking."

She had nerve. And she had him. With a gusty sigh, Hadwin said, "If I live to see another day, I shall *never* live this one down."

The girl's eyebrows arched, and he felt blood trickle down his throat

Dubiously impressed, the Pred began, "My name is Hadwin Rakefang, third son of Aurelius and Ulrica Harrow, and I surrender. *Again.*"

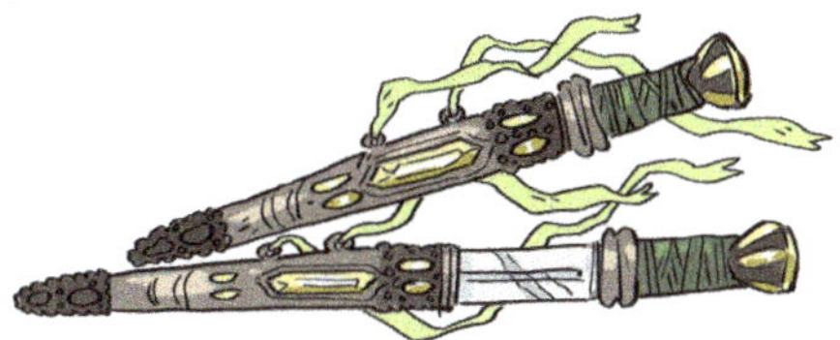

Kissing Graven's dawnstone nose, Tupper held up his finger. "One stranger. Find him. Stop him." The mosaic tiger's eyes actually widened, and no wonder. He was forever telling Graven *not* to stalk people—namely Aurelius. An invitation to hunt must have seemed a great treat. As the big cat slunk off, Tupper pondered the matter. Maybe Aggie could help him devise a game for Graven. She liked challenges.

In the six-sided chamber above the fountain colonnade, Tupper shed his boots and, with a careful series of twists, knotted his hair atop his head. Tapping his fingertips against the leather pouch belted at his waist, he took a deep breath, closed his eyes, and listened.

"Noisy," he sighed.

The whole mountain resounded with whispers of fear, questions unanswered, and even whimpers of pain. Tupper missed the Statuary's strong and steady silence. Its aura of peace.

Only one voice rang with confidence, and Tupper smiled even before he opened his eyes. Brand stood in the doorway at the base of the stairs, lantern upraised. "You came."

Brand's brows lifted, and even in the flickering shadows, Tupper could see his friend's bemusement. Of course he'd come. Hadn't this warrior pledged himself to the house of Meadowsweet?

Closing his eyes and tipping his head to one side, Tupper listened longer, waiting for the right sound to sift through the chaos. Eventually, a melodious cascade raised the hairs on the back of his neck, and he nodded to himself. Gesturing for Brand to join him, he said, "Don't worry. I know what to do."

Aurelius's first and only warning was a slight draft that eddied up from the staircase behind him. Darting away from the opening, he barely evaded what could have been a killing blow as his father-in-law's sword rang off stone instead.

Bringing up his blades, Aurelius commented, "You'll dull a fine weapon if you keep hacking at rocks."

Lyall sneered. "Your concern is misplaced, merchant. Your bones will feel its bite."

"Is this any way to greet kin?"

"Those ties are cut," Lyall growled. "And I shall cleave the life from your limbs."

Aurelius's eyebrows arched. "Do you mean to say you've had me banished?"

"Blotted out," he confirmed, blade cutting a wide swathe. With each slash, he snarled, "You. Have. Nothing."

"On the contrary," the younger man retorted, leaping lightly onto the balcony railing. "My conquests have left me rich beyond your wildest dreams."

To Aurelius's confusion, Lyall hesitated to deliver the next blow. The older man's dark eyes were fixed on a point below, where a bright beam of sunlight from the clerestories above illuminated those hiding amidst Thrall's coils.

"A nest of babies—pale, fragile, and noisy," their invader said, his voice deepening with his discovery. "Nay, *one* has potential. Did you rob me of both my daughter and her child?"

"Nay," Aurelius countered, looking for his next landing place. "In giving me your daughter, you robbed me of four sons."

"You aren't worthy of Ulrica!"

"If she wished to be rid of me, I'd be gone, sir."

"I will see you gone!" Lyall pledged, but he stopped short and backed up a step.

From below, Aurelius heard Arni cheerfully shout, "Tiggy-cat!"

Quintrell, who adored all things feline but held onto a healthy amount of filial loyalty, called, "Guard up, Papa!"

Enormous paws hooked the railing on either side of Aurelius's boots, and he teetered with the force of Graven's impact. Casting a wide-eyed look over his shoulder, he exclaimed, "This *isn't* a convenient time, you patchwork pariah! Begone!"

This balcony was certainly higher than the one in Frey's workshop, so the tiger's hind legs scrabbled against the wall below. Graven found purchase and lunged higher, hooking one leg over the railing. Lyall bared his teeth but swiftly retreated to the stairs as the stone guardian's paw shot after him, like a housecat fishing in a mouse hole.

For once, Aurelius wasn't the tiger's prey. But that didn't mean he wasn't caught. Jostled aside by Graven's efforts, the Pred was forced to grab onto him lest he topple into space. Planting a hand on the cat's broad muzzle, he tried to leap onto his shoulders but missed his handhold on the collar, instead sliding down the giant tiger's sleek back.

"Graven!" Freydolf bellowed, his voice echoing off the Cavern's walls.

Immediately, the tiger's tail wrapped tightly around Aurelius's right leg, halting his descent. Dangling upside down, the Pred glared up at the stone guardian, who gazed haughtily back.

Aurelius jabbed his dagger at the interfering cat. "Where are your priorities? We're in the midst of a hunt!"

After a considered pause—during which Aurelius could hear excessive giggling from the children—the Pred could tell he was being lowered. But then Graven performed a little swing, jerk, and release that sent him flailing into space. He landed with an ungainly *oof* in Freydolf's waiting arms.

The Keeper's face creased with concern, so Aurelius grimaced and grumped, "That was singularly undignified!"

Freydolf's features relaxed into wry smile. "Aye. Not your shiningest moment, lord governor."

From over the top of Thrall's coils, Quintrell waved frantically, and Arni begged, "Me next, Unca Ree!"

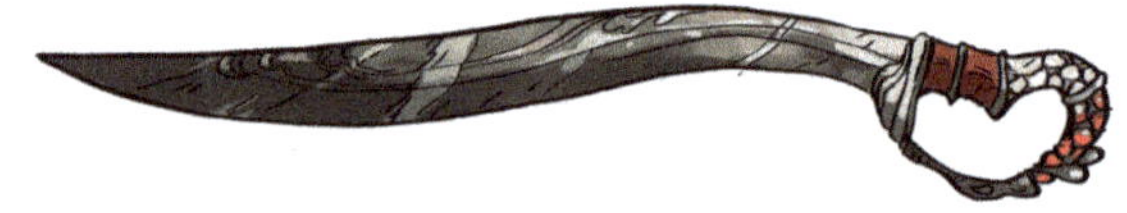

Tupper had belonged to Frey since he was ten. No, that wasn't quite right. They belonged to *each other*. Brotherhood went both ways.

On light feet, the Flox ran up another flight of stairs, climbing steadily into the Statuary's heights. All along the way, he met frightened statues, and he gave them each a touch, a smile, a whispered promise that their Keeper would see them safe.

Stopping to catch his breath at the end of the topmost hall, Tupper withdrew Snick from inside his tunic and traced each minute detail with his fingertip. The day Freydolf had made a present of this key and tied it to Tupper, he'd been irrevocably bound to Morven. Just like a Keeper. The others sometimes said that their mountain was greedy. But Tupper understood about Morven. In binding a Flox boy to herself, she wasn't taking a second Keeper. She'd given Tupper his dearest wish and banished Freydolf's lingering fear. Their mountain was generous through and through.

Brand's knuckles brushed Tupper's cheek, which was wet with tears.

"Morven," the boy mumbled with a sheepish smile.

They bypassed the room where the dawnstone Triad danced from sunrise to sunset, instead approaching the home of the Statuary's songstone guardian. Whistling shrilly, Tupper woke the green statue, who immediately stepped down from his ornate pedestal and bowed. An open hand. A heartfelt plea. A willing sacrifice.

Then the young man hurtled back the way he'd come. It was time to rejoin his bond-brother.

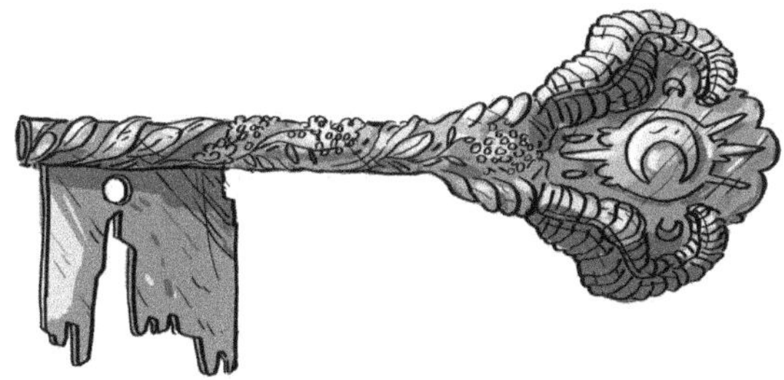

Freydolf and Haimish sat side-by-side on Thrall's hind foot outside her sheltering coils, giving Melina some privacy while she nursed Hanley. Fire-bearers and fire-eaters stood in ranks around them, a barricade of red statuary. The master sculptor peered at the light angling through the various windows dotting the Cavern's ceiling.

"It's hours until sunset," he reported.

Haimish followed his gaze and nodded sympathetically.

"Even longer for the moon to climb high enough to reach Thrall."

The brownstone Pred peered into his maker's face, an expression of helplessness lurking in his eyes.

"Don't fret, old friend. Neither of us was made for this sort of thing."

At least Aurelius was safe. The man had melted back into the shadows, rejoining Ulrica in their search for their trespasser. And Morven's mood could only mean one thing—Tupper was back. His mountain was always happiest when that boy's feet were set upon gray stone.

Their guards stirred, and Freydolf stood in order to see past them. From the direction of the tall double doors, Tupper darted fearlessly—or at least heedlessly—through the familiar forest of statues, Brand close behind him. The inner circle of fire-bearers parted before the Flox, who didn't stop until he collided with Frey, hugging him fiercely.

"Farley?" the sculptor asked.

"Safe."

"And Chelle?"

"Safe."

"Torio?"

"He's with Dessa."

Freydolf grunted. "Aye, that's as it should be."

"And I'm with you."

"*Also* as it should be?" he asked in teasing tones.

"Yes."

Just then, Arni's head popped up. "Hi, Unca Tupp! S'my turn ta hunt, Unca Doff?"

"Don't be galloping off just yet, Mister Meadowsweet. Is your little brother done eating?"

"Aye!"

"In we go," Frey ordered. "This is too exposed for my liking. My father already tried to take you from me once. I don't relish giving him another opportunity."

Tupper climbed obediently but pointed out, "There are too many fire-bearers for him to reach us."

"Aye, but Father's the one who taught Ulrica how to throw knives."

The remark was calculated to hurry the lad along, but Tupper stilled instead. Freydolf peered past him to where Melina dozed beside Hanley on a makeshift bed and the girls played with their dolls. In a tight voice, Tupper whispered, "Is Aggie taking Quintrell to the necessary?"

Frey's head whipped around, and he frantically scanned their surroundings. He'd instructed their statues to guard against strangers, but not to keep anyone from leaving. "Aggie took to the galleries hours ago. Melina backed up her choice, so I let her go."

Tupper nodded. "Quintrell?"

"... is being elusive. I need to find him before my father does!"

"No. Not you," he replied, wrapping his hand firmly around Freydolf's arm. "There's something else you need to do."

"But Quin's safety was my responsibility."

With a firm shake of his head, Tupper cocked his head to one side, then called, "Zev!"

In a moment, the gangling wolf pup trotted into view. Freydolf quickly descended to the floor and knelt before the sunstone guardian, who bounded in a circle before leaning into his creator's leg. Roughing up the wolf's fur, Frey took hold of his jaw and firmly directed, "Find Quintrell and bring him back."

The Meadowsweet girl held up her hand, and Hadwin scowled. He'd heard the soft rustle as clearly as she and was *quite* capable of responding appropriately. Folding his arms across his chest, the Pred gazed into the shadows from which they'd come, just in case. He wouldn't put it past his mother to bury a dagger in his back, assuming she'd returned to the Statuary. Judging by the progression of sun across stone, enough time had passed for his parents to have reentered the fray.

When the sunstone wolf's ears pricked, and he bounded off toward the enormous dragon on the far side of the Cavern, Hadwin tapped his companion's shoulder and pointed after the thing.

She went up on tiptoe to breathe, "Tupp called him."

"How did he know the wolf was here?"

Slim shoulders lifted. "Tupp knows."

Another soft sound came from their right, and the girl carefully eased around the raised pedestal against which they'd stopped. Hadwin saw her start to move forward, then hold herself back with a white-knuckled grip on the corner of the stone slab. He leaned past her for a look.

Lyall Rakefang had a small child by the collar, and judging by the wee lad's clothes and coloring, he was the Harrow Farley had mentioned. A baby brother.

Aggie spun, her fingers catching at his vest. Every trace of calm superiority vanished, leaving nothing more than a frightened girl. "Will he hurt Quinny?"

Hadwin nodded.

"Can we do anything?"

His brows drew together as he watched his grandsire stalk triumphantly toward the dragon. Taking the lead for once, he glided after them. They remained out of sight while Lyall leapt onto a stone slab not far from the phalanx of fire-bearers Freydolf had pressed into service. Holding the boy at arm's length, the Pred brandished his sword and called, "Show yourself, merchant!"

Aurelius immediately strode into the open, daggers sheathed and gaze calm. "I'm here, Quin."

"Papa," the boy whimpered.

Shaking his head once, Aurelius said, "Be still."

Lyall tucked the limp child under his arm and asked, "Do you want him back?"

"*My* sons are dear to me," the man replied in razor-edged tones.

"Return my daughter, and I'll yield the whelp."

Aurelius's brows arched. "You expect me to choose between my wife and my son?"

"Nay. She *is* mine. You're deciding whether or not this shivering babe lives." Lyall set his blade against Quintrell's neck. "Would you selfishly rob Ulrica of her child?"

Cold hands tugged at his, and Hadwin turned to his companion.

The girl whispered, "That's a bad bargain."

"Agreed. Let's make a better offer." Kneeling before her, he warned, "You'll need to surrender your daggers."

She swiftly divested herself of six blades, lining up her small arsenal on the floor between them.

When she straightened, Hadwin whispered, "He must believe I broke you. Stay close. Play along." For the first time he noticed that she wore bells at her ankles, and his opinion of her reached new heights. Flicking one of the bells with the tip of a claw, he said, "And walk like a Flox."

Tupper flung his arms around Freydolf's waist and sternly said, "No. You need to stay here."

"But he has Quin!"

"Yes. So you need to hurry."

"But I can't do anything from here."

"Don't worry. I have a plan." From the pouch at his waist, Tupper brought out the small tools Frey used for fine work—chisels and picks, rasps and rifflers. He pressed them into the sculptor's hands. "And it needs a master sculptor."

"I hardly think this is an appropriate thing to do when Quin is suffering," Freydolf argued, staring in disbelief at the tiny weapons with which his servant had provided him.

Tupper frowned. "I thought it was a good idea."

Freydolf shook his head in mystification. "What do you expect me to make with these?"

"A keyhole."

The Pred blinked. "Where?"

"Here."

"In the heartstone?" he asked, his gaze drifting to the egg. Melina and her children huddled beside it, watching him with more faith than he deserved.

"No. In Thrall."

"You want me to tamper with the Statuary's first guardian?"

Tupper rubbed at the base of one horn. "You changed Graven's mark."

"Aye," Freydolf grudgingly admitted. "But ...!"

"And you altered Phineas and Nerine."

"Aye."

"And the stone in my earrings was cut from ...."

Frey held up his hands. "Enough, lambkin. My record for tampering with my predecessors' works is well-established. But Thrall is not a door. What purpose would a keyhole serve?"

Tupper pulled his money cord from under his tunic and carefully detached the object hanging beside Snick. Offering his master the songstone guardian's key, he explained, "If you bind Thrall to this ..."

"She'll wake," Freydolf finished, pulling Tupper into a short, fierce hug. "Aye, lambkin. It's a *very* good idea!"

As Hadwin hoped, the rhythmic jingle of tiny bells warned his grandsire of their approach, and the stand-off between Lyall and Aurelius was momentarily set aside. "Look what I caught in the lower corridors," Hadwin gloated, lifting and twisting the girl's arm. She responded with an outraged squeak that might have passed for pain. Still, he was grateful that her spun-gold curls kept her expression hidden.

Aurelius softly inquired, "Did he hurt you, Aggie?"

"Is *that* her name?" Hadwin drawled, running his fingers through her hair. "She's been too shy to introduce herself."

Tupper leapt onto the dragon's coils and stared down at them, his expression thoughtful.

"Another Flox brat?" Lyall scoffed.

"Aye, but look how she's dressed." Hadwin knelt behind Aggie, his hands on her hips. "Hunting attire, twin daggers, and bells at her ankles."

"Wispy bit of nothing," his grandsire said. "No one would mistake her for a Pred."

"But the pet of a Pred?"

Lyall chuckled darkly and lifted his voice. "Ulrica, were you so lonely for home? Do you miss the company of your equals? Fear for nothing. I'll return you to your rightful place in the house of Rakefang!"

The woman stepped into view not far from her husband. "You deluded old fool! This isn't my prison. It's the only scrap of freedom I've ever known!"

"Then what of this girl and her ill-suited trappings?" challenged her father.

Ulrica took a step forward. "She is *my* precious daughter, and if either of you has injured her, I'll extract my vengeance from the marrow of your bones."

"Two bargaining pieces," Hadwin said, half-dragging Aggie toward Lyall. The silvery racket of her bells accompanied her ineffectual struggles, and she tried to hide behind him. Hadwin casually offered, "Allow me to free your hands, sir."

"Aye, take the whelp," agreed Lyall, his lip curling in distaste. "When the fight left him, he wet himself."

Hadwin wrinkled his nose and took hold of the back of Quintrell's tunic, swinging the youngster down into his chest. The boy was stiff and silent, but when Hadwin pushed him up over his shoulder, Aggie was able to show herself to the child. Whatever silent signal she used, it did the trick. Quintrell's arms locked around Hadwin's neck, and he clung fast.

Just then, a song began from Thrall's direction. Children were singing, and Hadwin soon recognized the lyrics as the learning verse for teaching children the Terse alphabet.

"What's that?" growled Lyall.

Aurelius glanced at his wife and asked, "Didn't anyone teach him Terse?"

"Languages were never father's strong point," Ulrica silkily replied.

While Hadwin's parents flung verbal barbs at their attacker, Tupper caught his eye and made a pushing motion with both hands. Hadwin frowned in confusion, but Aggie caught on and tugged at his belt loops, urging him to step backward.

Their silent retreat went unnoticed until Tupper calmly called, "Your turn, Graven. Up and out."

From just beyond the nearest sunbeam, the enormous tiger slunk into view. He dropped to his belly beside Hadwin and his prisoners. Leaping astride Graven's broad shoulders, the young man pulled Aggie up behind him and tucked Quintrell into the crook of his arm. As soon as the girls' arms clamped around his waist, they were in motion. Lights flashed by, and then the dark claimed them.

Still, it wasn't hard to keep his bearings. Graven arrowed along the main corridor leading to the Cavern, making for the fountain colonnade. They took a slight detour to bypass doors that were too narrow for their mount, but they soon burst into broad daylight and skidded to a stop.

Quintrell blinked several times, then whispered, "Aggie?"

"Here," the girl answered, standing on the tiger's back and leaning over Hadwin's shoulder to touch the boy's face. "Thanks to your Unca Tupp and this man, we're safe."

To Hadwin's chagrin, tears welled up in the little boy's golden eyes. "Brother?"

"Aye. Somehow."

"Love you, Winny," Quintrell declared before dissolving into hiccupping sobs.

Hadwin smoothed the boy's silky hair and smirked faintly. "Naturally."

Anticipatory power roared around Freydolf, making it difficult for him to even hear the children's nursery rhyme. Morven understood what was happening, and this adaptation pleased her greatly. The delicate key slid easily into the tiny hole he'd fitted between Thrall's scales, and he concentrated on building the bond that would allow a moonstone guardian to wake by day. Whether it was the nearness of Morven's heart, the urgency of Freydolf's need, or Tupper's conviction that this was a good idea, the link practically forged itself.

Pressing his thumbs over the mark surrounding the keyhole, Morven's Keeper whispered, "Welcome to a new day, Thrall. Do what you must."

The coils surrounding them shivered and grew supple, and high overhead, the dragon's head turned.

From somewhere above, Frey heard Tupper order, "Aurelius, Ulrica, get back!"

The Keeper quickly offered Melina and the children the shelter of his arms, bowing over them. To distract them from the fearsome stone guardian's movements, he rumbled, "I'm proud of you all. And grateful, since my rough, old voice isn't nearly nice enough to wake dragons."

Dulcie giggled and Yona reached up to pat his cheek. "You did your best. And so did we."

"Aye."

"What 'bout Quin?" Arni asked urgently.

Tupper dropped down and shouldered his way into the huddle. Tousling his nephew's curls, he said, "Quintrell's safe with Aggie. We'll catch up to them just as soon as Haimish comes back." Looking to Melina, he added, "Haimish will escort you to Frey's workshop. As soon as everyone's settled, I'll send Graven for Carden."

Freydolf peered warily up at Thrall, whose attention seemed to be fixed on the glimpses of blue sky offered by the various windows. Stretching out two of her four arms, she twisted and turned her elongated fingers in a shaft of light with an attitude of frank curiosity.

These were not the actions of a dragon driven to defend her egg.

"Is the bad man gone?" asked Dulcie.

Tupper quietly replied, "Yes."

Arni spoke up next. "Did Thrall eat him?"

Tupper shook his head. "Statues don't eat people. But people run away from dragons."

"Can we go?" Dulcie whined, boredom making her petulant.

"Soon."

Yona squirmed. "Mish?"

Tupper explained, "Haimish is bringing me water. It's my job to wash the floors."

Dulcie frowned up at him. "Uncle Doff even makes you clean the Cavern?"

"He doesn't make me. I want to," With a sidelong look at his bond-brother, he said, "It's for the best."

Unable to contain his curiosity, Freydolf stood. Tricky as it was to navigate over slithering scales, he surmounted them and peered at the remnants of his father's attack. Fire-bearers milled about or meandered toward their pedestals. Aurelius and Ulrica stood at a safe distance, heads bowed together. After some searching, he spotted his father. A single lantern illuminated his crumpled form—Brand's.

Tupper reached his side and pulled at his shoulder. "Frey, maybe you shouldn't look."

Red stone. Red blood.

"Aye," Frey managed, swallowing hard. Brand knelt beside Lyall Rakefang, grimly holding the Keeper's gaze. Freydolf nodded shakily to the warrior sworn to protect the house of Meadowsweet ... then fainted.

Late the following afternoon, Freydolf and Torio winced simultaneously as Ulrica drew a shocking and unnecessarily graphic comparison between robbing a Flox of his horn and ridding a fool of his ability to procreate. The two Keepers had returned to something resembling their usual routine— the Pred tapping away at Dessa's column, and the Grif idly paging through books. The rant emanated from Frey's kitchen, where his sister was holding court. From the sound of things, Hadwin's very life hung in the balance.

"Should I go in?" Tupper whispered.

Farley shook his head. "Let him sweat a little longer."

"He deserves it," Aggie agreed.

Tupper cringed and asked, "You don't really think Ulrica would … *you know*."

"Not if she wants more grandchildren," his younger sister replied breezily.

Freydolf found it funny that of the three Meadowsweet siblings eavesdropping outside the kitchen, Aggie was the only one not blushing. Just then, Carden leaned through the workshop door and beckoned. "Aurelius is back, and he wants to talk to Farley."

He straightened quickly. "How come?"

"You're *not* in trouble. In fact, I think you'll be pleased."

"In *that* case," said the lad, jogging out the door.

By the time Freydolf followed the Meadowsweets into the courtyard, Farley was exclaiming, "… brought 'em back with you!"

"Fine animals," Aurelius replied smugly. "'Twould have been a shameful waste to leave them wandering the desert."

Frey strolled over to the nearest of the four stallions standing in harness before a black carriage. Clucking and crooning to the spirited horse, he smiled when it thumped its nose against his chest, then snuffled at his apron pockets. "You made a fine acquisition, Aurelius."

"Nay," the merchant replied matter-of-factly. "Hadwin has agreed to yield them to Farley in partial recompense for damages."

Farley did a terrible job hiding how pleased he was. "The carriage, too?"

"Aye." Aurelius nodded to Torio, who leaned against the workshop's double-door. "It's a far sight finer than that rickety shamble of Kite's that's sagging in the stable. If I were you, I'd fit it out so when we're finally rid of you, you can ride out in a style befitting a Keeper and his mountain."

Farley flushed and grinned, and Tupper shrewdly inquired, "*Partial* recompense?"

"Negotiations continue apace. They've been at this since yesterday evening," Aurelius said, fiddling with his cuffs. "Ulrica must be enjoying herself to drag out the proceedings this long."

"Aren't you worried for Hadwin?" Tupper asked.

"I'd be more worried if he ran from the consequences of his actions," the man replied seriously. "The fact that he stayed to endure this ... I'm proud of him."

A yelp echoed from inside, and everyone hurried to see what happened. Aurelius sang out, "Ulrica dear, do you need assistance?"

"Aye. Come hold him down."

The Pred vanished into the kitchen, but his voice was pitched to carry. "You are as inventive as ever, my love."

A moment later, Hadwin roared, and Tupper bolted toward the sound, Freydolf right behind him. Ulrica struck a triumphant pose, holding up a bloody fang, while Hadwin drooped on the floor in the corner, shooting injured glances at his parents while cradling his jaw.

"I shall pierce it and wear it upon a ribbon," she exulted. But then a cunning smile appeared. "Nay, that would be too prosaic. I'll grant it to Aggie. Five years' servitude to the lass who set you flat."

"Mother," he groaned. "You know I could have ...!"

"Aye, but you *didn't*!"

Aurelius hummed. "This situation will prove most useful during our travels. We leave in a few days' time to inform my eldest that he's come into his inheritance. As new head of the house of Rakefang, he'll be in a position to overturn all that *preposterous* nonsense about my banishment."

Hadwin shook his head. "You'll bring me with you?"

"Aye. While I attend to filing all the necessary documents, you can show Aggie and Quintrell the ocean, the bazaars, perhaps even the white mountain."

"Lucky," grumbled Farley from the doorway.

Aurelius's brow quirked. "If it will further inconvenience my son, I'm sure my darling wife would extend an invitation to you."

The lad hesitated, then shook his head. "I can wait."

With a smirk for Torio, Aurelius murmured, "Admirable loyalty."

"A *rare* quality." Ulrica prodded her husband's arm. "Price and penance have been exacted, but there's one final matter to settle." Aurelius gestured for her to continue, and she glowered down at her son. "His name. It sets my teeth on edge."

"But love," he soothed. "You chose *Hadwin* yourself. A noble moniker meaning ...."

"Rakefang," she interrupted.

"Then change it," her son blurted. "I don't mind if you change it."

Freydolf could see the direction this was taking and chuckled over his sister's roundabout scheming. "How about Meadowsweet?" he innocently suggested.

Father and son grimaced in perfect tandem, and Aurelius quickly replied, "Nay. I'll see it changed to Harrow. Would that suit you, wife?"

"Aye. Admirably."

Aurelius straightened and rubbed his hands. "Which leaves us with one last matter of business. Later tonight, I want all able-bodied men in Frey's balcony. Bring your goblets. Bring your courage." Turning to Farley, he announced, "I'm going to pierce you."

"Really?"

"Aye." Bending closer to inspect the lad's broken horn, Aurelius said, "Right after I file these edges down. The jagged ends are sure to catch on fabric, and I can't bear to see good cloth snagged."

EPILOGUE

TWO YEARS LATER...

Farley carried a neatly-wrapped cheese into the workshop's kitchen and let it drop with a *thunk* onto the table. "Weather's taking a turn for the nasty."

A sleep-tousled Tupper turned from rummaging in the pantry. "A storm?"

"Yep."

"The one we need?"

"There've been too many false alarms. I wouldn't be here if I wasn't sure."

From his usual spot looped around Farley's neck, Nestor lifted his head, bobbing at Tupper. The young man reached out and gently tickled the snake under his chin. "Where's Torio?"

"He's been on the summit since ... I dunno. All night probably. The sunset was promising."

Tupper nodded. "I'll wake Frey."

His brother snorted. "The clouds aren't in a hurry. You have time to toast his mush."

Rubbing at the base of his horn, Tupper protested, "I haven't had to do that in a long time. And he'll want to know. There's lots to get ready."

Farley backed toward the door. "I'll warn Carden, then make sure Torio doesn't get cold feet."

Tupper considered that for a moment before saying, "He wouldn't go even if he could."

"More like he can't go until she can."

As soon as his brother let the door click shut, Tupper crossed to the statue standing against the far wall. Freydolf had finished Dessa near midwinter, but the season had been wrong for thunder. Their spring had been filled with slow, gentle rains—good for the gardens, but not for a certain Grif's mood. Now that summer was here, cloud-watching had become everyone's hobby, though in Torio's case it was more of an obsession.

"There's a storm coming, Dessa." Tupper knew she was listening, but the closer Freydolf had come to finishing the tempestuous heartstone, the quieter she grew. Gently touching the hands she clasped over her heart, he asked, "Why are you hiding?"

After nearly two years of painstaking work, Freydolf had coaxed a lovely person from the heartstone. She was much taller than Flox women, though not nearly as tall as Ulrica. Dessa and Farley were actually eye-to-eye, which meant she was a shade taller than Tupper. He searched her face, whose highly-polished perfection caught his own reflection. "Don't mind his grumbling."

When her reticence persisted, Tupper sighed and crossed the room to where Freydolf lay on his bed, one arm flung across his face. As soon as the Flox sat on the edge of the mattress, a dark eye cracked open. "Sweet-talking another man's mountain, lambkin?"

"Come, talk to Dessa."

With a faint smile, her sculptor said, "You know I can't hear her like you can."

"But she can hear you." Tupper plucked at the Keeper's nightshirt sleeve. "She thinks Torio will be disappointed."

"All their squabbling and rowing, but when it comes down to it...." Heaving a gusty sigh Frey waved Tupper aside and swung his legs out of bed. Striding across the room to the statue Aurelius had summarily declared his masterpiece, Freydolf took her by the shoulders and rumbled, "You already know what to do, Dessa sweet. Call to him. If he's meant to be your Keeper, he'll come to your side. It's as simple as that."

Farley oversaw the transfer of two gleaming black lionesses to the open pavilion in the outer courtyard. The structure's stone pillars were Carden's workmanship—his previous year's project as Frey's apprentice. Woven branches stretched over them, providing shelter from sun and rain, the handiwork of a whole family of basket weavers. In part, the addition had been made for this very day. They needed thunder to wake heartstone, but there was no reason for all those gathered to be soaked to the skin.

Tarps flapped in gusting winds, and the first heavy raindrops darkened stone.

Aurelius tested the edge of his blade and inquired, "How much blood will you need—drop, dribble, or dram?"

Frey blanched.

Torio blandly asked, "Are you really so eager to impale me?"

Aurelius's fangs flashed in time with a blaze of lightning, and Tupper's shoulder's hunched. Everyone else held their breath and counted, waiting for the answering thunder.

When it came, Freydolf shook his head. "Too far."

Torio tugged firmly at the brim of his hat. "The cats first, if you please."

Freydolf hesitated. "We may only get one chance. Don't you think Dessa deserves...?"

Shaking his head, the Grif said, "I want the guardians first, and I want Farley's blood used to wake them."

"Sure," agreed the young man in question.

"They'll be bound directly to Dessa," the sculptor reminded. Much thought had been put into the attachments, since the lives of men were so much shorter than those of statues. The lionesses had been created without pedestals, but they would be tethered by the will of their mistress. "They'll obey her, not Farley."

"But maybe they'll be grateful," countered the lanky sixteen-year-old. "Besides, Aurelius is antsy to pin me down. He hasn't had a chance since he pierced me."

The merchant reached over to flick the blue droplet dangling from Farley's ear lobe, sending the elegant jewel swaying. "There's no escape here, brat."

"Aye," Freydolf said, all business. "If the storm cooperates, I'll wake all three. Do you have a name for this one?"

Farley glanced at Torio, who said, "That one's Char."

"Very good. And her sister?"

The Grif replied, "She's Nyx."

A few moments later, the sky turned white, thunder clapped, and Farley yipped as Aurelius did his duty.

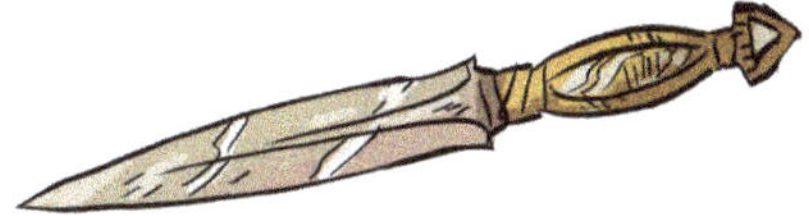

Torio wasn't sure he'd be able to tell when the next flash of lightning happened. Dessa's magic blazed around them in an incandescent display that left him half-blind and half-scared. Being tied to a lump of stone had been one thing, but his mountain was no longer a featureless block. She now had a proud nose, full lips, cascading hair, and dainty fingers.

More than a year had passed since Torio had dared to lay a hand on her. For reasons that were hard to explain, the act would have felt ... ungentlemanly.

"Show me your hands," Aurelius shouted next to his ear.

The Grif offered them without thinking but quickly came to his senses when pain seared across his flesh, and blood pooled in his palms. He started to jerk his hands away from the bloodthirsty Pred, but Harrow caught his wrists. "Don't waste it. Are you ready?" His nod became an uncertain bobble, and Aurelius chuckled. "I swear, you look like I felt on my wedding day."

"I doubt many brides cry for the blood of their grooms."

The man's laugh deepened, and he gripped Torio's shoulder. "If you'll recall, I'm blessed to call Ulrica my wife."

The Grif smiled weakly. "But this isn't a wedding."

"Nay, but it's a solemn bond that demands a lifetime of loyalty." Brows arching, Aurelius said, "And a man should bear in mind that even the most formidable of brides is still a maiden at heart."

"Th-this is *not* a wedding."

"True, but it's a deucedly good analogy." Leaning closer the Pred gravely added, "And from what Tupper told me earlier, Dessa's not crying for your blood. She's anxious for your touch, so make it a good one."

Torio glanced at his bloodied palms in dismay. Where should he put his hands? His gaze darted over Dessa's form. Freydolf had heeded his request for clothes sensible for travel, so the cut of her dress was simple, falling in natural folds from the swell of her hips. However, each delicate embellishment bespoke understated elegance and patient extravagance. The heart of the thirteenth mountain truly was Freydolf Meadowsweet's masterpiece.

Time for doubts ran out as the air sizzled with power, and a simultaneous flash-*BOOM* jolted everyone to attention. The sculptor thrust out his hand, and Torio bloodied the pad of his thumb. Tupper knelt under Freydolf's arm steadying the woozy Pred as he harnessed Dessa's jumpy magic and firmly coaxed them into the ties that would bind.

"*Now*, Torio," Freydolf commanded.

Taking a deep breath, the Grif cupped his hands over Dessa, then opened them, spilling their contents. Blood slipped over black stone as he rested his hands on the crown of her head. Torio had witnessed the waking of statues numerous times, but this was his first time on the receiving end. He blinked several times to clear the frissons of magic from his periphery, then noticed that the blood had dribbled down Dessa's face and was in danger of getting in her eyes. Catching the heavy drop with one finger, he simply oozed more onto her cheek.

Swiping at it with his knuckles, he mumbled, "I'm making a mess."

He curled the fingers of his other hand, and his talons caught in her hair. Torio snatched back his hands, paling when Dessa reacted with a tiny pout.

"Her name," Tupper prompted.

"Not sure he remembers," Farley remarked.

Torio cut a look at his servant, but the audacious young man with the snub horn just grinned and made a little shooing motion with his hands. Peering back down into the statue's face, he found her already searching his with pleading eyes. Torio stared in awe as the wind actually took her hair and blew it across her cheek, and her skirts flapped against his legs. He touched her face, and it was soft. He whispered her name, and she smiled.

Aurelius nudged him from behind. "Show some manners, Grif. Take the lady under your wing."

Grateful to fall back on familiar custom, Torio opened his cloak, tensing when Dessa swiftly accepted the invitation by winding her arms around his waist and nestling against his shoulder. She spoke his name, soft as a sigh in the depths of his mind, yet it pulled at his very soul.

Folding his arms around her, Torio answered the irresistible call with more confidence. "I'm here, Dessa."

Tupper found Freydolf sitting on a blanket under Brand's watchful eye. Several of the Meadowsweet youngsters who were worn out from excitement clustered within the circle of light cast by the redstone warrior's lantern. Ewert's three-year-old twins were sound asleep, their small hands clasped, and their silver curls mingled together. Frey held their newborn baby sister, and Quintrell leaned against his uncle's side, wholly absorbed in the basketful of kittens Arni had wheedled from his great-grandmother.

"You're not dancing?" his master asked in gently teasing tones.

"Hadwin asked Chelle," Tupper explained.

Frey chuckled. "He seems determined to conquer Floxish customs, including your folk dances."

"Yes." Gazing toward the whirl of music and laughter in the center of town, Tupper said, "Probably because Aggie said he couldn't."

"Strangest case of sibling rivalry I've ever seen."

"Maybe." After a lengthy pause, Tupper shook his head. "Probably not."

Aurelius strolled over, golden eyes assessing the state of Tupper's finery, his gift to the groom. The merchant passed along a goblet for each of them. Crouching before Freydolf, Aurelius gleefully whispered, "I found him."

"Who?" asked Tupper.

"Kite." Nodding toward the far end of the village square, Aurelius said, "He and Farley have hidden themselves away in your mother's garden with Dessa. They're trying to teach her how to dance."

Tupper smiled. "Good."

Pulling the corner of little Hanley's blanket up over his shoulder, Aurelius casually asked, "How is it that there's music in the air, yet you're not dancing?"

Freydolf blithely interjected, "Winny cut in."

"*Did* he?" In silky tones, Aurelius revealed, "There's a longstanding tradition in Pred society of kidnapping brides. Don't tell me you've let down your guard *again*, sprat."

Taking a long drink, Tupper calmly said, "I think Hadwin learned his lesson too well to even pretend."

"Aye, but I wouldn't put it past Ulrica to ...."

Tupper thrust his empty goblet into Aurelius's hands and hurried to rejoin his new wife.

Most of Tupper's plans for the next several days were a secret, even from Frey. All his bond-brother knew was that he'd be taking his bride on an extended tour of the galleries.

Several rooms had been prepared, each beautiful in its own right. In a way, they were Tupper's gifts, hidden along the way for her to find. Places with pretty views, bright flowers, spicy candles, dry firewood, stocked pantries, and fresh sheets. Every detail was for Chelle's comfort and for their enjoyment.

He was eager to share all his pent-up secrets, so he watched for his chance. As a dance ended and couples dispersed toward seats, the bonfires, or the many refreshment tables, Tupper held a finger to his lips and casually escorted his bride away from the merrymaking.

Once they were out of sight, Chelle fanned her pink cheeks and whispered, "Is this really happening?"

Tupper nodded confidently. They'd forged a bond as sure as stone. He couldn't see the magic, nor could he hear her voice deep in his soul, but the knot was tied. All he wanted to do was tend and strengthen the bond so there would be no doubts. This was really happening, and he couldn't be happier.

Taking her hands, he kissed her knuckles, then leaned down to whisper in her ear. The delicate point twitched against his lips.

She turned to look at him. "What did you say?"

He smiled and kissed her cheek, then traced letters into her palm. S - E - C - R - E - T.

Chelle's brows arched. "You're keeping the secrets you tell me a secret from me?"

Tupper kissed her nose to tease her, then kissed her lips because he could.

Weddings changed things, but they hadn't changed Chelle much. Catching the hand that had strayed to her waist, she pressed it firmly into her palm. "Tell me!"

S - H - O - W.

Curiosity piqued, she asked, "You have something to show me?"

So many things. Such good things. Too many to explain. Showing really would be better. C - O - M - E, he begged.

"Now?"

Tupper nodded, luring her toward the forest where Graven waited.

"Where are we going?"

H - O - M - E.

"Home," Chelle breathed, a soft look in her eyes as she trustingly twined her fingers with his.

And so Tupper Meadowsweet adapted a Pred tradition to suit his purposes by kidnapping his own bride. He carried her away to Morven's galleries long before the festivities surrounding their wedding day drew to a close.

A few days later, Freydolf sat alone in the balcony, ignoring the open book on his knees in favor of staring morosely into the dying embers of the fire. A soft knock sounded against the door frame, and when Tupper slipped out of the shadows, the Pred started guiltily. "You're not due back for four more days," he said. "Is anything wrong?"

"No." The young man gazed intently at him. "I missed you."

Frey rubbed awkwardly at the back of his neck, suddenly very conscious that he'd been skipping baths. "You shouldn't interrupt your marriage week."

Tupper strode across the carpeted floor and dropped to his knees beside the sculptor's chair. "I'll go back before Chelle wakes up."

Searching for something to say, Freydolf ventured, "You look happy."

"Yes." Tupper's hand lightly touched his bond-brother's knee. "You look sad."

"I suppose I am a little. I missed you, too."

"I can tell." Tupper took away Freydolf's book, carefully marking the page before setting it aside. "How long since you slept?"

"Melina made me take a nap with Hanley yesterday."

"Good."

Tupper pulled Frey's rough hand into his own, his face pensive as he smoothed his thumb over calluses and inspected the blunted tips of each claw. Soon, the lad began humming snatches of a tune, and the Pred recognized the stone song he'd taught him during their first weeks together.

Freydolf's heart ached, but the pain was sweet. He so clearly remembered when Tupper was barely taller than his boots, with bitty nubs peeking through his curls. Standing on a bucket to reach the sink. Chasing chunks and chippings across the floor as they fell. Taking on a man's responsibilities in order to keep one lonely Pred alive.

Now Tupper *was* a man, with curling horns and a calm demeanor.

"You stayed," Freydolf said softly.

"Promised I would."

"Aye." The Keeper turned his hand, capturing the lad's wrist with a firm grip. He was being childish and churlish and thirteen times a fool. But Freydolf didn't want to let go, even though he knew Tupper would never go far. The past few days had been *so* empty. Frey's throat closed, and his eyes began to water.

Tupper tutted softly and used the hem of his sleeve to wipe the Pred's cheek. "Have you been letting worries in again?" he asked.

"Aye. Pesky things."

When Tupper next dabbed at his own eyes, Frey realized that his lashes were damp. His lambkin was crying for him. Or with him. And that knowledge was his immediate undoing. A choked sob. A keening whine. And with fumbling hands, the Pred grabbed for his bond-brother and pulled him into an awkward embrace.

With a sniffle, Tupper clung to him.

Perhaps the lad hadn't come to scold, but for back-up. Freydolf would have loved to blame Morven for these tears, but she wasn't meddling. Their mountain laughed and crooned by turns, reveling in the excess of emotions.

The Keeper growled, "I'm happy for you, lambkin. *Happy!*"

"Yes. These are good changes."

But Tupper burrowed his face against Frey's old red tunic. Petting his fair curls, the man asked, "Why did you come to see me?"

"Because I wanted to tell you lots of things. But especially one thing."

"What's that?"

"Not here." Easing back, Tupper stood and said, "Come with me."

"Where?"

His lips quirked. "Not far."

"Aye, lambkin. Lead on."

He led Freydolf like a child down into the workshop and folded back the big bed's covers. "In," he ordered.

"Are you mothering me?"

"It's my job. It always will be. Did you forget?"

Meek as moonlight, the man obeyed. "Forgetting things is why I need a servant in the first place."

"If you forget to take your bath tomorrow, I'll drag you out to the horse trough."

"Aye." Frey folded his hands across his chest and waited. There was no sense rushing the lad. He always needed time to sort out his thoughts. And it was no use trying to guess what he wanted to say. Tupper was as unfathomable as ever.

"Dessa loves Torio. And Torio loves her."

Freydolf bemusedly replied, "Aye. As much as her Keeper likes to dance around the obvious, their attachment is more than magical."

Sitting on the edge of the bed, Tupper asked, "Do you love Morven?"

"Aye. In my own way."

"And Master Platt loved her. And all the other Keepers, all the way back, even before Master Tremont."

"Aye. The bond between a Keeper and his mountain is a precious thing. When someone takes responsibility for one of the Twelve—nay, the Thirteen—love and trust and loyalty are mixed in."

Tupper stared at his hands, then reached for Freydolf's again. "I think so, too."

"Does this have something to do with Morven calling you Chelle's Keeper?"

"No. But that was nice."

Freydolf couldn't track Tupper's thoughts, so he bit his tongue. Best to wait. But to his utter astonishment, the lad borrowed a new bit of Pred tradition. Taking Frey's hands, he pulled them up and pressed them against his cheeks in a show of utter trust.

Tupper said, "Before Dessa could love Torio, she needed a Maker. And that was you. She's your masterpiece."

"So says Aurelius."

"And before I could love Chelle, I needed to be yours. If I had never been yours, I would never be me. I needed a Maker."

The lad's cheeks were still wet, and Frey could feel a hint of stubble. Tupper might understand stone better than anyone in the world, but he wasn't a statue. "You're not a sculpture, lambkin."

"Carden says that guardian statues always carry a part of their sculptor's hopes for it. A maker's mark from a good man makes a good statue. I think ...." Tupper leaned into Frey's framing hands. "I'm *sure* I bear your mark."

With a soft grumble, Freydolf rubbed at the base of Tupper's horns, then tugged at a fair ringlet. "Your mother often remarks on a growing resemblance. But these changes were your choice, not my doing."

"I'm proud to bear your mark. Like Haimish, Rimbles, and Olexi." The lad's tone was stubborn. "So are Phineas, Nerine, and Thrall. Even Graven."

Frey's hands fell away. "There are a handful of statues who are grateful for my meddling, but I can't call them mine. They bear the marks of other sculptors. I only tweaked their ties so they'd be happy."

"Yes." Sounding surer now, Tupper said, "Like me."

Was it the same? If you looked at things from the lad's

perspective, both mountain and master had meddled on a grand scale. Affection. Affinity. Stealth. Style. After living atop Morven for the better part of a decade, Tupper fit in no better with the Flox than Freydolf did among Pred. Yet they'd found a sense of belonging. Brothering and mothering added up to kinship. And their family was growing every year.

"Aye," Freydolf finally conceded.

Tupper relaxed into a hopeful smile. "You understand?"

"You're the best pick I ever made, and you're as dear to me as any of my statues." To Freydolf's relief, Tupper seemed to take this as a compliment. Reaching up to tap one of the lad's earrings, Frey said, "These trappings are like bands of belonging. Aye, I've left my mark. And you've left yours."

"Probably."

"Undoubtedly."

"There will be more bands of belonging. Because I'm Chelle's. And one day I'll belong to my children. And then to my grandchildren." Tupper fussed with the blankets, tucking and patting. Eyes downcast, he said, "But I was yours first. And always."

Freydolf gruffly promised, "Always."

Tupper straightened his shoulders and nodded. "Should I make my pledge again? I haven't forgotten it. Not once."

He meant to refuse, but there was something in the lad's steady gaze that made Frey think that Tupper was the one who needed to hear the words. Pushing himself to sitting, the Pred leaned against his ornate headboard. "Remind this old fool what matters."

Pulling the money cord out from under his tunic, Tupper held out Snick. Frey accepted the gray key, and the lad enfolded his hand with both of his. Taking a deep breath, Tupper said, "I'm the one who sweeps your floor and keeps your water pitcher full. Your hearth is mine to tend, and I'll make sure your favorite tunic stays clean. All my life, I'll serve you."

"And make biscuits," Freydolf prompted.

A slow blink. A rare chuckle. A fond smile. "And make biscuits," Tupper promised, giving his master's hand a gentle squeeze. "Lots."

THE END

Thank you for purchasing *Rakefang*. I do hope the tale was to your liking. If so, I shall borrow from Flox tradition and say,

"THE TRADE IS GOOD; MAY OUR NEXT BE BETTER STILL."

C. J. MILBRANDT has always believed in miracles, especially small ones. A lifelong bookworm with a love for fairy tales, far-off lands, and fantasy worlds, CJ began spinning adventures of her own. Her family-friendly stories mingle humor and whimsy with a dash of danger and a touch of magic. Follow your curiosity to CJMilbrandt.com, where you'll find more stories and story art. CJ's books are also on GoodReads.

    Rakefang began as a personal writing challenge. The entire Galleries of Stone trilogy was written on the fly, posted in three hundred and sixty-six daily installments during 2012. Completely crazy. Entirely satisfying.

GALLERIES OF STONE
Meadowsweet
Harrow
Rakefang

GALLERIES OF STONE
PREQUEL
Deuce
C. J. MILBRANDT

www.ingramcontent.com/pod-product-compliance
Lightning Source LLC
Chambersburg PA
CBHW061055100726

47911CB00012B/232